**"I—I fear this game has
gone too far," she stammered.**

His mouth hovered a hairsbreadth above hers. "And I fear
it hasn't gone far enough."

The rustling of the leaves, soft as satin and lace, rose
above the hard-edged whisper inside his head. *Trouble,
trouble.* Ignoring the warning, Gryff possessed her in a
long, lush kiss. She tasted indescribably sweet, with a tart
tang of wild heather and some essence he couldn't put a
name to. He coaxed her lips apart, wanting more.

More.

To his satisfaction, her response was warmly willing.
She opened herself eagerly, twining her tongue with
his. Teasing, touching—like their bodies, the rules of
Polite Society seemed suspended as they hung high
above the ground, letting all rational thoughts dance
away on the summer breeze.

Eliza. The musical lilt of her given name rolled so
easily off the tongue. It suited her, decided Gryff, for
he sensed a simmering sensuality beneath her sun-kissed
skin. She was no cold-blooded prude, but rather a delightfully daring wood sprite. A creature of Nature—of
dark forests and sunny fields, of windswept moors and
swirling waters. Her eyes gave hint of primal passions
lurking deep down inside, just waiting to be released.

Acclaim for
Too Wicked to Wed

"Elliott packs the first Lords of Midnight Regency romance with plenty of steamy sex and sly innuendo...As Alexa and Connor flee London to escape vengeful criminals, their mutual attraction sizzles beneath delightful banter. Regency fans will especially appreciate the authentic feel of the historical setting."
—*Publishers Weekly*

"A surprisingly resourceful heroine and a sinfully sexy hero, a compelling and danger-spiced plot, lushly sensual love scenes, and lively writing work together perfectly to get Elliott's new Regency-set Lords of Midnight series off to a delightfully entertaining start."
—*Booklist*

"The Lords of Midnight, all sexy and dangerous men, are introduced in this series starter. The romance, adventure, and sensuality readers expect from Elliott are here, along with an unforgettable hoyden heroine and an enigmatic hero. She takes them on a marvelous ride from gambling hells to ballrooms, country estates, and London's underworld."

—*RT Book Reviews*

"A very entertaining tale...Well-drawn characters, an interesting plot, and plenty of passion kept the pages turning. Alexa and Connor are worthy opponents and even more worthy partners as they try to unravel the mystery at

The Wolf's Lair. Excellent and well-rounded secondary characters, both friend and foe, make for a superb tale."

—RomRevRoday.com

"Filled with suspense and passion. The mystery is delivered wonderfully and will have you guessing up to the big reveal...hilarious and downright charming...The romance element will have the reader on the edge of their seat...The mental tennis match heightens the all too present romantic chemistry to the point that it seems to jump off the page...If *Too Wicked to Wed* is an example of what we are to expect, this will be a series loved by many!"

—FreshFiction.com

"I really enjoyed Cara Elliott's writing. She hooked me from the start...kept me glued to the pages...an incredibly sexy and romantic read...I would read more by Cara Elliott based on this novel. I look forward to reading the next installment of the Lords of Midnight series."

—TheSeasonforRomance.com

Praise for the
Circle of Sin Trilogy

To Tempt a Rake

"From the first page of this sequel...Elliott sweeps her readers up in a scintillating and sexy romance."

—*Publishers Weekly*

"An engaging cast of characters...Readers who thrive on empowered women, sexy and dangerous men, and their wild adventures will savor Elliott's latest."

—*RT Book Reviews*

"Elliott expertly sifts a generous measure of dangerous intrigue into the plot of her latest impeccably crafted Regency historical, which should prove all too tempting to readers with a craving for deliciously clever, wickedly sexy romances."

—*Booklist*

"An exhilarating historical romance...a fast-paced tale...readers will enjoy dancing at this waltz."

—*Midwest Book Review*

To Surrender to a Rogue

"4 Stars! Elliott's ability to merge adventure, romance, and an intriguing historical backdrop will captivate her readers and earn their accolades."

—*RT Book Reviews*

"With mystery, intrigue, laughter, and hot, steamy passion...what more could any reader want?"

—TheRomanceReadersConnection.com

"Another fantastic read from Cara Elliott. Can't wait until the next book."

—SingleTitles.com

To Sin with a Scoundrel

"HOT...Charming characters demonstrate her strong storytelling gift."
—*RT Book Reviews*

"Has everything a reader could desire: adventure, humor, mystery, romance, and a very naughty rake. I was absorbed from the first page and entertained throughout the story. A warning to readers: If you have anything on your schedule for the day, clear it. You won't be able to put *To Sin with a Scoundrel* down once you start reading."
—*SingleTitles.com*

"Steamy...intriguing."
—*Publishers Weekly*

"Fast-paced...a fun tale...fans will appreciate Lady Ciara as she challenges her in-laws, the Ton, and love with the incorrigible Mad Bad Hadley at her side."
—*Midwest Book Review*

"Delightful...filled with fun and some suspense and lots and lots of sexual attraction."
—*RomanceReviewsMag.com*

ALSO BY CARA ELLIOTT

CIRCLE OF SIN TRILOGY

To Sin with a Scoundrel
To Surrender to a Rogue
To Tempt a Rake

LORDS OF MIDNIGHT TRILOGY

Too Wicked to Wed

Too Tempting
to Resist

CARA ELLIOTT

FOREVER

NEW YORK   BOSTON

This book is a work of fiction. Names, characters, places, and incidents are the product of the author's imagination or are used fictitiously. Any resemblance to actual events, locales, or persons, living or dead, is coincidental.

Copyright © 2012 by Andrea DaRif
Excerpt from *Too Dangerous to Desire* copyright © 2012 by Andrea DaRif
All rights reserved. Except as permitted under the U.S. Copyright Act of 1976, no part of this publication may be reproduced, distributed, or transmitted in any form or by any means, or stored in a database or retrieval system, without the prior written permission of the publisher.

Forever
Hachette Book Group
237 Park Avenue
New York, NY 10017
www.HachetteBookGroup.com

Printed in the United States of America

First Edition: May 2012
10 9 8 7 6 5 4 3 2 1

Forever is an imprint of Grand Central Publishing.
The Forever name and logo are trademarks of Hachette Book Group, Inc.

The Hachette Speakers Bureau provides a wide range of authors for speaking events. To find out more, go to www.hachettespeakersbureau.com or call (866) 376-6591.

The publisher is not responsible for websites (or their content) that are not owned by the publisher.

For Sherrie Holmes,
whose wonderful creativity and sense of humor
is a source of constant inspiration

Too Tempting
to Resist

Prologue

Oh, I'm *so* glad ye stopped by for a visit, sir. The Wolfhound has always said ye have a discerning eye fer art, so I'm anxious to get yer opinion on this." Sara Hawkins stripped the last of the wrappings from around a gilt-framed watercolor painting and let out an admiring whistle. "Don't ye think it will look lovely hanging in the Eros Bedchamber?"

Gryffin Owain Dwight, the Marquess of Haddan, shrugged out of his overcoat and came over to take a look. "You intend to hang *that* in *there*?" A dark brow shot up. "I wouldn't advise it."

"Why not?" Sara sounded a little crestfallen. "Roses are my favorite flower and this one is awfully pretty."

"Indeed it is. But in the secret language of flowers, red roses symbolize love—a sentiment that would likely make a number of your patrons rather nervous," said Gryff dryly. "Patrons" was putting it politely, seeing as Sara's establishment was one of the most notorious gambling hells and brothels in London. "If you must pick a rose for a decorative touch, make it an orange one."

"And what does that mean?"

"Fascination." He curled a wicked smile. "Better yet, find a print of a yellow iris, which means 'passion.' Or sweet pea, which means 'blissful pleasure.'"

She let out a snort of laughter.

"Or a peach blossom, which means 'I am your captive.'"

"Fancy that." Setting aside the painting, Sara perched a shapely hip on the sideboard and gave the marquess her full attention. "Now who would have ever guessed that flowers could talk."

Gryff nodded gravely. "And then there is the grapevine..."

"Which means?" Sara leaned forward, her eyes widening in anticipation.

"Which means, 'I am very thirsty so do you have any more of that expensive Scottish malt stashed away in your private cupboard?'"

A crumpled kidskin glove hit him square in the chest. "Oh, ye horrid man! Here I thought I was learning some fancy bit of knowledge. But ye was just pulling my corset strings." She gave an aggrieved sniff. "Now that I own this establishment, I can make my own rules. So I don't know why I let ye through the doors."

"Because of my *beaux yeux*, of course," quipped Gryff.

"Yer bows-yours?"

"That's French for 'lovely eyes,'" he explained, batting his raven-dark lashes. With all due modesty, the marquess knew that he was a great favorite with females, aristocratic or otherwise. And not only for his *beaux yeux*—though the unusual shade of green-flecked hazel did seem to have a mesmerizing effect on the opposite sex.

However, that fact was proving far less satisfying of late...

"Hmmph." Sara tossed her head, interrupting his private musings. "So Frogs have a language of their own, too, eh?"

Gryff gave a bark of laughter. "Touché." Seating himself on the edge of her desk, he loosened his starched cravat, and expelled a long breath. "Now about that malt, Sara."

The door of the Chinoise curio cabinet opened and shut. Glasses clinked as she passed him a silver tray. "Ye may pour me a taste as well."

"I take it that business has been good."

"Aye, very profitable," she replied. "Especially as I'm putting this bottle on your monthly bill."

Gryff splashed a measure of the dark amber spirits into two glasses. "I'd gladly pay double for the pleasure of conversing with you," he murmured, passing one to her.

She exaggerated a leer. "Pay triple and I'll pleasure ye with far more than words, sweetheart."

"Tempting." He eyed her over the rim of his drink. "But I thought you were too busy running the Lair to have private patrons anymore."

Until recently, The Wolf's Lair had been owned by Gryff's good friend Connor Linsley, the Earl of Killingworth. However, Connor had turned over a new leaf in life and had embarked on a new career as a goat farmer after gifting the Lair to his former employee.

Gryff swirled his whisky. His friend had also embarked on a new life as a happily married man, a fact which no doubt had much to do with his own current unsettled mood.

"Lud, I *am* busy," responded Sara. "You have *no* idea how much work it is to run a business." Despite the bantering tone, Sara was watching him carefully, a shade of concern clouding her gaze. "But fer you, I might make an exception."

A smile played on his lips. "Tempting," he repeated. "However, I value the relationship we have now far more than a fleeting tumble in bed." He turned away, his expression blurred by the soft shadows of the private parlor as he stared at the pale painted wall above the bookcase. "Next time I stop by, I shall bring you a picture of ivy to hang here."

"Oh? Does ivy have a special meaning, too?" she asked somewhat warily.

"It signifies friendship. Affection."

Sara slid over and planted a light kiss on his cheek. "That's sweet, no matter that you're teasing me with all this talk about roses and such having a language of their own."

"Actually, I'm not. The bit about the grapevine was a jest, but the rest is all true," he assured her. "Indeed, the concept has been around for centuries. Lady Mary Wortley Montague, wife of the British ambassador to Constantinople during the early 1700s, brought a Turkish book back to England entitled *The Secret Language of Flowers*. It's quite fascinating. If you like, I'll bring you a copy."

"Thank you." Sara twined a lock of his long black hair around her forefinger. "How is it that a rakehell rogue like you knows so much about flowers?"

Gryff felt himself stiffen. Pulling away, he stalked to the hearth and picked up the poker. Coals crackled as he stirred up a flame. "You know better than to ask your patrons about their private lives. And like them, I don't come here to answer personal questions," he snapped.

"Ye don't come here to dip yer wick or to drink yerself senseless anymore either," retorted Sara, eyeing the very modest amount of whisky he had poured for himself. "Is something wrong? Ye look a little niffy-tiffy. Is something eating at yer insides?"

He stared at the embers, the bits of glowing orange a stark contrast to the surrounding bed of gray-black ashes. *Dark and Light.* "Oh, I don't know. Perhaps I'm sick of..."

Sick of what? Seductions and sousing himself in brandy? Of late, neither swiving nor guzzling a barrel of brandy had held much allure. In fact, he had given up drinking heavily several months ago after his fuzz-witted carelessness had almost cost Connor his livelihood. As for women, strangely enough, these days, he was finding far more satisfaction in dedicating his energy to...other pursuits.

"Perhaps I'm sick of youthful folly," said Gryff slowly, thinking of the books on landscape design stacked up by his bedside and the unfinished essay on his library desk. "With age comes wisdom...or so one hopes." He made a wry face. "My birthday was last week, and when a man turns thirty, he is forced to take stock of his life."

Folding her arms across her chest, Sara subjected him to a searching stare.

"Ah, yes..."

Her eyes slowly ran the length of the marquess's lanky form, moving from the crown of his silky, shoulder-length hair, down over the broad slope of muscled shoulders and lean, tapered waist. She let her gaze linger for a moment on the distinctly masculine contours of his thighs before running it down the long stretch of legs.

"Yes," she repeated, raising a mocking brow. "I can see that teetering on the brink of senility can make a man repent of his past sins."

"Of which there are too many to name," he murmured.

"Ain't *that* the truth," drawled Sara. "You and your fellow Hellhounds have a terrible reputation for wildness." Society viewed Gryff and his two friends Connor Linsley and Cameron Daggett as dangerous because of their utter disregard for all the rules and regulations governing Polite Behavior.

"But you, of all people, know our deep, dark secret— we are harmless little lapdogs," replied Gryff. "Our bark is far worse than our bite."

"Ha!" Sara gave a snort. "The Wolfhound may have been domesticated…" Connor's nickname was the Irish Wolfhound, as his mother had hailed from the Emerald Isle. "But you and Mr. Daggett are still devilishly dangerous. And speaking of that devil, how is his leg mending from the bullet—"

A sudden urgent thumping on the door interrupted the question. It was punctuated by a gruff shout. "Oh, no—ye can't go in there, madam!"

"Oh, yes—" The latch sprang open. "—I can."

Gryff saw a willowy figure evade the porter's meaty hand and slip inside the private parlor. *Prim bonnet, dowdy gown, sturdy half boots, stern scowl.* An expert in assessing females, he need only an instant to recognize the type. She was not a lightskirt, but a respectable lady.

Definitely a harbinger of trouble.

But thankfully not *his* trouble. Taking a sidelong step out of the ring of firelight, Gryff slouched a shoulder to the storage cabinet, curious as to what sort of sparks were about to fly.

"Am I to understand that *you* are the proprietor here?" The intruder pointed an indigo-gloved finger at Sara.

"Yes." Sara extended a ladylike hand in greeting. "I'm Sara Hawkins. And you are?"

The intruder eyed it uncertainly, but after a moment, innate good manners prevailed. "Lady Brentford," she said reluctantly.

In contrast to her straitlaced appearance, her voice was low and lush, the sound sending an inexplicable shiver prickling down Gryff's spine. It was soft as silk, yet had a slight nub to its texture.

The effect was unexpected. *Erotic.*

Gryff gave an inward wince. *Erotic?* Good God, what momentary madness had stirred such a strange thought? The lady did not look as if the word "erotic" had ever entered her vocabulary.

And yet...

And yet, despite the severe chignon and the subdued, sober hues of her clothes, there was something sensual about Lady Brentford.

"Might I offer you some refreshment, Lady Brentford?" asked Sara politely. "If brandy is not to your taste, I can ring for some tea."

"Thank you." Her tone turned cooler—indeed, it could have chilled all the oolong in India. "But this is *not* a social call."

Gryff tried to shake off the odd current of attraction that kept his gaze held in thrall.

"Ah. Then I assume you are looking for Lord Brentford," said Sara.

"Good God, no." The lady grimaced. "Lord Brentford has been two years in the grave, and I devoutly pray that he remains there."

A small furrow formed between Sara's brows. "Then forgive me, but…"

"It is my brother I seek—Lord Leete."

A delicate cough sounded. "We have a full house tonight, and I do not know every patron by name. Perhaps you could describe him to me?"

Leete. The name stirred a vague flicker somewhere on the edges of Gryff's memory. He closed his eyes for a moment, trying to bring the fellow into sharper focus. *Yes, yes, it had been just last week—an obnoxious puppy, yapping some impertinent question about what type of tassel looked best on a Hessian boot.*

"Average height and reedy," he answered for her. "Blond hair brushed in an elaborate array of over-oiled curls." A tiny pause. "And sidewhiskers that make him look like a poodle."

"That's the one." Lady Brentford turned slowly to face him. "A friend of yours?"

"Not in the least," replied Gryff. "Actually, he was making a nuisance of himself. I was forced to be rather rude."

"He has a habit of doing that," she said. Her voice remained calm, but her eyes betrayed the depth of her emotion. Beneath the surface hue of azure blue rippled a darker current of stormy slate. "Is he here?"

Sara shot Gryff a questioning look.

"The gaming rooms," murmured he. "Try the

vingt-et-un tables in the West Parlor. Word around my club is that Lord Leete plays for high stakes." A pause. "Though only the Devil knows why, as he seems incapable of counting to ten when he's in his cups."

Looking a trifle uncomfortable, Sara cleared her throat. "Lady Brentford, there are, how shall I say it, some unwritten rules regarding establishments such as these. Gentlemen expect discretion from the management, especially concerning interruptions."

"I've come all the way from Oxfordshire to see him." Her tone had turned taut. "It's a matter of pressing importance."

Anger. Though she was trying hard to hide it, Lady Brentford was extremely angry, decided Gryff. *But was there also a touch of fear?* Repressing a frown, he angled a step to the side, trying to get a better read on her face.

"Yes, I can see that it is," said Sara quietly. "So in this case, I shall make an exception."

"Thank you," came the whispered reply.

"If you will excuse me for a few moments, I will go have a look."

Lady Brentford appeared reluctant to be left alone with an unknown gentleman. Slanting a sidelong look at him, she hesitated, and then seemed to decide that he was the lesser of two evils.

"Thank you," she repeated, signaling her consent with a curt nod.

As the door clicked shut, she expelled a pent-up breath and turned her back to him. *Swoosh, swoosh.* Her heavy skirts skirled around her ankles as she moved away to study the etching hanging above the bookcase.

Trouble, Gryff reminded himself. He had survived the

brutal Peninsular War by listening to the warning voice in his head. And right now it was drumming a martial tattoo against his skull.

Trouble, trouble, trouble.

The wise strategy would be to finish his drink and quietly take his leave. Whatever her reason for being here, it did not involve him.

Instead, he set his glass down and walked across the carpet.

"I apologize for the artwork, Lady Brentford." A whisper of warm breath somehow found its way through the knot of hair at her nape and tickled against her bare skin. "It isn't often that The Wolf's Lair entertains respectable ladies."

"No apology necessary," replied the Right Honorable Eliza, Lady Brentford, trying to ignore the lick of heat that was slowly sliding down between her shoulder blades. "I'm not about to swoon from shock. I have seen a penis before, sir."

The gentleman laughed. The sound was soft as a summer zephyr and yet it blew her skittering pulse up another notch.

Tracking Harry to a notorious brothel and gaming hell in the slums of Southwark was embarrassing enough, but why, oh, why did she have to find herself in a dimly-lit private parlor, ogling obscene art with the most sinfully attractive man she had ever laid eyes on?

It didn't seem quite fair.

"Yes," said the gentleman, once his low, lazy chuckle had died away. "But perhaps not quite so many of the offending organs at one time." As he shifted to stand beside her, she caught the twinkle of humor in his eyes.

His eyes. Eliza blinked. How unfair of the Almighty to bless a rogue with such arrestingly attractive eyes.

"Or in quite so many athletic positions of *amour*," he added.

Eliza inched away, finding that his closeness was having an unsettling effect on her insides. The prospect of confronting her brother already had her stomach tied in knots. "Rakes and rogues seem to devote all their waking hours to naught but gambling and bedsport," she answered rather tartly. "So, given your presence in this place, I imagine that you are familiar with all of them."

Rather than take offense at her deliberate rudeness, the gentleman laughed again. "No, not all." He made a show of studying the risqué etching for a moment or two longer. "And thank heaven for that. Some of them look deucedly uncomfortable."

She bit back a smile, unwilling to encourage any further flirtations.

He *was* flirting with her, wasn't he? Or was it merely wishful thinking?

"By the by, I don't believe we have been properly introduced," he murmured. He had come close again. Close enough that she could breathe in the faint spicy scent of his cologne. "I am Haddan."

Lord Haddan. Harry's hero.

Oh, of all damnable, despicable coincidences, thought Eliza wryly. He was handsome, he was humorous—and for a moment, she had actually been enjoying his company.

"*The* Haddan?" she inquired, shaking off her unreasonable disappointment. After all, what did it matter who he was? "One of the infamous Hellhounds, who takes such gleeful delight in breaking every rule of Polite Society?"

"I see that my reputation has preceded me," he said quietly.

Eliza answered by crossing over to the sideboard.

After a moment of uncomfortable silence, he followed. "Speaking of rules, you ought to counsel your brother to moderate his gambling. He's a callow country lamb compared to the wolves who play here at the Lair. He'll soon find himself fleeced to the bone."

With her nerves already rubbed raw from worry, his words were like a needle pricking against a tender spot.

"Why on earth would you imagine that I have any influence over my brother, sir?" she challenged. "He holds the purse strings and the power to make every decision concerning money and the managing of the family estate. Do you really think he cares a whit for how his sister would like for him to behave?"

She had snapped out in anger and frustration, but the marquess seemed to be giving her question serious consideration. His brow pinched in thought and his gaze dropped to the Turkey carpet, as if seeking an answer in the dusky swirls of color.

Not that she expected one. In her experience, gentlemen simply ignored any problem that was too difficult to deal with.

But again he surprised her.

"It seems that I owe you yet another apology, Lady Brentford. You are right—in retrospect, my question was asinine and absurd."

"A gentleman admitting to a fault? On second thought, I just might fall into a dead faint after all," murmured Eliza.

"I have far too many of them to deny," replied Gryff.

Damn the man for having such a sinfully attractive smile. And those eyes. Eliza had never seen such an intriguing hue of green—it was as if sunlight had melted forest leaves to a molten swirl of emerald and gold.

She quickly looked away. "Actually, it's ironic. Whatever your faults—and I'm sure they are legion—you are the only one whose words might penetrate Harry's thick skull."

"*Me?*"

"Yes, you. The Hero Hellhound. The manly paragon of Devil-May-Care Debauchery."

Gryff frowned. "I don't even know the pup."

"Well, he most certainly knows *you.*"

"Which in your books is apparently not a mark in my favor."

"I am sure that the opinion of a country widow is not of paramount importance to you either," she replied evasively. *A plain, impoverished widow*, she added to herself.

"I can see that I have sunk beneath reproach," he said lightly. "Is there nothing I can do to lift myself up into your good graces?"

The question was, she knew, merely rhetorical—a bit of banter meant to evoke a smile, not a real response. Yet, his words seemed to stir to life a strange flutter deep, deep within, and then suddenly a wild, wanton thought seemed to swirl up from nowhere.

Kiss me.

In all her life, Eliza had never experienced a *real* kiss—that sizzle of wild, wondrous heat described in novels. She had been married off by her father to an older, irascible baron—not for her looks but for her bloodlines—in return for money to fill the family coffers. It had been a cold, loveless match. And now Harry was wheedling to make it happen again.

Sensible, solid, serious—oh, how she was tired of living for everyone else's expectations. For once—*just once*—she wanted to do something different.

Something dangerous.

"Kiss me." *Oh, dear God, had she really whispered the words aloud?*

"I beg your pardon?" Gryff cocked his head. "I didn't quite catch that."

"K-kick my buffle-headed brother in the bum," she replied, this time putting some force to her feelings. "For a man who reportedly thrashed the stuffing out of Lord Fetters and Lord Bertram in the card room of White's last month, that shouldn't be a difficult task." She brushed a wisp of hair off her cheek. "Perhaps that would knock some sense into him."

"The newspapers tend to exaggerate these things," he replied. "In any case, it sounds to me as if Lord Leete needs more than a boot to the bum to steer him off the path of folly."

"I fear you are right." Eliza hoped her face wasn't flaming. Feeling horribly embarrassed at her moment of utter madness, she looked around desperately for some distraction—other than male and female privy parts.

"Oh." Her eyes fell on a handsome gold frame lying face up on the sideboard. "Oh, my goodness, that looks to be a watercolor by Redouté."

Gryff backed up a step, allowing her to brush past him.

She smiled as she touched the gilded wood, and he felt the breath catch in his throat.

It was as if the sun had scudded out from behind a scrim of clouds.

Her eyes warmed with a luminous light, and as her lashes lowered, he saw they were not mouse brown, but tipped with gold highlights. A glow seemed to suffuse her skin as well, brightening its lightly bronzed hue and accentuating the sculpted cheekbones that slanted slightly upward. On seeing a faint dappling of freckles on her nose, Gryff decided that she must spend a good deal of time outdoors.

It was a memorable face—not precisely pretty, but striking. *Unique.* Unlike so many of the London beauties, who all looked as though they had been cut from the same piece of pasteboard.

"D-do you think Miss Hawkins would mind if I shifted the glass just a touch? I should dearly like to see the texture of the paper he uses, and the detail of his brushwork."

"Go right ahead." A lady who recognized Redouté's work? "I am quite sure Sara won't have any objections."

Eliza began fumbling with the fastenings of her gloves.

"Here, allow me." Gryff took one of her hands and carefully worked the tiny buttons free. Turning back the hem, he peeled the soft kidskin from her fingers. They were slim and graceful, yet he sensed a certain strength to them.

"Now the other one," he demanded, taking hold of it before she could demur. "These feminine items of dress can be cursedly complicated to remove. But as you see, I have some expertise in the matter."

A deep blush colored her cheeks, turning her skin nearly as red as the painted rose.

This time, after folding back the leather, he stopped.

Trouble—trouble in the form of a small peek of smooth bare flesh—was staring him in the face. He inhaled, savoring the sweet, subtle scent of lavender and honeysuckle. The perfume tickled his nostrils, drawing him down, down, down...

"S-sir!" She pulled her wrist away from his lips, but not before he had tasted the beguiling softness of her skin.

"My apologies. That was very ungentlemanly of me," murmured Gryff, watching her yank off the half-peeled glove and begin fiddling with the frame. Had her whisper been naught but a figment of his fevered imagination? Strangely enough, he didn't think so.

"Feel free to slap me silly if you—"

Sara's return cut off the rest of his apology.

"Sorry it took me so long, Lady Brentford." She hesitated for an instant, fixing them with a quizzical look before adding, "I've told yer brother to wait in one of the private chambers at the end of the corridor. My porter will take ye to him."

"Forgive me, but I've shifted your painting's glass just a little," stammered Eliza. "I've never had the opportunity to see an original Redouté painting, so I wanted to examine his brushwork close up."

"A what?" asked Sara, craning her neck to see what she was missing.

"The painter," explained Eliza. "Pierre-Joseph Redouté. He served as court artist to Marie Antoinette."

"And later worked under the patronage of Empress Josephine," added Gryff.

Eliza looked at him in surprise. "You are familiar with his work?"

In fact, he was an ardent admirer of the Frenchman's

talents, but he took care to cover his enthusiasm with a casual shrug. Only his fellow Hellhounds Connor Linsley and Cameron Daggett knew of his private passion, and he intended to keep it that way.

"I may be a rake but I'm not a complete savage, Lady Brentford. I do know a little about art." Returning his attention to Sara, Gryff added, "Redouté is renowned for his botanical drawings, especially roses and lilies."

"And this is an exquisite example." Eliza paused and exhaled a small, soulful sigh. "No offense, Miss Hawkins, but I cannot help wishing that it might grace the walls of a different sort of place."

Sara nodded sagely. "Ye mean because of the secret language of flowers?"

"Yes. The red rose is symbolic of passionate love," she murmured, tracing a finger along the ruffled lines of the petals. A cynical quirk tugged at her mouth. "I don't imagine that sentiment would find much favor here."

"I suppose I should sell it," said Sara, sounding a little regretful. "And use the money to buy more pictures of naked ladies and gents."

"I would buy it if I had the blunt," said Eliza. She gave it one last, longing look, then turned away. "But I don't."

Gryff watched wordlessly as she drew on her gloves and flexed her hands, like a pugilist preparing to march into the boxing ring.

"I appreciate your kindness, Miss Hawkins," went on Eliza. Her chin rose, her spine stiffened. "I hope that I shall never have to trespass on your hospitality again." Without a glance his way, Eliza hurried through the pool of candlelight and into the shadowed corridor.

"She's got spirit," murmured Sara, as the door fell

closed. "I wish her good luck with the men in her life—she's going te need it."

Gryff found his glass of whisky and swallowed a small sip. But to his dismay, the spirits burned unpleasantly against the memory of the fleeting kiss. Damnation, the night was not going as he had planned. Perhaps his books would be the best company after all.

"Thank you for the whisky, Sara," he said abruptly, putting down the unfinished drink. "I think I shall be on my way."

"Leaving already?"

"Yes." His gaze fell on the painting, and for a heartbeat it seemed as if the delicate petals and arched stamens fluttered a secret signal. "And I'm taking this with me. Add it to my bill, along with the bottle."

"Yer going te run off with the Redoodie?" Sara gave a little laugh. "Have a care, milord. Aren't ye afraid that its whispers about true love might plant some strange thoughts in yer head?"

"*Moi*?" Gryff tucked the frame under his arm. "Sorry to disappoint you, my dear, but there's a purely practical reason I want this. And it has absolutely nothing to do with love."

Chapter One

Two months later

*T*he devil take it, stop nattering at me, 'Liza." His florid face screwing into a scowl, Harry, Lord Leete, slammed the bottle down on the polished table. "Leete Abbey is *my* estate and I shall run it as I please."

"That is *painfully* clear," said Eliza, trying to keep her temper in check. It was not easy. Four years her junior, Harry had been a thoughtful, sweet-tempered boy, but that had all changed when he had gone up to university. He had left an eager, engaging young man—and had come home an arrogant, selfish ass.

That he had no head for strong spirits only exacerbated the problem. As was amply evident now.

"Glad to see we understand each other." His supercilious smile showed that the subtle sarcasm had sailed right over his head. "As I said, I'm having a few of my friends come to stay for a few weeks. I expect you to see that everything runs smoothly." He gave a vague, fluttery wave of his hand. "You know, a fine array of courses at every meal, and all that. Plenty of beefsteaks. Legs of lamb. York ham. Oh, and Bushnell favors pheasant, so be sure the game room is well hung."

She couldn't quite believe her ears. Had he not heard a word she had said about the state of their finances? "Shall I have a wheel of green cheese flown down from the Moon as well? Or perhaps a fricassee of unicorn, spiced with silvery stardust."

That barb finally penetrated the haze of brandy.

"Dash it all, 'Liza, a fellow can't be a pinchpenny when it comes to entertaining," Harry turned his head to glower at her, and nearly poked out an eye on the starched tip of his shirtpoint.

Unsure whether to laugh or weep, Eliza set her elbows on the table and took her head in her hands. Otherwise she might have been tempted to hurl the earthenware jug of flowers at his head. *Was there a bloom that symbolized "bumbleheaded idiot"?*

"Harry," she said slowly. "Let me try to phrase this simply, so that even your fuzzed wits might understand. Our coffers are nigh on empty. The farmlands are in a state of shambles from neglect. The butcher is threatening to cut off credit, and…" She paused to pick up a stack of bills. "And your tailor and bootmaker are asking for a sum that would likely launch a four-deck ship of the line for His Majesty's Navy."

Her brother's lower lip jutted out in a petulant pout. "A fellow has to cut a fine dash in Town."

"Yes, well, your 'dash' is going to run us straight to the sponging house."

"Can't you do something?" he whined. "What about your paintings? I thought you made some blunt illustrating those silly little flower books."

Eliza looked away. The silly little flower books were, in fact, an impressive set of beautiful quarto-sized books on English wildflowers, written by a noted authority from Merton College.

And yes, she had been paid—quite nicely in fact. But she would be damned if a penny more of her hard-earned savings went to fund Harry's debaucheries. She was getting close—oh-so close—to saving enough to buy a snug little cottage of her own in the Lake District. A place where she could live independently at last, free from the grasping demands of the men in her life.

Another commission was pending, and if her work was chosen, the dream might actually be within her grasp.

"That money is long gone, Harry." It wasn't precisely a lie. She had given it over to the safekeeping of kindly Mr. Martin, a fellow member of the Horticulture Society who was a solicitor in the neighboring town of Harpden.

"What about doing more?" His tone had turned wheedling. "You're jolly good at it."

A sigh leaked from her lips. "What about spending less?" Eliza pointed to the shiny gold fobs hanging from his watch chain. "Look at you—you're like a magpie, snatching at every shiny bauble you see without a care of the consequences." Under her breath, she could not help but add, "Birdbrain."

Harry sloshed more port into his glass, spilling half of it over the table.

The rich ruby-red wine formed a sticky pool on the pearwood and was in danger of trickling onto the carpet.

An apt metaphor, thought Eliza, seeing as her brother was bleeding the estate dry.

He guzzled a swallow and fixed her with a red-rimmed stare. "Y'know, our problems would be solved if you would stop being so deucedly stubborn and marry Squire

Gates. He's willing to make a very handsome settlement on me for the honor of having your hand."

"*Our* problems?" repeated Eliza.

Harry had the grace to flush.

"Squire Gates is over sixty and confined to a Bath chair with gout," pointed out Eliza. "If you are so keen on marriage, why don't you find yourself an heiress?"

"I don't want to don a legshackle," he protested. "I want to sow my wild oats." His fist tightened around his glass. "So this is how you pay me back for taking you in and seeing to all your comforts? Lud, I am ill-used for all my kindnesses. You are cruel and ungrateful." A sniff. "And exceedingly selfish."

Eliza drew in a deep breath.

Another gulp of wine and Harry began to wallow ever deeper in self-pity. "I'm going back to Town for several days, and when I return, my friends will be coming with me. How the devil are we going to get the blunt for my party?"

"Oh, for God's sake, Harry." Seeing as he was already well into his second bottle, she knew it was useless to keep arguing. She pushed back her chair and stood up. "Sell your hunter instead of your sister."

Gryff looked up as a silver-tipped walking stick *tapped, tapped* against the newspaper he was perusing. "Well, well, the Prodigal Hound returns. When did you get back to Town?"

"Last night." Cameron Daggett, the third member of the Hellhounds, took a seat on the arm of the neighboring reading chair and crossed his long legs. As always, he was a picture of well-tailored elegance—save for a few personal touches that were deliberately designed to tweak the noses of Society's high sticklers. Today it was a lilac-colored cravat made of gauzy Indian silk, rather than a staid length of starched white linen.

"Where have you been?" asked Gryff.

"Oh, here and there."

Of the three Hellhounds, Cameron Daggett was perhaps the most enigmatic. And dangerous. A man of razor-toothed wit and deliberately outrageous style, he gave the appearance of viewing life as nothing more than a scathing joke. Gryff was among the few people who could stand up to his bite. But Cameron did not allow anyone, even his two close comrades-in-arms, to know what secrets lay beneath his show of worldly cynicism.

"You might have informed your friends of your travels," chided Gryff. "Connor and his bride were quite disappointed that you did not come to their estate while Sebastian was visiting from Yorkshire."

"Woof, woof, woof." With a silent snapping of his fingers, Cameron mimed a barking dog. "Don't growl at me. You know I rarely pay attention to such formalities. I was otherwise engaged."

"I shudder to think of the possibilities."

"Never mind that," murmured Cameron, who refused to join any of the fancy gentlemen's clubs in London. "Good God, this place reminds me of a crypt," he added, glancing around at the other occupants of the room. "Look at your fellow members—they all appear dead."

"They are sleeping off their midday meal." Yawning, Gryff turned the page. He, too, was feeling a little drowsy, having been up most of the night writing. "Feel free to leave anytime."

"I plan to, but I was hoping that you might like to accompany me. I have a pretty little pistol that I acquired in Paris, and I thought you would enjoy helping me test its accuracy at Manton's shooting range."

"Unfortunately, I have another engagement," answered Gryff.

"Ah." Cameron's mouth curled up at the corners. "With Linonia's lovely wife?"

"No, that was over long ago. I—" Gryff frowned as a flicker of candlelight winked off something lustrous tangled in his friend's sherry-colored hair. "Bloody hell, is that a *pearl* hanging from your earlobe?"

"Yes. And quite a nice one, don't you think? It belonged to King James, or so the legend goes." Brushing back a curling lock, Cameron fingered the filigree gold setting. "You should think of getting your ear pierced."

"Ha!" Gryff gave a low snort. "I'm not about to let you stick another cursed needle into my flesh. I'm still angry at you for convincing me to get tattooed by that Jamaican sailor in Bristol when I was three sheets to the wind."

"Why? Rufus is a very skilled artist." Cameron flashed a grin. "And you have to admit, the ladies find it rather alluring."

True. The fanciful dragon curling down from his navel seemed to fascinate the opposite sex. Indeed, Lady Chatwin had been so captivated that she had found an Indian artist to put a butterfly on her buttocks...

"So admit it, the pain was worth the pleasure."

At that, Gryff had to laugh. "Perhaps. But no earrings."

His friend smirked. "Jewels seem to drive the ladies wild. Just a small glimmer has them unlacing their corsets in a hot and lathered heartbeat."

"I manage to loosen corset strings without the aid of flashy baubles," said Gryff dryly. His gaze drifted to the tall case clock in the corner of the room. "Look, talk of sex is quite titillating. However, I have to be off."

"Anywhere interesting?" asked Cameron, rising as well.

"As a matter of fact, yes. If you must know, I'm paying a visit to Watkins & Harold."

Cameron lifted a brow. "The publishers?"

"Yes," answered Gryff. "They want to print my essays on The Great Estate Gardens of England—in an illustrated folio edition, no less. I'll need to add a few more new ones to finish the collection, but for the most part it is done. The most important thing is to pick an artist to do the paintings from which the engravings will be made. Watkins wants to show me a few examples this afternoon, so that we may make the final choice."

"Congratulations." For once, Cameron's tone was entirely serious.

"Thank you," he said, hoping the boyish excitement percolating inside him was not too obvious.

His friend spotted the wrapped package propped against the leather chair and picked it up before Gryff could stop him. "Is this one of them?" he asked, taking a peek beneath a corner of the brown paper.

"No, no, an artist of Redouté's fame would be unlikely to take on such a commission, even if he were residing in England." Gryff made a wry face. "Besides, his style is not exactly what I have in mind. I want something more... whimsical."

"Whimsical." Cameron looked a bit bemused. "Not normally a word I associate with you."

It was said lightly, and yet his friend's quick retort stung a little. "Just because I don't walk around looking like a bloody pirate..." Gryff's gaze flicked to Cameron's cravat, which, though knotted in a flawless Mathematical style, flaunted its wearer's highly irreverent attitude to the world. "That doesn't mean I have no imagination," he growled defensively.

"Having read your essays, I'm aware of that," responded his friend with a small smile. He shifted slightly and took a long moment to polish the single dagger-shaped fob hanging from his watch chain. "I was referring to the fact that hiding your artistic talents under a bush, so to speak, seems to be making you more and more tense and unhappy. Why not allow your real self to bloom?" The walking stick *tapped, tapped* against the painting. "There is, you know, nothing unmanly about having a love for flowers. Stop keeping it a secret."

"Ye gods, you are one to talk about keeping secrets."

The light died in Cameron's eyes as if a shutter of steel had slammed down over his gaze. "True," he said, assuming his most irritating drawl. "It's far easier to see faults in one's friends than in oneself."

"Since you are the one who brought up the subject of secrets, why the devil are you so close-mouthed about your background?" demanded Gryff. "Though we've known you for years, neither Connor nor I have a clue as to your family or where you were raised."

"That's because like the *djinn* in Scheherazade's Arabian tales, I simply emerged from a magic brass lamp in a puff of smoke." Then, with practiced ease, Cameron quickly deflected the talk to another subject. "Tell me more about the illustrations for your book. I am curious—

if Redouté's renderings are not to your liking, what sort of style do your seek?"

"It's hard to explain." Gryff abandoned his interrogation, knowing that it was pointless to press Cameron for personal revelations. "It may sound silly, but I'll know it when I see it. There is a certain...Oh, *merde*."

"What?" Cameron looked around.

"It's Leete, that obnoxious pup from the country. And he appears to be headed our way."

Sure enough, the viscount teetered in the doorway of the reading room for a moment before cutting a patter of quick, unsteady steps to intercept them.

"L'rd Haddan! Demmed fine show y' make at Jackson's yesterday. Lud, what I wouldn't give f' a right cross like yours."

Gryff flexed a fist, sorely tempted to stop the young man's tipsy yapping with a punch to the jaw.

"There's a big mill taking place near my estate in Oxfordshire next week—y' know, the Scottish Highland champion te fight the German Giant from Hamburg. A few of m' friends coming t' stay with me...don't suppose y' would care t' join the party?"

Actually I would rather break my knuckles one by one with a smithy's hammer than endure a fawning pack of puppies trying to win my regard.

"Thank you for the offer, Leete..." Gryff paused.

Leete.

"Perchance would your estate be Leete Abbey?" he asked.

"Yes," replied the baron eagerly. "Most of t' grounds are covered with cursed gardens 'nd crumbling ruins, but the manor house is a proper place of masculine refuge."

Cameron's mouth curled in contempt. "I doubt—"

"The mill sounds like it might afford some amusement," interrupted Gryff. "Thank you. You may count on my presence."

Leete's ruddy face split into a fuzzy grin. "Excellent, excellent! I promise y'll have a good time, sir."

"Have you taken momentary leave of your senses?" demanded Cameron as the viscount tottered away. "The fellow is an unmitigated ass. What in the name of Hades made you accept his offer?"

Gryff smiled. "I'm not going for the pleasure of the viscount's company. Leete Abbey is the location of a very fine example of Capability Brown's 'grammatical' landscapes." And unless he was much mistaken, it was also the location of the viscount's intriguing widowed sister. Both were worthy of a trip to the country.

"Grammatical landscape?" Cameron waggled a brow. "You are speaking a very odd sort of language."

"Brown added a new vocabulary to gardening," explained Gryff. "He spoke of adding a comma here, a colon there...What he meant was, he merely punctuated the natural landscape rather than force it into a formal layout."

"Interesting," murmured Cameron. As they reached the front portico, he gave a small salute with his walking stick. "I shall leave you to your commas and chrysanthemums. Enjoy your conversations with the local flora because you won't be getting any sensible talk from Leete and his pack of drunken cronies."

Eliza eyed the crates of wine that had come down from London and swore under her breath.

Their longtime butler coughed in commiseration. "It's a pity His Lordship wasn't born with your sense. Or rather, that you weren't born with his..." Another cough.

"With his plumbing," she muttered.

He bowed his head and remained tactfully silent.

"I suppose you and James had better carry these down to the cellars." An exasperated sigh leaked from her lungs. "Do your best to moderate the flow of festivities this evening, Trevor."

"Yes, milady. I shall."

As the two men hefted a slatted box and staggered for the stairs, Eliza cast a critical eye around the entrance hall. The two overworked maids had done their best in making the place presentable, but cobwebs could still be seen clinging to the corner moldings, and a dull sheen of dust coated the gold-framed scowling faces of her fore-bearers. Considering the musty aura of neglect pervading the once-handsome woodwork around them, they ought to be raising the roof slates with their scolding shouts.

Assuming the last storm hadn't blown most of them away.

"Don't look at me," she huffed, resisting the childish urge to stick out her tongue at the first Viscount Leete, whose weak chin and piggy little eyes had unfortunately been passed down to Harry. "It wasn't me who created a...monster."

A monster whose rapacious need for self-gratification was getting more and more out of control.

Turning away, she walked for the front door, her heels clicking over the stone tiles. At least they had been freshly swept—not that the expected guests would notice such niceties. Rich food and strong drink were all they cared about, along with enough vile-smelling tobacco to add another layer of grime to the plaster ceiling.

The echo of her steps reverberated off the paneling, urging her to hurry. The first of the revelers would be arriving at any moment, and the last thing she wanted was a face-to-face encounter.

Eliza was acquainted with most of the men on the guest list. Like Harry, they were crass, crude, spoiled young aristocrats, too old to be forgiven for their self-indulgent posturing, too young to have acquired any polish or charm. For the most part, they contented themselves with lascivious grins when she passed by, but several had been so rag-mannered as to attempt a few drunken gropes in the corridors. Impecunious widows were seen as fair game. Something to be used and tossed aside, like a soiled towel.

Oafs.

She kicked the door closed behind her, taking savage satisfaction in the loud *thunk* of the ancient oak slamming shut.

"Thank God I need not join them in the dining room," she informed a twittering sparrow. "While they drink and smoke and tell their stupid, vulgar jokes, I shall enjoy the civilized peace and quiet of my own chambers, along with a book." Perhaps one of Mrs. Radcliffe's novels. A crumbling castle filled with debauched wastrels, dastardly villains, clanking chains, and eerie noises would certainly complement her current mood.

Ducking behind a hedge, Eliza crossed the lawns and followed a winding gravel path to a small stone cottage screened by a high-walled garden. Half a century ago it had been the bailiwick of the under gamekeeper, but now it was her own private place of refuge. A safe harbor in a sea of storms. A place where she could let down her guard and be herself.

Whoever that may be.

For longer than she could remember, she had dutifully done all the things asked of her, allowing her own dreams and desires to be bartered, piece by piece, to pay for the pleasure of others.

"Maybe there is no real me left," she murmured, chilled by the depressing thought.

After fumbling for the key hidden under one of the flowerpots—filled with petunias, which meant "Your presence soothes me"—Eliza unlocked the door and stepped inside.

A warm, syrupy light spilled in through the west bank of windows, and as the first rays touched her shoulders, she felt the tension melt from her muscles. The sight of her worktable, a colorful confluence of paints, brushes, papers, and specimen clippings bunched in jars of water, was always a balm to her spirits. It was cheerful, a sentiment sadly lacking in the main house.

"To hell with Harry and his dissolute friends," she murmured, determined to keep her brother's follies from intruding on the rest of her day.

Hanging her shawl on a coat peg, she began to roll up the sleeves of her muslin dress. The garment was, she acknowledged, an unflattering cut and a bit worse for wear. The fabric had been worn by countless washings to a gossamer soft texture, and the sprigged roses had faded to pale pastels. But it was exceedingly comfortable—the paint spatters were like old friends, whose rowdy exuberance always made her smile.

Catching a glimpse of her face in the mullioned glass, Eliza had to look twice. It wasn't often that she saw her mouth curled upward in a smile. Spots of sunlight sparkled through the reflection of her cheeks.

"Why, I look halfway happy. Halfway carefree."

She stared at the unfamiliar image for another flickering instant before forcing her eyes away. "Yes, but if I ever hope to achieve the *other* half, I had better get to work."

Opening her paintbox, Eliza began to mix pigments on her palette. Perhaps on her next visit to the art emporium she would splurge on a few sheets of French laid paper. If Redouté favored the subtle texture for his watercolor washes then it must be—

Meow.

Eliza looked up with a frown. "Elf?" she called.

Another aggrieved yowl, this one sounding fainter.

Oh dear. What mischief was her cat up to now? Last week he had been sneaking into one of the botanical bandboxes and shredding all of her carefully dried fern plants.

Setting down her brush, Eliza quickly checked the storage closet. "Elf?" she called again.

The feline answer seemed to be coming from outside.

She opened the back door and stepped into the small stone-walled garden. A quick search among the climbing roses yielded no cat. The pink gerberas showed no sign of damage, and the silvery sage was likewise undisturbed, its purple-tipped stalks swaying softly in the gentle breeze.

"Hmmph." Mystified, Eliza unlatched the gate and walked a short way up the path.

Meow.

She looked left, and then right. And then up.

"Oh, you silly, silly creature!"

Elf's forlorn purr seemed to indicate his agreement.

"Can't you come down on your own?" she demanded.

His tail twitched.

"Very well." Rolling her eyes, Eliza edged around a patch of brambles and approached the stately oak overhanging the shaded gravel.

"Ye gods, why is it that I seem to be surrounded by bacon-brained males?" she muttered as she unlaced her half boots and tugged them off.

No answer floated down from above.

"I'm always expected to pull their fat out of the fire. You know, it would be nice if, for once in my life, some Paragon of Masculine Virtue would come to *my* rescue."

Meow.

"Yes, and if pigs could fly…" Heaving a wry sigh, Eliza reached up and grabbed hold of a branch.

Chapter Two

Gryff ran a hand over the weathered granite, savoring the contrasting textures of sun-warmed moss and wind-carved stone against his palm. It was one thing to study a portfolio of printed engravings depicting a historic building or landscape. But no matter how detailed, they were no substitute for experiencing the actual site. Bees buzzed in lazy circles around the wildflowers growing amid the Abbey ruins, the low droning a gentle counterpoint to the breeze whispering through the ancient stones.

Taking a seat on the remains of a wall, he shaded his eyes and admired the view. Fields of green and gold surrounded the knoll, the hawthorn hedgerows and stiles giving way to rolling hills and a ruffling of forest that darkened the valley. Outcroppings of rock dotted the meadow grasses, and in the distance a river meandered through the valley, sunlight glinting off the slow-moving water. Gryff drew in a lungful of the sweet-scented air and leaned back against a slab of granite, letting the pleasant warmth radiate through his coat.

It was good to be out of London, away from the gritty coal smoke and crowded streets. The light lilt of songbirds was far more soothing to the ear than the guttural curses of costermongers. *Country life.* The peace and quiet was a reminder that he should be spending more time at his own estate.

Not, he thought wryly, that Haddan Hall needed him. The estate steward, a man who had been there since Gryff was in leading strings, ran things with the well-oiled precision of a naval chronometer. And yet, over the last year, as he had become more serious in his studies of landscape design, he had begun to visualize some changes to the grounds. The view from the west wing of the main house could be softened with a more natural arrangement of plantings instead of the stiff formality of . . .

But before he embarked on any actual shaping of the earth, he must finish writing the last essay for his book. Seeing the finished words—black ink on white paper— would be a symbolic statement of sorts.

Looking up at the clouds scudding across the sky, he let out a small sigh. Cameron would call it a commitment to his real self.

But that all depended on whether he decided to use his real name as the author rather than a pseudonym. *Truth or* . . . Distractions and deflections.

After another moment of musing, Gryff edged around to study the subtle design elements that Capability Brown had added to the manor house grounds. The gardens had been sadly neglected of late, but the plan was still visible.

"No wonder Brown is considered a genius," murmured Gryff, as he pulled out his notebook and jotted down a few impressions, along with a rough sketch.

"Lud, I wish I possessed a talent for drawing," he muttered, staring at the pencil strokes.

The words provoked a sudden smile. Withdrawing a small watercolor sketch that was tucked between the back pages, Gryff held it up and angled it into the sunlight. It was only a quick, loose study of camellias, but the delicate colors and forms radiated with life. It was . . .

"Perfection," he said aloud, echoing the secret language of flowers depicted on the paper.

From the moment he had spied it peeking out from the portfolio of possible artists, he had known it was the perfect style for his book. He had gone through the motions of examining the other artwork, but the flower had already entwined him in its whisper-soft beauty.

Watkins had allowed him to keep it, and promised that working out a contract with the artist should be a mere formality.

A good thing, for Gryff had resolved that he wouldn't take no for an answer, no matter the cost.

Tucking the sketch safely away, he rose and resumed his walk, choosing a roundabout path back to the manor house that wound down through a copse of tall trees. Sunlight filtered through the leafy canopy, painting hide-and-seek shadows over the ground. Gryff slowed his steps, in no hurry to return to his rooms. Leete and his friends were already half sunk in a sea of claret, so the prospect of a long and well-lubricated supper did not hold much allure. A bunch of young fribbles spouting slurred jests and inane boasts.

Good Lord, was I really so crass and callow at their age?

Quite likely, he admitted with a rueful grimace. He paused to breathe in the woodsy scent of the surrounding trees.

"Elf! Elf!"

Were there mystical wood sprites at play in the ancient oaks? Gryff shook his head, half smiling at the thought. He was tired from traveling and the setting was obviously affecting his head. For an instant he felt like a child again, caught up in the enchantment of some fairy-tale story.

"Oh, hell and damnation!"

No, that was definitely *not* an ethereal forest spirit, but an irate human. Yet oddly enough, the voice did seem to be coming from out of thin air. He looked right and then left. And then, as a rain of leaves floated down from the spreading branches overhead, he looked up. Among the flicker of greens, there was a flutter of creamy lace and lawn cotton.

His brows arched. The sight of a lady's undergarments was hardly a shock, but the angle of view was a trifle...unexpected.

"Mmmph." A small thud was followed by another un-ladylike oath.

Biting back a laugh, Gryff watched for a few moments longer, then tucked his notebook into his coat pocket and shrugged out of the garment. He caught hold of an over-hanging limb and hoisted himself into the branches. Up, up he climbed, brushing aside the soft slap of the leaves.

"May I be of assistance?" he asked, joining the lady on her perch.

The breeze must have covered his approach, for she gave a sudden start. "*Oh!*"

Gryff steadied her balance. "Sorry, I didn't mean to startle you, Lady Brentford."

"W-what are *you* doing up here?" she stammered.

"I might ask the same of you," he replied.

"I—I am saving Elf," she replied over the chatter of the leaves.

"Saving elves?" She was either delightfully drunk, or delightfully mad.

"Not *elves*, sir. *Elf*." She jabbed a finger skyward.

There, a half-dozen feet above their heads, a small striped cat was curled in the crook of a branch.

"He's afraid to come down," she added.

"Ah." Gryff looked from the cat to her. "I might be, too, if someone was shrieking my name loud enough to wake the Devil."

"Ha, hah, ha." She didn't sound amused. "Be advised, sir, I am in no mood for levity."

"I gathered as much. Ladies don't usually swear like sailors."

Her cheeks turned a touch pink. "If you will kindly move aside, Lord Haddan. I need to see if I can reach around the trunk and wedge my foot—"

"No need." Gryff was already shimmying to a higher handhold. The cat was in a deucedly awkward position, but if he stood on tiptoes, one hand bracing a spread-eagle stance...

"I had better warn you, sir..."

"Don't worry, Lady Brentford. I spent my boyhood swinging from—"

His words gave way to a grunt of pain as the cat raked its tiny claws across his outstretched hand.

"Elf doesn't like men," she finished.

"Thank you," muttered Gryff. "A useful bit of information to know."

The cat hissed.

He reached up again, this time more gingerly. Elf

struck out with another swipe of his paw, raising a beading of blood, but Gryff managed to catch the animal by the scruff of the neck.

"Might I hand this imp of Satan down to you before he inflicts permanent damage?"

"Thank you," she said, clutching the squirming ball of fur to her chest.

Meow. Elf did not sound quite as grateful as his mistress. Wriggling free of her arms, the cat shot down the trunk and disappeared beneath a thicket of bushes.

"Thank you," repeated Eliza, steeling herself for an explosion of temper. In her experience, men did not react well to attacks on their pride. "I'm sorry you suffered an injury to your hand. Elf didn't mean any harm. He was simply frightened."

"Don't mention it," he replied lightly. To her surprise he had already started to shimmy up to a higher branch.

Good Lord, was he actually grinning?

"A little spilled blood is well worth this magnificent view." His boots slid across the smooth bark. "Is that the River Thames?"

"Yes."

An ominous crackling sounded as he shifted his stance.

She winced. "Lord Haddan, I really think that you should come down from there. Stout as English oak might be, I fear that particular limb is not quite up to your weight."

"In a moment." He crouched low. "Look, in this angle of afternoon light, the stones of old Abbey ruins turn the color of sun-drizzled honey."

Eliza craned her neck, trying to see through the scrim of ruffling leaves. "Oh, you are right." The color was indeed delicious—and how unexpected that he, of all people, should notice such a detail. "How lovely."

She leaned down, intent on imprinting the subtle hue on her mind's eye, but as she shifted again, her foot slipped. Arms flailing, she fought to regain her balance. However a gust caught her skirts and tugged her sideways. The world began to spin and Eliza felt herself falling, falling.

Falling—

And then a muscled arm suddenly caught her around the waist, halting her plummeting drop toward the ground.

"Mmmph." She gave a little kick, trying to free her snagged toes from the twigs.

"Don't move! One errant twitch and I might lose my grip."

With her head hanging straight down, and her legs twisted awkwardly in a froth of skirts, she was in no position to argue.

"Here, let me try to get you untangled." More crackling. And then she was suddenly aware of a thrum of heat pressing up against her derriere.

Whatever he was doing, it was most...improper.

"Sir—"

"Quiet—don't distract me." His hand skimmed along the ridge of her collarbone. "Just let me shift my position," he murmured, letting it slide lower. A callused palm cupped her breast and then squeezed. "Oops. Sorry."

She let out a sharp hiss. "Please hurry, I am getting dizzy."

A tug lifted her up and settled her right against his groin.

How in the devil had she come to be sitting between his legs?

"Stop squirming, Lady Brentford." Like his body, the marquess's breath was warm and tingly against her flesh. "Not that it isn't exceedingly pleasant. But certain parts of the male anatomy respond on their own to friction, and I don't wish to embarrass you."

"You are enjoying this, aren't you?" she muttered.

A zephyr of a laugh tickled against her neck. "I'm just trying to be a gentleman and help a lady in distress."

"Ha! A true gentleman would not take advantage of the situation to grope a lady's . . . chest mound."

"But it's such a very lovely chest mound," murmured Gryff. "Soft and yielding as a ripe peach." His voice dropped to a suggestive whisper. "I wonder whether it would taste as sweet."

Eliza felt her face heat from peach to pink to flame red. "Please get me down from here, Lord Haddan," she commanded. "This instant."

"I fear that's easier said than done," he drawled. "If you'll look down, you'll see that your tumble has landed us in a rather precarious position. There is only one way to descend. And you are not going to like it."

A glance showed he was not exaggerating. She would have to . . .

"Just get on with it," she said through gritted teeth, consoling herself with the fact that the embarrassing interlude wouldn't last long.

He set his big, broad hands on her hips. "Relax. I need to lift you up and turn you around."

Aware that she was no mere feather, Eliza's flush deepened. "Lord Haddan. I fear this is not going—"

"Trust me."

The leaves seemed to spin in a blur of chartreuse and emerald, and suddenly she was straddling his hips, the insides of her thighs kissing against velvet-soft buckskin encasing his thighs.

Oh, Lord, oh, Lord. But whether her inner self was voicing a plea or a prayer, she wasn't sure.

With naught but a scant layer of lawn cotton and leather between her and the overtly masculine bulge of his sex, Eliza was intimately aware of his long, lean body. The tapered waist, the chiseling of muscle, the corded legs, now serving as a wildly erotic saddle.

For a fleeting instant, all her wild, wicked imagination could picture was the image of skinny country spinster mounted on a big, dark stallion.

Her pulse began to gallop, sending a frisson of heat racing down the length of her limbs. Her flesh was tingling, and to her acute embarrassment her core was growing damp.

Surely he wouldn't—he couldn't—be aware of that.

Or did a rake possess a special sixth sense of seduction?

Her heart hitched and began to thud against her ribs.

Breathe, Eliza reminded herself. But sucking in a lungful of his spice-scented shaving soap only made her dizzy. Her brain seemed hazed in a swirling, silken fog. Light winked overhead, bright, brilliant flashes of jewel-tone blues and greens. She felt drugged. *Deranged.*

How else to explain how all reason went spinning helter-pelter as she clutched tighter to the broad slope of his shoulders and crushed her body to his. A blaze of sunlight melted through the interlacing of leaves, casting patterns of liquid fire over his long, curling hair. Threading her fingers through the silky strands, Eliza tipped up her chin to watch the play of emerald-shaded shadows dip and dart over his features.

Their gazes met, and the rippling intensity of his beautiful eyes suddenly seemed too deep to fathom.

I am in over my head.

"I—I fear this game has gone too far," she stammered.

His mouth hovered a hairsbreadth above hers. "And I fear it hasn't gone far enough."

Swoosh, swoosh. The rustling of the leaves, soft as satin and lace, rose above the hard-edged whisper inside his head. *Trouble, trouble.* Ignoring the warning, Gryff possessed her in a long, lush kiss. She tasted indescribably sweet, with a tart tang of wild heather and some essence he couldn't put a name to. He coaxed her lips apart, wanting more.

More.

To his satisfaction, her response was warmly willing. She opened herself eagerly, twining her tongue with his. Teasing, touching—like their bodies, the rules of Polite Society seemed suspended as they hung high above the ground, letting all rational thoughts dance away on the summer breeze.

Eliza. The musical lilt of her given name rolled so easily off the tongue. It suited her, decided Gryff, for he sensed a simmering sensuality beneath her sun-kissed skin. She was no cold-blooded prude, but rather a delightfully daring wood sprite. A creature of Nature—of dark forests and sunny fields, of windswept moors and swirling waters. Her eyes gave hint of primal passions lurking deep down inside, just waiting to be released.

Without thinking, Gryff moved his hand down over her breast and began a slow, circling massage over her peaked nipple. Its tip traced a spiral of fire along the inside of his palm.

He made a sound deep in his throat and the rumble seemed to break the spell of elfin enchantment.

Eliza's eyes flew open. "Please, sir..."

"Yes, yes." Gryff leaned back, reluctantly surrendering the feel of her feminine softness.

"D-down," she stammered. "We need to get down from here. It's dangerous—we might fall at any moment."

Why do I have the feeling that I'm already tumbling in a slow, spinning somersault? He dispelled the strange sensation with a small laugh. "Very well. Let's get your feet firmly planted on the ground."

Hitching her a bit higher, he swung around and braced his boots against the tree trunk. "Keep your arms around my neck, and hold tight," he cautioned. "This may get a little rough." Picking his way down through the branches was an awkward endeavor. Twigs snapped, bark scraped.

"Loosen your grip," he said—and then dropped her heavily the last few feet to the ground.

At the unexpected impact, Eliza lost her footing and sat down rather heavily on the mossy ground.

Grinning, Gryff dropped down lightly and offered her a hand up.

"Thank you for rescuing my cat," she said with injured dignity.

"And not your person?"

In the shadows of the overhanging leaves, her expression was hard to discern. "I think I would have managed quite nicely on my own," replied Eliza. She took a moment to smooth her skirts and pick a leaf from her bedraggled hair. "You distracted me with the mention of the light's effect on the stones."

"Yes, now that I get a better look at that fetching gown, I can see you have a keen interest in colors," he murmured, eyeing the paint-spattered muslin. "The design is quite...unique."

Eliza suddenly looked flustered. "I—I always wear old garments when I..." She let her voice trail off.

"When you paint?" he suggested. "Very practical. And what sort of paintings do you create? Portraits of feisty felines? Scenes of woodland Druids performing their pagan rituals?"

"I—I just dabble," she mumbled.

"I imagine you are being far too modest, Lady Brentford." He smiled. "All well-bred ladies are expected to wield a pencil or paintbrush with some proficiency, aren't they?"

She drew in a nervous breath, though he wasn't sure why.

"May I see them?" he went on.

"No!" she exclaimed in alarm. "Th-that is, I don't like to show my sketches to anyone."

"Oh, come now. Rest assured that I'm not a harsh critic. I enjoy looking at art and in my experience, most females are happy to show off their talents. And yours"—another look at her gown—"appear quite exuberant."

If anything, his teasing made her even more agitated.

"No, really. They—they aren't very good."

They must be truly awful to stir such a visceral reaction, thought Gryff. It would be ungentlemanly to embarrass her by pressing the point—not that his recent actions had been terribly honorable. A gentleman really ought not ravage his host's sister at the top of an oak tree.

"Forgive me," he said, sketching a small bow. "I did not mean to upset you. If you wish to keep your artistic talents a secret, I shall, of course, abide by your wishes."

"Thank you." Still, Eliza looked a little skittish. She grabbed up her half boots and made a shooing gesture. "If you don't mind, sir, I should like to get dressed, and it is only proper that I do so in private."

Gryff couldn't resist a bit more teasing. "But I've already seen far more than your graceful ankle."

"How very ungentlemanly of you to remind me, Lord Haddan," she tartly pointed out.

"One of my many sins, I'm afraid," he murmured. "I often say things that I shouldn't in Polite Society."

Eliza looked away, the curl of her wheat-colored lashes hiding any hint of what she might be thinking. "Yes, well, men are allowed to make their own rules. Alas, women are not."

She was right. He could laugh off the incident, while the consequences for her would not be so amusing.

He backed up several steps and went to stand behind one of the thick-trunked oaks. "There, propriety is satisfied," he called.

A scrabbling of leather sounded in answer.

"Will I see you at supper?" inquired Gryff.

"Are you *mad*?" she answered. "Sit down at a table full

of drunken, debauched louts? God forbid. I shall stay as far away from the lewd jokes and the overflowing piss pots as is humanly possible." He heard a rustling among the fallen leaves. "You may come out now."

He stepped out onto the path. "Has your brother no concern for your comfort?"

"Given our previous encounter, Lord Haddan, I should think it would be obvious that Harry thinks of little, save for his own pleasures." She picked a twig from her hair. "Enjoy yourself among such company, sir."

He frowned, realizing that she must think him part of their circle. He was, after all, here.

"You and my brother can drink yourselves witless, but I have better things to do with my evening." Eliza drew back her shoulders and assumed a regal pose—rather endearing given the disheveled state of her clothing and her half-laced boots. "Good day."

With that, she turned and began walking off...though the attempt at a dignified retreat was nearly upset by her tripping over a root.

Gryff waited a few minutes and then followed discreetly, curious as to where she was going. The manor house was in the opposite direction.

As the path wound out of the trees, he caught sight of her up ahead, hurrying to duck through the stone archway of a walled garden. The slatted gate slammed shut.

Again, he waited a moment and then approached for a closer look.

It appeared a very charming spot. The mortised stones glowed with a buttery warmth, the vines of wild roses adding an exuberant splash of color to the well-worn surface. Thick twists of ivy spilled over the top of the wall, the curls of green like slender fingers swaying in the breeze.

Beckoning him to enter.

Ivy—it signified friendship.

Not likely, given the liberties he had taken with her person, mused Gryff.

He was tempted to click the latch and enter for a closer look. However, despite his teasing comments, he *was* a gentleman. And the lady's privacy had been violated enough for one day.

"Damn." Gryff forced himself to walk on past the snug little cottage abutting the garden. "Damn, damn, damn," he added in a low whisper, reluctantly quickening his steps as he turned down the gravel walkway leading back to the manor house.

There appeared to be more to the widowed Lady Brentford than first met the eye.

But as she seemed determined to keep her secrets well guarded, he was obliged to respect her wishes.

"Oh, you witless, shameless idiot." Eliza wasn't sure whether the muttered castigation was meant for herself or the marquess. She kicked the cottage door shut, aware that every fiber of her body was still quivering with heat. It was anger that had ignited such sparks. Anger, and some hidden flame undulating deep down in a place she didn't wish to acknowledge.

Eliza rubbed at her arms, wishing she could dispel the prickling of her flesh. The imprint of his touch felt branded on her body, and the tickle of his breath seemed to have scalded her skin. Everything about Lord

Haddan—his scent, his shape, his sense of humor—was supremely sensual.

Sinful.

"Of course he is sinful, you ninny," she whispered. "He's one of the notorious Hellhounds."

From under the table Elf gave a throaty purr.

"A luscious, long-limbed Lucifer who wreaks the Devil's own havoc with women," she added, as if saying the words aloud would give them more force.

Lud, only an utter fool would refuse to recognize the danger.

But her body seemed intent on rebelling against her brain, even though in her heart, she knew it was supremely stupid to desire...things that could never be.

I have an artist's eye for shape and form, so I can see very well in the looking glass how my face appears.

Even now, she could see a faint reflection in the window glass. Thin and plain. Too strong, too sharp. Men preferred a petite Pocket Venus, not a gangling Diana, Goddess of the Forest Hunt, whose string-bean body was toughened from tramping the fields to gather flowers and herbs for her paintings.

I am hardly a specimen of feminine beauty.

So, Eliza thought wryly, experience should counter imagination.

A man like Haddan was merely bored and passing the time away from his usual distractions by playing silly games with her. If the newspapers and her brother could be believed, the marquess had his choice of lovely ladies in London.

For once, Harry probably had the right of it. Haddan was, in a word, a rake.

A sigh slipped from Eliza's lips. So was it wrong to want him to touch her? Even if it meant nothing to him?

Of course she knew the proper answer, and yet...and yet...

Yes, Haddan would forget her in an instant. But she would have the memories for a lifetime. A lingering taste of brandy-fired kisses to keep her warm when she escaped to a new life in that snug little Lake District cottage. She would be living alone and isolated, with naught but sheep and gorse—and Elf, of course—for company.

So why should I deny myself a teeny tiny taste of forbidden pleasure before I go?

Men certainly didn't. It was unfair that they should get to write all the rules. And then tear them up and toss them to the wind whenever Temptation waggled a come-hither finger.

The Marquess of Haddan offered a wildly wicked temptation. A chance to taste passion with a man who possessed wit, charm, and divine masculine beauty.

And he was nice, despite his devilish teasing. Would Harry or any of his wastrel friends have risked life and limb for a cat?

Not bloody likely.

Turning away from the window, Eliza sat down at her worktable and drew in a deep, deep breath. *Choices, choices.* At times, life seemed like such a daunting path, filled with confusing twists and choices at every turn.

Well, if I am going to go astray, I might as well enjoy it.

From the corner of the room came the playful crunch of papers and the flick of a feline tail.

As Elf darted under the storage cupboard, a wistful smile slowly tugged at her lips. Oh, be damned with the consequences, she decided. The chances were virtually nil, but if the opportunity arose to kiss Haddan again, she just might embrace it.

Chapter Three

Gryff peeled off his coat and tossed it on the dressing-table chair. He loosened the knot of his Belcher necker-chief and as it came free, he caught a faint whiff of Eliza's beguiling fragrance lingering on the fabric. Jasmine and clover, honey and heather—it was unusual. Just like the lady herself.

He couldn't help but smile. *Unusual.* He had experi-enced any number of exotic trysts, but he couldn't re-member ever having an amorous encounter in a tree before.

Moving to the casement, Gryff gazed out of diamond-paned windows, taking a moment to drink in the view of the sloping lawns and clustered plantings subtly shaped by a master of landscape design. It had been a good de-cision to come here, he decided, despite the prospect of a very tedious evening. The glorious gardens and the in-triguing widow more than made up for having to spend time with Leete and his circle of boorish friends.

He knew he had a reputation for rakehell behavior that attracted the admiration of would-be blades. And for the most part he was tolerant of pups who nipped at his heels, trying to attract his attention. However, there was something about Leete that made his hackles rise. The fellow was too loud, too loutish, too lacking in common sense.

Perhaps his opinion was colored by Eliza's comments and the fleeting ripple of fear he had seen in her sea-blue eyes on the night of their first encounter. It was clear that her feelings were more than mere exasperation with boyish escapades...

"What the devil?" Gryff made a face as he turned and caught sight of the tall, imposing four-poster bed in the center of the bedchamber.

"Sorry, sir." His valet stepped out from the dressing room. "The gentlemen insisted, and I wasn't sure whether you would want me to stop them or not."

"Christ Almighty, have you any idea what the bloody thing is, Prescott?" he growled, staring up at the exotic contraption of brass and rosewood that had been hung from a ceiling beam.

With a pained look, his valet handed over a note.

Gryff hesitated a fraction before unfolding the paper.

My Dear Haddan, he read—already offended by the obsequious assumption of friendship. *In honor of your acceptance of my invitation to stay at my estate, I wished to make sure you did not find country life too dull. Knowing your prowess with the opposite sex, I searched for a special gift that might provide some amusement, and found this Turkish slave bar in a shop that caters to gentlemen and their appetites for adventure. I'm sure you will find a willing wench to fill its shackles when we go to the local tavern tonight. As you see, I do not expect my guests to be monks when they visit Leete Abbey. (Ha, hah!)*

"Arse." Gryff crumpled the missive and tossed it into the fire.

"The staff here seems to be in agreement, milord," murmured Prescott.

"Indeed?" His valet, whose cherubic looks belied the fact that his former profession was that of a cutpurse, possessed many invaluable skills. One of which was the ability to gather information with the efficiency of a Bow Street Runner—a fact that had saved Gryff from a number of delicate situations in the past. "And why is that?"

"According to the housekeeper, the young master is a profligate wastrel who ignores the estate lands and is beggaring the family coffers with his gambling," answered Prescott. "Over the last year, a number of servants have been let go because of money. Those who remain are a small circle of loyal family retainers who have been here since before Lord Leete was born." A sniff. "They all disapprove of his inviting such dissolute friends here for drunken parties. It is thought to be extremely insensitive and improper, given that his sister is the lone gently-bred female in residence, and has no one to protect her from any untoward advances."

Gryff cleared his throat with a brusque cough. "Given that she is a widow, I wonder, why she is living here? Did her late husband not make provisions for her?"

"Apparently, he was a worse reprobate than her brother, and left her very little. The lands were entailed, and..." Prescott paused. "The housekeeper did not seem to know all the details, save to say that Lady Brentford did not wish to live as a dependent of her husband's heir."

No wonder she seems a bit cynical about men.

"It seems that she is very fond of the Abbey and its

gardens," went on his valet. "And it is through her prodigious efforts at economy that the place keeps function-
ing."

"Well done, Prescott," murmured Gryff. "It is always
useful to know the lay of the land."

"Thank you, sir. Shall I lay your navy superfine coat
for supper?"

"Yes, that will serve," he answered. "After that, you
may have the rest of the night off. I hear the King's Arms
has very pretty barmaids who serve a decent porter."

The valet allowed a tiny smile. "You are sure you shall
not need any assistance after supper?"

Gryff shook his head. "I have no intention of going out
to the tavern with Leete and his friends. I plan to retire
early and read, so I would rather not be disturbed. Enjoy
a few pints and I shall see you in the morning."

"Very good, sir." Prescott withdrew to finish putting
the marquess's clothing in order.

Gryff glanced up at the exotic sex toy, half-tempted to
climb up and take the dratted thing down. But on second
thought, he decided it wasn't worth the bother.

Turning away, he went to unpack his valise of books.

Eliza entered the manor house through the scullery, wishing to stay well away from the carousing going on in the
drawing room. An incident several months ago had taught
her that Harry had no ability—or inclination—to exert
control over his friends, and she didn't wish to repeat it.

It had been embarrassing. Humiliating. That a so-
called gentleman should behave like a beast with his
host's sister was...

Her mouth quirked.

Oh, but the encounter with Haddan had been, er, different.

Which begged the question of what the infamous Hellhound was doing running tame with Harry and his friends. She couldn't really imagine that the marquess had anything in common with such men, despite his reputation as a dangerous rake.

And yet, he was here.

It was a contradiction and a conundrum for which she had no answers.

Men. The marquess wasn't the only one whose intentions were puzzling. Lord Brighton, the leader of Harry's little group of wastrels, had suddenly begun to pay unsettling attention to her. It wasn't that he had made any overtly improper advances, but the cold, calculating look in his eyes was enough to send a chill snaking down her spine. His words had implied...

Shaking her head, Eliza shifted her thoughts from men to the set of essays that had arrived from Mr. Watkins in the afternoon post. Thankfully, they were far easier to understand and appreciate. The author wrote with a lovely, lyrical style, and his observations and insights on landscape were very thought provoking.

Or was it a "her"? Watkins had said that whoever had penned them wished for the time being to remain anonymous. To Eliza, that definitely indicated a female.

Her mouth compressed in wry sisterly sympathy. Oh, yes, females had a host of reasons to keep their talents hidden under a bush, so to speak. Money was, of course, one of them. It was grossly unfair that women had so little control over their own finances. And then there were the prejudices of the book-buying public. Art was an acceptable skill for a female to have. However writing—a discipline that demanded intellectual acumen—was considered not only unladylike but also too taxing for the female brain.

Ha! As if men were inherently smarter, simply because they possessed a p—

A hand suddenly shot out and snagged her sleeve as she turned into the shadowed corridor.

"What's the hurry, Lady Bren'frd?"

Snapped out of her musing, Eliza tried to pull away. In the flickering light she recognized him as one of the carousers Harry had come to befriend in London. Over the past year, he, along with his cousin Lord Brighton, had become a frequent visitor to the Abbey.

"Please let go of me, Mr. Pearce."

Instead, he pulled her closer. "Oh, come, 'Liza. We're old friends." His voice was fuzzed, and his breath reeked of brandy as he tried to capture her mouth with his. "Give me a kiss. After all, widows are allowed a little slap and tickle."

"I said, unhand me, sir."

He laughed and tightened his hold. "You ladies always like to make a little game of protesting. Very well, I'll play along."

Her heel came down hard on his instep, and as he grunted in pain, she twisted free of his grip. "Be assured, I don't consider accosting me a sport."

"Damnation." He added a more vicious oath under his breath. "You ought to be grateful for my attentions. Face it, you ain't in the first blush o' youth anymore." The undulating flame of the sconce lit the wine-red curl of his leering mouth. "And you're second-hand goods, if y'know what I mean."

"So I ought to be honored that you wish to toss up my skirts?" asked Eliza, rubbing at her wrist.

" 'Arry's always saying you're a clever lass." His leer stretched wider. "I see you unnerstand me perfectly 'bout the privilege o' having a real man in your bed."

"Aye, indeed I do," she replied softly.

"I'll come to your room later tonight. Discreet-like o'course. No one will know our lit'le secret."

"Mr. Pearce, listen closely..."

He leaned in unsteadily, groping for her breast.

She slapped his hand away. "If you come to my room, I shall slice off your cock with a rusty razor—discreet-like o'course—and then feed it to the crows who nest in the Abbey ruins."

His jaw dropped.

"Good—I take it you understand me perfectly. And if you don't..." Eliza shoved him aside and made to pass. "Well, I daresay it would be no great loss."

Pearce did not try to stop her, but as she turned the corner, his drunken growl followed on her heels.

"You think y'rself so high-'n-mighty clever, L'dy Brentford. But just wait an' see." His snarl turned into an ugly smile. "You're going t' pay—and pay d'rly for this."

"Lord Haddan, allow me to pour you a glass of brandy." Leete waved a bottle as Gryff entered the drawing room. "You shall have to swallow fast to catch up with the rest of us," he called. "While you were out tramping those dry, dreary gravel paths, we got a head start in washing the travel dust from our throats."

"So it would seem." Gryff accepted the drink but did not lift it to his lips. "The grounds are quite interesting.

I understand that Capability Brown designed some of the landscaping."

Leete stared at him blankly.

"Capability Brown?" repeated one of the viscount's friends. "I say, ain't he the jockey who won the fourth race at Newcastle? A *very* capable fellow if you ask me— I collected a hundred pounds on my bet!"

Everyone else in the room dissolved in drunken laughter.

"Ho-ho, Pearce! That's a rich one!" hooted Leete.

"The plantings look a little neglected," said Gryff, ignoring the hilarity. "You ought to keep them in better condition."

His host shrugged off the suggestion. "I'd rather spend my blunt on more interesting things than bloody flowers or shrubs." Leete sidled closer and gave a knowing wink. "Like gifts to ensure that my friends have a good time here at the Abbey."

Gryff saw all heads turn to him.

"Aye, we all thought you might enjoy getting a little *lift* to yer sexual performance, Haddan," chimed Pearce.

More chortles.

"I don't need any assistance in performing at my peak in bed," said Gryff coldly. "And if I did, I would not be turning to puppies for pointers."

"I—w-we—did not mean any offense, milord," stammered Leete. "It was a jest...all meant in good fun, y'know."

"Yes, yes, a jest," echoed the others.

Gryff sipped at the spirits, trying to quell the urge to plant his boot in Leete's backside.

One of the other men gave a little cough, breaking the

awkward silence. "I say, how many rounds do you think the German Giant will last against the Highland Hulk?"

A debate quickly began on the merits of the two pugilists and who would emerge victorious from tomorrow's combat.

Drifting to the terrace doors, Gryff looked out through the mullioned glass and watched the setting sun paint the distant heathered hills in dusky tones of pink and purple.

Temper, temper, he chided himself. His mood had turned prickly, exacerbated by his own less-than-laudable behavior and the schoolboy humor displayed by Leete and his friends in hanging the prurient pleasure bar over his bed. However, he had accepted the viscount's hospitality, and so far he had responded by snabbering over the fellow's sister and snapping at the hand that was feeding him.

Not well done, Gryffin.

Despite his outward disregard for rules and regulations, there was a certain code of gentlemanly honor that was unbreakable.

"My abject apologies if I have offended you, Lord Haddan." Leete sidled up to him, wearing a hangdog expression of remorse. "My friends and I were only trying to amuse you. If we went too far, we are sincerely sorry."

"Let us forget it," said Gryff. "I didn't mean to bite your head off. I'm a bit fatigued from the traveling, that's all."

His host exhaled in audible relief. "Of course, of course. Here, let me refill your glass. I've brought up a special vintage from the cellars—I hope it is to your liking."

Gryff allowed the viscount to pour out a generous

measure. Perhaps tonight he would allow himself a temporary return to his old habits of imbibing far more brandy than was good for him.

He had a feeling the evening was going to be exceedingly long and exceedingly dull.

"Fribbles and featherheads," muttered the housekeeper, slapping another linen serviette atop the growing pile on the table.

"Is something amiss, Mrs. Hillhouse?" asked Eliza, poking her head into the lavender-scented storage room.

"Your brother's brain," replied the elderly woman. "It must have sailed off to Cathay, taking with it every last shred of sense and moral decency. And Lord knows if it will ever return."

"Oh dear, what's he done now?"

"I'm not rightly sure," she said darkly. "Wilkins hinted at some hideously obscene item being put in the bedchamber of the new guest."

"You mean Lord Haddan?" she inquired.

"Aye. That's the one," replied the housekeeper. "It's supposed to be some sort of jest."

"I see," said Eliza. Her glance moved to the linens and she heaved a sigh. "Has Harry asked you to do yet more work for his guests?"

"The fancy gentlemen must all have fresh towels by their wash basins tonight—as if they were staying at the palace of Kublai Khan."

Eliza bit back a smile. She had been reading aloud from *Il Milione*, the exotic travels of Marco Polo, while Mrs. Hillhouse did her sewing, and now the housekeeper was enamored of all things from the Orient.

"Now that you have finished folding them, let me take them up and put them in the rooms," she offered. "So you don't have to climb the stairs."

The other woman looked aghast. "Allow you to near those dens of iniquity? Nay, I won't hear of it. Wilkins will do it, once he's returned from carrying wine up from the cellars."

"Wilkins has worse aches in his knees than you do," said Eliza gently. "I am going up to my quarters, and it is no great hardship to make a quick visit to the East Wing before returning to the safe haven of the West Wing."

Mrs. Hillhouse didn't look convinced. "I've seen the way that Mr. Pearce stares at you. And I don't like it one whit. He's got a nasty look about him."

"I am sure that he wouldn't dare try anything under this roof," replied Eliza. "There's nothing to worry about—the men are all at supper, and likely to be there for hours."

"Aye, but—"

Eliza swept up the linens before the housekeeper could voice further protest. "No buts. I'll see to it."

"Promise me that you will bolt your door," said Mrs. Hillhouse, nervously tucking a lock of silvery hair beneath her mobcap. "A young, virtuous lady isn't safe with these predators prowling the corridors."

"Good night, and don't fret. I can take care of myself." Eliza refrained from pointing out that she was not young. Nor, for that matter, could she claim to be virtuous. A virtuous lady would not be curious to see what sort of exotic item was sequestered in Lord Haddan's rooms.

Ducking into the servant stairwell, she hastened up a floor and then tiptoed down the guest room corridor.

There was no sign of life in the spreading shadows. The valets were all down in the kitchen having their meal, leaving the wing deserted.

One...two...three... Eliza quickly distributed the first half-dozen serviettes, saving the marquess's room for last. Drawing a deep breath, she tapped a light knock on the door.

No answer.

She eased it open, and winced at the sight of the lamp left lit, burning precious oil that they could ill afford. Damn Harry for his profligate parties. Mrs. Hillhouse was right—his brain might as well be halfway around the world, for all the good it was doing any of them.

Looking around, Eliza spotted several books and a portfolio of papers on the escritoire, but hurried into the bedchamber without giving them a second glance. She was already feeling a touch guilty about invading Haddan's privacy. Her own reaction would be one of outrage were anyone caught poking around in her private things.

I shall simply deliver the towel and have a quick peep at this wicked Implement of Sin, Eliza assured herself. And then she would take her leave.

A few minutes at most.

The glimmer of her candle showed the washstand in the corner by the dressing screen, a bar of scented bay rum soap set between the pitcher and basin. Unlike her brother, Haddan appeared to be a man of orderly habits. The dressing table was neatly arranged, with the silver-backed brushes and razor case aligned precisely in a row beside the looking glass. A dressing gown fashioned of coal black silk dotted with tiny scarlet dragons lay draped in careful folds over the back of the chair.

Y Ddraig Goch—the red dragon was the symbol of Wales, recalled Eliza, as she now remembered reading somewhere that his mother was descended from one of the ancient Welsh Kings. That explained his dark, smolderingly sensual looks and beautiful green eyes, not to speak of his unusual name.

Gryffin.

A strong name. Memorable, like the man himself. But from what she had read, it wasn't the lilt of his Welsh name that had the ladies of the *ton* waxing poetic over the Marquess of Haddan. It was his prowess in bed.

Releasing a soft sigh, Eliza turned to look at the immense tester bed, its carved oak posts age-mellowed to the burnt toffee hue of Highland whisky. She edged a step closer, running her eyes over the thick quilted coverlet and the plumped pillows resting against the headboard. A twinge of disappointment tightened her chest. Whatever the erotic plaything, it was nowhere in evidence. And she was not about to start rooting through the drawers or the dressing room. It was embarrassing enough that she had let vulgar curiosity lead her this far.

She was about to turn away when a whisper of wind from the open window stirred a tiny ringing of metal overhead. Her gaze shot up, followed an instant later by both brows.

"Good Lord," intoned Eliza, as she rounded the corner of the bed for a better view of the bizarre contraption hanging from the ceiling beam. "Good Lord."

Heavy brass manacles dangled from the center of a polished length of rosewood. Its dark, satiny surface was inlaid with mother of pearl, the tiny shards setting off winks of silvery light as the rod swayed to and fro.

Fascinated, Eliza took a step closer, and only then noticed the thick silk rope that threaded through the ceiling pulley and attached to a cleat on the head bedpost. As if by its own volition, her hand reached out and undid the knot. She let out the rope slowly, dropping the bar lower, and then snugged it tightly back into place.

Another puff of air brought the scent of jasmine floating in through the casement, and suddenly she could almost imagine that a magic carpet had carried her away to a Turkish harem.

Oh, what harm was there in allowing wild fantasies to fly free for a moment?

Without waiting for an answer, Eliza ruched up her skirts and climbed onto the mattress. Pushing up to her knees, she hitched her body under the manacles and turned to face the foot of the bed.

"I cannot believe I am doing this," she muttered, reaching up to finger the gleaming brass cuffs. They were cool and smooth to the touch, but as her hands felt inside them, she realized that they were lined with whisper-soft velvet.

Interesting. That must ensure a comfortable fit.

"This is wicked, this is wanton, this is—"

Click.

"Oh, no," she whispered.

No. No. No.

Eliza twisted her wrists, first to the left and then to the right. No luck. Surely there was a hidden catch—if she simply remained calm and logical, she would figure out a way to spring it.

Think.

Think!

A jiggle, a push. A wiggle, a pull . . .

And then a prayer. Nothing made any impression on the unyielding jaws of polished metal.

As if to add to her troubles, another little gust blew in from the night, snuffing her candle. Only a faint dribble of moonlight softened the dungeon-like darkness of the room. Steadying her nerves, Eliza redoubled her efforts to release the hidden locks.

Click.

Had the sound been closer, it would have triggered elation. However, as she heard the main door swing open and bootsteps move into the sitting room, Eliza felt panic rise, coiling around her body like a hot, humiliating serpent and squeezing the breath from her lungs.

And then even the low hiss faltered and fell silent as a shadow fell across the bedchamber threshold.

With a wordless growl, Gryff moved to the dressing table and set his candle on the corner. A gloomy silence seemed to hang heavy in the unlit room, though a ruffling breeze from the half-open window brought with it the softening scent of flowers.

He took a small sniff. Jasmine, and some faint perfume that smelled vaguely familiar. Closing his eyes, he inhaled deeply, and as he held the air in his lungs, an image suddenly flashed to mind.

A coil of honey-colored hair, long lithe limbs, breasts shaped like perfectly ripe peaches.

Swearing, Gryff released a sigh and put his glass of brandy down beside the wavering flame. He had drunk far more than he had wanted to, his resolve weakened by the banal chatter of Leete and his friends. A boring bunch of young men, with ordinary, uninteresting vices. His jaw ached from clenching back rude retorts. It was his own fault, for he had accepted the invitation, and so he had felt obliged not to be churlish.

But it had been damnably difficult.

Thankfully, he could now enjoy the rest of the night in peaceful solitude. He unknotted his cravat and stripped off his shirt...

An odd little sound seemed to stir within the room. Frowning, Gryff stilled for a moment to listen. Ah, it was just a flutter of the draperies, he decided, as the breeze puffed against the fabric.

He tugged off his boots and set them by the dressing table, ready for Prescott to polish in the morning. Unfastening the fall of his breeches, he brushed at a small smudge before peeling them off and tossing them carelessly onto the seat of the chair.

Another sound, this one more of a tiny squeak.

Gryff cocked an ear. Perhaps there were mice. Leete Abbey looked a little run down.

Whatever the problem, housekeeping was none of his concern. He quickly unknotted the strings of his drawers and let them fall to the floor. A casual kick pushed them aside, and then he took up his candle and swung around for the bed, intent on turning back the counterpane and plumping the pillows before fetching his book.

"What the devil..." The low, licking flame captured the flickering image of frothing skirts and tumbled curls.

"What the devil..." he repeated, letting his gaze move up the long, lithe stretch of female limbs.

"Elf," squeaked Eliza. "Have you perchance seen my cat anywhere in here?"

Chapter Four

$\mathcal{A}$h." Gryff slowly set his drink down on the corner of the dressing table. "It appears the little Imp of Satan has been up to mischief again."

Eliza nodded, her throat too tight with embarrassment to allow further speech.

"Perhaps you should consider a leash for the little demon."

"F-felines don't take kindly to such restraints," she managed to whisper. "They are too...curious."

"Yes, well there is an old adage about curiosity killing the cat," he drawled.

"That's why they have nine lives," she replied.

Gryff chuckled, seemingly unconcerned about the fact that he wasn't wearing a stitch of clothing. "An excellent point." He cocked his head, making a show of studying the swirl of shadows flitting around the ceiling beams. "I wonder how many lives females possess, for it looks like you might be stuck there for some time."

"That's *not* humorous, sir," she said tightly.

"Food, water," he mused, pretending he hadn't heard her. "Dear me, that could be a terrible problem."

Eliza licked her lips.

"Feeling a little thirsty?"

She closed her eyes and exhaled a ragged sigh. "Go ahead and have your fun, sir. I suppose I deserve the ridicule for being so bloody, *bloody* stupid," she muttered.

Picking up his brandy glass, he took a long swallow of the amber spirits. The candle flame spun a thread of gold through the rippling liquid and suddenly her mouth felt very dry.

"Would you care for a drop?" he asked, raising the cut crystal. Shards of light spilled across his torso, accentuating the chiseled contours of bronzed muscles, the dark peppering of midnight curls, the hard planes of flat belly, the...

Her eyes widened. "Is that..."

"A tattoo?" he finished. "Yes. A rather large one. Would you like a closer look?"

No. *Yes.*

He seemed to take her silence as an invitation to come closer.

The feather mattress shivered beneath her knees as he climbed atop the coverlet. A golden glow dipped and danced over the sleek stretch of masculine limbs. How was it that he could look so impossibly graceful? He reminded her of the temple sculptures brought back from Greece by Lord Elgin. Divine visions of Warrior Gods, carved out of smooth, perfect marble.

While in contrast, she had never felt so awkward and ridiculous in her life.

Gryff rose up and slid his knees to a wider stance. "See, it's a dragon."

"A-a very large dragon," she whispered, trying to keep her eyes glued on the tattoo.

"That's because I was largely unconscious during the process. My friend Cameron paid the artist double the agreed-on price to enlarge the design." He made a wry face. "So be assured, you are not the only one who has ever done something bloody, bloody stupid."

Eliza couldn't help but stare. The intricate pinpricks of ink etched a swirling pattern of dark against the light hue of his skin. The dragon's scaled tail twirled around his navel, while its lithe body uncoiled downward, the jaws opening wide to reveal curved teeth and a scarlet tongue that pointed...

Eliza jerked her gaze up.

"What do you think?"

Her cheeks turned uncomfortably warm.

"Of the art," he drawled.

Trying to sound as if admiring a man's nether region was something she did every day, she replied, "Quite imaginative. Did it hurt?"

"Like the devil. Especially here." Gryff indicated a spot below his navel. "The skin around the area of the head is particularly sensitive."

Eliza knew he was being deliberately provocative. *Don't react*, she told herself. And most certainly don't look.

But her ears were apparently deaf to all reason, for her eyes followed the waggle of his long, tapered finger.

The dragon's head really was rendered with great flair. The artist had combined line and detail to create the illusion of both power and delicacy. A curling, fire-tipped tongue seemed almost alive. It wiggled ever so slightly as a muscle twitched under his skin. And then, and then...

A larger movement stirred just below the thatch of

coarse dark hair at his groin. His arousal grew more ram-
pant, and as he shifted his weight, the flickering light
gilded the jutting outline of his cock.

"Come now, you have had your fun, Lord Haddan,"
she rasped. "You've displayed your wit, and exposed my
stupidity. Now, if you please, it's time to release these
dratted locks."

His brows arched. "Any idea of how?" he asked.

"No," she replied through gritted teeth. "You are the
expert on sexual peccadilloes, aren't you? Surely you
have some ideas."

"I'll have to take a closer look."

The marquess edged his naked body nearer to her, and
Eliza felt as if her gown had been lit afire. Sweat began to
trickle down between her shoulder blades, and the stays
of her corset pinched like red-hot pokers against her flesh.

"Hmmm." He reached up with his free hand to examine the rosewood bar, causing his erection to tickle
against her belly.

"Lord Haddan!"

"Sorry." Gryff leaned back a touch. "Look, it would
help if you could relax a little," he murmured. "I can't feel
around the brass cuffs with your wrists so tense."

"Relax?" A burble of half-hysterical laughter welled
up in her throat. "You may be very used to prancing
around, flaunting your nakedness, but I am not. This is all
very uncomfortable for me."

He dropped his arm. "First of all, I did not deliberately
disrobe to offend you, Lady Brentford."

"I—I grant you that."

"Secondly, I am not prancing, I am kneeling. In my
own guest bed I might add, where instead of sliding my

tired limbs between the sheets, I am trying to aid a lady in distress."

"It was just a figure of speech." Brass rattled against wood. Clenching her hands, Eliza arched her back, but the movement only pulled the bodice of her gown tighter over her breasts. "Might I ask you to try again?"

"Relax," repeated Gryff in a satin-smooth whisper. He lifted the glass to her lips. "Try a sip of this."

The splash of brandy provoked a sputtering cough. "Arrgh—it burns!" she gasped. "Good Lord, how can you gentlemen drink that vile stuff?"

"It's an acquired taste." Shadows swirled around his eyes, dark and dangerous. "Here, let's try it this way."

Gryff dipped his tongue into the spirits and then touched it lightly to her lower lip. "That should soften the effect," he murmured.

Eliza hesitated a fraction before taking a tentative taste. Her lashes quivered, stirring a glimmer of gold.

"There, that's not so bad, is it?"

She blinked.

He wet his tongue again and dabbled a bit more on the rounded swell of flesh.

As she licked off the trace of brandy, savoring the unfamiliar flavors, he watched the play of her mouth, the delicate flick of her tongue showing just a peek of pink. His cock twitched and hardened.

Trouble.

Heat sparked through his blood, its liquid pulse drowning out the low voice of warning. *Beware of the Siren's song, luring your ship toward the rocks.*

Heedless of the danger, Gryff lifted the glass again and

filled his mouth with the dark spirits, holding its potent fire for a moment before swallowing.

Trouble, trouble, trouble.

"This seems to be working," he murmured, teasing his tongue against the inviting little opening. "Shall we try a deeper taste?" He gulped down the last swallow and let the glass slip away.

As he pressed in, urging her lips apart with a probing thrust, Eliza flinched, but only a fraction. Then she drew him inside, enveloping him in a soft, suckling sigh. A dizzying warmth wrapped itself around him, the surge of sweetness far more intoxicating than any wine.

Their tongues teased and twined. She was kissing him—eagerly, exuberantly.

His self-control splintered into a thousand tiny shards.

The *thump* of glass hitting the carpet was lost in the surging *thrum* of his blood as he shifted his position, spreading his knees wider. The night breeze wafted in from the window, its sweet-scented coolness curling against the back of his thighs. The rest of his body was afire.

Dragging his mouth down, down, down, he traced the line of her jaw, the arch of her neck, seeking the pulse point in the hollow of her throat. Her skin was throbbing, each wild little twitch sending fresh heat spiraling to his groin.

She gave a tiny cry, hardly more than a whisper.

In answer, Gryff slid his hands over her hips and crushed her close. God, she felt good.

His lips tingling with the taste of her, he couldn't help himself. The taut fabric outlined the plump, perfect round-ness of her breasts, the tantalizing tips of her nipples.

He lowered his head and took the nearest one in his teeth.

Inhaling with a ragged groan, Gryff drew the bud in. Her scent flooding his nostrils, he nibbled and suckled, feeling the point grow hard beneath the damp fabric.

A ragged breath—a rasping sound—slipped from Eliza's lips. *Was it a word? A plea?* His senses were pounding with all sorts of conflicting messages—his head was drumming in warning, his heart was thumping in pleasure, his groin was throbbing in lust.

She is a lady, he reminded himself.

And I am a ravening Hellhound.

Her moans were a little louder, the sounds silencing any twinge of doubt. Eliza surged against him, her body speaking clearly that his touch was not unwelcome.

In response, Gryff left off his kisses, and began freeing the tiny buttons of her bodice.

"Oh, please," she said, her voice slightly fuzzed. "D-don't stop."

"No. I won't," he assured her, surprised at the waver in his own tone. "Not until you tell me to."

Her reply was lost in a breathy gasp as the muslin parted and his cheek touched the swell of naked flesh. His fingers hooked the top of her corset and eased it down, baring her rosy aureole.

"Exquisite," he growled, possessing the rose-pink point with a gentle little nip.

With a heated cry, Eliza undulated against him, sliding her belly back and forth against his rigid erection. The friction of the fabric against his cock was driving every sane thought from his brain. Cloth—all he could think of was removing the cloth that curtained her luscious softness from him.

Licking a slow, teasing circuit around the dusky circle, Gryff glanced upward. Release, and this mad, mad, moment might thud to an end. But what choice was there? His hands danced up her arms, found the ruffled cuffs of her prim gown...

Whooossssh. The light muslin yielded with surprising ease to his tug. *Rip, rip.* With their seams split, the sleeves fluttered like windblown petals to the carpet.

"Better," he growled, peeling the remains of her gown down to her waist. The laces of her corset came next, a task he could perform with his eyes closed. But he kept them open, loath to leave off watching her expressive face. "Much better."

Her mouth parted and she wet her lips.

Gryff sensed that despite being a widow, this was all new to her.

"Try to relax, sweeting, and tell me what you like. Sex is all about both people having fun."

Her eyes widened in surprise.

"Did your late husband never care about your pleasures?"

Eliza shook her head and answered in a very small voice. "He said proper females weren't supposed to enjoy the act."

"Lout," growled Gryff. "Trust me, it's the most natural thing in the world for women to take just as much pleasure in sex as men." He touched his tongue to her nipple. "Don't think. Just feel."

He heard her breath rasp into her lungs and smiled.

"I love the shape and the softness of your breasts."

She cried out as he sucked her tip into his mouth, and the sound sent a surge of savage satisfaction through him.

The heat of her skin triggered a scent of spicy florals mixed with an earthier feminine scent that was all her own.

As her body flexed beneath him, Gryff felt his own tension building. He was usually in control of his passions, but a powerful force seemed to have him in its grip, urging him on with an indescribable need...

Her body no longer seemed familiar. Eliza shivered as strange surges thrummed through her limbs, altering them in ways she had never imagined. It felt as if every wicked, wanton fantasy was coming true.

Not that in her wildest dreams she had *ever* imagined anything like this. Sex with her late husband had been a quick, furtive groping in the dark. Her night rail shoved up, his body shoved down in a few hurried jerks, leaving her wondering. Wanting.

She had *wanted* to respond to her physical stirring, but her late husband had found her eagerness...distasteful. He had made her feel ashamed of her desires. But Haddan seemed to like it.

"Oh, do that again," she gasped.

"Gladly." His teeth closed gently around her aroused nipple, sending a wave of pleasure coursing through her. As she arched against him, Gryff gave a laugh—a deeply male laugh that seemed to echo off the dark walls. "Let's get rid of the rest of these frills, shall we?" he said. "They are only in the way."

The crackling of the petticoat was like the sound of a dried husk being peeled away. *I am shedding my old skin and transforming...into a new and unrecognizable creature.* Dazed, Eliza looked down at her body, pink and taut with pleasure. She was naked, save for a thin pair of lacy drawers.

A surge of primal satisfaction welled up in her throat. She felt every fiber of her being was shamelessly, gloriously alive.

"Ah, that's better," murmured Gryff. He ran his palms down her sides, the slightly rough texture of his calloused skin abrading along every indent and curve. "Glorious," he murmured, settling his hands on the swell of her hips. A hitch drew her close, and suddenly the heat of his erection pressed up against her belly.

Oh, so good, so good.

Eliza arched into him, aware of a mad, pulsing fire building inside her that somehow needed to find release.

"Let's have nothing between the sensation of flesh against flesh," Gryff whispered. Her garters snapped, and her stockings yielded with a whispery rip. Air kissed the exposed skin as he peeled off the wisps of silk and tossed them over his shoulder.

An involuntary shiver coursed up her legs.

His hand was now caressing the inside of her thigh, moving higher, higher, higher.

Oh!

Eyes widening in wonder, Eliza bit back a cry as his touch threaded through her intimate curls. Gently, gently, his finger slipped inside her quim and found the tiny pearl hidden within the folds of flesh.

Heat rolled through her. It was good—beyond good.

"Spread your legs, sweeting," he urged, delving deeper.

Eliza opened herself, feeling wickedly wanton. "Oh, yes," she said, startled to hear her voice sound so lush, so smoky. "Yes." She could feel a liquid burning between her legs.

His strokes were growing faster, more demanding.

"Oh, Haddan!" His name trailed off in a throaty moan. "I—I don't know what I want—"

"Shhhhh." His mouth teased at the corner of hers. "Of course you know," he whispered. "Every woman does." And then he was kissing her, and all further thoughts skittered away.

She moved, pushing again and again against his hand. Heat spiraled up from her core, cresting higher and higher.

"Oh, God," he rasped. Eliza caught a glimpse of his eyes, gleaming like molten emeralds in the dim light, and was filled with a sense of wondrous power that she could ignite such a look in a man.

His fingers withdrew from her passage and Eliza, feeling suddenly bereft, cried out in protest. "Oh, Haddan, please!"

Gryff's response was a deep groan. She felt his muscles tighten and his hips hitch...

Then she was filled again, this time with a thicker, warmer blade of flesh, sheathing itself in heat and honey.

She thought she was going to expire with pleasure.

He was moaning, too, thrusting into her hard and fast. Never had she felt so fiercely feminine.

Elation bubbled up inside her, escaping as a throaty laugh. The room began to spin and then all at once seemed to burst into flames. A shower of sparks seemed to scorch her skin, and as she arched in pleasure, Eliza was dimly aware of a cry, covered by his hand.

A groan rumbled in his chest, and an instant later he

pulled back and she felt a splash of warm liquid on her belly.

"*Annwyl Dduw*," rasped Gryff in Gaelic as he slumped against her body, his arms wrapping around her waist. His sweat-sheened muscles melted to a softer shape, though in the wavering candlelight his broad back was still a stretch of chiseled strength.

He whispered something else, but the words were oddly muffled—all she was conscious of was the feeling of floating on air in some netherworld of spun-silver sugar.

Oh, it was delicious.

Gryff moved, and suddenly her wrists were released. Her body—gloriously boneless—slid into his arms.

Holding her tight, he collapsed onto the bed, their limbs tangling in soft linen and silken laughter. Eliza closed her eyes, savoring the closeness of his big body, redolent with the musky scent of their passion. Breathing deeply, she smiled and sunk into sweet, sweet oblivion.

Chapter Five

Darkness, still and silent, shrouded the corridor. Despite the lateness of the hour, Harry and his friends had apparently not yet returned from their revelries, leaving the rest of the Abbey slumbering in peace and quiet.

Holding her breath, Eliza crept down the unlit corridor and slipped into the servant stairwell, offering up a prayer to every Deity in Creation that no one had witnessed her descent into depravity.

The chill night air licked against her bare arms, stirring a stark horror of what she had just done.

Now that Reason had reasserted its normal place in her brain, Shame swathed her scantily clad body.

"Oh, you wagtail hussy," she whispered. Her aching loneliness, her longing need were no excuse for such wanton behavior. Clutching her torn gown, Eliza hurried her steps, desperate to escape to the sanctuary of her own rooms. A cautious peek showed the landing was deserted. She tiptoed across the parquet and darted into the dark corridor leading to her quarters.

As if I can outrun my misdeeds.

She was uncomfortably aware that her body was still

warm with the heat of *him*, every inch of her skin redolent with his musky scent and the raw, unmistakable reek of sex.

Sex. Her fingers found the latch to her bedchamber and yanked it open. Closing the door, Eliza slid the bolt into place and slumped against the paneled oak. Surely she would awake in a moment and discover this was all a bad dream. She wasn't the sort of wild, wanton female who swung nude in smoky boudoirs. But the trace of redness on her wrists said otherwise. Rubbing at the marks could not erase the fact that she had behaved like a jaded harem girl, a sexual sylph luring men to feast on forbidden pleasures.

Me? Seducing the opposite sex? Driving the notorious Hellhound wild with desire for my body?

No, thought Eliza with a shiver of disgust. The brandy had addled her wits. Haddan had simply been drunk. Bored. Randy. In such a state, any female would have suited the purpose of satisfying his lust.

So don't take it personally.

"I'm p-plain. And p-practical," whispered Eliza, her mouth curling in self-mocking contempt. "Indeed, *I* ought to have a tattoo displayed prominently on my person, announcing that fact." Squeezing her eyes shut, she threw her torn gown to the floor and pressed her palms to her forehead. "ELIZA THE IDIOT, emblazoned in large red letters. That way, every time I glance in the looking glass I could be reminded of my folly."

After several long moments of silently contemplating her sins, Eliza pushed away from the door and padded over to her bed.

"What's done is done," she murmured, looking down

at the shredded sleeves. She couldn't change the past, but she could—*she would*—control the future.

Not for all the velvet-lined manacles in Xanadu could she allow this strange, frightening infatuation for the Marquess of Haddan to ruin all her plans. Freedom, independence, control over her own destiny...

I must not—I will not—succumb again. And as her innate pragmatism slowly reasserted control over her rebellious thoughts, Eliza realized that there was one surefire way to put an end to any further temptation.

"Oh, bloody hell." Wincing as pain pitchforked through his skull, Gryff waited a moment, then lifted his right eyelid a fraction higher. His sight was still blurred, but his other senses were slowly coming into focus. *Feel*— he could feel that he was lying naked, twined in a rumple of sheets. *Smell*—he could smell the beguiling scent of verbena and cloves clinging to the linen. *Hear*—he could hear the faint rattle of metal swinging overhead.

Chink, chink, chink.

"What the devil is that infernal noise..." Frowning, Gryff flopped onto his back and forced his other eye open. Bold as brass, a dangling manacle winked back at him.

Satan's Ballocks. He sat bolt upright as the memory of the midnight hours finally pierced the brandy-thick muzziness wrapped around his brain.

Maybe it was merely a wild hallucination, a figment of fantasy stirred by the demons of drink.

But no—another sniff said her lingering scent was all too real. As was the tiny strip of torn fabric lying atop the bedsheet.

Good God. The sight of the sprigged muslin triggered

a rush of heated recollections. *Flaming candlelight, burning brandy, smoldering desires.* He groaned. *Willing flesh, eager passions, yielding secrets.*

Sweet, sweet ecstasy.

"Good God." This time he said it aloud. "How could I have been such a bloody, bloody arse."

His throat tightened in remorse. Regret. Not for the actual experience...which had been sublimely sweet. But for the shame of taking advantage of the situation. Gryff slumped back against the pillows, well aware that he had no right to castigate Leete for a lack of character.

I can hardly hold myself up as a shining light of gentlemanly honor.

Honor. He swallowed hard, trying to dispel the sickly, sour taste in his mouth.

The door opened quietly, though the sound was like another jab of sharpened steel against his skull.

His valet set down the tea tray and without a word began to straighten up the disarray. His coat and trousers were hung neatly over the dressing table chair...the wrinkled shirt and cravat were bundled and put away in a drawer...a lady's stocking was unwrapped from around the bedpost...

"Prescott, you will dispose of that discreetly," he muttered.

"Of course, sir." His valet cast a curious glance at the sex toy but was wise enough to refrain from comment. Tucking the scrap of silk in his pocket, he went to the windows and opened the draperies.

"And you will begin packing." Gryff winced as a blade of sunlight cut across his eyes. "Immediately."

"Will we not be staying for the mill?"

"No, I want to leave this morning. You may tell Leete…" He massaged at his aching temples. "Bloody hell, tell him whatever you damn well please."

"Very good, sir." His valet carefully smoothed a crease from Gryff's evening coat. "A pressing engagement calls us back to London—I shall take care of it."

"And Prescott…"

His valet paused.

"Might you inquire of the housekeeper whether Lady Brentford has yet risen this morning? I should like to arrange a private word with her before I go."

"Actually, I can answer that for you now, milord," replied Prescott. "The lady left at first light. It seems she is in the habit of paying regular visits to her former governess in Harpden in order to attend the monthly meetings of the Oxfordshire Horticulture Society."

Gryff propped himself up on his elbows. "And she was slated to depart this morning?"

"No, milord. She decided to leave several days ahead of schedule. But the housekeeper says that is not unusual, especially if the lady has supplies to shop for in town."

What sort of supplies? he wondered—and then repressed a guilty grimace. A new muslin dress to start with. Along with a pair of silk stockings.

"I see," he said aloud. Throwing off the coverlet, he swung his bare feet to the floor. "Then there is no need to delay our own departure. Kindly alert the stables to have my phaeton ready within the half hour. You may follow with the luggage carriage at your leisure."

Prescott nodded. "And will you be wanting pen and paper, sir?"

"What for?"

"I thought that perhaps you would wish to leave a note for the lady."

Saying what? *Oh, how delightful it was finding you trussed up in my bed. I had a lovely time tupping you witless. Indeed, I look forward to shedding my clothes— along with every last shred of gentlemanly scruples— and doing it again sometime soon. Respectfully Yours, the Heinous Hellhound*

"No note, Prescott," growled Gryff. "Just a cup of black coffee, if you please."

A short while later, Gryff was on the road back to London, jostling along with a spitting rain and his own equally stormy thoughts as company. *Reckless.* Gripping the reins, he slowed his matched pair of grays through a tight turn. He had been reckless. Heedless of all but the moment of pleasure.

Trouble. Once again, his devil-may-care disregard for the consequences of his actions had reared its ugly head.

It was a damnable weakness of his, and he was not proud of it. His drinking had nearly cost Connor The Wolf's Lair. His dalliances had nearly broken a lady friend's marriage. But they, at least, had known of his foibles, his faults. Lady Brentford did not. His taking advantage of her hidden passion had been shameless. She didn't know the unwritten rules of London games, so in a sense he had cheated by using his charm and humor to seduce her.

Oh yes, he knew the effect his smile had on women. And it had been unfair to use it on an unsuspecting lady, who was in many ways an innocent despite her widowhood.

Recklessness over responsibility—it was childish.

Bloody hell, he was no better than Leete, a selfish, weak lout.

The curricle's wheels jolted over the ruts, sending a stream of chilly water splashing from the brim of his hat down beneath the collar of his coat. The drops trickled down his spine, stirring a shiver of reproach.

Strangely enough, it hadn't been just a game at the time. Both unusual encounters with Lady Brentford had been unique—and not simply because they involved acrobatics and branches of wood. She made him feel...

"Be damned with feelings," he muttered, shifting his sodden boots to steady himself against the bounces of the road. "The interlude was a moment of inexplicable madness. Lady Brentford is a sensible, smart female—I am sure that she is just as anxious as I am to forget that it ever happened."

The ancient carriage lurched to a halt. Stuffing her sketchbook into her valise, Eliza wrenched the door open and dropped down to the ground before the coachman could come around to assist her.

"Thank you, Johnson," she called to her longtime servant. "You may come collect me on Thursday."

"Aye, milady," came the reedy answer. A flick of his frayed whip set the lone horse into a shambling walk. "Assuming we are all still in working order."

She watched the wheels wobble, knowing it was a miracle that the vehicle was still in one piece. It was only through Johnson's ingenuity—and a pot of his mysterious glue—that the worn metal and wood held together.

Yet last month, Harry had purchased a showy new hunter.

Sighing, she turned and unlatched the garden gate.

Soon the only road they all would be galloping down was the Path to Perdition.

"Eliza!" A tiny figure dwarfed by her white apron and oversized mobcap emerged from a tangle of wisteria vines, setting off a shower of pale purple petals. "How lovely to see you!"

In spite of all her worries, Eliza couldn't help but smile at the vision in white with pastel speckles. Her old governess looked like an elfin sugar confection dotted with candied violets.

"I hope you don't mind that I am here a day early. I should have sent word, but it was an impulsive decision," she replied. *Like a number of other recent actions.* "Harry has a houseful of idiots and, well..."

"Oh, pish. I'm always delighted to see you," said her old governess.

"Thank you." Eliza looked away quickly, horrified to feel tears prickling at the back of her lids. With exaggerated nonchalance, she bent over a clump of flowers. "How lovely your daisies are looking."

There was a moment of silence. "Are you feeling ill?"

"No!" She carefully brushed a bee from one of the curling stems. "W-why do you ask?"

"Because you are admiring the purple coneflowers."

"Oh. Right." Eliza quickly shuffled a step to her right. "I suppose that I'm a little...fatigued."

"I don't doubt it. Harry's friends would exhaust the patience of Job." Miss Augustina Haverstick's soft smile belied the sharpness of her gaze. She would put a hawk to blush with her perceptive powers. And right now, Eliza was feeling like a field mouse caught far from any protective cover.

"Come, why don't we go inside and fix a cup of tea."

"I don't wish to interrupt you—I can put my things away and make myself at home."

"Yes, but I'm feeling in need of a bit of sustenance myself. There are strawberry tarts, fresh from the oven. And walnut shortbread as well."

Eliza's stomach growled. She had fled home without a bite of breakfast. "I adore your shortbread."

"I do know you rather well, my dear," came the dry reply.

Which was, fretted Eliza, a mixed blessing. The elderly lady was more like real family to her than any flesh-and-blood relative. If Gussie were to find her behavior beyond the pale, then she might have to crawl down a rabbit hole.

And hope that it burrowed all the way down to the pleasure palaces of Xanadu.

The comfortable clatter of making tea—the bubbling kettle on the hob, the *chink, chink* of the chipped Staffordshire pottery—helped ease the knot in her chest. For years now, this snug little cottage on the outskirts of town had been a safe haven from all the pressing doubts and fears that had encircled her life since leaving the schoolroom. Gussie had been a sage counselor, a patient confidante, a loyal friend.

But even the closest friend might shy away from the awful secret that she carried inside her.

As Eliza rummaged through the cupboard, gathering the trays and linens, she was sure that she could still feel the imprint of Haddan's body on hers. No amount of scrubbing or scouring would remove the trace from her skin. Like a brand from a red-hot poker, it would mark her forever.

"Oh, stop being so melodramatic," she whispered to herself. On second thought, perhaps she could take up novel writing, and illustrate the perilous Path to Perdition with drawings of fallen flowers. Geraniums for stupidity...

"Did you say something, my dear?"

"No, nothing," mumbled Eliza, quickly moving to put out the forks and spoons on the kitchen table.

Augustina set the tea tray down, and performed the soothing ritual of pouring the fragrant brew. A plume of steam wafted up from the spout, its warmth punctuated by the cheerful rattle of the sugar and cream pots.

"Here you are." Her friend passed over a double helping of shortbread along with a cup. "You look as though you need an extra bit of food to fortify your strength."

Eliza was sure that she could not eat, but broke off a piece to hide her confusion. To her surprise, the buttery crumbs were ambrosial on her tongue. The woodsy tang of the nuts and spices reminded her of Haddan—

Stop mooning like a silly schoolgirl. Hadn't she sinned enough without seeing the Hellhound's seductive presence in everything around her?

"Oh, what would I do without your delicious sweets?" murmured Eliza. She reached meditatively for the second piece, but this one remained pinched between her fingers.

"Something truly must be amiss, if you have lost your appetite for my shortbread," remarked Augustina.

Eliza swallowed hard and essayed a wan smile. "Is it that obvious?"

Her friend eyed the small pyramid of crumbs on the plate and merely lifted a brow.

"Right." A tremulous sigh. "I—I am unsure of how to start."

"At the beginning, of course," said Augustina in her best schoolmistress manner.

And where was that? In a brothel? In a tree?

"Come, come, it can't be that bad." A frail hand covered hers, the pale skin looking as delicate as old parchment. "If you've murdered Harry, the local squire might hold a fête in your honor."

Eliza's laugh was a little rough around the edges. "The only thing I've slain is my own reputation." Her mouth quivered. "You see, I did something Exceedingly Stupid."

"Ah," murmured Augustina. She took a moment to add another small spoonful of sugar to her tea. "I take it you did not do this Exceedingly Stupid thing alone."

She shook her head. "No, the Exceedingly Stupid thing to which I refer *definitely* requires two people."

A marmalade kitten climbed up on the table and began nosing around the cream pitcher. Her friend tactfully refrained from making the obvious analogy. Instead she merely said, "My dear Eliza..." Her knife sliced off a tiny morsel of tart. "You have been obliged to exist for many years on a diet of bread and water, so to speak. If at this point in your life you crave a taste of sweets—say, a rich, decadent confection oozing with toffee and cream—that is only natural."

Eliza stared at her spinster friend and felt her jaw drop a fraction.

"We females are not cut from pasteboard, much as some men would like to make us believe. So forget what you have been told. It is *not* wrong to have...carnal desires."

"It isn't?"

Augustina thumped her spoon on the scarred wood. "Most definitely not!"

The kitten gave an indignant squeak and jumped down to the floor.

"Oh." Eliza reached for a fresh piece of shortbread and swallowed it in one bite. "That is a great relief to hear."

"I am glad that I may still teach you a few lessons." The spoon began drumming an expectant *tap, tap, tap* on the tabletop. "Now, far be it for me to pry, but if you wish to elaborate on this Exceedingly Stupid thing you have done, I am happy to listen."

"It's like one of those ridiculous, horrid novels—you know, the ones with dark, creepy dungeons, and manacles, and whips." Eliza knew that she was babbling, but decided it didn't matter. The story defied coherence. "Only it didn't happen in a dungeon, but in the Burgundy Suite, which is only used to entertain important visitors to the Abbey."

"Whips?" said Augustina faintly.

"Well, no—no whips. Just manacles."

"He put *manacles* on you?"

"No, I put them on myself. It was . . . a mistake."

Augustina's silvery brows shot up. "Have you perchance been nibbling some of the mushrooms you collect for your paintings? Because you are beginning to sound as if you are hallucinating."

"I know, I know." Eliza hung her head. "There is an old adage about truth being stranger than fiction. If you remember, we once read Scheherazade's exotic Arabian tales—"

"If you are about to tell me that a handsome genie popped out from one of Harry's brandy bottles and ravished you on the spot, I am going to summon the apothecary."

Eliza bit her lip to keep from laughing. "The *he* in question wasn't a puff of scented smoke. He was definitely a flesh-and-blood Englishman."

Propping her elbows on the table, Augustina leaned in a little closer. "Well, go on. Is *he* handsome?"

"As sin," she confessed. "Tall, with divine muscles and the most beautiful eyes in Creation." A sigh slipped of its own volition from her lips. "And he has a large dragon—"

"Is that what you young people call it these days?" interrupted Augustina. "In my time, some gentlemen referred to their privy part as Abraham's Rod."

Eliza's eyes widened. "How perfectly dreadful. That does not bode well for him believing a female should enjoy the act, does it?"

An unladylike chortle. Which was one of the reasons she loved her friend.

"It was also called a pizzle, a prick, a potato finger," confided Augustina. "And a pump handle."

Oh, she liked that. Haddan had quite a lovely pump handle. One that made her wish that she were a wanton tavern maid, whose duties included frequent trips to the trough in order to fill her bucket...

"You know, I hadn't really thought of it before, but it is interesting how all those euphemisms for penis begin with the letter 'P,'" mused her former governess.

"Very interesting," agreed Eliza. She cleared her throat. "Um, speaking of which, you seem to be, er, quite conversant in the subject."

Chuckling, Augustina gave an airy wave. "Prinny did not invent sexual dalliances, my dear."

Eliza joined in her friend's laughter, but as the mirth

died away, she suddenly felt a stab of guilt that she had never thought to ask a certain question before.

"Were you ever in love, Gussie?"

"Oh, yes," replied Augustina softly. "Deeply. Madly. But my family had no money for a dowry, and his family demanded that he marry wealth. We were going to defy them, once James had saved enough from his parish earnings to afford a wife on his own." She looked down at her plate and carefully rearranged the three remaining slivers of strawberry tart in a neat row. "However, an epidemic of influenza swept through the village, and he refused to stay away from his sick parishioners." The ivy leaves twining around the window casement fluttered in the breeze, sending patterns of light and dark skittering across the glass.

"So that, my dear, is why I say there is nothing wrong in seizing the moment when you have a chance. I am at an age where I can say with some authority that one rarely regrets the things one has done. But as for the things one hasn't done..."

A silence—comfortable as only one between two longtime friends can be—filled the time it took for Augustina to add hot water to the pot and refill their cups. Eliza stared pensively at the bits of tea leaves settling in the depths of the sherry-colored liquid. *Was the future written there, or in the riddles of a Gypsy fortuneteller, or in the runes of some ancient Druid spell book?* And if it were, would she want to know it?

Her sigh dissolved the curl of vapor. "You're right. I am so sorry that I never asked you more about your life before you came to Leete Abbey,"

"Oh, pish. I wouldn't have told you. The time wasn't

right until this moment," replied Augustina frankly. "Speaking of which, we have somehow strayed from the subject at hand." She edged forward in her chair and set her elbows on the table. "Do tell me more about the manacles."

After gulping down several sips, Eliza gave a halting description of the room and finding the sex toy that Harry and his friends had hung over Gryff's bed. "I was curious," she explained. "In a theoretical way, that is. So I simply intended to have a closer look."

"Quite right. It isn't every day that one gets to examine such an interesting apparatus," said Augustina gravely.

"And then..." Heat rose to the ridges of her cheekbones as Eliza recalled watching Gryff strip off his clothing and turn around, the candlelight gilding his masculine profile. "Um, and then..." She glossed over all but the bare facts in admitting her transgression. "Afterwards, I slipped away while he was sleeping, and left at first light to come visit you." She pressed her palms over her eyes, feeling a flush of heat singe her cheeks. "I couldn't face him in the light of day."

"You have no reason to be ashamed," said her friend stoutly.

"I suppose I am, just a little," she admitted wryly. "But most of all, I'm confused. I find myself attracted to him, and I don't want to be."

"Ah. A friend of Harry..."

"He says that he is *not* a friend of Harry. I—I don't know precisely what brought him to Leete Abbey, but he didn't seem interested in spending time with the others." Her brows pinched together. "There is the mill, of course, which might explain it."

Augustina nodded sagely. "Yes, men do seem to take delight in watching brutes pummel the stuffing out of each other."

"Would that some paragon of masculine muscle knock some sense into Harry," mused Eliza. "But that would not be a mill—it would be a miracle."

"Stranger things have happened."

Like me making love to one of the most notorious blades in London.

Her expression must have given some hint as to her thoughts, for Augustina hid a grin behind her hand. "Did you like him? Not Harry, of course, but the Lord of the Manacles."

Eliza tried to think. "He makes me feel rumpled."

"Rumpled?"

"Delightfully disheveled. Like I looked better with everything slightly askew." Her hand gave a vague wave before hooking an unruly curl behind her ear. "Like I didn't have to have every stay laced tightly and every hair pinned in place. He looked at me as if I was Delectable." She blew out a sigh. "I know, I know, I'm not making any sense."

"You are making perfect sense, my dear. The man makes you feel like you can be yourself."

"He makes me laugh," she added in a small voice, feeling her mouth crook up at the corners. "He's funny, and doesn't take himself so seriously."

"He sounds utterly charming. Does this Paragon of Perfection have a name?"

"Haddan."

"*The* Haddan. The Hedonist Hellhound?"

Eliza nodded.

"Oh, dear," murmured Augustina. "That could be trouble."

Trouble. As if I need any reminder.

"But then," mused her friend. "Life can be awfully boring without the prospect of a little piss and vinegar."

A snort of tea nearly went up her nose. "What would I do without you and your wise, witty teachings, Gussie?"

"You would manage just fine, my dear. Though neither of us would laugh quite as much. Which would, of course, be a great pity, as humor is what helps make the sun shine."

"Right." A flicker of light on the ivy outside the window reminded her of Gryff's lazy, lidded gaze. "I have learned a lesson, at least. Men like the marquess have no place in my life." She forced herself to look away from the glints of shadowed green. "You see, Haddan is not the only threat of trouble. Harry's debts are getting worse, and I fear that things are truly getting out of control."

Augustina's look of amusement sobered to one of concern. "I take it he won't listen to reason."

"He turns a deaf ear on all my pleas, and...I don't quite know what to do. I am powerless to control him. I was in Town last week, staying with Margaret while I met with Mr. Watkins about a commission, and..." She had to pause, in order to wash the taste of fear from her throat with a tiny sip of tea. "Lord Brighton stopped me in Bond Street."

"Did he threaten you?"

"Not in so many words. But he hinted that Harry was...making promises about my future."

Augustina swore under her breath. "The bastard."

The oath made Eliza feel a tad more cheerful. Brighton

had struck her as a thoroughly dirty dish during the times he had visited the Abbey. That he and the odious Mr. Pearce were cousins only confirmed her intuitive reaction.

"The bastard," she echoed, finding that saying it aloud helped loosen the knot in her chest.

"Come, let us continue this discussion outdoors, where the breeze will dispel the noxious fumes formed by mention of that smarmy man's name." Augustina rose and began to gather up the plates. "I think better when I am wielding my pruning shears." Eyes narrowing to a martial squint, she added, "Never fear, we'll figure out what to do."

Chapter Six

$\mathcal{A}$ bump of the wheels jolted Gryff's attention back to the road. "Damnation," he growled, fisting the reins and guiding the horses through a tight bend. Despite trying to set his emotions on a straight line, he found his mood veering back and forth between self-loathing and self-serving excuses.

"For God's sake, I didn't despoil her innocence," he muttered, playing the Devil's Advocate. "She said herself that she had seen a penis before."

Though her late husband had obviously not been very skilled in its use.

"That's beside the point." The snide observation prompted a snappish reply from his Better Half. "Your behavior was unworthy of a gentleman."

A pause. "Who said I was a gentleman?"

The horses snorted and suddenly shied away from an overhanging branch, nearly knocking him off his perch.

"I've never claimed to be a saint, but that does not mean I have sunk to the depths of utter depravity." The dialogue with his inner demon continued. "Without some code of honor, a man is no better than a slimy earthworm who dwells in the dank, dark dirt."

The Devil had no clever retort.

"So if I wish to hold my head out of the mud, honor demands that I face Lady Brentford and offer my apologies, instead of crawling back to Town."

Gryff listened for any rebuttal, but heard only the whistle of the wind. Swerving onto the grassy verge, he turned the phaeton around and flicked his whip over the heads of his startled pair of grays.

"Yes, yes, I know you fine fellows are confused," he called, settling their skittish trot. "That makes three of us."

An hour later, Gryff rolled into Harpden, where a few quick questions at one of the local shops elicited directions to a small cottage on the outskirts of town. Tying his team in the shade of a beech tree, he unlatched the wooden gate and, mustering his resolve, headed straight for the front door. It wasn't as if he was going to face a firing squad—though the lady might be tempted to put a bullet through his ballocks.

Several knocks brought no response, so he stepped back to see if he could spot any movement through the upper windows. After coming all this way, he was loath to leave without speaking to Lady Brentford.

Meow.

The muffled sound seemed to be coming from behind the shutter of the attic dormer. A marmalade paw poked out from between the wooden slats.

Meow, meow.

"Why is it that felines choose to get themselves into trouble when I am near?" he grumbled. Another glance up showed that the heavy iron hinge holding the shutter in place had loosened and was wedged in the thatch.

The kitten's cries were becoming fainter.

"Oh, blast." Tugging off his coat and waistcoat, Gryff found a handhold on the age-blackened timbers and started to climb.

Charming as the snug little cottage appeared from afar, its weathered little quirks of character were not conducive to a quick ascent. His highly polished Hessians scrabbled over the rough-textured stucco, leaving streaks of white-wash on the dark leather, and the finespun linen of his shirt snagged in the thorns of wild roses, tearing a rent in the sleeve. Prescott would likely burst into tears on seeing the damage—for all his flexibility in other things, the valet took matters of wardrobe to heart.

Soot smudged his breeches as Gryff edged around the chimney pot and caught tentative hold of the dormer shutter.

"Ouch!" he muttered as his scraped fingers brushed against the rough straw of the roofing. "You had better appreciate this more than the other dratted cat did," he growled. "Else I might feed you to the chimney storks."

The kitten hissed as Gryff gently freed its tail from the wooden trap, but instead of darting away, it pawed free the fastenings of his shirt and climbed inside.

"Oh, now I am supposed to serve as your horse and carriage?" he murmured, his lips tipping up as the soft fur tickled against his chest. "Who do you think you are—the Prince Regent?"

Meow.

"The Sovereign of Scrawny Runts?"

At first Gryff heard only a loud purring, but a moment

later he was suddenly aware of voices. Agitated feminine voices.

A rock sailed by his ear.

"You think to rob my house, thief!" The next missile plunked him on the shoulder. "Think again!"

"Truce!" Seeing the silver-haired spitfire about to wind up for another throw, Gryff waved a white sleeve in surrender. "I assure you my intentions are naught but honorable, madam!"

She lowered her arm. "Then what are you doing on my roof?"

Gryff was about to answer when a second female emerged from the shrubbery. As she tipped up her chin to meet his gaze, he saw that her cheeks went very pale, and then very pink. The color reminded him of sun-ripening peaches.

"I think he was rescuing Mouse," said Eliza to her companion.

"Actually I was rescuing a cat."

"Mouse is a cat," replied Eliza.

"Ah. I should have guessed."

"Do you know this intruder, my dear?" asked his assailant.

"Yes," said Eliza flatly. "Gussie, allow me to present the Marquess of Haddan. I think I can safely say he's not out to purloin your silver." Looking back at him, she continued. "Lord Haddan, this is Miss Augustina Haverstick."

"My apologies, young man," said Augustina. "However, if you had announced yourself properly, I would not have been forced to defend my property."

"My fault entirely," he said dryly. "Be that as it may, while I am up here . . . have you a hammer?"

"A hammer?" Eliza fixed him with a wary squint. "What for?"

"The shutter's hinge has come loose from the window frame. If you hand me a hammer, I shall renail it."

"Oh, Mr. Reading has been promising to fix it for an age, but he's not yet had time." Augustina sighed. "It bangs loudly enough to wake the dead when the west wind blows."

"I shall be happy to serve as a surrogate to Mr. Reading."

"You know how to fix a shutter?" demanded Eliza.

"I know how to do a great many things, including wield a hammer," drawled Gryff, taking ungentlemanly delight in watching her face turn a luscious shade of strawberry red. "Pounding in a few loose nails is a simple task."

"Don't move a muscle, milord," piped up Augustina. "I shall be right back."

Eliza's eyes widened in alarm. "I'll fetch it—," she began, but her friend had already disappeared around the corner of the cottage.

"Miss Haverstick is remarkably spry," he remarked, rubbing at his shoulder.

The attempt at humor didn't provoke a smile. As her lashes lowered, and her lips pinched to a crooked line, he, too, suddenly felt a little awkward. "I apologize for intruding without warning, but—"

"But why are you here?" she blurted out.

A good question. And one not easily answered.

He was rescued by the cat. A paw poked out from inside his shirt, followed by a tiny, tufted ear.

"Sorry. I hope you have not suffered further injury to

your person," muttered Eliza. "Mouse has a habit of getting into mischief."

"Cats have a habit of getting into trouble." He had meant it innocently, but the comment sparked a fresh flare of embarrassment.

"Lord Haddan, I am aware that my...actions of last night must have led you to believe that I—"

"I found it!" called Augustina, raising the hammer aloft as she trotted through the opening in the privet hedge. "Took me a moment to recall where I had put it."

Eliza shot a scowl at her friend, which the spinster cheerfully ignored.

"Here you are, young man," went on Augustina, blithely handing the tool up to him.

Extracting the ball of fur from inside his shirt, Gryff held out the kitten in exchange. "Mouse would probably prefer not to return to the scene of the crime." He heard a sharp intake of breath from Eliza. "Not," he added softly, "that he should feel any remorse about being adventurous."

"Thank you." Eliza snatched the kitten from his hands and stepped back.

Taking the hammer, Gryff scrambled back up to the dormer and made quick work of refastening the shutter in its proper place. Seeing that several pieces of the windowframe were loose, he called, "Have you some extra nails, Miss Haverstick?"

"Yes!" came the reedy answer.

"Perhaps Lady Brentford could climb up the stairs to the attic and pass them out to me." She would likely resent the manipulation, but it seemed the best way of getting a private word with her.

A few minutes later, the mullioned window swung

open with some force. "That…" A small canvas sack sailed into his lap. "…was a dirty trick."

"If you are truly angry, you can go ahead and cosh me on the head with the hammer."

Eliza looked out from the shadows. "Fix the frame first."

He laughed. "Very practical." Shaking a few nails from the sack, he stuck them in his mouth and set to work.

"I *am* practical," she said after a hitch of hesitation. "Exceedingly practical. Most of the time, that is."

"Could you hold this strip in place?" he mumbled around the nails.

Expelling a little whoosh of air, Eliza leaned out of the opening to do as he asked. Her scent—that sweetly spicy blend of verbena and cloves—tickled at his nostrils, stirring an immediate, primitive response.

He shifted slightly to hide the bulge in his breeches. "Thank you, that's it…now just a little higher."

Wiggling around, she stretched her arm higher.

Oh, I am evil. Gryff shimmied closer, his shoulder brushing up against her breasts. *Evil.*

"What are you waiting for? Gideon's trumpet blast to signal the Resurrection?"

"It's important…" *Tap, tap.* "To choose…" *Tap, tap.* "The right spot…" *Tap, tap.* "Else the wood might split." Gryff took another nail from his mouth. "You can let go now."

She leaned back and set her hands on the sill. The weathered wood framed a charming picture. Sunlight painted her features with a soft, shimmering glow. Glimmers of gold gilded her lashes and the curls that had come loose and now danced in the breeze.

Gryff smiled. She did not smile back.

"Lord Haddan—"

"My name is Gryffin. Or Gryff for short."

"And it would be most improper for me to call you by either," she snapped. A sigh followed, and then a rueful quirk pulled at her mouth. "Not that I have any right to speak of propriety after last night. I—"

"That depends on whose definition of propriety one chooses to recognize," pointed out Gryff.

"Stop interrupting me, sir. It's difficult enough trying to apologize for my wanton behavior, without having you prolong the agony."

He handed her the hammer. "Are you saying that you regretted the interlude?"

Her mouth went through a series of strange little contortions, making it impossible to tell whether the jumbled sounds meant "yes" or "no."

"If by 'wanton,' you mean something sordid or squalid, I beg to disagree," said Gryff.

"I behaved like a strumpet. A shameless hussy." Eliza looked down at her hands, which were gripped so tightly around the hammer's handle that her knuckles had gone white. "I...am usually so practical and level-headed." Her expression screwed to a look of slightly dazed disbelief. "I am n-not in the habit of shedding every scrap of m-morality along with m-my clothing."

"There's nothing shameful about having a passionate nature, Lady Brentford." He reached out and gently tipped up her chin. "We are two sensible adults who decided to embrace our mutual attraction. There is really nothing fundamentally wrong with that. In fact, I thought that what happened between us was quite wonderful."

Eliza gave a small laugh, though her eyes betrayed a suspicious glitter. "From what I have heard, you find embracing a mutual attraction quite wonderful with *anyone* who wears skirts. So I won't take it personally."

The remark rendered him momentarily mute. She was right—and yet utterly wrong. Making love to her *had* been different. Wildly, wonderfully different, though how or why was something that defied any attempt to capture it in words.

"Well, you should." He touched the corner of her mouth and slowly traced the curve of her lower lip. *So sweetly, sweetly lush. So perfectly, perfectly pink.* And the slight tremor beneath his fingertip made him ache to still her quivering doubts. "Because at this moment I want nothing more than to lean in and kiss you witless."

She recoiled, confusion coloring her face. "R-really, sir, you must stop teasing me with your silly flirtations." Edging back, she retreated deeper into the shadows, until her features were naught but a blur of grays. "If you have finished here, Gussie wishes to serve you tea and pastries in the kitchen. Her walnut shortbread is a special treat."

"How can I resist such a tempting offer? I'll be down in a moment."

"Delicious, Miss Haverstick." Sparkles of sugar danced in the slanting sunlight as Gryff dusted his hands. "I've never tasted such sublime shortbread."

Good God, was Gussie actually simpering?

Eliza stirred another spoonful of honey into her tea. The man could probably charm the scales off of Satan if he so chose. A fact she would do well to remember. The devilish desires stirring inside her must stay smoldering in the deepest, darkest recesses of her being. It was too dangerous to let them see the light of day.

Too wicked to feed their flames with secret fantasies.

"Do help yourself to another piece, Lord Haddan," said Augustina, pushing the plate across the table. "It's nice to see a man who has a healthy appetite for sweets."

Caught in mid-swallow, Eliza let out a loud sputter. "Sorry," she apologized, clearing her throat with a quick cough. "It must have been a trifle too hot."

Gryff looked at her with a lazy, lidded gaze and smiled, prompting her stomach to do a series of herky-jerky flip-flops against her ribs. "Would you like to share a bite?"

"Thank you but I've had enough," she said. "Too many of Gussie's rich butter and sugar treats will make me fat as a Strasbourg goose."

He ran his gaze slowly along the length of her body. "Your figure looks perfectly shaped to me, Lady Brentford."

"And no doubt you are an expert on the female form," she said under her breath.

Augustina elbowed her in the ribs as she reached for the cream pitcher. "More tea, Lord Haddan? Or perhaps you would like to sample a slice of strawberry tart."

"I'm very fond of tarts…"

Eliza found herself blushing furiously.

"But alas, I, too, had better watch my figure."

Augustina eyed his tapered waist and flat stomach, which showed indecently well through the light-as-a-feather weave of his shirt, and let out a low snort. "I daresay you have plenty of others watching it closely, milord."

His eyes lit with unholy amusement. "Why, Miss Haverstick, you are making me blush."

Rising abruptly, Eliza began to gather up the empty plates. "I'll clear the table while you two…" *Flirt*, she thought rather ungraciously. "…while you discuss the variety of entertainments available in Town."

Gryff was up in a flash, and somehow she found her hands empty. "I insist that you sit. Having enjoyed the toils of your labor, the least I can do is carry the dishes to the counter."

He turned, the broad stretch of his back crowding out all else in her line of vision. Sweat had dampened his shirt, accentuating the rippling of muscles beneath fabric.

Feeling a little queasy, Eliza quickly looked away, only to encounter Augustina's speculative gaze.

Don't, she mouthed, *Say A Word.*

Her friend flashed an impish grin, but friendship won out over mischief and she remained mum.

The marquess's baritone voice rose above the clatter of the crockery. "If you ladies will excuse me, I really ought to go outside and fetch my coat. It's been terribly rag-mannered of me to sit half-dressed in your presence."

"You are forgiven, milord," called Augustina cheerfully. "At my age, it's rather delightful to sin with a handsome scoundrel."

His answering chuckle blended into the breeze as he sauntered out the back door. "I shall take that as an invitation to return in a moment."

Chapter Seven

So *that* is Haddan?" said Augustina, once the sound had died away. "My goodness, you didn't mention that he—"

Eliza frantically fluttered her hands, trying to signal her friend to silence. "Ssshhhhh! He'll be back at any moment and—"

"Look who else is hungry." Gryff reappeared with the kitten cradled in his coat. "Having awoken refreshed from a nap, he's now demanding his share of treats."

The throaty purr—from Mouse, not Haddan—made her start to squirm in her chair. It made no sense that he was having such a very odd effect on her peace of mind. By all rights, the longer she was in his presence, the calmer she should become. Instead she was turning more and more nervous. Jumpy was perhaps a better description. Like a cat trying to dance across a hot griddle. As he came closer, the balls of her feet began to bounce ever so slightly against the floorboards.

On second thought, a cat would be far too intelligent to keep going once its paw touched heated metal.

"I can't say I blame him," went on Haddan. "There are

so many delectable morsels in here, a man can't help but be tempted to sin."

Augustina covered her mouth to stifle a chortle.

Flustered, Eliza quickly rose and went to pour a saucer of cream for the kitten. *Up-down, up-down.* She was beginning to feel like a child's jack-in-the-box. "How do you know Mouse is a he?" she demanded, trying to distract herself from thoughts of sin.

"I checked. He has a pizzle."

A pizzle. Bending down to place the cream on the floor brought her eye level with the fall of Gryff's breeches.

So much for keeping thoughts of sin at bay.

"You know, Eliza and I were just discussing the fact that so many euphemisms for the male privy parts begin with the letter 'P,'" offered Augustina. "I find it rather interesting."

"It sounds like a fascinating topic," agreed Gryff, a roguish twinkle lighting his eyes. "Actually, I can think of several that don't—but I shall refrain from saying them in *Polite* company."

"I am always in quest of broadening my intellectual horizons," responded Augustina. "Even if it means transgressing beyond the bounds of so-called *Propriety*."

"*Pardon* me," interrupted Eliza. "But this notebook fell out of your coat pocket." She picked up the leather book and brushed off the cat hairs clinging to its covers.

"Thank you." Gryff was no longer looking quite so amused as he plucked it from her grasp.

"A lexicon of naughty words?" she asked, gratified to see that the sun-bronzed slant of his cheekbones had turned a shade redder. Tit for tat, she thought, spotting the hammer lying atop the jelly cabinet. He wasn't the only one who could hit a sensitive spot. "A collection of passionate *billet-doux*?"

His smile was back in place, though it looked a little crooked at the edge. "Sadly, no. Sorry to disappoint you, Lady Brentford, but it contains far more boring material than that."

"Like what?" she pressed.

"Notes," he said gruffly. "Mere reminders of some mundane tasks that need to be done."

Eliza sensed he was evading the question. But before she could inquire further, Augustina suddenly rose. "Well, seeing as my kitchen is in good hands, I shall return to pruning my roses."

"I shall—"

"You shall stay here and keep His Lordship company," said her friend firmly. "It would be quite rude to leave him alone."

Eliza scowled, a look her former governess cheerfully ignored. "You wouldn't want him to think that I taught you bad manners."

"Right," she muttered. "We certainly wouldn't want him to be shocked at my behavior."

Augustina merely winked as she swanned out the door.

Gryff waited until the footsteps on the flagstones faded. "Sorry, I don't mean to tease you into a tither," he said softly. "I can see that my presence is making you uncomfortable, so I'll not prolong it. Might I ask you walk me out to my phaeton?"

Seeing her hesitation, he added, "You asked why I came here, Lady Brentford, and as of yet, I've not answered you. It was to make my apologies. Not, I must repeat, because I regret anything about our interlude, but because I took advantage of your...position. That was wrong of me."

She looked away, a loosened curl falling to hide her downcast gaze. "Let us leave off the arguments of right and wrong. There is no point in parsing the past."

"And the future?" he asked quietly.

Eliza started putting the remaining shortbread away in a tin. "Would you like a few squares for the trip back to London, sir?"

"Ah, a dismissal, no matter how sweetly phrased." Gryff smiled. "Thank you, but I shall survive without sustenance." He buttoned his waistcoat and smoothed the wrinkles from his coat sleeve.

"Nonetheless, Gussie would be disappointed if you did not take some along." She folded a few of the pastries in a square of linen. "Come along, sir."

They walked through the herb garden and circled around to the front of the cottage.

"Miss Haverstick has a good eye for color and texture." Gryff studied the border plantings. "Though I daresay you've had an influence in this."

"How—" she began and then stopped abruptly.

His suspicions confirmed, he replied, "Because they are similar in feel to the plantings around your hideaway at the Abbey. You clearly have a feel for landscape design."

"I—I dabble," she admitted. "I like flowers, and how they fit into their surroundings."

"The earth does not lie. There is something elementally refreshing in the truth that Nature must provide nourishment for life to sprout, green and wonderful, full of potential."

Her brows drew together, as she thought for a moment. "That sounds vaguely familiar," she murmured, looking faintly puzzled. "Is it by one of the Lake Poets?"

He shook his head, feeling a little bemused. "No, it was written by someone unpublished."

"It's a lovely sentiment." She walked on several paces and then slanted him a sidelong look. "I am surprised that you noticed the nuances of the gardens here and at the Abbey, sir. Most men don't."

He shrugged and exaggerated a laugh. "I appreciate Beauty in all its glorious guises."

Her gaze flicked to the silvery stalks of columbine, but not before he caught a glimpse of her eyes.

Gryff felt his chest tighten with a sudden clench of anger. Damn the men who had made her feel less than lovely or desirable. On impulse, he reached out and took hold of her wrist.

"Lord Haddan..."

He couldn't help it. At the sight of her quivering lips, he tugged her into the shade of a coppery beech tree. Sunlight drizzled through the leaves, painting her face in shades of gold and amber. She tried to shy away, but he pulled her close, heat drumming through him as the touch of her body set his skin afire.

"Kiss me," he rasped, his hands caressing her shoulders.

Eliza lifted her chin, her breath quickening to ragged little gasps.

Leaning in, Gryff gently touched his lips to hers. One, two, three heartbeats, and then she pulled back, breaking the bond between them.

"Y-you had best go, Lord Haddan," she said.

"Why?" he murmured. "Because you want to make love with me again?" It was half question, half seduction.

He felt her stiffen against him, and then relax into a reluctant laugh. "Yes, I suppose that I do," she admitted with delightful frankness. "But it would not be wise."

She was right—and it was wrong to seduce her into temptation. But he couldn't quite make himself let her go.

"Are you always ruled by your head?" he asked, stroking a thumb along the line of her jaw.

"I can't afford to throw caution to the wind," replied Eliza. "It's too dangerous."

Like a serpent, the word coiled itself around his conscience and slowly squeezed. *Danger wasn't all that frightening—it added a spice to life*, he told himself. It couldn't really hurt either of them. She was a widow, and if they were discreet, the worst that could happen was a bit of unpleasant speculation.

"If we are careful, there is no reason for anyone to know," he murmured. "If we both take enjoyment in it, there is nothing wrong in enjoying an intimate relationship, Lady Brentford."

"I see now why you are so successful at seducing women." She said it lightly but the reply lanced through his skin.

"Being far more experienced in dalliances, you are no doubt right that the consequences are not very serious—for you, that is," she went on. "However, they are for me. I cannot risk such a distraction in my life right now."

"Why?" he asked.

She wouldn't meet his gaze. "Because I have other plans."

Which she clearly did not intend to share with him.

Not that it was surprising. He was a near stranger, who had spent most of their time together pawing and snabbering over her body. The thought didn't make him feel proud of himself.

You are a gentleman, Gryffin. And a gentleman ought to honor her wishes and walk out of her life.

And yet...

"Will you see me again? Perhaps just to take a walk, if that is what you prefer."

"I...I will have to think about it," answered Eliza.

"Of course."

Her words were a reminder that he, too, should keep his mind on serious pursuits. He had vowed to leave his rakehell days behind him. And do something meaningful with his life. A fleeting tryst with a country widow would be a mistake. A step backward when he had vowed to march forward in a new direction.

Gryff took a moment longer to get his wayward longings under control, then untied the long phaeton reins from one of the low-hanging branches and turned back to take his leave.

Eliza had moved a step back and was staring away into the distance, a pensive look shading her face. Several curls had slipped free of their pins and were dancing in the breeze. Her collar was askew, her skirts were dusty, and yet there was a simple, natural beauty to her slightly ruffled appearance. She made the London ladies in all their fancy fineries look like naught but bits of polished glass. Smooth and glittery, but possessing no depth or substance.

While she had intriguing angles and textures, hints of hidden facets, all the more alluring for their uneven edges.

He came up quietly beside her, and in one quick flick, looped the leather around her wrists.

She gave a squeak of surprise. "S-sir!"

Pulling her close, Gryff slanted his mouth over hers, cutting off her protest with a long and lush embrace. "If that is to be our last kiss, it should at least be somewhat memorable." With that, he released her and vaulted up to the perch of his phaeton.

"Give my regards to Miss Haverstick. I hope the two of you enjoy your afternoon in the gardens." The horses snorted and started forward, anxious to be off. "I suggest you trim back the *perovskia* by the back wall. It's getting a little leggy."

Augustina looked up as Eliza came around the high hedge and paused in its shadow. "You are mad—" she began.

"I know, I know," said Eliza softly. "It was utter madness to have given way to impulse and succumbed to the charms of a rake."

"You are mad not to set your cap for Lord Haddan," corrected her friend. "Why, if I were fifty years younger, I'd be lifting my skirts to run after him. And I'd be whacking at your legs with a cricket bat to keep you from chasing after him, too."

"I should never do anything as undignified as chase after a rogue," huffed Eliza. "No matter how charming or well-muscled."

"You are mad," repeated Augustina. "He is worth the trouble. A man who rescues cats and fixes broken shutters does not grow on every tree."

No, just the large oak outside my cottage workroom window, thought Eliza wryly.

"Haddan is absolutely perfect for you."

"I doubt that he sees the match in quite the same light as you do." Her mouth quirked in a mirthless smile. "He bedded me, Gussie. As he has a great many other women. It doesn't go any deeper than that."

"He looks at you with more than lust in his eyes," insisted her friend with endearing loyalty.

"You aren't wearing your spectacles," pointed out Eliza.

"Ha! It's clear as crystal that he makes you laugh."

"And he will probably make me cry if I take your suggestions to heart," she answered softly. "Do you really think a man like Haddan is seeking anything more than a roll in the hay? At the moment, I seem to have caught his fancy. But once the novelty of our tryst wears off, he'll tire of country pleasures and move on to something else."

"To me, Haddan appears very different than Harry and his rakehell friends," said Augustina.

"That's because you insist on viewing him through rose-colored lenses." Eliza pressed her hands over her eyes, hoping to banish the picture of Haddan and his sinfully seductive dragon from her brain. Unfortunately, they seemed tattooed on the back of her lids.

No wonder the Bible prophets thought that graven images were wicked. *Beware lest you act corruptly by making a carved image for yourselves, in the form of any figure, the likeness of male...*

She offered a swift, silent prayer to the Heavens to deliver her from temptation, ending it with a chuffed sigh. "Please, Gussie, I have trouble enough with trying to keep Harry in check and my own dreams alive. So let us drop the subject of Lord Haddan and his rakish repertoire of charms. They are, I confess, potent. But it would be foolish in the extreme to pursue the relationship, and I like to think that I'm not a fool."

To herself, she added, *For only a fool makes the same mistake twice.*

"If you insist," grumbled Augustina, though a stubborn tilt kept her chin angled at a mulish jut. "But trust your elderly teacher—you've still a number of lessons to learn about men."

"I'd rather you teach me how best to avoid them." Cats, she thought. Cats and paintboxes made far more comfortable companions. "Once I'm settled in my own solitary little place overlooking the lakes and hills, independent and free from the machinations of men, I shall have everything I want in life."

Her friend made a rude sound. "Sunshine and soft summer breezes can only go so far in warming your cockles. The winters in the Lake District are long and cold, my dear."

"And a man like Haddan isn't about to settle by the hearth and kindle a cozy little fire," pointed out Eliza. She paused for an instant, picturing his naked body painted in bold, bright red-gold flames. "He would probably burn the whole house down."

"I can think of worse ways to go than being consumed by a burning passion," quipped Augustina.

"Aren't you," said Eliza slowly, "supposed to be acting as the Voice of Reason? The Wench of Wisdom?"

A smug little smile crept to her friend's mouth. "My point exactly."

"Oh, Gussie." A laugh welled up in her throat. Really, the conversation was too absurd for the tears that had been prickling at her lashes.

Brushing a leaf from her wide-brimmed hat, Augustina lifted her shears. "But enough said on the subject for now."

Eliza sighed and dabbed a sleeve to her cheek. "Drat, a bit of pollen seems to have lodged in my eye."

"A wet washcloth should soothe away the problem," said Augustina tactfully. "Once you return from the kitchen, let us get back to pruning the garden. Barring any other feline folly or marauding marquess, we should manage to have a peaceful afternoon."

Chapter Eight

It had started raining just a few miles after leaving Miss Haverstick's cottage, the squalling clouds and rumbled thunder capturing the agitation of his own unsettled mood. Right and wrong—his assessment of his recent behavior continued to rise and fall with the bumps of the roads.

In a truly foul temper by the time he reached his townhouse, Gryff stomped into the entrance foyer and flung off his sodden driving coat and gloves with a loud oath.

His butler appeared from the corridor and surveyed the puddles with a poker face. "Tea, milord? Or would you prefer something stronger?"

"A hot bath, if you please," muttered Gryff. *And a large brandy to warm his conscience.* But he snapped his mouth shut. His lapse in judgment had gone on long enough. No need to make a fool of himself in front of his staff.

"Very good, sir." The butler picked up the marquess's soggy hat and gingerly shook the mud from its brim. "Mr. Daggett is in the library, sir. He said you would not mind if he looked through several of your books."

"Books." Gryff made a face. "I didn't know he could read."

"I wouldn't know about that, sir." A cough. "He appears to be perusing ones that have mostly pictures."

"Bloody hell. You had better stubble the order for a bath." Gryff ran a hand through his lank locks. "Send tea to the library, Mifflin. Along with a nice, dry towel."

Cameron looked up on hearing the *squish* of steps crossing the Aubusson carpet. "I thought you were staying in Oxfordshire for another two days."

"Change in plans," said Gryff curtly, sinking into the armchair by the hearth.

"Any particular reason?"

"No." A hiss of steam rose up from the coals as he propped his boots on the fender. "Yes."

"Do you care to elaborate?"

"Actually, I'd rather not."

Cameron returned to his perusal of the lavishly illustrated book that lay open on the worktable. A page turned with a whispery flutter. "I assume that means a lady is involved."

"What makes you say that?"

His friend heaved a long-suffering sigh. "Most of your escapades involve females or alcohol, and since you claim that you're only drinking in moderation these days..." Another page turned. "Is it Leete's intriguing sister?"

"How the devil do you know about her?" Gryff straightened from his slouch. "I swear, sometimes I think you were birthed by a diabolical *djinn* spirit rather than a flesh-and-blood female."

"One does not need any special supernatural powers to

discern your foibles. One only has to pay a visit to The Wolf's Lair." Cameron flipped yet another page. "Sara told me all about your interesting encounter with the Widow Brentford."

"Nothing *interesting* happened there," protested Gryff. "We exchanged a few words is all."

"Then why are you blushing like a schoolboy who's been caught with his breeches down around his ankles?"

"Because..." The flames wagged, silent, scolding fingers of fire. "Because I'm not very proud of myself about what happened afterward," he blurted out.

"Ah."

Gryff waited for him to go on, but his friend leaned down, seemingly engrossed in the colored engraving.

"Ah? That's all you have to say after I bare my soul?"

Cameron twitched a tiny smile. "I daresay your soul was not the part of your person that was bared to the lady."

In spite of himself, Gryff let out a harried laugh. "Unfortunately, you are right. Trust me, I had no intention of getting into trouble." *Trouble—that word was beginning to haunt him.* "But I did."

"This is beginning to get moderately interesting," remarked his friend. "Go on."

"You will probably think that I am making it up if I tell you the truth of it," muttered Gryff.

"Better and better." Cameron stretched out his legs and crossed one elegantly shod foot over the other. "I am waiting."

Gryff shook his head. "Bloody hell, Cam. You know that honor forbids a gentleman from discussing any intimacies with a lady."

"I should love to hear all the delicious details, but of course, the widow deserves her privacy." Cameron tapped his fingertips together. "And you are feeling a trifle guilty because of whatever happened between you?"

A gruff nod.

"Yet I am assuming that she was not an unwilling participant in any amorous act."

"No. But…"

"But what? Sara described Lady Brentford as a very intrepid, intelligent female. I doubt she would appreciate your patronizing attitude."

"*Patronizing?*" sputtered Gryff.

"Yes, patronizing," replied his friend flatly. "Give her a little credit for being able to decide what she does and does not want. It sounds to me like she might be heartily sick of men controlling her life."

He blinked.

"It's not as if she were a virgin," pointed out Cameron. "Had you deflowered the young lady, it would, of course, make matters much more complicated. But a widow is allowed to take a lover, if she is discreet."

"I know, I know. She did say that she had seen a penis before." He flashed a wry grimace. "Though not a tattoo."

"Found it fascinating, did she?"

"She said that she admired the artist's skill." Gryff rose brusquely as a servant brought in the tea tray, suddenly anxious to wash the sour taste from his mouth. "Look," he said gruffly, once they were alone again. "However we might jest about the subject, and however she may say that the interlude is best forgotten by both of us, I still can't shake off the feeling that my behavior was less than honorable."

"In what way?"

"I . . . I can't really put it in words."

"How odd. Your essays display a great deal of eloquence on the subject of emotions."

Gryff darted an involuntary glance at his desk, where the drafts of his recent writings lay atop the blotter. "Damnation, you ought not be poking your nose in my private things," he muttered, though in truth he was rather touched by the praise. Cameron rarely expressed anything other than biting sarcasm.

"Yes, well, the Hellhounds are not known for paying much attention to the strictures of Polite Society."

"That seems a rather self-serving excuse, don't you think?" he muttered, though the scolding was meant more for himself than for his friend.

Cameron didn't reply right away. Pushing back his chair, he went to pour himself a glass of port. "Forgive me, but if we are going to discuss morality, I find myself in need of something a little more fortifying than tea."

Cradling his cup between his palms, Gryff fixed a brooding stare at the burning logs in the hearth. The cracking seemed a chorus of chidings. Even the tiny tongues of fire seemed to be growing more and more vociferous in reproach.

His friend came to lean a hand on the mantel, and as he stood in profile, the fire cast light and dark flickers over his features. "Now, assuming your question wasn't simply rhetorical, I'll give you an answer." His expression turned even more pensive. "Don't be too hard on yourself. It is not easy for a man to change."

"Is that spoken from experience?"

Cameron's mouth formed an ironic curl. "Of a sort."

Gryff released a pent-up breath, the small sound echoing the stirring of the ashes. "Why are you so deucedly determined to be cryptic?"

A brusque wave deflected the retort. "This isn't about me." Then in a moment of candor that took Gryff by surprise, his friend added, "I've plenty of foibles, but unlike you, I'm not eager to address them at this moment." The shadows dipped and Cameron's eyes lit again with their usual glint of mocking detachment. "You've talked about *your* feelings. But what did the lady have to say when you saw her this morning?"

"I didn't see her right away," replied Gryff. "She left to visit a friend before I could arrange a chance to speak with her."

"But I take it you pursued the matter?"

He nodded. "I—I didn't plan to at first. But then it seemed cowardly to simply slink on back to Town."

"So you managed to have a *tête-à-tête*." A pause. "Or perhaps you put together other bodily parts—"

A warning growl cut off Cameron's quip.

"Yes, we talked," he went on. "But it would be ungentlemanly of me to reveal any of the particulars."

"Do you plan to see her again?"

"I—I haven't decided. Even if I do, she's made it clear that…" Suddenly anxious to change the subject, Gryff broke off in mid-sentence as his wandering gaze fell on the open book of engravings. "I trust that you are not thinking of taking that with you. It's a very valuable edition, and I frequently use it for reference." He scowled. "Place your purloining paws elsewhere if you are in need of funds."

"I was merely having a look," answered Cameron. "I

saw a similar volume the other day and wished to confirm
that my instincts were correct."

"Where?" asked Gryff. "There are very few in existence."

"At one of my dealers."

"You mean a flash house?" he pressed, referring to a
place where thieves brought their stolen items to sell.

"Yes, if you must know. A fellow wanted to sell it to
me, along with several other items. I wasn't overly interested, but the incident piqued my curiosity."

"In what way?" asked Gryff.

"Oh, just a few little details that would be meaningless
to you," answered Cameron vaguely. He set down his
glass of port and slowly walked back to the worktable.

Pages riffled, releasing the pungent scent of printing
ink and old paper into the air.

Soothing smells. Unlike the seductive whiff of feminine florals that had been teasing at his nostrils for much
of the day. Damnation, the perfume of Lady Brentford
must contain some secret ingredient more intoxicating
than drink, for it had left his wits feeling strangely
fuzzed.

Another deep inhale of the familiar library scents
helped clear his head. Books—they reminded Gryff that
he wanted to pay a visit to Watkins & Harold as soon as
possible. He was anxious to learn whether the unknown
artist had accepted the commission to illustrate his essays. Not that he intended to take "no" for an answer.
Over the last few days, the sample sketch had grown dog-
eared from constant handling. The more he looked at it,
the more he was sure that style was a perfect match for
his words.

Oddly enough, the artist seemed to understand his feelings for nature even better than he did.

And so he was determined to make the match. Every man—or woman—had a price, thought Gryff sardonically. He was wealthy enough to afford whatever it might be.

An abrupt question from Cameron drew him back to a less pleasant subject. "By the by, how well do you know Lord Leete?"

"Curse it, I don't know him bloody well at all." He rubbed at his temples, feeling a dull throb begin to twitch beneath his fingertips. "Look, even at the best of times, your convoluted questions tend to make my head ache. If you've something specific to ask about the fellow, go ahead. Otherwise, I wish to change out of my wet clothes and pay a visit to my publisher."

"It's not important," said his friend with a nonchalant shrug. "Run along and seek solace in your pastoral pursuits." A pause. "Maybe next time you should make love to the lady in a garden. A ray of sunshine might rub off."

"Arse," he grumbled. "I assure you, come rain or shine, it's highly unlikely that there will be a next time."

Clip. Clip. Eliza lowered the blades for a moment to dab the beading of sweat from her brow. The glare of the sun had seemed to bring all her worries into brighter focus. *Clip, clip.* If only she could cut off Harry's fingers, so he could not hold cards or throw dice. *Clip, clip.* Or maybe some other appendage should be first to go, she thought ruthlessly, suddenly recalling the bill she had seen for some fancy bauble purchased at Rundell and Briggs.

Clip. Clip. And while she was at it, if only she could

cut off this cursed, crazy longing that stirred inside her. Haddan was a Hellhound. And the fact that he made her want to descend to the Devil's own Lair of Depravity with him was a little frightening.

"Perhaps you ought to move on to another bush," said Augustina dryly. "Before that one is reduced to a stubble."

"Sorry. I was thinking of Harry, and yet another asinine expense he's made. A sapphire bracelet, which I assume went to some opera dancer." She grimaced. "No matter what I say, he seems oblivious to the fact that we are sailing down the River Tick, and the bilges are fast filling with water."

"That's because he expects you to bail him out, as you usually do."

"It's not as if I've had much choice," replied Eliza. "I love the Abbey, and cannot bear to let it sink into utter ruin. I've no other home." She stopped there, afraid of turning too maudlin. Indifferent parents, a stranger for a husband—in truth, she had never felt truly welcome anywhere. A home should hold warmth, laughter. Love.

"Since you are asking about choices…" Augustina stepped into the shade. "I do hope you are not considering sacrificing your future to Sir Brighton."

Eliza turned away to watch a bee buzz around the fragrant petals of a honeysuckle vine.

If only there were a patch of hellebores to stare at, she thought wryly. Which in the secret speech of flowers meant "relieve my anxiety."

Instead, her gaze strayed to a flash of geranium red—which cheerfully shouted out "Folly! Stupidity!"

But it also meant "true friend," Eliza reminded herself.

Ha! She quickly quashed the thought with a silent scoff. As if Haddan had formed any sort of *lasting* attachment to her.

"My dear," said Augustina, interrupting her musing on botanical language. "I feel that I must speak up. I stood aside in silence the first time you let your family barter your happiness to fill their coffers. It was not my place to voice an objection when your father was alive. But now, I feel no compunction to keep quiet."

A lump in her throat kept Eliza from responding.

"You were unhappy with Brentford," pressed on Augustina. "You would be even more miserable with Brighton." The cuttings crackled underfoot as she shifted her stance. "From what I have heard, he's a lout and a bully."

"I—I can deal with that, if need be," she managed to whisper. "I need not look to a husband for happiness. I have my art."

"And what if he takes that away?" demanded her friend. "He can, you know. He would be well within his rights to toss your paints and papers into the fire."

"I know, I know. I'm not a complete ninnyhammer." Despite the sunlight, she felt a chill settle in at the nape of her neck. "For some time now, I've realized that much as I love Leete Abbey, it is not mine to protect. And so, I..." She swallowed the hitch in her voice. "I have been working on a plan to make myself independent from Harry and his wheedling. But I'm not yet in a financial position to act on it. Perhaps after another few commissions."

Assuming her brother hadn't added any major expenditure to the growing pile of debts.

"I've just been offered a very lucrative one," she went

on. "And if I pinch pennies very carefully, it will bring me very close to my goal."

"Which is?" asked Augustina.

Eliza hesitated. She had refrained from talking about her dream, even with her closest friend, for fear that giving voice to it might cast some black magic spell over it. *Shadows and superstitions.* But she was tired of living in constant trepidation, of tiptoeing in silence, hoping some silly talisman would ward off disaster.

Augustina is right—it's time I paint in the colors of my future with my own brush.

Drawing a deep breath, she said, "I have been saving a portion of my earnings and investing it with Mr. Martin, that very nice man of affairs who is a member of our Horticulture Society. We have worked out how much I need to purchase a small cottage in the Lake District." A remote spot, far, far away from Harry's whining. "And to have enough left over to live on." Closing her eyes, she could see the subtle hues of a mountain sunset dancing over the wind-whipped lake waters. "Once I have that amount in my account, and combine it with my income from art, I should be able to make it work."

"Hooray for you," applauded her friend. "I'm delighted that you shall finally profit from your own talents, rather than allow Harry to keep gobbling them up."

"As of yet, I have not earned enough, so let us not celebrate too soon," she cautioned.

"I have every confidence in your abilities, my dear." Augustina swatted a fly from the brim of her straw hat. "You know," she added a softer tone. "Even if you don't get that commission, Sir Brighton need never be an option. You are always welcome to come live with me."

It was a lovely offer, and the sentiment sent Eliza's heart skidding up against her ribs. *Love—she had experienced so little of it in her life.* Crooking a smile, she looked around at the snug little cottage and well-tended garden, still enchantingly lovely despite her earlier hackings. "It's a beautiful offer, Gussie. And I'm profoundly grateful."

But it was a tiny space, and she knew that the elderly spinster subsisted on a very modest income. No matter how close their friendship, such tight quarters might cause them to rub together a little *too* closely. The idea of anything fraying their special friendship was unbearable. Besides, she was tired of always living as someone else's dependent.

Freedom to be herself, independence to make her own decisions.

In a flash of awareness, bright as the afternoon sun, Eliza suddenly realized that she was willing to fight tooth and nail to have what she wanted.

"However, I have decided on what I want, and I mean to have it." The assertion was profoundly liberating. She felt the knot in her chest unravel and the skeins of worry float off in the scudding breeze.

"That's the spirit," said Augustina. "It's time you took your own happiness to heart."

"No, I have not yet heard an answer, milord."

"No answer?" Gryff frowned. "The remuneration we are offering is generous, is it not, Watkins?"

"Extremely generous, milord," assured the publisher. "It's just that this particular artist can be somewhat eccentric."

The furrow in his brow deepened. That news did not bode well for a smooth working relationship.

"No, no." Watkins hastily corrected himself on seeing the marquess's expression. "I didn't mean to give you the wrong impression. It sometimes takes longer than usual to hear a reply, for the artist can be a trifle eccentric about what projects to accept. But once a commission has been agreed on, Linden is completely reliable."

Linden. The small, elegant signature in the corner of the watercolor had been bedeviling his thoughts for days.

"Who is this cursed Linden?" he growled. "A man? A woman? A pixie from the primeval forest?"

"Please don't ask me to betray a confidence, milord." Watkins eyed him unhappily. "You have asked me to protect your own privacy, and would not want me to renege on my promise."

Gryff could not argue that point. There were, he knew, any number of reasons why a person might wish to use a pen name. Bloody hell, for all he knew, this fellow Linden might be a member of his club, and just as anxious to keep his artistic sensibilities a secret for now.

"Very well," he conceded, expelling a sharp sigh. "I shall not badger you about that. But I do expect you to do your utmost to convince the shadowy specter to accept the job. The style is perfect."

"That it is, milord. I shall send another letter, with a lengthy explanation on why I think the project is a perfect collaboration, and will result in a magnificent book."

"Sweeten the pot, if you wish," said Gryff. "Money is no object."

The publisher nodded. "That may have some bearing."

"What about a face-to-face meeting?" He was reluctant to reveal his identity at this point, but if his title and position in Society might help influence Linden's decision, he was willing to set aside his scruples. "Let us be frank—many people are swayed by superficial things like rank and wealth."

The publisher's face went through a series of odd little contortions. "I shall be frank as well, milord. That would not be a good idea. In fact, it might do more harm than good."

The response was not what he expected. "Has Linden a dislike of me personally? Are we acquainted?" Gryff wracked his brain, trying to recall a Linden from his Eton or Oxford days, but came up blank. Perhaps a check of his Debrett's when he got home would refresh his memory.

"Not that I know of," answered Watkins, looking even more uncomfortable. "Let us just say that Linden has no great love for Tulips of the *ton*." A discreet cough. "*Not*," he added hastily, "that I mean to cast any aspersions on your character, milord. But from reading the newspapers and scandal sheets, one might, er, easily get the wrong impression of your character."

"You need not cringe behind your desk, Watkins. I am not about to leap like a rabid cur over that stack of galley proofs and bite your head off for saying the truth."

No matter that the truth stung more than he cared to admit.

"I shall leave it to you to decide the best way to proceed," added Gryff as he rose and began to pace along the line of bookshelves. It was damned unnerving, this compelling need that was gnawing at his insides. He felt like a hungry dog who had spotted a juicy bone, only to have it whisked away at the last moment from his open jaws.

And now, with terrier-like stubbornness, he wouldn't be satisfied with any other sustenance.

"But bloody hell, Watkins," he growled. "I am counting on you to get the deal done."

"I assure you, milord, I shall do my very best."

"I am anxious to proceed on the project," he added, hoping to cover his querulous mood with a professional reason.

"Of course, of course." The publisher looked equally relieved to change the subject from paintbrushes to pens. Blotting an ink-smudged handkerchief to his brow, Watkins quickly asked, "Have you given any more thought to the subject of your last essay?"

"As a matter of fact, yes," answered Gryff. "In fact, I've just returned from a preliminary visit to the estate that I wish to write about. It inspired some...new ideas."

That further fieldwork within its picturesque confines might prove a problem was something he left unsaid. How *would* Lady Brentford react to his reappearance at Leete Abbey?

Not by serving herself on a silver platter, he thought with an inward wince, recalling her reluctance to continue the relationship. *Or in any other way that involved smooth, shiny metal.*

Which was a shame, since the thought of feasting on her luscious body was stirring an involuntary reaction in his nether region. Her mouth had held beguiling traces of a nutty sweetness when he had last kissed her. The Siren of Shortbread, luring men to their doom...

"Then you think it possible that we might stick to our original plan of publishing the book in the spring?" asked Watkins.

"I see no obstacle," answered Gryff. "Save for the elusive Linden." And a long-legged lady with breasts as sweet as sun-sweetened peaches and eyes as alluring as brandy-deep sin.

Keep your mind on landscape, not lust.

Cameron was right. It was damnably hard for a rake to reform. But he was determined to make himself a better man.

"Then it is imperative that we finalize arrangement with the artist as soon as possible," mused Watkins. "I'll send off the letter this afternoon."

Landscape, not lust. Work, not play. The massive pearwood desk in his library sat in readiness for the final drafts to be done. Quills and penknife aligned in sharp order, paper and ink lay at the ready, scholarly volumes stood ready to offer up the answers to any research questions.

Gryff cleared his throat and steadied his resolve. *Yes, this is what matters to me.* "In that case, I had better make plans for returning to the final estate in order to work on my notes."

"We don't have a 'yes' yet," cautioned the publisher.

"Let us not worry about Linden," he said slowly. "If your appeal fails, you will have to turn the matter over to me. When I put my mind to something, I can be very persuasive."

Chapter Nine

The sound of polite applause snapped Eliza out of her reveries. Heaving a rueful sigh, she realized that much of the last hour had been spent woolgathering, rather than picking up on the fine points of pistil and stamen shapes in *Lavandula stoechas*. "A fascinating talk, was it not?" said Lady Fanshaw, the elderly wife of the local squire.

"Indeed," agreed Eliza, quickly gathering up her notebooks before any further queries could unmask her inattention to the lecture. Lady Fanshaw's bulging eyes and chubby jowls gave her the appearance of a well-fed pug, but woe to anyone who underestimated the lady's intellect. "Oh, look, Augustina is waving for me to join her. Mr. Simpson must have a question regarding what watercolor pigments to purchase."

"I didn't see—"

"Yes, yes, there it is again," assured Eliza. "A discreet hand signal, which means she is in imminent need of rescue."

"She could have employed an even more discreet way of communication by waving a nutmeg geranium," quipped Lady Fanshaw. "Which, according to a book I recently read on the secret significance of botanical blooms, means 'I expect a meeting.'"

Good heavens, thought Eliza. The language of flowers seems to be more popular than French these days.

"How very interesting. Though I daresay sending messages that way could be slow going in winter." Leaving her fellow member pondering the point, Eliza slipped behind Mr. Kennan and Mr. Semple, who were arguing over the right type of winter compost for rose bushes, and made her way to the tea table.

"Ask Mr. Simpson about paint pigments," she said under her breath as Augustina offered her a cup of tea. "Loudly."

The odd request didn't cause her friend to bat an eye. "How are your garden sketches coming along, Mr. Simpson?"

"Why, I am very glad you asked," answered the curate. Eliza had heard him grousing earlier about the quality of paint to be found at the local emporium. "I am having great difficulty mixing a proper shade of Hooker's Green."

"Have you tried the pigments made by Newton? Their ingredients are superior to any others I have tried..." Out of the corner of her eye, Eliza saw Mrs. Fanshaw pause for a moment and then sweep by into one of the side parlors.

"What was that all about?" inquired Augustina, once the conversation had ended and Mr. Simpson had moved off to the pastry table.

"I've enough tempests in my teacup without offending the patroness of our Society." The monthly meetings were usually a safe harbor, a tranquil haven from the storms threatening her life. But today, she found herself feeling at cross-currents with the genial mood and chatter of her fellow members.

"I am in sudden need of some fresh air," Eliza added in a low murmur. "Do you mind if excuse myself and run a few errands while you enjoy the refreshment hour?"

Augustina started to set down her cup. "I would be happy—"

"No, please. You always enjoy the tea and cakes. I would just as soon take a solitary stroll."

"In that case, run along," replied her friend. "I shall tell the others that you are exhausted from having Harry and his friends down from London for a visit. Everyone knows that your brother would try the patience of a saint."

And God knows I am no saint, thought Eliza.

"Thank you, Gussie." Her words spilled out in a rush of relief. Gathering her shawl, she edged into the entrance foyer, the shafts of sunlight slanting through the front windows beckoning to her like beacons.

Solitude, and a chance to reflect on the last few days.

Perhaps she would sit for a while in the shade of the graveyard wall, and sketch the morning glory blooms that dotted the mossy stones with vibrant shades of blue.

Impelled by the thought of peaceful quiet, Eliza hurried her steps and turned down the rectory lane. Up ahead, the way narrowed and wound past a row of stucco and timbered buildings. Over the roof slates, she could see the top of the towering yew that marked the lynchgate. A crow rose from the branches with a raucous cawing, its big black wings stirring the still air.

A movement in the shadows suddenly drew her gaze back to earth. Two figures stepped out from the narrow alleyway between the middle buildings.

Harry and Brighton?

All three of them stopped short and stared at each other.

"'Liza!" Harry sounded drunk, and a little nervous. "Didn't 'spect to see you here."

"But meeting up with you is always a pleasure," said Brighton smoothly over her brother's stutter. He smiled, looking very much at ease, and inclined a polite bow.

Eliza acknowledged the greeting with a wordless nod. "It's the regular meeting day for the Horticulture Society," she replied to Harry. "So my presence should come as no surprise." She left the obvious implication hanging heavy in the air.

Harry was foxed—but not so foxed as to miss it. Like a wary turtle, he drew his head down into the fussy folds of his cravat and avoided her eyes. "Right-o. Well, we'll be on our way."

"What were you doing here?" Eliza blurted. There was no sign of any tavern or other haunt for gentlemen, which stirred a prickling of alarm. Not that Harry couldn't get into trouble anywhere, but something about the quiet of the surroundings seemed so out of character for him.

"We simply stepped into the alleyway to blow a cloud," replied Brighton. "We know you ladies find the smell of tobacco noxious, so we didn't wish to offend any delicate sensibilities by strolling down High Street sporting lighted cheroots."

And yet Eliza could smell no hint of smoke in the air.

"If I have led your brother astray, I beg your pardon," continued Brighton. "I just came down from Town this morning to join the party at the Abbey, and Harry agreed to meet me here in Harpden."

"As I have no say over Harry's activities, there is no need for any apologies to me," she replied caustically.

"Quite right," agreed Harry in a querulous slur. "I'm m'own man."

Oh, how I wish you were a man, Harry, rather than a sulky, spoiled child.

"Yes, but it is to your sister's credit that she expresses a concern for your well-being," observed Brighton.

Harry's mouth took on a mulish set, but he didn't retort.

"Shall we walk with you for a bit?" went on Brighton. "You look as though you might welcome some assistance in carrying your things."

Shifting the small satchel of her papers and paints from one hand to the other, Eliza waved off the request. "Thank you but there is no need for that. I'm only going as far as the rectory, where I plan to sit and make a few sketches of the flowers." That information ought to hurry the two gentlemen on their way.

But Brighton did not seem in any rush. "Ah, yes, your brother often sings praises for your impressive artistic talents."

Ah, yes, and pigs often fly to the moon for tea.

Eliza eyed the baronet warily, wondering what had sparked such a show of attentive pleasantries. Nothing good, she decided, though what his motives might be were a mystery to her.

Brighton smiled at something Harry muttered, showing a set of perfect, pearly teeth. He was, she admitted, a man whom most females would consider handsome. His glossy chestnut locks were thick, showing only a touch of silver at the temples, and though some years older than her brother, he cut a more impressive figure. *Taller, broader, heftier.* Only an artist's discerning eye would see the telltale signs of dissipation—the sagging mouth, the thickening jowls, the chest muscles turning to fat.

A clench of disgust tightened her hands.

He noticed the tiny movement and lifted a brow. "I assure you, we would be happy to relieve you of your burden and offer an escort to the churchyard."

"But we're headed in the opposite direction, Freddy," whined Harry ungraciously.

A quelling look from his companion warned him to silence.

"Thank you, but I'm perfectly capable of carrying my bag the short distance," replied Eliza. She couldn't help but add, "I daresay I won't encounter any ravening wolves along the way."

Perhaps it was merely a scudding of the clouds, but Brighton's expression seemed to darken for an instant. Had his cousin mentioned the encounter in the Abbey corridor? Men seemed to brag about such things among themselves...but likely only when they could trumpet success rather than failure.

"Of course y'won't," piped up Harry. "Don't think there are any wolves left in England."

"How very clever of you to recall your history lessons," said Eliza sweetly. "Good day to you."

Brighton tipped his hat. "And to you, Lady Brentford. Will I see you at Leete Abbey on the morrow?"

"I—I have not yet decided on when I shall return," she replied. "Miss Haverstick has been feeling a little unwell, and I wish to stay with her until she is fully recovered."

"Your loyalty is commendable. Though I am disappointed to hear that a more extensive interlude together may have to wait for a future date. Alas, your brother and I must return to Town for a previous engagement the day after tomorrow." Another doff of the curly brimmed beaver. "Enjoy your sketching."

Eliza watched the two men walk off, dismayed to discover that the premonition of danger lurking somewhere close did not trail along with them.

Harry had appeared guilty and Brighton had looked smug—an unsettling combination if ever there was one. She expelled a long breath. But worrying over unknown threats was pointless.

If mischief was afoot, it would catch up with her soon enough.

Her own steps brought her abreast of the wrought iron gate to the graveyard. The cheerful chirping of the sparrows helped dispel her mordant musing. In the shade of a leafy oak, she found a tumbled block of stone from the old wall and took a seat. Sunlight dipped and danced over the weathered granite, teasing tones of pale grays and greens from the lichens growing in the shadows. In contrast, the variegated blues of the morning glory blossoms glowed with an exuberant life.

Eliza took out her paintbox and canvas roll of brushes, but after a hitch of hesitation, she set it aside, deciding there was no point in delaying the real reason she had sought some time to herself. Reaching into her satchel again, she withdrew the packet that had arrived that morning from Mr. Watkins.

Damn Harry and his debauched friends for distracting her from the pending commission. She had been meaning to draft a suitably flowery acceptance of the terms and generous fee, but for the last few days her attention had been elsewhere. Mentally ogling the muscled abdomen and lean loins of a notorious rake, she admitted with a guilty grimace. It would serve her right if the author of the essays had changed his mind.

But no, a quick perusal of the publisher's letter informed her that the author—who, like herself, preferred to be known by a nom de plume—still wanted to engage her services and was anxiously awaiting her decision.

As if there was any doubt in her own mind as to whether she was going to accept the offer from "Owain."

Heaving a small sigh of relief, Eliza unfolded the accompanying pages. Clever Mr. Watkins—having worked closely with her on several projects, the publisher apparently knew her soft spots better than she had imagined. He had forwarded one of the finished essays, saying that he hoped the ideas would appeal to her artistic imagination.

Up to now, she had read only a short excerpt of the writing...

The paper crackled softly beneath her fingers as she began skimming over the words. It was a short piece, sensitive yet strong, and once again, Eliza found herself impressed with the author's perceptive eye. Owain saw textures and nuances that most people missed. And she liked that the ideas and observations were expressed with such grace and wit.

She stifled a chuckle over one particular passage. The words had a certain joie de vivre that made her want to shuck off her corset, like a butterfly breaking free of a confining cocoon, and dance around in her shift to the music of a spring breeze riffling through newly unfurled leaves. Tilting her face skyward, she closed her eyes and imagined the rhythm of raindrops, the melodies of birdsong. Warmth whispered against her cheeks. The air was still, silent, and yet in her head she heard a symphony of sunshine, in harmony with nature.

Strangely enough, Owain, the Poet, made her feel... well, much like Haddan, the Rake, made her feel. *Free. Alive. Exuberant.* Both touched her in ways that stirred a passionate response...

Oh, don't be foolish, she chided herself. Owain was probably female. Or an octogenarian with a humpback and a squint.

Still, she couldn't help but think of the Poet as a kindred soul.

If circumstances were different, she might even be tempted to ask for a meeting. But seductive as the idea was, it held far too many dangers.

And of late, she had taken enough impulsive risks to last a lifetime.

Banishing any further wayward thoughts, Eliza pulled a pencil and notebook from her satchel, and began composing a letter.

Dear Mr. Watkins,

After careful deliberation, and a lengthy study of the essay you sent me, I have decided to accept your generous offer. The timing will leave little room for error, but with luck it should work out...

After several drafts, she was satisfied and copied out a final draft. Now, if only she could structure her feelings about Haddan in the same orderly, logical fashion.

Haddan—forget about Haddan!

"Don't be pathetic," she muttered. "You can be sure that the marquess is not pining over the memory of a country widow." Not when he had legions of lissome beauties eager to make the fleeting interlude fade to an indistinct blur. A colorless, shapeless blur.

For the next few minutes, she busied herself in uncorking her water bottle and mixing colors on her palette. But after two or three desultory tries at capturing the flowered wall, she abandoned the effort and turned to a fresh page.

Perhaps the nearby gravestone would provide better artistic inspiration—she could draw a monument to girlish dreams that were best left dead and buried in the earth of the past.

As her brush floated over the page, Eliza mused on gentlemen of the *ton*, and how quickly they grew bored. For them, life seemed naught but one passing fancy after another. It took a brash challenge to excite any sort of enthusiasm—racing a curricle from London to Bath, downing a half-dozen bottles of brandy in the space of an hour, picking which raindrop would reach the bottom of a window first—and even then, heated passion often turned to jaded indifference within the blink of an eye.

"And that," she reminded herself, "is why you would be a complete and utter lackwit not to put Haddan out of your head."

The drawing of the dragon seemed to wiggle in response.

Eliza snapped the book shut. Poppies—she need to find a patch of poppies for her sketching.

In the secret language of flowers, they stood for oblivion.

* * *

Gryff set aside his razor and patted his cheeks dry. The mundane tasks of dressing and shaving himself proved surprisingly soothing, making him glad that he had left his valet in London. Prescott had not been happy about the decision, no doubt fearing that the marquess's elegant clothing was journeying into mortal peril.

Wrinkles could be pressed, smudges could be laundered, mused Gryff as he picked his driving coat up from the floor and hung it over the bedpost. He was more concerned with mending any damage that his recent behavior had done to Lady Brentford's feelings. Games of flirtation could be harmless, assuming both parties knew how to wield the implements of play and understood the rules. No matter her enthusiasm, the widow was an obvious novice, and as such it was ungentlemanly to take advantage of her lack of experience.

Not that her performance had left anything to be desired. He felt his groin clench at the memory of her eager kisses, her throaty moans.

She had reacted with innocent abandon. Which was why, despite all his rationalizing, he felt slightly soiled.

"I like her," he murmured, casting a sidelong glance at his reflection in the looking glass to see if he had spouted horns and cloven tongue. Encouraged that voicing such sentiments had not turned him into the Devil Incarnate, he added, "I like her feisty spirit, her tart humor, her quiet strength." Not to speak of her shapely long legs, her glorious body, her expressive face. She was Beauty who saw herself as merely Ordinary.

Clenching a fist, Gryff found himself wanting to crack the skulls of the men who had failed to make her feel attractive. Alluring. Desirable.

She deserved better.

Ignoring the serpentine slither of guilt that suddenly slid down his spine, he tucked his notebook in his pocket and hurried for the door.

It was a short ride from the inn to Leete Abbey, and for most of it he kept his mind rooted in landscape design. Vistas, ha-has, classical follies—he had a long list of specific elements he wished to see. But as his horse turned into the winding approach to the manor house, Gryff found that his normal sense of self-assurance seemed to have stayed behind in London.

"It's absurd to feel nervous," he growled. So what that he had said nothing to Leete about a return visit? By all accounts, the viscount had returned to Town and was once again submerged in the hellholes of Southwark, gaming away what little assets were left to his name.

Gryff felt a surge of sympathy for the supporters of Mary Wollstonecraft's radical ideas on female equality. Possessing a pizzle did not give a fellow the right to piss away centuries of careful stewardship.

Glowering at the unpruned hedges, he rode into the courtyard. The harsh glare of the midday sun accentuated the unwashed panes of the mullioned windows, the chipped pediments of the colonnading, the broken noses of the ornamental lions. The grand house was like a beautiful lady gone to seed. Once-lovely lines sagged, stretches of smooth, honey-colored stone were riddled with fine cracks.

"Leete ought to be hung by his ballocks from the crumbling roof slates," he muttered, looking around for a groom to take his mount.

"Alas, if you are looking for revelries, you have arrived

several days too late." There was no mistaking the sarcasm in the lady's voice. "My brother has left for London, and you would do well to follow, sir. Without him in residence, things are dreadfully dull here at the Abbey."

He turned in the saddle. "I'm not seeking a party."

Eliza's eyes widened as he lifted the broad brim of his beaver hat. "Then why are you here, Lord Haddan?" In a lower, tighter voice she added, "As I said, the revelries have come to an end."

Gryff dismounted, causing her to retreat a few steps. "I have no intention of intruding on your privacy, Lady Brentford. I would simply like your permission to have a look at the Abbey grounds."

Her brows pinched together. "What for?"

Not that he could blame her for questioning his motives. If Leete's cronies ever ventured into the gardens it was likely not to smell the roses but to piss in the bushes.

"I assure you, my intentions are quite benign. I promise, I did not come to further provoke you." Gryff had assumed that someone would ask for an explanation, so he was prepared with an answer. "A friend of mine has read about Capability Brown's designs for the Abbey grounds. He's thinking of making some similar landscaping changes on his own estate and wished for my opinion on certain looks before he undertakes such extensive renovations."

If anything, her expression turned even more doubtful. "Why would he ask you?"

"I have eyes, Lady Brentford. And an estate of my own," he replied. "Not all titled gentlemen are indolent idlers. I have plenty of faults, but ignoring my lands is not one of them."

Eliza flushed at the set-down. "I did not mean to imply—"

"Of course you did." He softened his words with a smile. "And with good reason, I would guess."

Her lips twitched. "The last time one of Harry's friends decided to take a stroll through the grounds, he fell into the lake—but not before setting fire to the boathouse."

"I trust there was no lasting damage."

"The beams were merely singed." Eliza paused. "As for Lord Vestry, I cannot vouch for what scars are left by a lighted cheroot falling on brandy-soaked buckskins."

Gryff chuckled. "I have no plans for arson. Or for planting gunpowder bombs in the Abbey ruins, decimating your specimen apple trees with an ax, or, for that matter, indulging in any other sort of puerile pranks." He let his words sink in for a moment before adding, "In short, my intentions are completely honorable."

The tips of her half boots suddenly seemed of far more interest to her than his own paltry presence. Perhaps, he thought dryly, she was looking for some cryptic message in the powdery patterns of dried dirt. The secret language of the Dust Motes.

Or, more simply, Your Name is Mud.

Eliza's gaze angled from the ground to the sky. "When clouds are rolling in from the west, it usually means that rain is in the offing. And judging by their color, I would say that it's going to be more than a passing shower." The breeze was already rising, setting her skirts to flapping around her ankles. "The choice is yours, of course, but unless you enjoy getting soaked to the skin, you might want to return on the morrow."

"Is that an invitation?" he murmured.

"Call it a reprieve." Though she didn't say from what.

"There is an old saying about discretion being the better part of valor. So I think I shall heed your advice. I might survive a downpour, but my valet would likely turn murderous if my garments were ruined. He is very attached to this coat."

"Then maybe he ought to be wearing it," she suggested, the corners of her mouth framing a telltale twitch of humor.

"Prescott would no doubt agree with you." Gryff made a show of inspecting the sleeves and lapels. "He says it makes me look fat. What do you think?"

At that, Eliza laughed, a light, happy peal that momentarily chased the chill from the moist air. The sound seemed to take her by surprise, for she quickly pressed a gloved hand to her lips.

The unconscious gesture gave hint that she didn't have much occasion for merriment in her life.

"I think," she replied, slowly lowering her fingers, "that you are incorrigible, Lord Haddan."

"Agreed," he said. "Seeing as you didn't say 'insufferable,' dare I hope that you will consent to guide me around the grounds? I would be happy to provide a picnic, which we might eat down by the lake. It would be a cold collation, of course." He waggled a brow. "No errant lucifers to spark any trouble."

She ducked her head, the wind loosening several tendrils of hair from her hairpins. They danced in the scudding light, setting off flashes of red-gold fire. From beneath the poke of her chip-straw bonnet floated a low murmur. "The devil, you say."

"I was referring to the phosphorus-coated matchsticks, Lady Brentford, not any compatriot of Satan."

"Yet wherever you go, the Devil seems to follow."

"I'll keep him at arm's length with a pitchfork. I trust the gardener's shed here has an extra-sturdy one."

"Incorrigible," she repeated, trying to tamp down the note of amusement in her tone.

More laughter? A good sign.

"I know that you asked for time to think about any further contact, but please say you will come," pressed Gryff. "What is your favorite treat—besides Miss Haver-stick's walnut shortbread? Kumquats? Caramel apples? Candied violets?"

"*My* favorite?" Surprise squeezed her voice to a squeak.

"Is that a no to the violets?" Gryff kept nattering non-sense to keep a growl of pure, primal anger trapped in his chest. *Good God, had no one ever asked about her likes? Her needs?*

"Vile things, those sugar-coated purple petals," he went on. "The Turks have an almond confection flavored with rosewater. But I daresay I'd have to journey to Con-stantinople, and that would mean putting off the picnic by a few days. So perhaps we could compromise on goose-berry tarts, and keep our appointment for tomorrow?"

"I haven't said 'yes' yet, Lord Haddan," she pointed out.

"Yes, but you will," he replied. "Won't you?"

"I...oh...why not?" A passing cloud cast her in shadow. Held in the grip of the iron-gray shades, Eliza looked achingly alone and vulnerable. "I—I suppose there's little harm in casting propriety to the wind." She made a wry face. "Though considering the fact that our first encounter was in a brothel, it's rather absurd to speak of us and propriety in the same breath."

"You will have no cause for complaint."

She lifted a brow but did not retort.

"I shall call tomorrow at eleven, if that suits you, Lady Brentford."

"Yes. Fine." She started to walk away.

In the distance, a grumble of thunder echoed through the hills. Gryff turned up his collar and turned to his horse.

"Custard tarts."

He stopped abruptly and looked back over his shoulder.

"I like custard tarts. Topped with cinnamon and apples."

Gryff snapped a salute. Had she asked for sugared moonbeams, dusted with spiced starlight, he would gladly have found a ladder long enough to reach up to the black velvet heavens.

"And you shall have them."

Her tentative smile was more dazzling than any celestial orb.

"Tomorrow, at eleven," she confirmed. "And be forewarned, I have a very unladylike appetite."

Chapter Ten

$\mathcal{E}$liza rose at first light, nervous as a green girl before her first ball.

"I'm not about to waltz across a parquet dance floor in a stylish swirl of satin and lace," she reminded herself, catching a glimpse of her decidedly frumpish night rail in the cheval glass. With a self-mocking curtsey at her scarecrow reflection, she rose on her bare toes and pirouetted around the rug. "I'm going to slog through a muddy field in worn muslin and half boots."

A sweeping bow to Elf sent him scurrying under the bed.

"Thank you, Fair Prince, for your company, but I have another admirer waiting to take me into supper," she said in a high falsetto. "What? You would like another dance after I've plied myself with lobster patties and champagne?" She picked up a washcloth and gave it an airy wave. "La, I'm sorry, milord, but my dance card is completely full."

The strange feline sounds emanating from beneath the bed hangings seemed to imply that Elf was just as happy to forgo a country gavotte.

"I know, I know—I've gone quite mad." Eliza padded across the floor and propped her hands on the windowsill. The world outside the glass was still painted in shades of gray. Mist floated over the gardens, pale swirls silhouetted against the pewter-dark foliage.

But a glimmer of sunlight behind the distant hills gave hint that the day would brighten.

Brighten.

Somewhere inside her, a spark seemed to flare and send a tiny flame of warmth tickling up to her face. Eliza felt her lips curl up in an involuntary smile.

A picnic—the last time she had been on a picnic, she chased butterflies and made herself sick eating too many sweetmeats. She had been five at the time.

Then her mother had died, and there were no more picnics, just her father's querulous complaints about the uselessness of daughters, and the damnable expense of a dowry.

"It doesn't matter," she whispered. "It's time to break free from the fetters of the past." She rubbed her wrists, recalling the brass cuffs that had recently encircled her flesh. In its own bizarre way, perhaps that had been the first step to shucking off the guilt and the meek acceptance of Fate in the form of a spendthrift family.

"I'm tired of being treated like a hound on a leash, tugged this way and that by some male master." Her voice rose, the force of it fogging the panes. She wiped the mist away with her sleeve. "From now on, I'm not going to roll over and play dead on command."

Her nails drummed a martial tattoo against the glass. So it was imperative to remember that however handsome and charming, Haddan was a danger to her dreams if she let girlish longing get out of hand. The attraction was merely skin deep, she assured herself. It could not—would not—go any further.

"I'm going to listen to my own instincts and allow myself...the freedom to follow my dreams."

A cottage in the country, not a castle in the sky. A cat for a supper companion, not a handsome marquess. Her dreams were modest. And realistic. Better yet, they were possible, but only if she worked very, very hard for the next few weeks.

This coming painting commission was critical.

One last day of play, and then she must buckle down and forget about green-eyed lords and sinuous dragons. This wasn't a fanciful fairytale. It was real life, and if anyone was going to write a happy ending, it would have to be her.

"I'm sorry, but you will have to put your horse away in the stable on your own, Lord Haddan," said Eliza in curt greeting as the marquess reined to a halt in the courtyard. "The groom was needed to help with repairing a fence in the west pastures."

Gryff swung a large hamper off the pommel of his saddle. "That is not a problem, Lady Brentford. Conditions on the Peninsula were far more grim than these and I managed quite adequately."

Surprise flickered across her face. "I—I didn't know you were in the military."

"The Rakehell Regiment." He snapped a mock salute. "The Major of Mayhem and Mischief at your service."

She stepped closer, her stare sharpening as she tilted her head to one side. "Is that a saber scar?" she asked.

Gryff touched his brow. "A mere scratch. I fell off my mount. It was all rather embarrassing."

"I see."

Anxious to forestall any further comment, he lifted a corner of the checkered cloth covering the hamper, allowing the scents of sugar and spice to waft up from the wicker. "Custard tarts, fresh from the oven."

The drab wool of her gown tightened over her breasts as Eliza inhaled deeply.

"Made just the way you like them," he murmured, trying not to salivate at the sight of her breasts plumped to perfection. His privy part was now straining to stand at ramrod attention.

"Tarts?" Her tongue teased over her lower lip.

"Hot and juicy," he rasped, feeling as if his body was being griddled over hot coals.

"Do you think they will last until nuncheon? Or should we gobble them down here and now?" Eliza grinned. "No doubt the warm cream would dribble down our chins, but part of the fun of a picnic is throwing manners to the wind and licking up the excess."

The devil keep me from temptation.

Gripping the reins, Gryff ducked to the other side of his horse's head and quickly led the animal into the cool shade of the stable. Was she deliberately trying to torture him with talk of tongues and buttery sweets sliding over bare flesh?

Sweat had beaded on the back of his neck, and was shivering its way down his spine.

"I think they will hold out," he rasped. Though the same could not be said for his self-control. He had vowed to be a gentleman. But like the pastry's flaky crust, that resolve was in imminent danger of crumbling.

"Very well," she said, far too cheerfully. "Anticipation often makes things taste even sweeter."

"Right," he growled. Thankfully, the pungent smells of horse and hay helped quash his lustful thought. By the time he had unsaddled his mount, his wayward body was under control.

Eliza had wandered out to wait by the paddock. Her back was to him, giving him an excellent view of her shapely derriere perched on the top rail of the fence. She had removed her bonnet and had her head tipped up to catch the blade of sunlight cutting through the thinning clouds.

On hearing his approach, she jumped down and jammed the headcovering back in place. The slightly squashed poke of straw looked faintly ridiculous atop her glorious, honey-gold hair.

He was tempted to pluck it off and feed it to his horse.

"Aren't you worried about getting freckles?" he asked. "I thought ladies lived in mortal peril of spots marring their perfect complexion."

"You are used to the refined sensibilities of a London belle," replied Eliza. "The two of us are as different as chalk and cheese. She has elegance. I have spots." Her chin rose a fraction. "I like the feel of the sun on my face," she added, her tone daring him to make a snide comment. "And since men are never going to swoon over my looks, why should I care whether I have a dusting of freckles over my nose?"

"Why, indeed?" The fact was, Gryff found her freckles rather endearing. They gave her face character. In contrast, the smooth, marble-white perfection so favored in Town suddenly seemed colorless.

Or perhaps "lifeless" was a better word.

"Is there something specific you wish to see on the estate grounds, Lord Haddan?" she asked, struggling to retie the flapping satin ribbons.

"I have a list…" On impulse, Gryff reached out and snagged the strings. He had left his own curly brimmed beaver hat in the stable with his saddle, preferring to feel the wind in his hair as he walked. "If you don't like it, why don't you leave it off?" A yank lifted it off her head. Catching it in midair, Gryff sent it sailing through the breeze, where after several lazy somersaults, it landed neatly atop a fencepost.

"How did you do that?" she asked admiringly.

"It's all in the wrist," he explained, demonstrating a quick flicking motion. "One learns it through casting a fishing line and throwing a cricket ball. As well as hammering a broken shutter."

"You are a man of many talents," she murmured.

Should he feel insulted that throwing a hat and fixing a cottage window seemed to be at the top of her list? Oddly enough, it made him smile. "I'll take that as a compliment, even if it wasn't meant to be."

She looked a little embarrassed. "Your list," she said, abruptly changing the subject. "Shall we begin?"

Paper cracked as he unfolded the note and read off the areas he wished to visit.

"An interesting selection." Eliza thought for a moment. "Your friend understands landscape design."

And so do you, thought Gryff. Only someone well versed in the nuances of the art would see the connection.

"Follow me," she said. "We'll start at the south ha-ha and work our way around to the lake."

He fell in step beside her.

They walked in companionable silence, the crunch of the gravel a pleasant counterpoint to the rustling leaves and chirping songbirds. Somewhere close by, an owl hooted, the sound sending a rabbit skittering for cover within a tangle of blackberry canes. The stones ended, and as Gryff walked over the soft grass, he could feel the warmth of the earth seeping up through his boots.

The crowded, dung-spattered cobbles of London suddenly seemed to hold little allure. Breathing in the clean-scented air, he was reminded of the choking soot, the noxious smells of the city.

Country. Earth and wind. Sun and foliage.

Perhaps it was time to go home. Home to a place where countless Dwights had trod the land before him. Home to a place where living things took root and grew. Home to a place he could take pride in improving and then pass on to a future generation.

"As you see, sir, the use of a ha-ha wall allows a clear vista down to the river."

Eliza's words pulled Gryff out of his reveries.

"Capability Brown left this line of bushes to define the left opening," she pointed out. "Clever, is it not?"

"Indeed." He took out his notebook and pencil. "It's also interesting how he used..."

For the next few hours the two of them traversed the fields and climbed up and down the slopes, studying the contours of the land, and how the celebrated designer had used shape, texture, and color to guide the eye through the natural setting. It was a sublime experience, made even more enjoyable by the company of his companion. Gryff found himself admiring not just her lovely body, but also her clever mind.

Eliza was intelligent, knowledgeable, articulate. But most of all, she was passionate. He liked watching the fire light in her eyes when she described an element that appealed to her imagination. Their color turned to flame-kissed sapphire, a molten shade of blue so vibrant, yet so ethereal, that it defied a solid name.

Her features were equally expressive, once she relaxed enough to let down her guard. She had a certain way of quirking the corners of her mouth when she disagreed with him. And rarely had he seen the arch of a brow convey such scathing skepticism. A crinkling, a flutter—it was all very subtle. One might easily miss her signals.

But then, he guessed she had learned to disguise her feelings. Hide her passions.

Intrigued, he provoked her into arguments over details, taking pleasure in the fact that she wasn't afraid to challenge his opinions. In London, so many of his acquaintances were either sycophants or seductresses. It was refreshing to be with someone who was simply herself.

Finally finished with their survey of the south section of landscaping, they skirted a copse of beech trees and made their way down to the classical Greek folly set on the edge of the lake.

"Mmmph." Eliza passed through the row of fluted columns and plopped down on one of the stone benches with an audible sigh.

"Tired?" he asked, feeling a little guilty that he had forced her to cover so much ground.

"Hungry," she replied, eyeing the hamper. "I hope you brought plenty of food."

"Enough to feed an army."

"Ha!" she grinned. "An army of hummingbirds, perhaps. I've seen how the fine London ladies dine." Sucking in her cheeks, she gave a frightfully accurate imitation of how the reigning belles of Society took dainty little bites of a morsel no bigger than a pea. "Sorry, but after all that exercise, I could eat a—"

"Please don't say horse," interrupted Gryff, exaggerating a grimace. "I am quite fond of Demon." He set the hamper down. "And I don't think he would taste very good."

"Too tough," she agreed. "I hope you have something better tucked under that cloth. Else I might have to nibble on your..."

Gryff felt his body give an involuntary clench.

"...boot," she finished.

"You might have to settle for an elbow. Hoby's footwear costs an arm and leg," he responded, greatly enjoying the verbal give and take.

"I thought you were rich."

"I am. But no amount of money could compensate for losing Prescott and his secret champagne polish for my footwear. Have you any idea how hard it is to find a good valet these days?"

Eliza rolled her eyes. "What a Macaroni you are."

He couldn't remember ever having enjoyed conversing—really conversing—with a lady this much before. Probably because his exchanges with the opposite sex were mostly sultry, sexual word games aimed at winning an invitation to tumble between the bedsheets.

"Good God, does your valet control your life?" she remarked, once her facial gymnastics were done.

"He controls my clothing, which is much the same," answered Gryff. "I can't very well walk around Town stark naked."

She fell silent at that, her gaze dropping to watch a grasshopper's progress across the mossy stones.

Damnation. He gave himself a good, swift mental kick. Her downturned face and loosened ringlets could not quite hide the telltale flush of her embarrassment.

"Would you like a breast or a leg?" he quipped, quickly unpacking the roasted chicken in hope that humor might restore the mood of relaxed camaraderie.

Her shoulder blades stiffened.

Oh, bloody hell...It took a moment for him to realize she was trying not to laugh.

As a stifled chuckle slipped from out from the folds of her shawl, the knot in his chest loosened, allowing his breath to release in a rush.

"I imagine that you would choose the breast," said Eliza, her lips still quivering with mirth.

"I like both." He grinned, feeling ridiculously happy at seeing her smile. "Why don't I carve up a little of each for us?"

Eliza nodded in assent. "What else is in there?" After a peek under the cloth, she took out a loaf of crusty bread, a wedge of crumbly cheese, chutney, and a jug of cider in quick succession. A last foray produced the tart, which she set down ever so carefully beside her.

"Am I forgiven for all my past transgressions?" he asked, passing her a plate.

"I'll tell you after I've tasted the tart."

What with the fresh air and exercise, Gryff found that he, too, had worked up a good appetite. Shrugging out of his coat, he fixed a generous helping of the food for himself and dug in.

"This is delicious," murmured Eliza, breaking off another wedge of the buttery cheddar and topping it with a dollop of pickled fruit.

He liked how she ate with gusto. There was an earthy sensuality to her uninhibited enjoyment of the taste and textures of the food. The sight of her mouth savoring the—

Gryff made himself swallow his lecherous thoughts.

Taking another swig of the potent cider, he leaned back on his elbows and watched the gentle undulations of the leaves overhead. The breeze had softened, and with the stones radiating the heat soaked up from earlier in the day, he felt his mood turning even more mellow.

"You were right," he heard Eliza announce. "Well, half right. There are enough pickings left for at least a regiment." A fork clinked, followed by a soulful sigh. "Sorry, though. I'm not sharing the tart with anyone but you."

"Is it good?" he asked drowsily, not opening his eyes.

"Absolutely divine." Her skirts brushed up against his thighs. "Here, you have to try a bite."

He lifted a lid. Her almond-shaped eyes were rich with merriment, and he was suddenly, hungrily aware that of late he had come to have a craving for nuts. "If you insist."

"You won't regret it. "

She leaned in closer, and all he could see was the cupid's bow curve of her mouth and the sinuous stretch of her smile, made a touch lopsided by the dab of creamy custard clinging to the corner of her lips.

"Open wide," she said, teasing a forkful of tart in front of his nose.

Gryff obeyed the order. But before she could feed him the morsel, he straightened slightly and flicked out his tongue to lick away the excess pastry. "Sorry, you had a spot." He smacked his lips. "Mmmm, you're right. It's delicious."

Her throat convulsed. "I—I have lots of spots."

"So I see," said Gryff softly. He touched his lips ever so gently to the bridge of her nose. "Hmmm. They seem to be stuck there. Perhaps I should try harder."

Eliza caught a dancing lock of hair and smoothed it behind her ear. "Ladies are told to use lemon juice to erase them," she murmured.

"I can think of a far sweeter method to try."

Sunlight played over the curl of her downswept lashes, winking like bits of burnished gold. Despite the brightness, her eyes remained hidden in shadow. "I thought you promised that your intentions were honorable."

"So I did." Reluctantly he leaned back. "And a gentleman always keeps his promises."

Her expression pinched as she let out a sardonic laugh.

Gryff wouldn't have thought that a fleeting whisper could express such a multitude of emotions. *Anger. Exasperation. Doubt. Hurt.*

"Do they?" she replied after the sound had died away. "How odd to hear you say so." Eyes narrowing, she stared out over the lake. "In my experience, a gentleman always does exactly as he pleases, regardless of what flowery words he's spoken."

"Perhaps you've been consorting with the wrong sort of gentleman, Lady Brentford."

She carefully set the plate and fork down on the stone and dusted the crumbs from her fingertips. "Yes, well,

I don't seem to know any who aren't rakes, roués, and reprobates."

How could he argue when honor demanded that a gentleman not lie to a lady?

Wind ruffled her hair, loosening another pin. Curls floated free, like drizzles of honey against the blue sky.

"You deserve better," he said, breaking the sliver of silence.

"Life is rarely fair." Her mouth tipped into a crooked smile. "I may deserve better..." She drew in a breath and let it out slowly. "But I'll settle for you."

Chapter Eleven

*M*aybe it was the fizzy cider, or the surfeit of butter and sugar that had addled her brain. Whatever the reason, Eliza felt reason slipping away. For so much of her life, dreams and desires had been far out of reach. She had learned to keep them bundled up and stashed away in a dark place, where they wouldn't bother anyone. Only sometimes late at night would she sneak a peek beneath the coverings and let herself think about what if.

What if. What if she had spent a Season laughing with suitors and dancing til dawn? What if her marriage had not been a cold, loveless match?

What if, for once, she dared to grab at something before it became just another *what if*?

Boldly, before reason reasserted its grip, Eliza placed her hands on the slope of his shoulders. Sleek muscles met her touch, their sculpted contours smooth as marble through the soft-textured linen.

"Lady Brentford," he began.

At that instant she wasn't Lady Brentford, she was…some nameless longing dancing in the slanting sunlight.

Dipping her head, she kissed him full on the mouth.

He tasted of apples, that forbidden fruit of temptation. Oh, no wonder females had been seduced into sin. The tart-sweet spice held hints of an earthier, distinctly masculine flavor.

Under her hungry assault, his lips parted, and then their tongues were touching. Twining, twirling, teasing in sensuous play. Eliza hitched closer, reveling in the lush heat flooding her senses. Her body was once again transformed. She was no longer a drab widow, but a sensual sylph, capable of driving men mad with desire.

She could have gone on forever, lost in this haze of fantasy, but he shifted beneath her, just enough to jar her back to reality.

"Sorry." She broke away, blinking against the glare of the sunlight as she sucked in a shivering breath. "So, *so* sorry."

"For what?" asked Gryff, his voice sounding just as dazed as hers.

"For acting like a wanton strumpet. A shameless hussy." Did he think her disgusting? Depraved? "I know it's very wrong to succumb to sinful urges. I—I apologize for subjecting you to such unwanted advances."

His beautiful eyes reflected the shimming swirls of green and gold around them. "Unwanted?" he repeated in a husky whisper. He caught her hand as she tried to scoot away. "Unwanted?"

Gently unfisting her fingers, Gryff pressed her palm to the fall of his breeches. "Trust me, Lady Brentford, I've been wanting to kiss you witless all day, but was trying to restrain my beastly lust."

"Oh." Eliza sighed as she felt the contour of his rigid

cock hard against her yielding flesh. "Oh, I like your beastly lust."

Gryff chuckled, and then captured her mouth in a ravening embrace. "Mmmm, I like your sinful urges," he murmured some moments later.

Turning her head, she lay her cheek against his, feeling the faint stubbling of his whiskers. "I don't know how to explain them. You stir such wicked thoughts in me."

"Like what?"

Dare she say them aloud?

"Like what," he prompted.

"Like the mad desire to fill your navel with custard and slowly lick out every last drop."

His cock twitched hard against her hand.

"Like the wild urge to trace my lips along the curling, ink-dark lines of your dragon tattoo."

He groaned, and the thrumming echo seemed to linger in the air.

"Is that so terrible?" Her cheeks were hot as hellfire.

"No," he rasped. "You know what fantasies I am having?"

Eliza held her breath.

"First I would unravel the ribbon from your hair..." His fingers pulled the silky strand free. "Then I would tug each and every hairpin free and toss them into the lake..." A tinkling of tiny splashes followed. "Next I would take off my shirt..." His muscles rippled as he tugged the fabric over his head. "And then I would lie back on this warm stone and beg you to do with me as you will."

Eliza watched in fascination as the light played off his bronzed skin and the dark, curling hair peppering his chest.

Gryff propped himself on his elbows, his eyes following her finger as she scooped up a dollop of the tart's creamy filling and filled the dimple in his belly.

"Sweet Lord," he said, his voice a little unsteady.

Oh, she liked that. With a few playful strokes, she shaped the custard, then leaned down, letting her breath tease against his skin.

Did she dare?

"It is unfair to taunt and torture me," he rasped.

At the look on his face, Eliza suddenly felt a surge of power. "You mean you want me to do this?" A light flick of her tongue circled the sweet, barely grazing.

He let out a quivering hiss.

"Or this?"

"God give me strength."

Emboldened, she traced her lips round and round, suckling, nibbling. There was a hint of salt on his skin, which heightened the sweetness of the custard. And the wisps of silky-soft hair added an intriguing texture. The dark frizz led down, following the curl of the dragon's sinuous neck...

Her hands moved tentatively to the fall of his breeches and, one by one, worked the fastenings free. He squirmed ever so slightly as she pulled the buckskin several inches lower on his hips. "I want a closer look at your dragon—may I?"

A groan—or was it a growl?

She flattened her palm on the plane of his belly, feeling the liquid pounding of his heart beneath the skin. *Or was it her own?* It didn't seem to matter. The thrum drew her down, and then her tongue was tracing the dark swirls of ink.

Gryff slumped against the back of the bench, his eyes closed, his breath coming in hoarse little rasps.

Wicked—this went beyond wicked.

Growing more confident, Eliza grasped the soft leather and inched his breeches and his drawers down from his thighs.

Released from restraint, his cock sprang up. "You," Gryff gasped, his eyes opening, "are a vision of ethereal beauty with your goldspun curls dancing against the clouds." One large hand reached up to tangle in her hair, while the other guided her grip around his manhood.

Haddan called her beautiful? Deep down inside, Eliza knew it was likely just a pretty phrase that he said without thinking. But it didn't matter. No man had ever called her beautiful.

Sighing, she let his heat suffuse her palm. He was so soft, yet so hard.

"You feel like velvet over steel," murmured Eliza. Enchanted by contrast, she feathered her fingers along his length, up and back, up and back. Circling him again, she squeezed.

His whole body clenched.

"Am I doing this right?" she asked, watching the play of sunlight over the planes of his face. Tightening her hold, she quickened her stroke just a little, reveling in the heat thrumming through him.

"Exquisitely right." His voice was a ragged whisper. He swiveled his hips and thrust up against her with a groan.

"I like touching you, Haddan," announced Eliza, surprising herself with the bold statement. Oh, but she *did* like it. Eager to explore the nuances of his shape, his feel, she changed her tempo, her stroking. It was all so new, so intriguing...

Catching her wrist, Gryff suddenly wrenched free and grabbed a cloth from the hamper to cover himself as he released a rumbled growl through his teeth.

After a moment, he fell back, his chest heaving, his body going limp.

"Haddan?" The brusque movement had broken the erotic spell. Uncertainty swirled up inside her as she realized how impulsive her actions had been. Should she apologize?

He looked up with a lidded gaze, as if reading her thoughts. "Don't try to think, Lady Brentford. Just feel."

She drew in a deep breath of the clean-scented country air and held it in her lungs. *I feel happy*, she decided. However fleeting it may be.

Trouble. Gryff felt the afterglow of their intimacy give way to shadows. He should have listened to the first little warning. Now he was in deep, deep trouble. And in danger of sinking deeper.

All the familiar rules seemed to explode into myriad pieces when he was with Lady Brentford, leaving him feeling conflicted and confused. A part of him—the honorable part—feared that once again he was leading an innocent into ruin.

Unfortunately, Honor's voice seemed to be growing fainter and fainter.

"Would you mind turning," he said softly, feeling a little ashamed of himself. "So that I may put myself to rights."

Eliza scooted around, nervously smoothing her unruly

curls and tying them back in with the ribbon she retrieved from the flagstones. By the set of her shoulders, he saw that she was embarrassed.

Pulling on his shirt, Gryff quickly refastened his breeches. The clatter of the cutlery and cider jug as she repacked the hamper was a little overloud.

"Lady Brentford—Eliza…"

She looked up through her lashes.

"Might I ask you to step over here for a moment?"

She hesitated.

"Please."

Her steps scraped over the stone.

Reaching up, he framed her face between his palms and drew her down for a quick, chaste kiss. "There is no reason for a stormy face. A man and a woman just indulged in a mutually delightful intimate game amid a sparkling of glorious sunlight." He smiled. "That's cause for celebration, not recrimination."

Her mouth crooked. "I seem to turn into the W-whore of Babylon when I'm around you."

He pressed a finger to her lips. "Your passions are nothing to be ashamed of."

"They aren't?"

Gryff laughed lightly. "Good heavens, it would be awfully hypocritical of me to say otherwise."

Her mouth quirked up at the corners. "That's one of the things I like about you, Haddan. You are honest about who you are."

The comment stirred an inward cringe. But in truth, he hadn't really *lied* to her—he had just told a small fib concerning his real reasons for visiting Leete Abbey. But as they had nothing to do with her, there was no reason to confess. It would only make things more...complicated.

"Hmm—I think I'd like to hear some of the other things you find attractive about me," joked Gryff, anxious to deflect the talk away from morality.

Eliza rolled her eyes. "I'm sure you get far too many flatteries as it is, sir. I shall keep my thoughts to myself."

"How cruel," he murmured, and tucked the last remnants of the meal into the hamper. "Are you tired of walking, or could we return to the manor house by way of the ruins?"

"As you pointed out, it's a lovely day for a stroll, and unlike your London ladies, I'm a country-bred female, so I am hearty as an ox," answered Eliza. "We can leave the basket here, and it can be fetched in the morning."

Her self-deprecating quip made him frown for a moment. "There is nothing ox-like about you, Lady Brentford—"

"I'm hardly a Pocket Venus," she countered.

"True—rather you are a magnificent Diana, Goddess of the Forest." He rose and offered his hand. "Lead the way through your realm."

Chapter Twelve

The Abbey ruins came into view, the crumbling walls still radiating a certain grandeur in the slanting sunlight. Gryff hurried up the last few turns of the path, while Eliza maintained a more leisurely pace in climbing to the crest of the knoll. She smiled, watching him run a hand over the weathered stone. Strangely enough, she didn't feel too awkward around him. Which was rather odd, considering...

Don't try to think, she reminded herself. *Just feel.* Feel the caress of the wind, the tickle of the long grasses against her skirt, the happy thrum of her heart.

"What a marvelous vista," he called, climbing to a vantage point atop the highest wall.

"Yes, isn't it?" Eliza shaded her eyes and watched the shadows from the scudding clouds play over the distant hills. "The river adds a certain shimmering quality to the light."

He nodded and scrambled up a different perch.

"Careful," she warned. "Some of the stones are loose, and the footing can be treacherous."

"Hmmm." Gryff took out his notebook and began writing.

He had been doing that throughout their meanderings, she mused. His friend was lucky to have someone who took such meticulous notes on what he saw.

Climbing up to the lower wall, Eliza watched him, interested to see the concentration in his face. Boyish laughter had given way to a more serious mien, and the expression added depth of character to his handsome face. She had begun to notice the subtle little nicks and scars—he was no indolent fribble and she liked him more for it. Just as she liked the way his hair fell over his cheek, and curled around his collar. He had a habit of tugging at his earlobe, which made the right corner of his mouth curl up.

An oddly endearing quirk.

She bit down hard on her lip to keep from smiling.

He pursed his lips in thought, and as her heart gave a little lurch, Eliza made herself look away. *Dangerous.* Even without the inner whisper of warning, she knew that things were taking a dangerous turn...

Just then, a sudden gust caught the page and snatched the book from his hand. It spiraled up, and Gryff cried out an oath as it plummeted toward a swampy section of the old cistern.

Eliza grabbed for it, and just managed to catch a corner of the cover. But a loose stone tipped, throwing her off-balance. Arms flailing, she fought to maintain a hold on the precious notebook.

The wall tilted, the sky spun in whirligig circles, and in the next instant she hit the ground with an undignified thump that knocked the wind from her lungs.

"Don't move!" Gryff's voice sounded very far away, but as she opened her eyes, Eliza saw he was already scrambling down from his perch.

Oh, wonderful. If ever the marquess needed a resounding reminder that she was not a graceful goddess from glittering ballrooms of Mayfair, this was it. In spades.

She lifted her head, woozily aware of the bits of straw and mud caked on her cheek, and tried to sit up.

"Don't move!" cried Gryff again, looking worried.

She tried to brush him off, embarrassed at making a spectacle of herself. It was as if some wild woodland sprite had slipped into her skin and taken control of both body and spirit for the day. The real Eliza, Lady Brentford, hung in the shadows, happy to go about her life unnoticed. She did not seek to wrest the crown from the reigning Queen of Sin.

"Stop squirming." Gryff held her shoulders down, ignoring her querulous protests. "You took a hard fall. Lie still and let me check on whether you've broken any bones." His fingers probed gently along her arms. "Do you feel any pain?"

"No, luckily I landed on my head," answered Eliza wryly. "It only hurts when I try to think. And since I haven't been attempting that today, I'm quite comfortable."

Gryff's head was bent, so all she could see was the tangle of his dark hair dancing in the breeze. "Hush." His voice was gentle, and she found herself choking back further sarcasm. He shifted, and, moving his hands down to her lower legs, hitched up her skirts just enough to feel around her ankles.

"Ouch."

"I feared so," he muttered. "I saw your leg twist as you fell."

"It's only a twinge," she said quickly, feeling like a

clumsy ox. "It will pass in a moment." Clenching her hands, she suddenly remembered the little book. "Here are your notes. I trust they didn't suffer any injury."

"Your safety is far more valuable than my scrawls."

"I have been curious. What have you been writing—"

He hastily snatched it out of her hand. "Nothing nearly as important as getting your ankle properly treated."

"I can easily shake it off."

"No, there's already a bit of swelling. But if I remove your boot, it will only get worse." Gryff unknotted his cravat and started to wrap the length of linen around the sore spot. "I'll bind it tightly for now. It may be uncomfortable, but it will help later on. Once you are home, you must lie down and keep it elevated with a pillow. No walking for at least a day." After snugging a firm knot in place, he sat back on his haunches. "Let me help you to a more comfortable spot while I go fetch my horse."

"No!" Eliza caught hold of his sleeve. "Please, it's not necessary to make a spectacle of my folly."

His brows drew together.

"I would rather walk back to the manor." In truth, it hurt like the devil, but she was determined to salvage some of her pride. "Help me up."

The marquess hesitated, but after studying her face for a long moment he heaved a sigh and did as she asked.

"It's quite manageable," she said through clenched teeth. "Just give me your arm, and I'll be fine."

"You know, sometimes discretion is the better part of valor, Lady Brentford. You have nothing to prove to me."

"Valor." A mirthless half-laugh slipped out. "Any attempt to paint myself in a heroic light would be rather lame, don't you think?"

He stopped abruptly and angled to face her, his hands seizing her shoulders. "Let's not tiptoe around what happened between us this afternoon," he said softly. "I promised to behave, so if anyone deserves censure, it is I. But that's not to say I'm sorry about what happened. I'm not."

Sunlight gilded the rueful curl of his smile. "There seems to be a powerful physical attraction between us," he went on. "We are two rational adults—"

"That could be considered questionable," interrupted Eliza.

A glint of humor warmed his gaze. "I concede that emotion did overpower reason for a short interlude. However, my point is, there's nothing shameful about having a passionate nature."

She longed to believe him. And yet...

"That may be true for a rake, Lord Haddan. But for a lady, it's rather more complicated." She watched a pair of mourning doves flutter through the rustling leaves, their pale wings a blur of light against dark. "And confusing."

"If I have embarrassed you, I am truly sorry."

"Fine, fine. Now, let's...let's just forget it," she gabbled, wanting nothing more than to limp home as quickly as possible and nurse her wounds. "Could we please keep moving?"

"Of course." His expression was unreadable as he tucked her hand in the crook of his arm. "Have a care, it gets a bit steeper here."

Eliza picked her way down the winding path, holding back a hiss at every step. Oh, the pain served her right, she told herself. It was a paltry penance for her sins.

Thank God for small mercies. At least she hadn't been struck down by a thunderbolt.

A shallow stream was the last obstacle before they reached the sloping lawns leading up to the main house. Eliza gritted her teeth in preparation for picking a path across the slippery rocks.

Slowly, slowly, and mayhap by some miracle she could avoid another embarrassing tumble from grace.

She lifted her skirts, and then suddenly was floating in air as Gryff swept her up into his arms.

"But, sir, I can make it across on my own!"

"Hush," he chided. "Don't you ever allow someone to help carry you over rough spots?"

How to answer? Other than Gussie, there was no "someone" in her life to make such a gallant offer.

Ignoring the stepping stones, Gryff splashed right through the shallow water.

"Your expensive boots are getting ruined," she pointed out.

"I shall give them a suitable funeral," he replied. "With full military honors." *Bang, bang, bang*—loud stomps punctuated his words, kicking up silvery plumes of spray. "Including a twenty-four gun salute."

She smiled in spite of herself. "You have a very odd sense of humor, Lord Haddan. Most men take themselves far more seriously than you do."

"Another of my faults," he murmured.

"Laughter is never a fault," replied Eliza. "Unless," she amended, "it comes at someone else's expense." They had reached dry land. "You may put me down now."

He kept walking.

Though the soft wool of his jacket was proving a seductive pillow, she felt compelled to protest. "Lord Haddan, I'm heavy as a horse."

"Especially as you consumed the lion's share of the custard tart," he teased.

"That was very bad of me." The scent of the sun-warmed grass and the rhythm of his long, loping stride suddenly had her feeling very sleepy. "Oh, but it was the most delicious thing I ever ate."

His laugh tickled against her hair. "I'll bring you another the next time I visit."

"There mustn't be a next time." Eliza's half-hearted whisper was lost in the buzz of bees circling through a patch of wild figwort. She regarded the dark purple blooms through half-closed eyes, watching the tiny flashes of yellow weave in and out of the long, slender stalks. "That's what you are telling me—there mustn't be a next time."

"Actually figwort means 'Take a chance on future happiness,'" said Gryff.

Her insides clenched. *Yes, and to do that, sir, our paths must diverge. Sooner rather than later.*

"However you phrase it, the message is much the same for me." Eliza shifted in his arms. "I really must insist that you put me down, Lord Haddan. We are close to the manor house, and I'd really prefer not to be spotted in such a compromising position."

This time, the marquess bowed to her wishes without argument.

"Thank you." Eliza shook out her skirts, aware that the air all around her suddenly felt several degrees colder now that the heat of his body was gone. "Let us take the right fork up ahead. It's the shortest route to the front courtyard."

He offered his arm, careful to keep his distance.

She limped along in awkward silence, her downcast gaze fixed on their feet. Mud marred the once-shiny surface of his boots, and gorse thorns had left deep scratches in the leather.

Gorse. Surely it must have a meaning. A prickly one, no doubt, despite its cheerful yellow blooms.

"How do you know so much about the language of flowers?" she asked, wanting to fill their final moments together with more than the sound of crunching gravel.

"I have an interesting little book from the last century in my library," he replied.

"Not the one by Mary Wortley Montague?" she exclaimed.

"As a matter of fact, yes."

"Oh, I have heard about it from members of my Horticulture Society."

"You don't have a copy?"

Eliza shook her head. "They are rather rare." And rather expensive. But that did not begin to explain why a Tulip of the *ton* would bother reading the volume. She was about to ask when a hail from the housekeeper interrupted the exchange.

"Ah, there you are, Lady Brentford! I was wondering where you had wandered off to..." Mrs. Hillhouse stopped short as she rounded the corner of the rose bower, her eyes widening slightly at the sight of the marquess.

"I was at the Abbey ruins and foolishly lost my footing on the stones. Lord Haddan kindly offered his assistance. He likes flowers, you see." Embarrassment had her gabbling like a goose. "And trees," she added lamely.

"Leete kindly gave me permission to visit the grounds and make some notes on the landscape design," explained

Gryff smoothly. "Luckily I was close by and was able to come to Lady Brentford's aid."

Mrs. Hillhouse maintained a poker face, save for a tiny twitch of her right brow.

It was, knew Eliza from long experience, the housekeeper's I-smell-a-rat look.

"Lucky, indeed," commented Mrs. Hillhouse after another appraising look at the disheveled state of their clothing. "I'll fix a soak of arnica leaves for that ankle." Setting a hand on her hip, she asked, "Would you like a cloth to wipe the smear of custard from your breeches, milord?"

"Thank you but no, I might feel a trifle peckish during my ride back to the inn."

The housekeeper's gimlet gaze softened slightly.

"Was there a reason you were looking for me?" asked Eliza quickly, before any further culinary questions could be asked. The mention of custard had her face burning.

"Aye. Two letters just arrived for you. Seeing as one is from your brother, I thought you would want to see it right away." Both of them knew that Harry never wrote unless he was in dire straits.

Eliza reluctantly accepted the missives. "Oh, Lord, what scrape has he gotten himself in now?" she muttered, frowning at her sibling's near-illegible scrawl. The sight of Mr. Watkins's neat handwriting stirred slightly more positive sentiments.

"Lady Brentford, I fear I have trespassed on your hospitality long enough," said Gryff. "I shall take my leave and allow you to attend to your family concerns."

Whatever the news from London, it could wait a few moments longer. Shoving the unopened letters into her pocket, she gave a brusque nod. "Yes, I suppose that it would be best. Mrs. Hillhouse, kindly ask Jem—"

"Jem has not yet returned from working in the fields," replied the housekeeper.

"I shall see to my horse," said Gryff quietly.

"And I shall see to steeping the herbs for your ankle," said Mrs. Hillhouse. "Unless you need me to help you up the stairs to your room."

"No, no, I can manage," mumbled Eliza. It might have been wiser to let the marquess go without a last private word. Trite formalities seemed absurd—and it wasn't as if she could blurt out, "Oh, thanks for the jolly lovely sexual tryst in the folly by the lake."

Folly.

Eliza quickly thrust the thought aside.

"Did you see all you came for?" she began—and then quickly wished she could seize the words and cram them back down her throat. *So much for trying to sound as cool and sophisticated as a London belle.*

"Yes, thank you," replied Gryff, kindly ignoring the obvious innuendo of her question. "I would, of course, enjoy seeing the whole estate, but I must return to London first thing in the morning. I have other obligations that I must attend to."

Her fingers brushed against the stiff folds of paper in her pocket. She, too, had pressing matters to sort out. This mad, mad interlude couldn't be allowed to interfere with her plans.

Step by step. It had been a struggle to overcome all the obstacles in her way. But she had persevered, sacrificed, endured.

"Yes, of course you do," answered Eliza, deciding to

make no mention of the fact that Harry's troubles and her own business might also require her to leave for Town at first light. God forbid that he think she was following him. He would tire of it, and quickly. A fleeting dalliance with a country widow was one thing. The city was another world entirely. Silky smiles and satin laughter. All was so seamlessly smooth and polished within the highest circles of the *ton*. Gilded wheels turning within wheels.

Eliza looked away. She didn't want to think of that. Let this enchanted afternoon remain etched on her memory as...perfect. It was, after all, no more real than a fairy tale.

Concern cut through her reveries. "Will you be well?" asked Gryff.

She forced a cheerful smile. "But of course. I'm a rough-cut country miss, Lord Haddan. I've suffered plenty of bumps and bruises. By tomorrow they will be gone. Forgotten."

"Your letters—"

"Harry is likely up to his usual nonsense," she assured him. "It's nothing that I can't deal with."

A frown creased his brow. "You shouldn't have to deal with it."

"But I do," she said practically. For only a little while longer.

Gryff plucked at his cuff and smoothed a wrinkle from his sleeve. "Goodbye then."

"Yes, goodbye." Eliza essayed a smile as she jiggled her injured ankle. "You had best be on your way before I destroy any other articles of your clothing."

He eyed the dust-covered cravat and chuckled. "I shall inform Prescott that it marched to its death with great fortitude."

Oh, I would miss his quirky humor. She stilled the fluttering in her chest with a deep breath. "Thank you for the picnic."

"It was my pleasure."

Their eyes met for a moment as she sought to memorize the smoky hue of gold-flecked hazel. *Haddan's Green.* To be placed in her paintbox next to the standard hue named Hooker's Greens.

"I had a lovely time, Lord Haddan," she went on. "I wish your friend the best of luck in altering his landscape. I hope you came away from the afternoon with some good ideas."

He lifted her hand to his lips. "Nature is infinitely inspiring."

"Quite so."

He hesitated a fraction and then touched his brow in salute before turning for the stable.

Eliza hobbled toward the back terrace, but some irresistible impulse made her linger behind the privet hedge.

A short while later, hooves clattered over the cobbles and she watched him ride off, waiting until the bend swallowed him from view before turning away.

A welling, hot and bitter as bile, rose in her throat as she trudged up the stone stairs.

"Don't be a goose." She swiped a sleeve across her cheeks. "At least I shall never have to say 'what if?' I have a memory, not a regret."

And she would hold that memory dear, and keep it close to warm countless windswept nights on the lonely moors.

Chapter Thirteen

Gryff hurried across the busy street, carefully following the path cleared by the sweep. He had changed his clothes and his water-stained boots on arriving back in London earlier in the day—an act accompanied by several long looks of silent reproach from his valet—but had been too on edge to tarry for more than a short stop at his townhouse.

Throughout the journey back from the country, he had reminded himself that fleeting dalliances were no longer important in his life. More serious pursuits now took precedence over frivolous pleasure. *Think of your work, not a beguilingly freespirited widow.*

He quickened his steps, trying to outpace the memory of a graceful ankle, a lilting laugh, a lush mouth.

"Bloody hell," he muttered. "It's time for an old dog to learn new tricks." Paramount of which was thinking with his brain, not his pizzle.

And so, to keep his mind focused on the task at hand, he had decided to pay a visit to Watkins & Harold, rather than send a messenger to inquire whether any reply had come from the elusive Linden.

Yes or no.

It was a bit bemusing how nervous he felt. "No" was not a word that normally answered a request from the Marquess of Haddan. An august title and a glittering fortune were powerful incentives to voice an affirmative. Grease to keep the wheels of life turning with nary a squeak, he thought ruefully, dodging a lumbering dray cart.

But then, Linden was not aware that the commission was coming from a lofty peer. The artist would decide based on the merits of the essays alone.

Which was both frightening and exhilarating.

Turning down a sidestreet, Gryff drew a quick, calming breath before he entered the publisher's modest brick building.

"Linden has said yes," said Watkins without preamble as the door to his private office fell shut.

Gryff sat down rather heavily in the chair facing the desk. "Excellent." He clapped his hands together, trying to look as if he hadn't been worried sick. "Excellent."

"That it is. However, we've a tight schedule to stick with," pointed out the publisher. "As I've told you, I'd like to have the volume printed in time for the botanical symposium that is to take place next spring in Oxford."

Gryff swallowed hard. The project was suddenly more than just an idea floating around in his head, more than just scribbles on a scrap of paper. It was taking shape as something real. Ink and paper, bound in calfskin with a gold-stamped title and the author's name.

A new step. A new dream. Was he truly ready to turn over a new leaf?

"Deadlines, milord—we will have deadlines," continued Watkins. "I know this is all new to you, but I do run a business."

"And you are asking whether I can be professional?" said Gryff.

Watkins looked a little uncomfortable but nodded. "In a nutshell, yes."

"You may count on it," he replied. "And what of Linden?"

"Having worked with the artist before, I am confident that we will have no reason to rue our choice."

"Well then, the work should go smoothly as silk."

The publisher allowed a small smile to bloom on his craggy face. "I am not sure I would phrase it quite that way, milord. Creativity does not always twirl along with the same precise steps as an elegant Mayfair waltz. Artists—and authors—tend to dance to their own music. I've learned to expect a stumble or slip along the way. What's important is to end on the same beat, if you take my meaning."

"I'm an excellent dancer," quipped Gryff.

"I don't doubt it, Lord Haddan. But as an author, you must be prepared to improvise."

Improvise. He caught himself thinking of custard tarts and a sun-dappled smile.

"Now, since you are here, let us review the essays you have submitted so far, milord..."

Don't be daft. Her eyes must be playing tricks on her. Slipping into the shadows of a recessed doorway, Eliza watched a tall, elegantly attired figure stride out of the print shop and turn in the direction of Piccadilly Street.

Stop seeing ghosts, she chided to herself. Or in this case, Gryffs.

Marquess Madness seemed to have seized her brain. Even in the half-light of dawn, she had seen his shape in the flitting shadows of the trees and hedgerows along the route to London. She had thought it was merely the dust on the ancient carriage windowglass that had distorted her vision...

But no, this approaching apparition was not a figment of her imagination. The profile beneath the high crown beaver hat was definitely fashioned from flesh and blood. The aquiline nose, the chiseled lips, the glint of green...

Cringing deeper into the corner of her refuge, Eliza prayed that the marquess would pass by without a side-long glance.

To her relief, Gryff did not seem to notice that he had company on the quiet sidestreet. Head bent, brow furrowed, he appeared to be lost in thought as he hurried past her.

Eliza waited until she could no longer hear the click of his bootheels on the pavement before venturing out of her hiding place. How strange, she thought, casting a searching look over her shoulder before continuing on her way. The marquess had mentioned having pressing engagements. So why was he visiting an out-of-the-way publisher? Watkins & Harold did not offer popular novels or sporting books.

Perhaps he was purchasing one of the shop's pretty little gold-stamped books of poetry for a lady friend, to make up for his absence from the ballroom. And boudoir.

She squashed the stirring of jealousy. The thought of rumpled sheets and naked limbs provoked other naughty ideas. Mayhap he was bringing a set of erotic etchings to be bound in soft, smooth calfskin. A prickling of goose-flesh stole up her arms. No, she couldn't really see the straitlaced Mr. Watkins agreeing to handle such a commission. He wouldn't agree to be part of anything immoral.

The bells over the front door jingled, reminding her that she wasn't here to pine over Lord Haddan. There was work to be done.

"Good morning, madam," greeted the clerk. "Is Mr. Watkins expecting you?"

"Not exactly." Eliza assumed he had received her agreement to take on the project. "But I would be grateful if he could spare a moment to see me."

The publisher didn't keep her waiting long. "Lady Brentford! Please come in," he exclaimed, gesturing for her to enter his private office. "Er, what a surprise."

"Not an unpleasant one, I hope," she replied.

"Not at all, not at all." And yet, despite the coolness of his office, a beading of moisture had formed along his hairline. "Please have a seat."

As he hastily rearranged his papers. Eliza thought she caught a glimpse of one of her sketches.

"Thank you," she murmured. "A family matter has required an unexpected trip to Town. But if this is an inconvenient moment for you, I can return at another time."

"Not at all," he repeated, but his smile looked a little strained. "By coincidence, I was, er, just putting together a packet of the final essays for illustration to send to you."

"Perfect timing," she remarked.

He dabbed a handkerchief to his brow. "Indeed."

Eliza refrained from comment on his bizarre behavior, deciding that any mention might only exacerbate his discomfort. The poor man must be suffering from a mild fever, or perhaps a touch of gout, which would explain the odd little bouncing of his foot against the rug.

"Speaking of timing, that is the reason I am here," she explained. "I am anxious to complete this commission as quickly as possible."

The publisher's fidgeting stilled somewhat. "I am happy to hear it. I have set a very tight production schedule in order to have the finished book ready for an important botanical symposium." His craggy face suddenly spasmed in alarm. "You aren't hinting that there may be a problem in completing the paintings, are you?"

"No," she answered quickly, careful to sound confident. "I have no intention of letting you down."

He blew out his breath. "That is a relief. The author would be greatly disappointed. And you know how temperamental artists can be—yourself aside, of course." Another dab to his brow. "It is never easy to shepherd a project of this sort through the various stages."

"And I don't suppose we make it any easier by insisting on keeping our identities a secret for now."

Watkins reached for his water glass. "That," he said tightly, "is putting it mildly."

"I admit, I'm rather tempted to forego the secrecy and ask for a meeting. From what I've read so far, it appears the person who penned the essays has a delightful sense of humor." Eliza paused. "My guess is that the author is a female."

A loud croak sounded as Watkins nearly choked in mid-swallow. His face, already a flushed pink to begin with, turned an alarming shade of red. "A f-female?" he sputtered. "W-why would you think that?"

"There is a whimsical note to the writing. In general,

men are not whimsical, though there are, of course, exceptions to the rule." That she could think of one right away was an irrelevant detail that need not be mentioned.

"In general, I would agree with you," said Watkins carefully.

"But by your reaction, I'm assuming that in this case I am wrong," she probed.

Sweat now sheened the publisher's cheeks. "I did not say that," he protested.

"Forgive me. I did not mean to make you uncomfortable," apologized Eliza. "I'm curious, that's all."

"As is the author," conceded Watkins with a harried grimace. "I have promised both of you that I would guard your real identities. But it is proving to be a deucedly difficult pledge to keep."

"I'm sorry. I shall cease pestering you." She shifted her reticule in her lap. "Indeed, I don't want to take up any more of your valuable time. But since I am here, might I take those finished essays with me? That way, I could begin work on the art."

Papers moved in a whispery shuffle over the ink-stained blotter. "Unfortunately, I've not yet had a chance to have the lads make copies for you. But they should be done by the end of the day. If, as usual, you are staying with Mr. and Mrs. Frampton, I can have them sent around to Hart Street as soon as they are ready."

"Thank you. I—I am not sure how long I shall be in Town, so it would be best if they could arrive today."

Eliza rose. She had put off thinking about Harry's unsettling summons for as long as possible, but unfortunately it could no longer be avoided. A request for a meeting was unusual in itself. That he had chosen

Gunter's of all places, a café famous for its iced confections, was even odder. Considering his other haunts, such a respectable venue should be welcome. Instead it sent shivers down her spine.

Harry trying to turn her up sweet?

She couldn't help feeling a foreboding.

"I shall escort you out, Lady Brentford, and drop off these papers at the copy desk," said Mr. Watkins. "Just give me a moment."

As he gathered the sheets and sorted them into order, Eliza caught a fleeting glimpse of a boldly slanting script.

No—the idea was absurd.

Blinking, she pressed the heel of her hand to her brow. *Stop seeing Haddan in every flutter, every line, every shadow.* The ghost of Gryffin must not be allowed to haunt her head.

"There," he announced, paging through the stack one last time. "All is in order."

When Eliza looked again, she saw nothing that resembled the handwriting in the marquess's notebook. She wasn't sure whether to feel disappointed or relieved.

"By the by," she said as she followed him to the door, "was that Lord Haddan I saw coming out of here earlier?"

"Haddan?" The publisher's voice was muffled by the papers in front of his face. "Perhaps he was picking up a book from one of the clerks. Gentlemen sometimes order a special binding from us."

There was certainly nothing havey-cavey about that. Eliza felt herself relax. Her nerves were on edge, that was all. Yes, the marquess was knowledgeable about landscape design, but he had offered a perfectly plausible explanation. He was a careful steward of his lands, and it was foolish to read anything deeper into his interest.

"Thank you again for your time, Mr. Watkins," she said. "In the future, I shall try not to barge in on you unannounced."

"I look forward to seeing your first paintings, Lady Brentford." The publisher patted absently at his hair, which was sticking up in spiky little silver tufts. "I have every expectation that when all is said and done, the results of this collaboration will have been well worth the effort."

"Bloody hell, Cameron, since when have you become the bibliophile?" Gryff paused in the doorway of his library, a little growl of irritation edging the greeting as he saw the branch of candles perched perilously close to a rare volume of seventeenth-century etchings. "And bloody hell, do move those cursed flames away from the paper. Don't you remember signing a solemn pledge at Oxford not to burn the books?"

"You forget that I did not attend your fancy schools. And from what I have heard, you and Connor paid no heed to the university rules and regulations, so stop your barking," drawled Cameron. He did, however, shift the silver candelabra to the corner of the worktable.

"Then what in Hades has sparked such an interest in my collection of art books? Or dare I ask?"

"I've always been interested in art," came the cryptic reply.

Abandoning any further interrogation as pointless, Gryff continued on to his desk. "Please note that I use a glass-globed lamp to illuminate..." His words trailed off in a hiss of air. "Damnation, you really must stop pawing through my personal correspondence, Cam."

"I didn't think you had anything to hide."

"That's not the point," he snapped. Scowling, he carefully lifted a letter off the corner of the watercolor sketch by Linden. "I have valuable art sitting here, which apparently escaped your notice."

"On the contrary, I had a good look at it." A pause. "I daresay the artist has a high regard for its value as well."

"What is *that* supposed to mean?"

"I'll get to that in a moment," answered Cameron. "What do you know about this Linden?"

For a moment, Gryff was tempted to tell his friend to go to the devil. He was touchy enough about this part of his life without having Cameron's caustic comments making him even more uncomfortable.

"There's a reason I'm asking." His friend sounded more serious than usual. "But I'd rather get a few facts straight before I explain."

The candle flames quivered, and Gryff watched a tiny drip of molten wax slide down one of the tapers. The faint scent of honey mingled with the earthier smells of parchment and leather.

"I know nothing about Linden," he admitted. "Save for the fact that the person in question is a damn fine artist."

"A rare talent, from what little I've seen." Cameron rose and came over to have another look. "Have you any other examples of Linden's work?"

"No, not yet. But Watkins does."

"I should like to have a closer look at them."

"I could arrange that, I suppose." Gryff smoothed

down the curling corner of the thick laid paper. "Assuming I agree with your reasons for asking."

"I could, you know, simply arrange to get at them on my own."

"What makes you think that Watkins will let you see them?"

"What makes you think I would ask him?" countered Cameron.

"You..." *Smack*. "Are a Bloody..." *Smack*. "Pain in the Arse." *Smack*.

The whack of his palms to the polished pearwood helped release some of his pent-up frustration. The pointed innuendos from his friend had only exacerbated his own unsettled emotions. "I am in no mood for playing your taunting little guessing games."

"So I see." Cameron had placed a hand on Gryff's shoulder, and now exerted a light pressure to push him back down in his seat. "I told you I would explain."

"Then please do so. Before you find yourself forced to extract your teeth from your gullet."

Seating himself on the tufted arm of the facing leather chair, Cameron made a quick inspection of his well-buffed nails. "Who would lose his ivories is a matter of debate. But we'll leave that discussion for another day."

"Yes." Gryff gazed down at the confident brushstrokes, the delicate detailing, the subtle washes of color. "Let's stick to the subject of art."

The case clock ticked off several long moments before his friend began.

"I can see that you've acquired an eye for the nuances of artistic style. I suspect you've spent many hours studying landscape and botanical works from both the past and the present."

"You're correct," replied Gryff tersely. "I consider myself fairly knowledgeable in the field of prints and watercolors. Perhaps not an expert, but close enough."

"I, too, consider myself well educated in that particular subject. So when I saw an original watercolor painting by Maria Sibylla Merian being offered for sale—at a very high price—I was naturally interested in having a close look at the master's technique."

Despite the blazing fire at his back, Gryff felt a chill steal down his spine. Very few of the Swiss artist's original paintings had survived from the seventeenth century, and those that had were collector's items. He knew, for he had recently inquired about obtaining one himself, only to be told by the dealer that none were available at the moment.

"I really can't see where this is going, Cam," he muttered, hoping his premonition was wrong.

"Patience, Gryff. I'm getting there." His friend shifted to a more comfortable position on the chair. "As you know, Merian is now recognized as one of the first true masters of botanical illustration."

"Along with her rendering of insects," mused Gryff. "Her ability to render lifelike detail is quite astounding."

"Indeed. Merian's talents are even more extraordinary considering that she was a woman. Females in the 1600s were not exactly encouraged to develop their God-given gifts."

"Nor are they today," growled Gryff.

"A good point, but one that is irrelevant to the discussion."

"What *is* your point?"

"That the painting I saw for sale was a forgery." Cameron held up a hand to cut off Gryff's sarcastic retort. "I know, I know, items for sale in the flash houses do not come with the most reliable of provenances. There are often forgeries offered. However, what caught my eye was that the painting was among a group of items that also contained a rare book from Lord Leete's library. And before you demand how I know that, it's because of the bookplate."

Gryff sat up straighter.

"Now, it's not uncommon for a gentleman to sell off such items under the table, so to speak, especially if the contents of the library are under the entail. But the fact that it's being offered with a forgery piqued my attention." He rose and went to the desk. "As you know, I am always curious about what illegal activities are going on here in Town. So I borrowed the forgery—"

"What you really mean to say is you stole it," snapped Gryff.

Cameron made a pained face. "Actually I didn't have to. The owner of the flash house is a friend. He trusted me to return it." Seeing Gryff's expression darken, he hurried on. "To make a long story short, I happened to spot Linden's sketch on your desk and was struck by the similarities in style to the forgery. My suspicion is that both works were done by the same artist."

"You think Linden is a criminal?" For some reason, Gryff felt as if he had been punched in the gut. The art had struck a chord inside him, and he had come to think of the unknown artist as a friend. "I don't believe it. You're not an expert in art."

"I have more experience that you might think," countered his friend. "However, you are correct. I do not wish to make a final pronouncement based on a single sketch. That's why I'd like to see several more examples."

When Gryff didn't answer, Cameron added, "It's not that I give a damn whether someone gets fleeced in making a purchase of the painting. When one deals at the flash houses, it's buyer beware." He touched a finger to the Linden sketch. "What I do care about is that your first book not be tainted by any scandal, Gryff."

It took a moment for the clench of conflicting emotion to loosen in his throat. "I am grateful for that, Cam. But ye gods, this comes as a damnable shock. I greatly admire Linden's style, and think it a perfect complement to my writing." He let out a mirthless laugh. "I know it sounds ridiculous, yet I can't help feeling betrayed."

"That's why I want to be very sure of things," said Cameron. "If you can get the rest of Linden's sketches from Watkins, I'll have a much better idea of whether I'm right. Then we can decide what to do."

"I'll go back to the offices now."

Cameron held up a hand in warning. "I'd advise you to say nothing about the real reason you want them. Let's keep this quiet until we are sure of what we are dealing with."

Something in his friend's tone set off another alarm bell in his head. "What else aren't you telling me?"

A vague wave dismissed the question. "Nothing other than a hunch. Let's just say, if I were you, I'd avoid having anything to do with Leete or anyone associated with him."

"Leete isn't clever enough to be a criminal," muttered Gryff. As for his sister...

Impossible.

"I agree," answered Cameron. "But several of his gentlemen cronies are thoroughly dirty dishes."

Gryff pushed up out of his chair. "Then let's get to the bottom of this, before it soils the whole damn project. According to Watkins, timing is of the essence." Slanting a sidelong look at the sketch on his desk, he expelled a sharp sigh, finding himself conflicted on how he should feel. "If you are right, what the devil are we going to do about it?"

"I have a few ideas," said Cameron. "But first things first. I'm anxious to get my hands on the sketches as quickly as possible, for I have to return the forgery to my friend before I leave Town. Why don't we meet at a spot close to the publisher, and you can pass me the portfolio."

Gryff gave a grudging nod. "Grosvenor Square is just a short stroll away from Watkins & Harold..."

Chapter Fourteen

*E*liza plucked nervously at the hem of her glove.

"Shall I fetch you a glass of lemonade, milady?" asked her childhood friend's abigail, who had accompanied her to the fashionable tea shop.

"Thank you, but no," she replied tersely, her stomach too unsettled for food or drink. "My brother should be arriving shortly." Assuming he wasn't too jugbitten to remember the appointment. "I shall wait."

She didn't have long to fret, for with uncharacteristic promptness, Harry strolled into Gunter's at the appointed hour.

"Ah, 'Liza," he called with forced joviality. "You are looking exceeding well this afternoon. Is that a new bonnet?"

Harry not only on time but also offering compliments on her appearance? Her insides clenched...and then tightened into a hard knot when she saw that he wasn't alone.

Her brother and Lord Brighton seated themselves at the table.

"Please buy yourself a sorbet, Symonds. I shall find

you when I am finished here." Eliza passed the maid several coins and waited until the girl had moved off before offering a clipped greeting to her brother. "What *Important News* have you to tell me?" she asked, accentuating the heavily underlined words of his letter.

Harry bared his teeth in a weak semblance of a smile. "Oh, come, let us get you some of shop's special ices first. The sweets here are very popular with the ladies."

"I'm not hungry for sweets, Harry." Her gaze flicked to Brighton, who in contrast to her brother looked completely relaxed in his chair as he brushed a speck of dust from the hat in his lap. "I would rather you explain the reason for your urgent summons to Town."

"What-ho, can't a man miss his lovely sister?"

She stared unblinking, and after a moment he dropped his eyes. "Things is, 'Liza, I've got some excellent news."

Her sense of foreboding grew more pronounced.

"Which is?" she asked softly.

"Can't come to Gunter's without having their famous ices and some pastries," Harry said abruptly. "Let me go choose a few for you, along with a dish of burnt filbert sorbet. I know how fond you are of nuts."

He rose and walked—or rather, fled—toward the ornate glass display case in the front of the café.

"I assume you have some idea of what Harry's momentous news is, sir," said Eliza to Brighton.

His mouth curled up at the suggestion. "I do, Lady Brentford. But let us not rush our enjoyment of the afternoon."

"It has been a long time since I've associated the words 'enjoyment' and 'Harry' with each other," she said.

Unlike her brother, Brighton did not flinch from eye contact. "Perhaps that is about to change."

A flutter of unease quickened her breath. "I don't see how."

Harry returned with a plate of lemon tarts and a large fluted glass of nut-studded sorbet.

"Seeing as it's a lovely afternoon, why don't we take a stroll around the square while you consume your treat," said Brighton smoothly as he picked up two spoons and gestured at the large front window. "As you see, it's quite popular to do so."

Eliza rose without a word. Much as she resented being maneuvered into accepting the proposal, to protest would only stir an embarrassing scene. Stepping outside, she hurried across the wide street and entered the center garden before turning to confront Harry and his friend. To her dismay, only Brighton had followed.

"Allow me." He offered his arm and started to move, giving Eliza no choice but to place her hand on his sleeve. "You really should try this confection before it melts, Lady Brentford."

She accepted the sweet. "I'm sure it's delicious. However, at the moment I have no stomach for pleasantries. Harry has commanded my presence here in London, at no small inconvenience and expense to his household, I might add. And now he skulks behind a platter of lemon tarts while sending you to walk me around and ply me with sweets." The glass was cold against her gloved palm, and as she looked down at the creamy confection, she couldn't help thinking of warm custard.

Swallowing hard, Eliza took a quick breath to compose her emotions and went on. "I assume you are going to tell me why."

"You have a tart tongue, Lady Brentford." Brighton's

tone was faintly mocking. "You might want to consider exercising more discretion in voicing your opinions. It would make you more attractive."

"You wish for me to sprinkle sugar on my sentiments so that they can feed a gentleman's hubris?" Eliza tried to keep a grip on her fraying temper. "Thank you, but as I couldn't care less about winning the regard of the opposite sex, I have the luxury of saying what I think."

He gave a curt laugh. "Plain speaking, indeed." He cocked a brow. "So, you don't wish to remarry?"

"No," she said flatly. "I most certainly do not."

Still smiling, Brighton turned down one of the graveled walkways and continued on at the same leisurely pace. Rather than take offense at her deliberate rudeness, he drew her a touch closer.

She stiffened, ruing the fact that anyone watching from afar might assume there was an intimacy between them.

"What a pity you feel that way, seeing as I was counting on you to consent to becoming my bride."

Eliza stumbled, and would have dropped the sorbet, had he not caught her and steadied her hand.

"Careful." He leaned down and licked a small splash from her wrist.

From him, the gesture was faintly repulsive. She tried to pull away but his hold was surprisingly strong. "I suggest you don't make a scene," he warned. "It would not reflect well on any of us."

She went very still. "Is this some sort of jest, Lord Brighton? A wager put in the betting book at White's that I am supposed to go along with?"

"I assure you, I am quite serious."

"But *why*?" Eliza felt her throat constrict. "No, wait,

you need not answer that. The reason doesn't matter, for whatever it is, my answer is no."

Brighton's eyes were opaque, emotionless. "Some men might take offense at that."

"But this is absurd," protested Eliza. "We hardly know each other, and...and I cannot see that we have anything in common. There is no earthly reason for a match between us. So, please, whatever your game, let us put an end to it. I have no intention of agreeing to your proposal." She drew in a gulp of air. "And that is final."

"Have you finished expressing your sentiments?" he asked softly.

She nodded, not trusting herself to say more.

"Excellent." Brighton drew her beneath the shade of a linden tree. The long, leafy shadows accentuated the sharp angles of his face and lines of dissipation around his full-lipped mouth.

"Excellent," he repeated. "Now it's my turn to be frank, Lady Brentford. As you know, your brother has developed a number of profligate habits here in Town and has gotten himself into deep financial trouble. He owes a great deal of money, mostly to me." Brighton let his words sink in for a moment before continuing. "I am willing to forgive his gaming debts and loans. But only on the condition that you agree to become my wife."

Eliza's legs suddenly felt as if they were made of *blanche mange*. The fear crept up her limbs and to keep her hand from shaking she gripped the glass so tightly that she feared it might crack. "I—I don't understand. This makes no sense. Why would you want me, of all females? I'm not a stunning beauty, I'm not a wealthy heiress."

"No, but you are an exceedingly talented artist."

* * *

Spotting Cameron standing by the square's east gate, Gryff cut between two carriages and hurried across the cobbled way.

"Any trouble?" asked his friend, straightening from his slouch against the wrought iron curlicues.

"Perhaps I should become your partner in crime," he muttered as he followed Cameron into the gardens. "I seem to have a skill in duplicitous deceptions."

"You've a knack for seducing favors," agreed Cameron. "But as for the darker aspects..." He let his words trail off in a cryptic shrug. "How many examples did you manage to obtain?"

"A half dozen, which was all that Watkins had." He passed over the small portfolio of paintings. "Damnation, don't lose them."

"I shall be extremely careful." Keeping his gaze locked straight ahead, his friend circled around the central fountain and cut down one of the shaded side pathways. "Nothing would please me more than to discover I am wrong about my suspicions."

"But you don't think you are," said Gryff after several silent strides.

"No, I don't."

A pair of pugs growled and snapped at Gryff's boots as he kicked up a scattering of gravel. "Sorry," he apologized to the irate owner, who added a grumble of her own.

"Hmmph! You young gentlemen are always in *such* a confounded hurry." Her cane jabbed at the border bushes. "You ought to learn to stop and smell the roses."

If only the plantings included Christmas roses, which signified "relieve my anxiety."

Gryff inhaled sharply but waited until they were out of earshot before saying, "When will you have a chance to compare the artwork and come to a decision, Cam?"

"Hard to say. My contact is sometimes a bit difficult to track down. I'll be in touch as quickly as I can." His friend paused at a fork in the walkways. "In the meantime…" Cameron hesitated as his gaze followed the curve of the pruned bushes to the far end of the garden. "I'd avoid rubbing shoulders with Leete and his cronies, if I were you. You have naught to gain but a soiled coat by associating with the likes of Brighton."

Gryff followed his friend's eyes to a clump of trees shading the walkway, where half-hidden by the hanging branches, a couple were engaged in what looked to be an intimate discussion. As the man reached up to brush a curl from the lady's cheek, he let out a low hiss.

"I take it you recognize the baronet's fair companion?"

"Perhaps," said Gryff, but he did not elaborate.

Cameron stared thoughtfully at the shifting patterns of light and dark for a moment or two before looking away. "I'm heading east, so I'll part ways with you here."

Gryff nodded absently, his attention still on the swirl of shadows. Cameron's voice faded away, as did the clatter of the carriage wheels and the yapping of the little dogs. All he could hear was a strange sort of thrumming in his ears.

He balled a fist, fighting off the urge to go grab Brighton's hand and yank it away from Eliza's face.

Quelling the flare of temper, he turned on his heel and chose the perimeter path. He had been intending to return home to work on his writing, but suddenly a stop at his club for a taste of its famed French brandy seemed a far more attractive alternative.

Why the devil hadn't Lady Brentford mentioned that she was coming to Town?

The question had no sooner taken shape in his head when he dismissed it with a rueful grimace. He had no right to feel possessive. Their mad little moments of intimacy were just that—sweetly serendipitous lapses of sanity. Pursuing the acquaintance would only lead to trouble.

"Trouble," he muttered under his breath.

Frowning, two elderly matrons gave him a wide berth.

"Trouble." Gryff said it again, hoping the audible reminder would carry more force than his mental scold. Repressing the urge to dart another look at the trees, he kept on walking.

"A talented artist?" Eliza was totally bewildered by Brighton's words. "I can't imagine why that would matter to you. I'm under the impression that you prefer to pursue more mundane activities than the quiet contemplation of drawings or watercolors, sir."

"Correct, Lady Brentford. I like endeavors that make me money. Preferably a lot of money." He looked at her expectantly. "And you will help me turn a handsome profit for precious little investment."

"Are you drunk?" she demanded. "Or simply demented?"

"Neither," replied Brighton, the sneer thinning from his face. "Enough of your nattering, Lady Brentford. Let us get down to business."

She waited.

"Listen, and listen very carefully. Your brother owes me a fortune, and he's offered you as a means of paying it back. You're right, I don't find your gangly looks or shrewish temper attractive. But then…" His lips formed a curl of contempt. "I don't need a wife for pleasurable pursuits."

Eliza maintained a stoic silence, trying to pretend that he wasn't frightening her.

Brighton seemed a little disappointed that she didn't react. His voice hardened. "Do as you're told, and I'll leave you to rusticate in the country, once I beget a brat or two on you."

Her skin began to crawl at the thought.

"And just what is it you want me to do?" asked Eliza softly.

"A very simple thing for a lady of your prodigious skills." He was enjoying this taunting. Malice intensified the color of his eyes, adding a reddish glint to the pale brown hue. "All you have to do is copy some prosy old paintings of flowers and bugs."

"I won't." It took Eliza only an instant to grasp his meaning. "I won't be party to your plans."

"Oh, but I think you will."

"Forgery is crime. I've no intention of going to prison."

"Then I'd think twice about making an enemy of me, Lady Brentford. You see, your first endeavor is already in the marketplace."

"Impossible!" whispered Eliza. And then bit her gloved knuckle as she remembered a long-ago practice painting…

"That's right," gloated Brighton. "A lovely rendition of a Maria Sibylla Merian botanical painting, done so masterfully that even the experts have been fooled."

"But I did it as a *learning* exercise," she protested.

"Copying is an age-old practice in art. It's meant to teach an artist about technique and brushwork."

His laugh was sharp as a razor's edge. "Perhaps the magistrates will appreciate a lecture on art history. But I rather doubt it."

Dear God. For an instant, Eliza went numb with shock. She had always dismissed the baronet and his oily attempts at charm as simply an unpleasant wastrel. But apparently she had underestimated his capacity for cunning cleverness.

"As I said, think on it, Lady Brentford. Refuse me and your brother will end up on the sponging house and you—well, at best you will be reduced to abject poverty, your family name in deep disgrace. But it's far more likely you will be residing in Newgate Prison."

"Accept you and I shall be enslaved in a marriage where I am forced into criminal activity, with no control over my person or my purse."

A wicked grin. "Pick your poison."

He had her trapped between a rock and a stone, and no matter which way she turned, it seemed that the rough-cut slabs were squeezing in with unyielding force.

No, I won't let myself be crushed, vowed Eliza, though in meeting Brighton's gaze, it was hard not to let her resolve waver.

Swallowing a surge of panic, she made her mind focus. "H-how much does Harry owe you?"

The question seemed to take him by surprise. His brows pinched together as he growled. "Why do you ask?"

His wary expression encouraged her to press on. "How much?" she repeated a little more forcefully.

Brighton hesitated and then named a figure that nearly made her swoon.

Steady, steady. Eliza forced herself to think. "That's a great deal to recoup through selling forgeries. I wouldn't imagine that you are taking the chance to offer my copy at a legitimate auction house, so I am curious—where do you seek a buyer?"

"I don't see that such information is any of your concern," he replied slowly.

"On the contrary, sir. You are asking me to enter a lifetime business arrangement, so I have a right to know whether it has a chance of being profitable." The past few years of dealing with Harry had taught her to put on a brave face. "I'm not nearly as stupid as my brother. If I am going to put myself under your thumb, I want some assurances that I'm going to get something in return."

He narrowed his eyes in a calculating squint. "You may prove even more useful than I thought. Very well, there's little harm in satisfying your curiosity." His self-assurance was back. "The painting is currently being offered for sale at a flash house here in London."

Eliza remembered overhearing Harry use the term when he and his friends had been discussing a rash of robberies in Mayfair. "That is a place run by some unscrupulous person who sells stolen goods brought to him by thieves."

"A private emporium," agreed Brighton with a smirk. "Open only to a select clientele."

"I see." An idea—an admittedly wild idea—was beginning to take shape in her head. But conventional wisdom wasn't going to save the day. Lowering her lashes, she swirled the spoon in the now-melted ice. "Please, sir, this quite a lot to digest. I—I need some time to think about it."

"Go ahead. But keep in mind that there's only one choice that will save you and your brother from ruin."

"Harry knows about your offer?" she asked.

"But of course. And he's given it his enthusiastic blessing."

Eliza expected no less, and yet it still hurt. Taking care to keep the hollow ache in her chest from echoing in her voice, she said, "If there's nothing further to discuss, I would like to return to Gunter's."

The baronet leaned in as she accepted his arm. "Smile, Lady Brentford. You wouldn't want people to think we weren't the happy couple, would you?"

A patch of pale lavender petunias caught Gryff's eye. *Damnation—Nature seemed to be sending mixed messages regarding Lady Brentford*, he thought wryly. The flowers said "your presence soothes me," while his brain was communicating exactly the opposite signal to his body. He tried to dispel the strange prickling sensation on his skin by loosening the knot of his cravat. The grit from travel was rubbing a bit raw, and the sooner he returned home to a bath and fresh linen, the better.

Seeing that Eliza and her companion had moved out of the shade, Gryff turned up a parallel path and moderated his pace.

"I'm not spying," he muttered slowly. "I'm merely observing."

And he didn't much like what he saw.

Her face looked like a marble mask, a pale, lifeless stretch of stone, save for two hot spots of color painted along the ridge of her cheekbones. Despite the sunlight, her eyes were dull, reflecting a hard-edged glimmer that lacked any inner fire.

He knew her well enough by now to sense that something was wrong.

His gaze flicked to Brighton, who in contrast appeared smugly satisfied with whatever had just passed between him and the lady.

The couple left the garden and crossed back to the tea shop. Gryff halted inside the gate and under the pretense of consulting his pocket notebook, slanted a sidelong look through the wrought iron bars. A few moments later, a grinning Brighton and Leete emerged from the interior and sauntered off, looking for all the world like two schoolboys who had just stuffed themselves with sweets.

Recalling the night he met Eliza and her half-jesting wish that he kick some sense into her brother, Gryff was tempted to follow them and thump a pair of rumps. But then, the jingle of the tea shop's bells drew his eyes back to the ornate entrance. Eliza was leaving, followed by a young abigail.

Let her go. Bloody hell, he had enough trouble of his own without seeking more.

"Yes, but a gentleman does not turn his back on a damsel in distress." As the low mutter trailed off, his lips quirked up. And rescuing *this* particular damsel had become something of a habit.

Slipping though the opening, Gryff hurried to catch up with his quarry.

"Lady Brentford! What a surprise to encounter you." He touched the brim of his hat. "I didn't realize you were planning a trip to Town."

The greeting drew a slanted glance. He saw only a flicker of her shadowed lashes and then her eyes snapped back to staring straight ahead. Her unladylike hurry had her bonnet ribbons flapping around her cheek, further obscuring her profile.

"Why would you?" she replied coolly. "I am not in the habit of confiding my personal plans with strangers, sir."

Gryff gave a pointed look at the abigail, who immediately dropped back a discreet distance. "I should hope that we are rather more than strangers, Lady Brentford," he murmured, hoping to soften the jut of her chin.

His words drew no hint of a smile. Instead she tightened her jaw and started walking faster, despite the limping hitch in her stride. "Oh, and just what exactly are we, Lord Haddan?"

The visit to Gunter's appeared to have left a sour taste in her mouth.

Without giving him a chance to answer, she went on in a rush. "As far as I can see, men are wont to see a female as naught but another of their countless toys, to be used until it breaks or ceases to amuse." Her half boot scraped against the pavement as her lingering limp caused her to stumble over a rough patch of cobbles. Gryff reached out a steadying hand, but she jerked back out of reach.

The misstep seemed to goad her to greater ire. "A toy can simply be discarded, and a new one acquired to take its place."

Leete must have done something to strike a very raw nerve.

"I saw your brother leaving Gunter's," he said. "I take it he has done something to upset you."

She kept walking.

That the baronet may have stepped in to try to comfort her did not improve his own mood. "It may be none of my business, but I would counsel you not to seek solace from Sir Brighton. His reputation is not one that should engender much confidence in a lady." As he spoke, Gryff was uncomfortably aware of the irony in his words.

Eliza did not throw them back in his face. She merely replied, "You are right, sir. It's none of your business."

Gryff refused to be brushed off. "Lady Brentford, you are clearly upset. Is there anything I can do to help?"

Satin snapped in the breeze, the ribbons tangling and pulling her bonnet slightly askew. A sharp exhale blew them clear of her pinched mouth.

"Forgive me for sounding shrill, Lord Haddan," she answered after a moment. "I appreciate your concern, but it is a private family matter."

There was little he could say to that, save to incline a polite nod. "It is I who should apologize. I did not mean to cause you further distress."

"It's not you who are to blame." A nonchalant shrug punctuated the reply, but as she stepped through a patch of sunlight, he caught a quicksilver glimmer of moisture clinging to her lashes.

Repressing a frown, Gryff pretended not to notice. Looking up at the carved cornices and mortared brickwork of the building up ahead, he spent the next few strides mentally pummeling her brother for upsetting her. A bleakness had wrapped itself around her, snuffing out every bright spark of her spirit.

And what of Brighton? Surely he deserved some of the blame, for whatever he had said to Lady Brentford, it had brought her no comfort. Gryff thought of her hands clenched around the dish of melting sorbet, and was suddenly reminded of Cameron's comment about the baronet being a thoroughly dirty dish.

Gentlemanly scruples demanded that he honor the lady's request to respect her privacy. But no such code covered the baronet. Another glance at Eliza's stiff-legged gait and steeled spine and Gryff made up his mind.

Brighton needed further scrutiny.

"I turn here, Lord Haddan." Eliza paused just long enough to let the abigail catch up. "So I will bid you adieu."

"Are you staying long in Town?" he inquired politely. "If so, perhaps you and your friends would like to attend the theater?"

"No, my business is finished here," she said brusquely. "I intend to return home on the morrow."

"Ah. Another time, then."

"Yes, another time." She turned, her dark skirts flapping like stormclouds around her legs. "Goodbye, sir." Reverberating off the surrounding stone, the words took on an echo of finality.

Gryff watched until the two figures were swallowed by the slanting shadows. "Goodbye," he repeated. "But only for now."

Chapter Fifteen

*I*n the mist-swirled darkness of the midnight hour, her plan seemed even more absurd than it had in broad daylight. Eliza lingered at the mullioned window, tracing a random pattern on the fogged glass. If only she could spot a pinprick of light through the pall of coal smoke hanging over the London rooftops. A star to help her find her way.

The ticking of the mantel clock did not offer much encouragement. Amplified by the nighttime silence of her guest bedchamber, the sound took on a doleful rhythm. *Hope-less, hope-less.*

"It may be hopeless," she whispered. "But I have to try."

She lifted the flickering candle and carefully drew the numeral "2" through the silvery vapor that had reformed on the pane. Her plan had two parts. First, she had to raise enough money to pay off Brighton. Second, she needed to locate the incriminating painting and somehow get it back.

"Oh, and while I am at it, why don't I conjure up a turbaned genie who will crown me the Queen of Sheba and whisk me away to a land of milk and honey."

For a lingering moment, she let the image of a magical

hero wrap around her like a swirl of sweet-scented smoke. He had long, dark hair, green eyes, and a musical laugh that made her heart dance against her ribs...

Eliza blew away the thought with a mirthless laugh. Fantasizing that Haddan would swoop in to rescue her was just as unrealistic as dreaming of magic lamps. That she had, against all reason, against all resolve, allowed her emotions as well as her body to succumb to his charms, was only further warning that he was a dangerous distraction.

"I can't afford girlish dreams," she whispered. "Not when reality requires every ounce of my strength." The challenges facing her were daunting, to put it mildly.

Her hard-won savings would cover maybe half of Harry's debts. As for the other half... The reflected light caught the rueful quirk of her lips. "I suppose I could make more forgeries and sell them on my own," she said to herself, drawing another little squiggle on the glass. "At least I would profit from my crimes, and have control over my own destiny."

Unfortunately, what she knew about the fine points of engaging in illegal activities could be painted on the head of a pin.

"Money," she muttered, focusing on the problem in front of her rather than the nameless longing fluttering inside her chest. "There aren't many ways for a female to earn more than a few paltry pennies..."

The flame shivered in a whoosh of breath as she suddenly thought of someone who might be willing to offer her advice.

After all, the battle would not be won by the faint of heart.

* * *

Swoosh, swoosh, swoosh. Gryff paced along the silk-fringed perimeter of the Turkey carpet, his slippered feet kicking up a soft, sinuous whisper. Left abandoned in the shadows, the empty desk chair sat in silent reproach as he passed it yet again. He gave a guilty glance and kept going, too restless to settle down with his pens and papers.

Damn. He knew he should be obsessed with his writing and not with a country widow whose troubles were none of his concern. She did not want his interference, and had said so in no uncertain terms.

And yet her eyes had sent a far more ambiguous message.

Her anger could not quite overshadow the ripple of longing, as if for one instant she had been tempted to confide in him.

"Damn." Out of habit, his steps veered to the side table, where he poured himself a large tumbler of brandy. Several months ago, solving a troubling conundrum was simple—all he had to do was simply pickle his wits in several bottles of potent spirits. "It is far easier to be a rogue than a man of conscience," he muttered, lifting a baleful salute to the marble bust of Socrates set atop the manuscript cabinet.

Perching a hip on the corner of his desk, he twirled the glass between his palms. The color of the liquid, spinning from deep bronze to amber gold in the glow of the argent lamp, reminded him of Lady Brentford's unruly curls dancing free in the fresh country sunlight. A bold, bright spirit ought not be dimmed by dark shadows. They had hung beneath her eyes like bruises.

His gaze moved to the gilt-framed watercolor by Redouté that was leaning against the curio cabinet. It was still half-wrapped, with only a hint of the rose showing.

"Have you any advice to offer on the situation?" he growled. "A rose ought to feel an affinity for a lady in trouble."

The leaves hung limp and lifeless.

A sigh—or was it a snarl—slipped from his lips. After a brooding moment, he set the glass down and turned to ink instead of brandy.

Inspired by the memories of her unfettered reactions to the landscape of Leete Abbey, he began to write, the words flowing fast and furious. For nearly an hour the only sounds in the library were the hurried scratch of the nib and the faint hiss of the glowing coals burning down to dark embers in the hearth. When finally he put down his pen and scraped back his chair, the skewed stack of papers on his blotter held a finished essay.

"She is my Muse," he murmured, slowly skimming through the scrawled pages. "Like Linden, Lady Brentford helps me see things that I would miss on my own." This essay was his best yet, the tone both lyrical and down to earth. It bothered him that the laughter had died from her voice, and he felt helpless to do anything about it.

"What are you doing holed up like a monk doing penance in his cell?" Cameron lit the candelabra by the doorway with his single taper. "Ye gods, don't you find it rather depressing to be sitting here in near darkness?"

"I'm brooding," he shot back. "So the ambiance is appropriate."

"Oh?" His friend raised a brow. "About what? Linden?"

"And a lady."

"Ah. I should have guessed that a female would be in-volved." Cameron crossed to the hearth and propped a boot on the brass fender. "The one you were watching outside of Gunter's? With a look, I might add, that would have melted a hogshead full of iced chocolate cream."

"I can't explain it. I seem to be besotted," admitted Gryff. "Smitten like a schoolboy."

"You who have resisted the charms of every Beauty and Temptress in Town?" His friend sounded amused. "I take it the lady in Grosvenor Square was Leete's sister—the one with whom you had that tasty dalliance."

A growl warned Cameron that any risqué remarks would not be welcome. "Yes, that was Lady Brentford," added Gryff. "And I fear that she may be in some trouble."

"Seeing as Leete is her brother, I don't doubt it."

"Stubble the jests. This isn't a subject for levity," he snapped. The image of Leete laughing with the baronet prodded him to ask, "What do you know about Brighton?"

"Not much, save that he and his cousin are considered very unsavory fellows by some of my acquaintances."

"Why?"

Cameron shrugged in response. "I've never asked. But I can make some inquiries if you like."

"Thank you, that would be helpful," replied Gryff. Pursing his lips in thought, he drummed his fingers on the blotter. "Speaking of Linden, have you learned anything more?"

"My friend has taken a little jaunt to the country. But I've another idea on how to get information," replied Cameron.

"I think I'd rather not know what it is," he said.

"I think you are right," quipped his friend.

Once his chuffed laugh had died away, Gryff stared moodily at the barely glowing coals. "I feel so bloody useless. Is there naught I can do but sit and wait while you take action?"

"You *are* in a strange mood." Cameron came over to the desk and eyed the glass of brandy. Seeing it was untouched, he lifted it to his lips. "May I?"

He gave a curt wave.

"Might I ask another question?" Without waiting for an answer, Cameron continued. "Why do you care so passionately about Lady Brentford and her problems?"

Gryff didn't quite know how to articulate his feelings.

"Well, I had better get to work," said his friend after downing the brandy in one quick swallow. "You are far more entertaining company when you're not blue-deviled."

"I appreciate your touching concern for my state of mind," he said gruffly. "By the by, is there a reason you stopped by in the first place?"

"I just happened to be in the area and saw a light in the library window," answered Cameron vaguely.

"To see the library, you have to be in passing through one of the back alleyways."

His friend merely smiled. "I'll stop by again as soon as I have anything to report."

"Blue-deviled," muttered Gryff as the door clicked shut. Perhaps it was because he was tormented by the sparkle in his mind's eye of rich sapphire, its brilliance clouded by the shadow of men—

Men. He suddenly sat up a bit straighter. Had Lady

Brentford's sarcastic comment of men and their toys been directed at *him*, as well as her brother? At the time, he had been too concerned by her troubled face to give the words any heed. But now, in the dark, quiet depths of the night, with no distractions save for his own introspective thoughts, the statement came back to haunt him.

"Oh, surely she doesn't think that *I* see her as simply an object of amusement."

In answer, the oppressive silence in the room seemed to grow louder.

Gryff made himself think back on their encounters. And in each one there was no denying that he had behaved like a snapping beast, pawing, poking, prodding— entirely for his own pleasure.

No, not entirely, he amended. She had seemed to enjoy their intimacies as well.

Still, despite the self-serving platitudes, he was for a moment overwhelmed with a sense of shame.

Picking up his little notebook, he slowly thumbed through the pages, rereading his scribbled record of her comments throughout the afternoon.

"I need to clarify some things between us, Lady Brentford," he muttered. "Whether you want me to or not."

Eliza added a small splash of water to her mixing palette and carefully wet her paintbrush. "A touch of burnt sienna," she murmured, drawing the soft sable bristles over a square of dried pigment, "will tone down the brightness of the cerulean blue..."

She had arrived back at the Abbey at a little past noon, and for the moment, there was nothing more she could do to put her plan into action. On the morrow, she would ride over to ask Gussie for a council of war. Her old governess would be eager to help do battle against Brighton and his terrible ultimatum.

With her sharp mind, of course, thought Eliza wryly, and not with her frail body.

Though on second thought, she could picture Gussie seeking to slice off the baronet's potato finger with her pruning shears.

The image cheered her mood considerably.

As did the wash of color taking shape on the thick sheet of watercolor paper. Painting allowed her to escape from her worldly worries, if only for a short interlude. The act of creating shapes and textures, of mixing shades and hues, of adding line and detail was supremely satisfying.

Sitting back, she studied the specimen she had clipped from her cottage garden. It was a purple columbine, whose message was "I intend to win." "Perhaps later, I'll cut a bouquet of chrysanthemums," she said to Elf as the cat jumped up onto her worktable. "Which mean 'abundance and wealth.'"

Meow.

"Right, this columbine does look a little wilted. Shall we go gather a fresh one?"

Meow.

"How refreshing to be in the company of such an agreeable male," she quipped, watching the marmalade tail disappear out the door. "Harry and his friend are beasts."

As for Haddan the Hellhound...

She gathered her paintbox, sketchpad, and water jar, deciding the day was much too nice to remain cooped up inside. Besides, Haddan made her think of sunlight drizzling through leaves like liquid honey, of breezes soft as a whispered laugh, of meadowgrasses dancing to the freespirited notes of the songbirds.

To be sure, the marquess had a devilish charm, but the moniker of "hellhound" did not really fit the man she had come to know. *Her* Haddan was no hard-hearted predator, no rapacious rogue. He was funny, sensitive, compassionate, and...

Nice. That summed it up succinctly.

"He's nice," said Eliza loudly. "But I'm never going to see him again." She drew in a lungful of air and held it, waiting a moment for the pain in her chest to subside.

"I can live with that," she murmured, setting down her things and moving to the flower beds. Forcing herself to forget his kind offer to help, she plucked a freshly fallen oak leaf—which symbolized bravery—and stuck it in the twined coil of her hair. "I cannot depend on anyone else to fight my battles. If Brighton is to be beaten, I must find a way to do it myself."

Gryff reined his horse to halt by the stone cottage and dismounted, careful to keep the well-wrapped bouquet from being squashed. It had taken several stops to find a flower shop that offered purple hyacinth, which said "please forgive me" in the language of flowers. He would add his own embellishments to the basic message—he glanced at the age-blackened oak—assuming she didn't shut the door in his face.

Leaving his mount to graze in the shade of the trees, he approached the entrance and gave a soft knock.

No answer.

Frowning, Gryff waited a few moments, uncertain of what to do. Not wanting to cause her any embarrassment at the manor house, he had decided to pay a discreet visit to her hideaway, hoping to find her alone. Given what he had to say, a private meeting would be best. *Just the two of them.*

Clearing an odd nervousness from his throat, he knocked again.

Still no stirring from within.

"Hell and damnation," he muttered. "Some imp of Satan must be conspiring against me—"

Meow.

Speak of the devil. Looking up, Gryff saw the cat curled atop the gated archway. "Halloo, remember me?"

The cat twitched its whiskers.

"Why, thank you for the kind invitation," he said, trying the iron latch. It released with a raspy *clink.*

He opened the gate just enough to squeeze through and pushed it closed behind him. The high, weathered walls with their earthtone lichens and twines of gray-green ivy gave no hint of what was hidden within the mortised stones. Gryff stopped short and blinked at the riot of textures and colors, feeling a little drunk, a little disoriented. In the space of a few small steps, he had been magically transported from staid Oxfordshire to an exotic pleasure garden in some unknown land.

The impression was accentuated by the sight of a fanciful female figure twirling in circles on the soft grass. A garland of oak leaves and daisies crowned her hair, which, freed from its pins, spilled over her shoulders in glorious honey-colored waves. The curling ends danced across the back of a white peasant blouse, its gauzy cotton liberally embroidered with bright flowers.

His gaze slid lower, taking in the billowy scarlet trousers, snugged at the ankles with turquoise ties, and her bare feet.

She must have heard his sharp intake of breath, for she stopped humming and spun around.

"You make a very striking Gypsy sorceress, Lady Brentford."

Her mouth opened and closed several times before any words came out. "I—You—W-who in the name of the Devil gave you permission to invade my privacy?"

"Imp of Satan bade me to come in," replied Gryff. "Though I admit, I might have misunderstood his invitation."

She bit her lower lip. "Oh, never mind that. More importantly, *why* are you here?"

The crackling sounded like crickets chirping as he held out the odd-shaped package wrapped in thick brown paper. Strangely enough, he felt a little tongue-tied, so all he said was, "To bring you this."

She made no move to take it.

"It won't bite," he murmured.

Pushing back her sleeves, Eliza gingerly plucked it from his outstretched hand.

"Sorry, it's a little like carrying coals to Newcastle," he went on as she started to undo the wrapping. "Had I known, I could have brought gold bangles and a floral headscarf. But that would not have sent quite the right message."

"Which is?"

The paper fell away, revealing a bouquet of pale purple blooms.

"Please forgive me," they both said at once, reciting the secret language of lavender hyacinths.

A breeze ruffled through the tall spikes of lavender, filling the air with its sweet herbal fragrance. He watched the rise and fall of her chest as she breathed in and out.

"Forgive you for what?" she asked softly.

"I thought maybe...that is, I worried whether you might..." It was his turn to stammer. "Hell's bells, I am making a complete mull of this, aren't I?" He shifted his weight from foot to foot. "I haven't felt this awkward since I was a spotty-faced schoolboy trying to ask the milkmaid for a kiss."

Her lips twitched. "I bet you didn't have to ask twice."

"Actually she turned me down flat," replied Gryff. "I was short for my age, and a trifle plump."

Eliza arched her brows in disbelief. "That rather defies the imagination."

"So does this." A sweep of his hand encompassed the profusion of the colorful plantings. "It's remarkably unique—in a wonderful way." *As are you*, he wanted to add.

"Thank you. But—"

"But I still haven't explained my presence," interrupted Gryff. Her hint of a smile had loosened the knot in his tongue. "Yes, right. Well, the thing is, I was thinking about what you said yesterday about men and their toys."

Her lashes flicked down, hiding her eyes.

"And I wanted to assure you that I've never thought of you in such a way," he went on in a rush. "If I've given you the wrong impression—" He tipped his chin at the bouquet in her hands. "I beg your forgiveness."

Eliza touched a fingertip to one of the petals. "I was speaking of men in general. There are always exceptions to the rule." She finally looked up. "Most people would say it's *my* behavior that is unforgivable. I've acted like a shameless hussy, a wanton jade."

He started to protest but she cut him off. "And you know something—I don't care!" She tilted her face to the sun. "I don't care that my face has unfashionable spots, or that I dance barefoot in gypsy trousers, or that I've stolen scandalous kisses with a notorious rogue. It makes me feel happy."

Gryff felt a smile bloom on his lips. "I am glad. You have nothing to be ashamed of, Lady Brentford."

"Ah, well, a Hellhound *would* say that."

"That wasn't a Hellhound speaking," he replied softly. "It was simply…" *Who was he?* "…an old dog who would like to think he can learn new tricks."

Eliza blinked, as if trying to bring him into sharper focus. "I should put these lovely flowers in water," she said abruptly. "Will you excuse me for a moment?" Turning in a blur of jewel-tone colors, she hurried for the back door of the cottage.

Still smiling, Gryff shucked off his hat and coat, wanting to feel the perfumed air tease through his hair and the sunbeams suffuse his skin. All of his senses suddenly felt heightened—he was intimately aware of the colors, the smells, the textures, the sounds.

Drawn to the buzzing of a honeybee close by, he crouched down to study the artful array of border plantings. The garden had been planned with a masterful eye for detail. The effect was enchanting.

Rising, Gryff wandered along the pathway, drinking it all in. In the far corner of the wall was a stone bench, and on it was a sketchpad and wooden paintbox. Recalling her remark about having no artistic talent, he couldn't help but be curious. Quickening his steps, he decided to steal a quick peek before she returned.

Alas, there was nothing on the page but a flat background wash of light blue.

"Lord Haddan!"

He set the pad down. "Your secrets are still safe, Lady Brentford. There's naught here to betray your talents." He chuckled. "Or lack of them."

Chapter Sixteen

That may be so." Eliza sought to still the pounding of her heart. There was no reason to be alarmed. Even if Lord Haddan saw a finished sketch, it would mean nothing to him. "However, you have no right to look through my private things without permission."

He acknowledged the scold with a solemn nod. "You are right, of course. Having recently chastised a friend for doing much the same thing, I should be sensitive to such transgressions."

"No harm done," she murmured. It was strange how the enclosed space of the garden, which seemed quite large when she was alone, suddenly felt crowded with his presence. The stretch of his shoulders blocked all but the tips of the tallest bushes and the light citrus scent of his cologne overwhelmed all of the floral perfumes. "I would offer you some refreshments, but I'm afraid I have nothing but a jug of water and a bowl of walnuts."

"Thank you, but I am happy just to linger here for a bit and feast on the marvelous sights and smells you have created." His gaze circled the space and came back to her. "I take it you designed all this."

"The basic plantings have been here for ages. I just added a few embellishments."

"You are far too modest, Lady Brentford." Gryff took another leisurely look around. "It takes a true artist to make such imaginative use of colors, shapes, and texture. Clearly you have an eye for creating beauty."

His praise stirred a tingle of heat inside her. "Thank you. Most people don't really notice how flowers can be arranged and combined to…make a statement, as it were."

He grinned. "Perhaps that's because most people don't understand their secret language." He pointed at a stand of graceful calla lilies. "They say 'magnificent beauty' and I heartily agree."

She paused and regarded him thoughtfully. "You know, sir, during all of our outdoor interludes here at the Abbey you have shown yourself to be very articulate on plants, and the subtle shapes and nuances of Nature. It speaks of more than a casual knowledge of landscape design."

It may have been the scudding of a leaf or a cloud, but it seemed to her as if a slight shadow flitted across his face. "Does it? I'm flattered that you think so," replied Gryff evasively. "Ah, walnuts!" he exclaimed an instant later, spotting the bowl in her hands. "How nice."

"Yes, but Elf seems to have dragged off the nutcracker to some feline hiding place."

"Never fear, I know an old soldierly trick." He took a seat on the grass and stretched out his leg. "If you would kindly help me remove my boot, Lady Brentford."

She regarded him quizzically. "Your boot?"

Pointing to the decorative stone tiles set around the sundial, he mimed a hammering motion. "One simply places a nut on the flat stone and *whack*!"

"With a boot?"

"Hoby crafts a very fine heel."

Eliza grasped his ankle and gave a hard tug. "Does he charge extra?"

"Oh, no, not for English walnuts," said Gryff with a straight face. "Only for Spanish almonds and French filberts."

A laugh welled up in her throat, and all at once her worries seemed to loosen their grip. "What about American pecans?"

"That's double."

As he spoke, the boot suddenly slipped free, sending her tumbling backward onto the grass.

He began to laugh.

"Oh, you odious man! You did that on purpose, didn't you?" Untangling herself, she sat up and took aim at his head with the shiny leather. However, a fit of giggles ruined the threat.

The gesture made Gryff start laughing harder. "You look like an enraged Earth Goddess, sprung to life from a bed of flowers." He raised his hands in mock surrender. "What offering must I make to placate your wrath?"

The boot landed by his side. "Nuts," commanded Eliza. "Shelled and fed to me as I recline on my grassy throne."

Leaning back on her elbows, she closed her eyes and let the warmth of the sun-dappled ground suffuse her body. A swirl of sweet perfumes tickled her nostrils, the soft serenade of the garden birds and bees danced on the breeze. It would, she reflected, be wonderful if some magical moments could be captured in a bottle and saved forever.

"Dream on," she whispered.

Whack, whack, whack. The sound of Gryff's labors snapped her back to the present, and with a rueful smile she reminded herself of an old adage. *Eat, drink, and be merry, for tomorrow . . .*

Tomorrow—she would not think of tomorrow.

Lifting a lid, she watched him gather up the cracked walnuts and come take a seat beside her.

"Lean back and open your mouth, Your Majesty."

A nutmeat touched her tongue. "Mmmmm." She chewed slowly and swallowed. "Ambrosial. I could get used to this."

He popped a piece into his mouth. "The High Servant of Shoe Leather is at your beck and call anytime."

"Mmmmm." Eliza accepted another offering. "Have a care, Lord Haddan. You might find yourself shackled into a lifetime of service." Belatedly realizing the implication of her words, she flushed. "That is, I—"

Another morsel silenced her stammering.

"I can think of worse fates," he said lightly. Stripping off his stocking, Gryff wriggled his toes in the grass. "I can see why you come here. It's very peaceful."

"Do you spend much time at your country estate, sir?" she asked.

"No," he answered. "I've been neglecting it for too long." He inhaled a deep breath and released it very slowly. "But London is losing its allure."

"I think you would be happy in the country."

He cocked his head. "And I don't strike you as happy now?"

She didn't answer right away.

One dark brow rose in question. "Well?"

"It seems to me that you would be happier at this moment if you took off your other boot." She, too, could evade an uncomfortable query. "Your left leg must be hot as Hades."

He waggled his foot. "The Limb would be very grateful for your kind assistance."

A few quick pulls removed the boot without further mishap. "The Limb now owes me a custard tart."

Gryff chuckled. "Done."

They sat for a bit in companionable silence, their shoulders touching, their toes playing in the same patch of fragrant grass. His closeness was strangely comfortable. It seemed to fit like a familiar shoe.

"Why are you smiling?" asked Gryff.

"I was imagining Your Lordship as a well-worn shoe."

He gave a feline stretch. "And here I thought I was the very *soul* of Manly Magnificence."

"Are you always this silly with ladies?"

"No. I know so very few who dare to let themselves laugh." There was an odd note in his voice. "Or wear gypsy trousers, or eat custard tarts in the wild."

"We are a very odd couple," she mused.

A rumbled sound, impossible to interpret. It might have been a laugh, or merely a cough to clear his throat.

"By the by, how did you come to have such a fetching ensemble in your wardrobe?" asked Gryff.

"There is a Gypsy caravan that comes through Harpden each summer. I've become friends with one of the women, a healer who is skilled in the use of medicinal herbs and plants," replied Eliza. "She gave these clothes to me as a gift in return for some paintings I did for her."

"Ah. And yet, you've told me that your talents with a paintbrush were sadly lacking."

Damn. "Th-they weren't very good."

He looked down his nose at her for a long, thoughtful moment. "Once again, I think you are being far too modest, Lady Brentford. And I can't help but wonder, what secrets are you hiding from me?" And why?

"We all have secrets, Lord Haddan." She recalled his little notebook, and how reluctant he was to share its contents. "Are you going to tell me that your private life is an open book?"

"No, indeed." His mouth quirked. "Though a good deal of it has been splashed on the front pages of the scandal sheets."

Eliza didn't want to think about those exploits, many of which involved sparkling champagne and voluptuous women. She suddenly felt very dull and plain.

"Feed me another nut, High Servant of the Shoe Leather." Might as well enjoy the fantasy while it lasted. Illusions had a nasty habit of disappearing in a puff of putrid smoke.

"As you wish, Your Majesty." Shells crackled. "Close your eyes and open your mouth."

"If you put an earthworm inside it, I shall turn you into a frog," she warned.

"Then I shall beg a kiss from a fairy princess and turn into a handsome prince."

"Don't press your luck." Sitting up a little straighter, she primly parted her lips.

"Eyes closed!" he repeated. "No cheating."

"Oh, very well." Eliza squeezed off her peeking, though she felt a little foolish sitting there like a flytrap.

A piece of walnut hit softly upon her tongue, followed by another.

"Very clever," she said after swallowing the morsels.

"I'm a dab hand at cricket," he replied. "Let's try a spin pitch."

The next nut bounced off her lip and fell beneath the open collar of her shirt. Her eyes flew open as it rolled inside her chemise.

"Oops."

The marquess's laughing face was just inches from hers. His green-gold eyes glinted with unholy mischief and his lordly mouth quivered with boyish merriment.

"Oops," she whispered.

As his laugh grew louder, the ground began to tilt and spin beneath her. Reason blew away in the breeze, and suddenly Eliza pitched forward, capturing him in a shameless kiss.

"Mmmm, you taste good," she murmured, after enjoying a long, leisurely embrace.

Gryff nipped her chin. "Mmmm, so do you." Framing her face with his sun-warmed palms, he teased his teeth along the swell of her lower lip. "Delicious." A sigh tickled her cheek. "But I didn't come here to seduce you, to use you for my own selfish pleasure."

"There is a question of just who is seducing whom," she murmured, twining her arms around his neck and scooting into his lap. "If you are afraid for your virtue, Lord Haddan, I give you leave to withdraw."

"Oh, I think my virtue is up to the challenge, Lady Brentford." A stirring beneath her bottom punctuated his reply.

"Is it?" She shifted slowly from side to side.

"You," he rasped, "are very...very..." Her wriggling reduced his words to a gasp.

"Wicked?" she offered. "Wanton?"

"Alluring," he answered. "Enticing. Enchanting."

Her breath caught in her throat. "*Me?*" No one had ever seen her as such.

"Yes, you. And do you know what I intend to do about it?"

Her skin began to prickle all over. "What?"

"Listen very carefully, Lady Brentford." He inched a little closer. "First, I am going to take the tassels of your shirt and untie them." His fingers worked the strings free. "Then I am going to ask you to raise your arms to the sky."

Her hands shot up. Slowly, slowly, the embroidered cloth slithered up over her head.

"Now for your chemise. Let me think." Gryff cocked his head, his gaze studying her breasts. "I could suckle your perfect little nipples through the cloth. The friction of the wet fabric would set them afire."

Eliza let out a little moan.

"Or I could tear the delicate fabric straight down the middle..." He drew his thumb from her breastbone down to her navel. "And peel it away, like a harem slave disrobing a plump, sweet grape for the sultan to devour."

She shivered, aware of a honeyed heat forming between her legs.

He teased his touch lightly over her nipples. "Choices, choices. I can't seem to decide."

"*Haddan*," she gasped in throaty protest. "Stop. No—that is, *don't* stop."

He leaned back, and their bodies were no longer touching. "What is it you want, sweeting?"

"I—I want you to make love to me," she whispered. The ground felt deliciously warm as she raked her fingers through the fragrant blades of grass. "Without delay."

A husky chuckle teased a thrill along her spine. "Then perhaps you had better help things along." Gryff folded his arms across his chest. "Why don't you undress yourself. I'll watch."

Her eyes widened. What he proposed sounded indecently…intriguing. She hesitated, but on catching a glimpse of the smoldering heat in his gaze, she slowly stripped off her chemise, baring her breasts to the tickle of the breeze.

"Go on," he rasped.

Eliza loosened the strings of her trousers. Oh, it was exquisitely erotic to be taking off her garments while he watched. The sinuous slide of fabric aroused every inch of her skin to heightened sensations—the currents of the breeze, the softness of the grass, the heat of his gaze.

Her hips lifted, allowing the gypsy trousers to slither down past her knees. A little kick freed them from her ankles. Gryff made a strange little sound in his throat as she inched off her drawers, leaving her entirely naked.

Reaching out, she caught the tail of his cravat and gave a tug. "Now it's your turn."

Smiling, he complied, drawing out the dance with a lazy, languid grace.

"You," she chided, "are a very maddening male. Perhaps I've changed my mind in the interim."

"Then I shall have to exercise the powers of my persuasion." Gryff pushed her back in the grass and covered her body with his. "And make you think again."

"I don't want to think," she said dreamily, as his cock nudged up against her passage. "I just want to feel."

"Hmmm." He nibbled her earlobe. "How does this feel?" he whispered, entering her with a slow, smooth thrust.

"Heavenly," she responded, staring up at the sky. "I wish it could..." *Last for a lifetime.* "...go on all afternoon."

"Very well—we'll take it very slowly."

He set a leisurely rhythm, and Eliza followed his lead, matching his movements, letting her imagination wander along with the flickering sunbeams. It was oh-so scandalous, to be lying outside in broad daylight, twining her hands in his hair, exploring the chiseling of his body, the texture of his muscles, the taste of his mouth. *And oh-so exhilarating.* Kissing and caressing him made her whole being thrum with pleasure.

Shifting his weight, Gryff slipped his hand between their bodies and touched the soft curls between her legs.

"Oh, Haddan."

"Gryff," he corrected. "Say it."

"Gryff," she whispered, his name like honey on her lips. "That feels so *good.*"

His fingers dipped and danced against her flesh.

Liquid fire coursed through her, the heat of it growing unbearable.

"*Gryff!*"

He surged into her, his cry joining hers.

And then...and then she was floating—floating on a warm, zephyrous bed of lighter-than-air spun gold, its winking shimmers of light brighter than the sun.

Coming back down to earth, Eliza opened her eyes from a drowsy half-sleep to see Gryff was still deep in repose, his long, lithe body stretched out, face up, on the grass. The leaves of the foliage painted shades of light and shadow over his belly and the dragon tattoo.

On impish impulse, she crept over to her paintbox and set it up on the grass beside him. Choosing a pointed sable-hair brush, she wet it in water, and twirled it to a fine point.

He made a snuffling sound in the back of his throat, but didn't wake.

She mixed up a deep azure blue and with quick, bold strokes, began painting a second dragon around the tattoo.

His eyes flew open.

"Don't jump," she cautioned, "or you'll ruin the snout."

"Snout is not a term I use for..." He gingerly lifted his head. "Oh, I see what you mean." He watched her sketch in a long, curling neck and wings. "Very clever," he murmured. "You are exceedingly skilled with a brush."

"Art requires diligent practice," said Eliza, ducking her head to hide her grin. She flicked the bristles lower, brushing soft sable against the head of his cock.

His reaction was immediate—and physical.

"I think your two dragons need another playfellow," she teased, taking up a smaller brush and dipping it in a pool of scarlet paint. With a few more strokes she drew in fanciful slanted eyes, and a mouth with curved fangs.

Roused from repose, his privy part was now standing at attention.

Giggling, Eliza switched to alternating hues of turquoise and emerald to draw in an intricate pattern of scales beneath the flanged head.

Gryff was growing more and more aroused by the moment. "Have a care. Your new beastie seems to be waking from a nap and may have an urge to show off his new-found splendor."

"Maybe the beastie only wants to play with the dragons," she said.

"My beastie a molly beastie?" he exclaimed in mock outrage. "No, I assure you, he only waggles his scales for women."

They were laughing too loudly to hear the faint creak of the gate hinges. It took a loud cough to catch Gryff's attention.

"Forgive me for interrupting."

Gryff sat up and snatched for his breeches. "Bloody hell, Cam, you ought to knock before barging into a private place."

"I did. Several times." He inclined a curt nod to Eliza. "Milady."

She had her shirt clutched to her chest.

"Might I have a word with you, Gryff?" went on Cameron. "Outside if you please."

Chapter Seventeen

What the devil do you mean, barging in on us like that," demanded Gryff. His initial shock had been replaced by equal measures of anger and embarrassment. "This time your cursed sense of humor has overstepped its boundaries."

Cameron's face was oddly expressionless. "I'm aware of the fact that you consider this no laughing matter." Taking Gryff by the arm, he drew him away from the wall. "The thing is, you pressed me to find out certain information as quickly as I could, so I assumed you wished to hear it without delay."

"Given the circumstances, another hour or two would hardly have made a difference," he growled.

"I beg to differ." His friend's gaze had grown shuttered.

Gryff felt the small hairs on the back of his neck stand on end. "Why?"

Cameron answered with a question of his own. "Just how involved are you with Leete's sister?"

"What do you mean?"

"*Must* I spell it out in graphic detail?" A martyred sigh.

"It appears that you are in much deeper into this dalliance you indicated. And that, I fear, may present a problem."

Gryff clenched his jaw. "My private affairs are none of your concern, Cam."

A tense silence quivered between them for a moment before his friend expelled another sharp breath. "Lady Brentford is your elusive Linden," he said without preamble.

"Impossible," whispered Gryff. "You must be mistaken."

"I assure you, I'm not. I had a look at Watkins's correspondence last night, and it's all there in writing—every last detail about the commission."

"But she claims to have no artistic talent."

"Then she is not being truthful," replied Cameron. "According to the letters, Watkins considers her to be one of the finest botanical artists in all of England."

"Bloody hell," whispered Gryff.

"I'm sorry," said his friend softly. "But you did ask, and I feel an obligation to tell you all the facts, no matter how unwelcome." He paused. "You do realize that this colors your query about Brighton. If Lady Brentford is Linden, that also means..." He let his voice trail off.

"That means she is working with the baronet on selling art forgeries," Gryff finished for him.

"So it would seem."

Despite the dappling of light that softened the leafy shadows, Gryff felt chilled to the bone. Hugging his arms to his bare chest he turned to stare at the garden wall. The ivy-covered stones no longer seemed to wave a friendly invitation. They now appeared an ominous barrier, a false front.

"Damnation," he muttered. "Why—why would she do such a thing when her talents allow her to earn an honest living? I'm paying a very generous sum for her paintings."

"Money has a powerful attraction," said Cameron. "Some people simply can't get enough of it."

"But Lady Brentford seems the very opposite of a greedy, grasping criminal."

His friend waited until the last little echo of the protest died away before asking, "How well do you really know her?"

"Apparently not well at all," replied Gryff tightly. His chest felt as if an iron band was squeezing into muscle and sinew, slowly forcing the air from his lungs.

Cameron clasped his hands behind his back. "I'm sorry."

Gryff forced himself to inhale, once, then twice. "So am I." He was a worldly Hellhound, a jaded rogue who had seen every shade of good and bad. It was ridiculous to feel disappointed or disillusioned.

"I doubt that you want to ride back to London barefoot." His friend's voice somehow penetrated the harsh humming in his ears. "Shall I fetch the rest of your clothing?"

Boots—his boots were still lying in the grass, along with his coat and the other testaments to his folly. "No." He chafed at his arms, only to find them as cold and unfeeling as marble. "Thank you but I'm not quite that much of a coward."

"I'll wait for you here."

Gryff walked across the path, ignoring the painful press of gravel against the soles of his feet. *Pain is good,* he told himself. It provided a welcome physical distraction from his mental turmoil. He pushed the gate open and drew it shut behind him.

"Bad news?" Eliza stood still as a statue by the edge of the grass. She was fully dressed, her hair hastily caught up in a simple twist at the nape of her neck. Loose tendrils danced in the breeze, finespun threads of gold lacing the dark greens of the background foliage as she held out his carefully smoothed garments. Her face was very pale and concern clouded her eyes.

A consummate actress as well as artist, he thought rather bitterly. He felt conflicted. Confused. Betrayed. Though that was perhaps a bit unfair. She had no idea he was the author of the essays, so deliberate deception was not a sin he could lay at her feet.

Lifting his gaze from the ground, he replied with a curt, "Yes."

"I—I'm sorry," she whispered. "Is there anything I can do to help?"

He restrained the urge to laugh. "No. Nothing." Reaching for his shirt, he quickly pulled it on and shoved the tails into his breeches. "I'm afraid that circumstances demand I return to Town without delay." A fleck of paint spotted the back of his hand, prompting him to add grimly, "Enjoy your painting. Judging from the example I have on my person, you have been much too modest about your talents."

A shadow of alarm seemed to ripple in her eyes as Eliza wordlessly handed him his coat.

Avoiding her gaze, Gryff stuffed his cravat into his pocket and pulled on his boots. Uncertainty gripped his throat. A part of him wanted to confront her, to demand an explanation. He had never been one to turn tail and run in the face of a challenge, but what was there to say?

Are you a crafty criminal on top of being a liar, Lady Brentford? In truth, he would rather not hear the answer from her lips.

"Godspeed, Lord Haddan," she said softly. "I hope that whatever the trouble, it resolves itself quickly."

Unable to loosen his tongue, he simply nodded and turned away.

Eliza winced as the gate fell shut. Faint though it was, the clink had an ominous finality to it. Or was it merely her imagination that Lord Haddan's eyes had turned colder, harder, during the short meeting with his friend?

"But why?" she whispered. Why would he have such a sudden change of heart?

The chirping of the linnets gave no answer.

Trying to shake off a sense of foreboding, she began to gather up her paints and brushes. "It makes no sense," she mused to herself. One moment they had been sharing intimate laughs. And then the next, he fixed her with a grim, stony-faced stare.

As if I were a criminal.

Eliza sat down rather heavily and drew her knees to her chest. *Enjoy your painting*, he had said. *You have been much too modest about your talents.*

Oh no, surely he couldn't have any idea...

A rustling in the nearby planting drew her out of the unwelcome thoughts. She looked around to see a marmalade tail waving among the pink gerberas. A paw flashed, followed by a hiss and a thump.

"Oh, Elf, what have you got there? A dead vole?"

Heaving a sigh, she scooted over to the flower bed. "I'd much rather it be a magic frog. If ever I needed a fairy-tale prince to appear, it is now."

The cat's newfound plaything had neither furry claws nor webbed feet. It was a small leatherbound notebook tied shut with a familiar green ribbon.

"Drat it." It must have fallen from Haddan's pocket when he had tossed his coat onto the bench. She had seen him scribbling in it often enough to guess that the contents would be sorely missed.

Elf purred loudly, sounding immensely pleased with himself.

"Oh, you naughty, naughty creature. Haddan might think that I did this on purpose, to lure him back here." A hot flush rose up to ridge her cheekbones. She had, after all, been alone with his coat.

The cat batted at the small emerald bow.

"I ought to box those pointy little ears of yours," she muttered. "It's all because of you that push came to shove."

Elf gave an aggrieved hiss.

"Oh, you're right," she admitted. "The fault lies more with me and my own ungovernable urges. I should have been satisfied with life in the shadows. But no, I had to spread my wings and try to fly to the brightest burning orb in the sky." Eliza held back a sniff. "And we all know what happened to Icarus. When dreams are fashioned of naught but wax and feathers, one should know better than to get too close to the sun."

Meow.

Eliza felt a little like whimpering, too. Much as she tried to convince herself that the marquess's abrupt departure was not personal, she couldn't dispel the memory of his eyes, and the look, however fleeting, that had dulled their lovely color.

Disappointment? Nay, it had been worse than that. *Dismay. Disgust.*

"I don't understand," she said again, stroking a finger over the worn leather cover of the notebook. "But then, what do I really know of men and how their minds work?" Her jaw tightened. "Save that somehow, since the time of Adam and Eve, females are always the ones who must suffer the worst of the serpent's bite."

Her hand came to rest on the ribbon, and it seemed to twitch beneath her painted palm. "Hell's bells, since I already seem to be hurtling down the Path to Perdition at full speed, what's another little sin to speed me on my way? I may as well have a look inside." The tiny knot slipped free. "What deep, dark secrets can the Marquess of Haddan have?"

After soothing her conscience with the reminder that he had claimed to be making notes on the landscape, Eliza slowly opened the cover.

A page turned, then another.

"Oh." A single syllable was all she could manage. Tracing a finger over the penciled script, she wished that she could deny the truth. But there it was, writ plainly on the paper.

Haddan was the author of those lyrical essays?

No, it wasn't a question, it was a cold, hard fact. The only real conundrum was why Haddan would wish to hide his talents from the public. Why choose a pen name?

Why, why, why?

Her mouth crooked. "I, of all people, know there are

reasons for keeping secrets. But the marquess need not worry about money. He has control over his destiny while I…"

Elf nudged up to her, rubbing his whiskered face against her hand. "Yes, I know—I should not succumb to self-pity." She stroked his soft fur, seeking some measure of warmth to take the chill from her bones.

"I wish that Haddan and I might have shared…"

Ah, if wishes were pennies, I'd be rich as Croesus.

"And then I could tell Brighton to go to the Devil."

Meow.

"Yes, and take Harry along with him."

For a moment, the thought of her brother with a red-hot pitchfork burning his bum brightened her spirits. Just as quickly, the spark fizzled and died, leaving naught but cold ashes.

The sun was sinking, the lengthening shadows cutting like knife blades across the garden. Her sanctuary suddenly felt more like a prison than a refuge, and as she stared at the dark bars, Eliza had to escape.

There was only one place in the world where a smile would make her feel welcome. Wanted.

She stared down at her hands, but the sight of the whimsical painting nearly made her come undone.

Scrubbing her palm on her pantaloons did not erase the stubborn image. Averting her eyes, she tossed the notebook into her paintbox and snapped the lid shut.

If only it were so easy to lock away her own bruised heart.

Crystal clinked against silver. "You look as if you could use a drink," said Cameron, pouring out two generous measures of spirits and carrying them over to the hearth.

"I don't want brandy," muttered Gryff. "I want…"

He paused in mid-sentence, unsure of how to finish his thought. What *did* he want? An apology? That was rather hypocritical, considering how often he had bent Society's strictures on right and wrong. Maybe she didn't see her artistic deception as wrong—if the painting was exquisite, and the buyer took pleasure from it, what did it really matter who had created it?

A sticky philosophical question. However, he was in no mood to ponder abstract questions of morality.

"I want some answers about what Brighton is up to."

"Knowledge is a dangerous thing," answered Cameron, lifting the drink to his lips. Glints of fire-sparked gold winked off the faceted glass, a mocking reminder of Lady Brentford's sun-lit hair. "Are you sure that you haven't already learned enough?"

A grunt sounded in answer.

"I'm not sure whether to take that as a 'yes' or a 'no.'" Cameron took a long sip. "But if I might offer a word of advice, think about why you wish to pursue this, Gryff. Ask yourself what you are looking to gain." A pause. "Other than trouble."

"It's not about me," he snapped. *Or was it?* "Not entirely," he amended. "Yes, call it selfish, but I would like to see the project come to fruition. All questions of morality aside, Lady Brentford is an extraordinary artistic talent, and her illustrations add depth and beauty to my words. There is no doubt in my mind that the whole would be better than the two parts."

Cameron took another silent sip of his brandy.

"However, I'm talking about more than ink on paper. There is something about this that just…" Gryff placed his palms on the marble mantle and tapped a brusque tattoo. "…feels wrong."

His friend watched him intently for a long moment. "If you squeeze any harder on that stone, it will crack into a thousand little shards."

Gryff answered with a low oath.

"She has really gotten under your skin."

His hackles rose. "Bloody hell, Cam. From the moment I met her, I could sense a wariness in her—call it fear, if you will."

"A damsel in distress?"

He curled a fist. "I swear, if you laugh at her, I shall knock your teeth into your gullet."

"Seeing as I value my pearly smile, I'll not test your prowess." Cameron then eased the amusement from his tone. "Are you, perchance, in love with her?"

Love. Gryff drew in a deep breath, unsure of how to answer. "I—I'm not sure what to call it. All I know is that she is my friend, and needs my help."

"If you mean to pursue this, I'll see what I can find out about Brighton," replied Cameron. "But unfortunately, it will have to wait for a few days. I have a previous engagement that cannot be put off."

"Be assured, I'm not afraid of getting my paws dirty," said Gryff. "You are not the only one who can dig around for information. I have some sources I can turn to."

"The sort of things you wish to learn will not be common knowledge at any of your clubs."

"It may come as a surprise to you, Cam, but not all of my time is frittered away in gaming hells or boudoirs. My range of contacts may not be as extensive as yours, but a few of my acquaintances have less than lily-white hands," replied Gryff.

"I was not questioning your mettle, merely the means for deciding how to use it."

"I have an idea where to start looking. If that cur Brighton is threatening Lady Brentford, I'll pull out his claws, one by one."

"I don't doubt you would emerge victorious in a dog-fight." Cameron hesitated just a fraction before adding, "Just keep in mind that you may be barking up the wrong tree."

"Thank you for the warning. But I'm a little like a mastiff—once I have a bone between my teeth, I am loath to let go."

"Well, try not to choke on it."

Gryff gave a reluctant laugh. "You can make me eat my words if I end up looking like a gudgeon. But I don't think I will."

Cameron regarded him thoughtfully, a well-tended forefinger stroking absently at the dangling earring in his left lobe. This one was a dark Persian turquoise, set in gold. "Don't try to snout around the flash houses by yourself. You'll learn nothing without me, and may scare off any potential informers. Wait, and we'll make a trip together when I return."

"I don't suppose it would do any good to ask where you are going."

"Never mind," responded his friend. "Though I do plan to stop for a brief visit to Connor and his new bride." After a last little swirl of the amber-colored liquid, he set the glass down. "Lady K will no doubt find it vastly amusing that another Hellhound has been tamed by an unexpected female visitor to The Wolf's Lair."

"I wouldn't look quite so smug," warned Gryff. "The time may come when you meet your match."

Cameron dismissed the jibe with a sardonic laugh. "I think I can safely say that the odds of that happening are virtually nil."

"Stranger things have happened." *Like Connor becoming a goat farmer and me writing essays on landscape design.*

"Not many," drawled his friend. "I'd better be off. I need to be at Execution Dock at midnight."

"Watch your neck," counseled Gryff. "One of these days..."

"Watch your back," riposted Cam. "You did promise Connor you would stay out of trouble."

"The Lair is in capable hands. Assure the Wolfhound that there's no need to worry about the place. Sara doesn't need me to offer any guidance. She runs the place even more efficiently than he did."

"I think I'll let you pass on that message." A cocky salute and then Cameron was gone, leaving only a momentary glimmer of blue and gold lingering in the shadows.

"Trouble," muttered Gryff. "As if *I* am the only one of this flea-bitten trio to ever get himself into a scrape."

Chapter Eighteen

$\mathcal{A}$ flicker of lamplight shone though the window, its glow a beacon, guiding her to safe harbor in a storm.

Twisting her shawl tighter around her shoulders, Eliza hurried through the garden gate and knocked on the kitchen door. Through the glass panes, she saw Augustina put aside her sewing and rise from the table.

"It's me, Gussie," she called softly, and heard the bolt slide back. The sound seemed to release all her pent-up emotions, for at the first crack of light, she practically threw herself into the warm, sweet-scented air.

"Eliza!"

"I'm sorry for showing up at such an ungodly hour. I was planning to wait until tomorrow, b-b-but..." To her dismay, her lips were quivering too badly to go on.

Frail arms wrapped around her shoulders and pulled her close. "My dear, you know that you are welcome here at any hour."

Eliza sniffled, feeling all of eight years old again. "I—I didn't know where else to go, and I—I couldn't bear to be alone. So I saddled Boadicia and rode here to you."

"I should hope so! Now, sit down and let me fix you

some tea and a plate of walnut shortbread," ordered Augustina in her best don't-you-dare-disobey voice. "Then you can tell me all about it."

The familiar clatter helped calm her jangled nerves. Placing her hands face down on the waxed wood, Eliza let the steam and the scent of the cut lilacs in the earthenware jug by the stove envelop her in the sense of snug good cheer that pervaded the little cottage.

She had dreamed of having just such a setting, and now it seemed so impossibly out of reach. Tears welled up again.

"Drink this." Augustina added a splash from a small silver flask into the cup of tea. "It's for medicinal emergencies, and this appears to qualify."

"Arrggh." Eliza nearly gagged on the potent brew. "What is it?"

"The Scots call it *uisge-beatha*—or water of life. It helps cure any number of ills."

"If it doesn't kill you first."

"A dollop of honey will soften its punch." Augustina put a plate heaped with shortbread down beside the teacup. "Once you have fortified yourself with whisky and walnuts, we'll talk."

Walnuts. Eliza's lips began to quiver at the memory of Haddan's earthy kisses.

"Oh, dear. This must be serious indeed, if the mention of walnuts is bringing that look to your face."

Blinking back tears, she gulped down another swallow of the whisky-laced tea. "Oh, Gussie, after all your wise teachings, how is it that I've been such a bloody fool of late?"

Augustina reached over to squeeze her hand. "Come,

dry your eyes and tell me what's happened. I promise you, it won't seem half so bad when you share it with me."

Sniffs yielded to a watery smile. "Or it might seem twice as horrible when said aloud."

"Go ahead and spit it out," said her friend.

Eliza sucked in a deep breath and then let it out in a rush. "Haddan hates me!" she blurted out, letting her fears tumble out helter-pelter. "And now he thinks I'm a criminal as well as a strumpet. His friend must have found out...and...and it gets even worse."

"Worse?" murmured Augustina.

"Yes, much worse! I-it turns out that he's the author of those beautiful essays."

"Hmmph." A pensive pause. "So he's not only handsome as sin, but smart as the devil?" said her friend with a wry smile. "I should think that would be cause for dancing on the table, not crying into your teacup."

Sniff. "He hates me!" *Sniff.* "I saw it in his eyes. That's because of Brighton and his dastardly plan of art forgeries—oh, and the baronet wants me to marry him."

It was Augustina's turn to blink. Pulling a handkerchief from her apron pocket, she passed it over. "Blow your nose, my dear, and then let us start at the beginning and go through this a little more slowly."

Eliza explained about Harry's summons to London and the baronet's two-pronged proposal.

"The dastard," growled her friend. Her fingers curled around the butter knife. "As for Harry, his cods should be cut off. A brother should be protecting his sister from predators, not throwing her to the wolves."

"Yes, well, we both know I can't look to Harry for any help." Letting her shoulders slump, Eliza leaned forward and pressed her palms to her brow. "I feel as if I'm trapped between a rock wall and a slab of stone," she said in a small voice. "There seems no escape, Gussie. Any way I turn, I see only disaster looming."

A swirl of wind rattled the casement, and rain began to patter against the panes. "It's so confusing. Do I let Harry go to debtor's prison? Do I let Leete Abbey and all the people who depend on me sink into ruin? Do I accept Brighton's odious offer and hope that he doesn't crush me like a bug?" In the quiet of the kitchen, the drops sounded like bullets ricocheting off the glass. "I can't even decide which is the lesser of all the evils."

"We'll find a way out of this crevasse," said Augustina stoutly, but her face betrayed a shade of worry. "But before we turn to that, tell me how Haddan fits into all this."

Eliza explained about the meeting in Grosvenor Square, and how the marquess had come to Leete Abbey earlier that afternoon.

Her friend caught the faint flash of color as she lowered her hands from her face. "What's that on your palm?"

"A dragon," she admitted.

"Ah. I take it that songbirds were not the only winged creatures fluttering in the sunshine of your garden."

Her cheeks grew uncomfortably warm. "I seem to throw all common sense to the wind when I am around him."

"I can't say that I blame you, my dear," quipped Augustina. "He is a *very* attractive man."

"Yes, and I couldn't resist temptation," said Eliza with a hollow laugh. "So now I find myself cast out of my little Garden of Eden—in a manner of speaking. It was actually Haddan who left in a rush, and on thinking back over his curt comment on painting, I fear it's because he learned of my sin."

"It's Brighton who has sinned, my dear, not you," objected Augustina.

"But in Haddan's eyes, I'm painted with the same tainted brush as the baronet," she pointed out. "And that is how everyone will see it."

To which her friend had no reply.

"It's awfully ironic that I should discover we have more in common than physical lust," went on Eliza, trying to keep her voice from cracking. "Haddan and I share an appreciation of nature." She bit her lip. "But that doesn't really matter anymore."

"You don't know that," insisted Augustina. "From what you described, Haddan's bad news could have been unrelated to you. 'Enjoy your painting' could have meant...enjoy your painting."

"Oh, I know it was me," said Eliza, recalling the shadows that darkened the green-gold gaze. "And 'enjoy your painting' had a darker meaning. I saw it in his eyes. Whatever he learned, it was very personal." She stared at her hands, unable to keep from thinking what they had been doing earlier that day. "Now that I know he is the author of the essays, I would guess he feels he's been tricked into buying tainted goods."

"Well then, we simply have to show him he's wrong."

"I don't know how." Eliza heard the hollow echo of defeat in her tone. It wasn't like her to surrender without a fight, but at the moment, she just wanted to crawl under the table. "Oh, Gussie, I'm feeling a little desperate. It seems to me that the only way to get out of this chasm is to do something drastic." *Something dangerous.*

"There is no need to panic yet," counseled Augustina. "We will think of something."

She didn't argue, but the reality of it was that things looked very grim. The ride over had provided plenty of time to ponder every possibility. At first, the idea of simply packing up and heading north to lose herself in the Lake District seemed a viable solution. But without Haddan's commission, she didn't have the funds to purchase a cottage. Worse, if scandal darkened her name with Watkins and the other London publishers—an all too likely possibility—she would have no future way of earning a living.

Destitute. She would be destitute, penniless and disgraced. Gussie would offer shelter, but the idea of being a burden on her friend's limited finances was...unbearable.

Looking up, Eliza found Augustina watching her with a troubled look. "Perhaps I will have to consider Brighton's proposal," she said slowly. "How bad can it be?"

Her friend reached for the whisky and took a small sip straight from the flask. "How can you ask that? You've already endured a forced marriage to a man you did not love or respect."

"Yes," said Eliza. "And I survived."

"Hmmph! Marry that miscreant? Over my dead body!"

Eliza smiled in spite of her worries. "Oh, Gussie, what a fierce dragon you are! I am very grateful that you are willing to fly to my defense, snorting smoke and breathing fire. However, I refuse to let you risk being singed by my family's scandal."

"If anyone is going to get burned, it is Brighton," said her friend resolutely. "So let us put our heads together."

* * *

"Lord Haddan!" Watkins looked up in surprise from his morning tea. "Er, if you have come to inquire about whether Linden has sent any finished artwork, the answer is not yet. I only passed on the first set of final essays a few days ago."

"No, I didn't come to ask about Lady Brentford's progress on the paintings." Gryff took a seat facing the publisher's desk and waited for him to finishing mopping the splash of tea from his blotter. "I have some other queries, if you don't mind."

The publisher's face had turned a touch ashen. "Milord, please understand that I—"

Gryff silenced him with a curt wave. "Nor did I come here to rake you over the coals about keeping her identity a secret. I can hardly complain about your integrity in honoring a confidence."

Watkins blew on his burned fingers, looking visibly relieved. "How did you come to discover her secret?"

"Never mind," Gryff answered, more curtly than he intended. Tapping his fingertips together, he looked around, trying to decide how to begin. He had come here intending to probe more into Eliza's character. But what had seemed like a good idea in the sleepless hours just before dawn now took on a different light.

Outright questions on whether she was capable of committing a forgery would cast a pall of suspicion over her, whether she was guilty or not. To blacken her name would be not only unfair, but also ungentlemanly.

Damnation, Cameron was right—he hadn't a clue as to how to conduct a discreet investigation.

"I trust that there is no problem with the sex of the artist?" asked Watkins hesitantly.

Sex. Gryff snapped to attention.

"That is, the fact that Linden is a female," amended the publisher.

"I—I haven't decided," he muttered, aware that he was making a hash of this. He stood up, and put on his hat. "Thank you for your time."

"Milord..."

Gryff paused, his hand on the latch.

"I hope very much you will give the matter careful consideration, and not hold it against her that she isn't a man." Watkins spoke very slowly, choosing his words with care. "It is not my place to speak of her personal life, but it is my impression that she is caught in a very difficult family situation. Not that she breathes a word of complaint. In spite of that, she is unfailingly reliable." A cough. "I hold her in the highest regard."

"Thank you, Mr. Watkins," muttered Gryff. The statement stirred a fresh wave of guilt for believing the worst of her without asking for an explanation. Without further word, he left the shop and turned west heading for Bond Street, determined to do better at his next stop.

Footsteps crunched along the narrow pathway leading around the cottage.

"Ah, thought I might find you here, 'Liza." Harry swatted a vine of climbing roses out of his way and walked unsteadily into Augustina's back garden. His face was flushed and the cocked brim of his stylish beaver hat showed a forehead sheened in sweat.

"You're foxed," said Eliza flatly, and went back to watering the potted herbs.

"'M not," he protested. "An' even if I was, it's no business of y'rs."

It was a good thing Gussie was in the shed. Otherwise, her brother would have blistered ears to go with a bilious stomach.

She, too, felt like breathing fire and brimstone, but instead, she simply asked, "What do you want?"

Harry stretched his mouth in a sickly imitation of a smile. "I need t' have a word with you. In private."

"We *are* in private, Harry. Gussie went to fetch her pruning shears and watering can, so you can speak freely." Not that he would make any coherent sense.

"The thing is, I need y' t' come back to London with me. Today."

"I can't," she snapped. "Unlike you, I don't have quarters at a fashionable hotel, or a fancy curricle at my beck and call."

"You always stay with Margaret, and she's happy t' have you anytime," he whined. "Especially now, with her husband on a diplomatic mission t' St. Petersburg."

"Yes, I'm fortunate to have such a generous childhood friend. But of late I've been abusing the privilege. I can't just keep showing up on her doorstep and imposing on her generosity whenever I choose."

Harry's expression turned mulish. "But this is important."

"It always is." Breaking off a few spiky leaves of rosemary, she crumbled them between her fingers and inhaled the soothing fragrance. "Tomorrow, perhaps."

The concession suited her own plans. It had taken a long discussion late into the night—along with a few fibs—to convince her friend that there was no need to spring into action quite yet.

Dear, determined Augustina. The elderly spinster had

been all for picking up a poker and banging her way into Brighton's townhouse, demanding the return of the copied painting. She had reluctantly agreed to give Eliza a few days to make some inquiries in London... supposedly with Watkins, about the possibility of other art commissions.

But the real reason was to...

"What's keeping you, Leete?"

Eliza felt her insides clench. She now knew why her brother was so nervous. Turning, she saw Brighton's odious cousin, Mr. Pearce, saunter past the trellis.

"Really, Eliza, you ought to be wearing a bonnet out here in the sun," he said. "Spots are so unfashionable on a lady, but then, you have always been eccentric in your habits."

"Please refrain from using my given name, sir. There is no connection between us that allows such intimacy," she replied coldly, deliberately raising her chin a notch.

"Ah, but we are about to be family," he sneered. His crop flicked against Harry's shoulder. "Go see to the horses, Leete. I wish to have chat with your charming sister."

Her brother slunk away.

Pearce darted a quick look around the garden, then took a step closer.

Eliza calmly took up a pruning knife from her basket.

His eyes glittered with malice as they swung around to meet hers. "As I recall, you were awfully sharp-tongued the last time we met."

"I'm surprised you remember the encounter, given your state of drunkenness."

"Oh, I remember, Eliza," he said softly.

"What do you want?" She began cutting a bouquet of lavender to keep him from seeing the tremoring of her hands.

Pearce shifted his stance, throwing her into shadow. "I suggest you start being nicer to me, Eliza. Cousin Reggie and I are good friends. We share a good many of our possessions with each other—horses, curricles, walking sticks." He was enjoying himself. "If you take my meaning."

She didn't give him the satisfaction of an answer.

"And speaking of sharing..." His voice dropped a notch. "Reggie and I also are partners in that profitable little business he mentioned to you. We've just acquired another rare painting that needs copying, so I suggest you don't dally with your decision to become Lady Brighton."

"I've been wondering something," said Eliza, making herself focus on gathering information, rather than react to his taunting innuendos. "Why does your cousin insist on the charade of marriage? Blackmailing me with Harry's debts seems a sufficient threat to make me do your bidding."

Pearce's smirk stretched wider. "A wife cannot give testimony against a husband."

"I see you have thought this through." *Good God, the two of them really were slimier than garden slugs.* "Well, so have I." Eliza forced a show of confidence, though her insides were quaking. "So I have a proposal for you and your cousin to consider. For the sake of keeping Leete Abbey and my brother from utter ruin, I am considering the idea of aiding and abetting your criminal activities. But the only way I will say yes is if your cousin drops the demand of marriage. That I will never consent to."

"You are in no position to bargain," said Pearce.

"No? Then go ahead and find yourself another artist."

His eyes narrowed. "Picture this, Eliza. With no money, the servants would leave, the larders would empty. Leete Abbey would become an abandoned ruin. You would soon find yourself out on the street, and with your brother's disgrace and rumors of your own misdeeds swirling through the *ton*, what would you do to survive, heh?" He let out a nasty laugh. "Sell your scrawny body?"

"I am not so helpless as you think."

Pearce gave long, leisurely look around. "This is a pretty little place. But alas, these old cottages can so easily go up in flames. I doubt that a decrepit little spinster living on a tiny annuity would find it easy to recover from such a disaster."

The depth of the pair's depravity was truly frightening.

A wave of nausea churned in her stomach. Choking down the sour sting of bile, Eliza steadied herself against earthenware planters. "You like to play rough, don't you."

"The sooner you understand that, the better." Pearce smoothed the cuff of his expensive glove. "As long as you cooperate, things will go easy for you. Indeed, you might even come to enjoy the arrangement."

This had, she knew, nothing to do with desiring her body. It was all about breaking her spirit.

Clenching her teeth to keep from retorting, Eliza busied herself with putting the cut lavender in a jar of water until she had composed herself enough to speak. "You have made yourself perfectly clear, sir. I will give your cousin my answer shortly."

He looked about to say more when Augustina rounded

the corner, her arms filled with flowerpots. "I didn't realize we had company," she said, fixing their visitor with an
unfriendly squint.

"Mr. Pearce was just leaving," said Eliza softly.

His mouth thinned, but after a moment's hesitation, he
touched the brim of his hat. "Good day, Eliza. We'll speak
again soon."

"What did that smarmy man want?" asked her friend,
watching the tails of his coat disappear behind the bushes.

"To annoy me," she answered tightly. Filling her lungs
with the scent of the herbs, Eliza stared at the pale purple
hue of the flowers, reminding herself of their unspoken
message. *Be calm.*

"Pay him no heed, Gussie."

Tools clinked and clattered as her friend began arrang-
ing them on the potting bench.

Despite the heat and the healing properties of the
plants, a deathly chill began creeping up her arms, turning
her blood to ice.

"My dear, are you all right?" Augustina's voice
sounded very distant. "You look as if you are going to
faint."

Eliza shaded her eyes. "Mr. Pearce was right—I should
be wearing a bonnet. The sun must be too strong for my
head. Excuse me for a moment while I go inside for a
glass of water."

"G'day, milord." The towelman bobbed his head in greeting. "Looking fer a match? Ain't yer regular day, but I
may be able te find ye a skilled enough partner."

"Actually, I stopped by to see you, Georgie," answered
Gryff. Here, at Gentleman Jackson's Boxing Saloon, he

felt on firmer ground than at Watkins & Harold. Over the last few years, he had developed an easy rapport with the hired help. The men who worked there tending the leather bags, cleaning the changing rooms, and supervising the sparring were all former pugilists, willing to let their guard down for a lord who was generous with his bawdy jests and free rounds of porter at the nearby alehouse.

Lowering his voice, Gryff asked, "Are you and your friends interested in making a bit of blunt on the side?"

Georgie's expression sharpened. "Does a right cross to the kidney hurt like bleeding hell?"

He smiled. "Excellent. Let's go somewhere a bit more private to talk, shall we?"

A twitch of the ex-boxer's broad jaw indicated an alcove near the far corner of the saloon. "I was jest about te go fold the towels, sir."

Gryff followed along into a narrow nook behind a storage cabinet. The still air was rife with the smells of lye and soap and sweat.

Muscles rippled as Georgie cracked his massive knuckles. "Need a few heads bashed, milord?"

"Perhaps," answered Gryff. "But to decide that, I first need to gather a bit of information about the fellow in question."

"Who?"

"Brighton."

The towelman spit on the floor. "Clutch-fisted bastards, both him and that smarmy cousin he hangs around with. Thick as thieves, they are. Unlike you, sir, they never leave a farthing for us hard-working coves."

"Yes well, Brighton's not only a nipcheese, but I have

reason to suspect that he's putting the thumbscrews on a friend of mine."

On the walk over from the publisher's office, Gryff had been mulling over the situation. Watkins, a man of sound common sense, had an intuitive faith in Lady Brentford's character. And despite all the evidence to the contrary, he simply could not imagine her being involved in any criminal activity, especially one involving art. Her love of the medium was too honest, too joyous. She would never disrespect it in such a sordid way.

And yet Cameron had a discerning eye, and would not make allegations lightly.

There was only one explanation that could reconcile the conflicting facts—Lady Brentford was working under duress.

"Oy." Georgie spat again. "I don't much like it when someone tries te bully one of me friends."

"Neither do I." Gryff took a small purse out of his pocket, the *chink* of gold making a heavier sound than copper. "I imagine you know a few people who are privy to what's going on in the flash houses in Town."

Georgie's eyes widened as the money plopped into his hand. "Aye, milord. That I do." He caressed the soft leather. "And with this to grease a few palms, I should be able te learn whatever ye need."

"I want to know what rig Brighton is running," replied Gryff. "Quickly, but discreetly. I'd prefer he have no inkling that anyone is making inquiries into his activities."

The towelman touched a finger to the side of his mashed nose. "Don't ye worry, sir. I'll keep it silent as the grave."

"Excellent. There will be more for you and your friends when you're done."

"This be plenty, milord. I don't want te pick yer pocket. Not when yer already so free in spending yer blunt on the likes of us."

"Don't worry, I'll consider it money well spent." Gryff patted him on the shoulder. "You know my direction. Send word to my townhouse as soon as you know something."

The purse jingled as Georgie fisted his fingers. "Don't ye worry, sir. Ye won't have long te wait."

Chapter Nineteen

The ooze of decay rose up from the river in thick curls of dirty gray fog. Eliza hunched deeper into the seat of the carriage, wincing with every *clip-clop* of hooves upon the bridge. The sounds struck her as a funeral dirge of sorts. Indeed, it felt like her spirit was crossing the River Styx, moving out of the land of the living and into a world of gloomy shadows where the dead floated in ageless lament for their sins.

"And there's no doubt that I have sinned," she whispered.

Strange though, she didn't feel as if her soul had shriveled and died. Despite the surrounding darkness, her lovemaking with Haddan was a small, bright flame, a flicker of warmth that she kept alight in her heart.

Even though his opinion of her had turned black and cold as yesterday's embers. A visit to Mr. Watkins had confirmed that the marquess was aware of her identity. The publisher had also admitted that the book project was in jeopardy, for Haddan had appeared angry and undecided about whether to continue.

The marquess's change in heart was not hard to pin

down. His friend must have heard something about Brighton's plan. Men talked among themselves—perhaps even more than women—especially while they were in their cups.

"We're here, madam," called the driver from his perch, his voice muffled by the inky gloom. His boots scraped against the footboard and the butt of his whip knocked against the seat. "I'll wait for you here."

Thank God for her stalwart friend Margaret, who provided a coachman and horses without any questions. Had she been asked to explain her mission, Eliza would have had a hard time putting her thoughts into words. "That's because I ought to be taking myself to Bedlam, instead of a brothel," she murmured wryly, gingerly setting a foot down in the foul-smelling mud. "Clearly my wits have wandered to the very edge of dangerous delusions."

The alleyway was deserted, the impenetrable shadows still and silent. Hurrying across the short distance to the iron-banded door, Eliza mustered her flagging resolve and knocked with more authority than she felt.

If ever a foray could be described as a fool's errand.

The beefy porter gave her an unfriendly look and reluctantly ushered her down a dimly lit corridor and into the same small back office where she had been sequestered on her previous visit to The Wolf's Lair.

"Wait here," he growled.

Eliza pushed back the hood of her cloak and shuffled her feet, breathing in and out as she watched the flames of the sconce candles undulate in the draft from the door. The red-tinged light played over the erotic etching, teasing her thoughts to an unwilling recollection of her first encounter here with Haddan.

He had jested about the oversized phalluses, the inventive positions. And then he had pressed a gossamer kiss to a spot of bare skin just above her glove...

Rubbing at her wrist, Eliza quickly moved away to the sideboard. The Redouté rose was nowhere to be seen. Miss Hawkins must have taken the advice to sell it.

A wise decision. In any language—secret, silent, or spoken aloud—love was a very uncomfortable sentiment.

She blinked. *Love.* Oh yes, love hurt. Like the thorns of a rose, it could prick painfully into the flesh. But of course, it could also be softly sensual, like the touch of a velvety petal or the whiff of an ethereal sweetness. Perhaps the contradiction was part of its allure.

Love. What an odd place to be thinking about the subject. So far, she had managed to avoid delving too deeply into her feelings. What she had experienced with Haddan was lust, pure and simple. Their bodies had coupled for a fleeting interlude, and then come apart to go their separate ways...

"Lady Brentford." Sara Hawkins closed the door quietly behind her. "If you are looking for your brother, I can tell you he's not here tonight. Indeed, I haven't seen him for the last week or so."

"No, I'm not looking for Harry," she replied. "I—I was actually hoping that I might have a word with you."

"Of course." Sara gestured to one of the chairs by the desk. "Shall we sit? If ye don't mind me saying so, ye are looking a little shaky on your pegs."

"I suppose my knees are knocking just a bit. It isn't every day that I enter an establishment like this one."

Sara chuckled. "I should hope not."

Eliza's fists clenched even tighter in her lap. "H-how do your girls come to you?" she stammered, not daring to look up from her whitening knuckles.

The sound of amusement stopped abruptly.

"And h-how m-much can they make a week at a place like The Wolf's Lair? I—I have heard that men are willing to pay a high price for pleasure at the most exclusive places in Town."

Sara allowed only the tiniest flicker of surprise before masking her reaction with a quick cough. But Eliza had a great deal of experience in watching facial expressions. What she saw was enough to make her wish she could sink through the floorboards. *What madness had made her come here?*

"Ye can't be thinking of seeking employment here, Lady Brentford," said Sara gently.

No, of course not—it was a ludicrous idea. Eliza looked away. "I know I'm not pretty—"

"Now wait a tic. Ye think yer not pretty?" exclaimed Sara.

"I *know* I'm not pretty."

"Ha! Take my word fer it, you've got the type of looks that drive a man wild."

Eliza opened her mouth to protest.

"No, hear me out. First of all, physical appearance isn't what makes a woman desirable. Look at me—I'm no raving beauty, but I had gentlemen fighting fer my favors. And ye want to know why?"

Eliza nodded. "I . . . Yes, very much so."

"Gentlemen like . . . well, Lord Haddan calls it spirit—a girl's inner spark that lights up her whole being. It's hard te describe, but it's wot makes a man want te be around her, ye know? They aren't just looking te have their pump handles diddled. They like te talk. Te laugh."

"Oh." Eliza stared thoughtfully at the lamp flame's sinuous dance.

"Ye got fire, Lady Brentford. In spades."

Her mouth quirked. "Is that a good thing?"

"Very," Sara assured her.

"Then why can't I work here?"

Sara rose and moved to the sideboard, where she uncorked a decanter and poured two measures of sherry. "Look, we are both practical females," she answered, once she had set down a glass in front of Eliza. "Te be frank, even if I was tempted te let ye ruin yer reputation, such a move would be very bad fer my own business. Men would find it horribly uncomfortable te be around a lady of their own class—someone who might be their own sister. They would go somewhere else."

After pondering Sara's words for several long sips of the wine, Eliza let out a long sigh. "I see your point." She swirled her wine, and its spinning seemed to suck her deeper into confusion. "But the trouble is I need money. Lots of it. You are clearly a good businesswoman. Have you any ideas what I might try, other than shackle myself to a lifetime of crime—which at this point seems my only choice?"

Sara smoothed her skirts. "Ye had best start at the beginning, and tell me all about it."

Eliza haltingly explained about her brother's debts, her own hard-fought struggle to save enough for her dream of independence, and Brighton's terrible ultimatum. "I won't marry him, of course. I'd rather starve in the streets. But I thought that if I could find lucrative employment, I could pay off Harry's debts and salvage something of the family reputation by keeping him out of debtor's prison. I have half the funds from my artistic endeavors, and I figured Brighton would accept the rest in installments, if you will. It's that or nothing, and given the baronet's greed, it seems likely he would agree to the terms." She let out a sigh. "And then perhaps I can start saving again for that little cottage in the Lake District."

"I can see you have thought this out very carefully," said Sara slowly. "But unfortunately the question of, er, wages is not quite so simple. Ye see, without dipping into a great deal of detail, there is a wide range of positions within the demimonde, as well as a wide range of remunerations."

Eliza inched forward in her chair. "I suspected as much, but to tell the truth, I am not as clear as I should be on the differences."

"I shan't describe the most primitive parts of the business—I daresay you can imagine that on your own. Let's just say that the girls here are well cared for and make a decent living. But only the most expensive courtesan could aspire to make the sort of sum you mentioned."

"A courtesan?" repeated Eliza. The evening was proving educational, if not a financial success.

"A *cher ami*, a ladybird high flyer, who has a single protector," said Sara. Seeing Eliza's questioning look, she blew out a small sigh and went on. "It works like this—a gentleman offers such a female a slip on the shoulder. That is, he sets her up in a snug little house, pays for servants, showers her with fancy clothes and baubles. In return, she entertains him. Exclusively, if ye get my meaning."

"I see." Eliza pursed her lips. "So courtesans are the aristocracy of the lightskirts."

"Aye, that's a good way of putting it. And it takes a rich man to afford the best."

She twitched at the hem of her glove, thinking back to a lordly smile gilded in the smoky lamplight. "I imagine a gentleman like the Marquess of Haddan has a finely feathered friend tucked away in some love nest."

Sara's brows pinched together. "Haddan? No, actually he doesn't." A soft laugh stirred the shadows around them. "I suppose the Deerhound was always too busy running to and fro in Town. Chasing the does, ye see." She set her glass down. "Though in truth, he was never quite as much of a Hellhound as the gossipmongers made out. Beneath the rakish reputation, he's always had a heart o' gold. His quiet acts of kindness fer the girls here aren't talked about in those fancy newspapers. They just want to report on the scandals." She tapped meditatively on the table. "And even those have died down. Of late, he seems to have tired of all that. He says that he's grown older and wiser."

Eliza looked away, hoping to swallow the lump in her throat without making a complete fool of herself by sniveling.

Sara sat in sympathetic silence, letting the low flicker of flame and shadow dance across the walls, until Eliza composed herself enough to quirk a wry smile. "Would that age automatically brought wisdom. Unfortunately, it feels as if my thinking has been growing more muddled by the minute. Please forgive me for coming here and taking up your time."

"I'm sorry te disappoint ye, Lady Brentford, but the truth is, lifting yer skirts ain't going to earn ye the blunt yer looking for." She paused. "For what ye've told me, I gather that ye possess special talents as an artist. Is there no way to use them to earn the funds ye need—legally, of course?"

Eliza shook her head, seeing no point in mentioning Haddan's book commission. The afternoon visit to Mr. Watkins had all but confirmed that the project would never make it to paper and ink. The marquess had been gentlemanly enough to imply it was because of her sex rather than her criminal activities.

"There are not many opportunities for a female. My publisher is one of the enlightened few, but even though my work garners accolades, I have to hide my real identity with a pen name."

"How unfair. Ye ought te be recognized for yer talents."

"When males make the rules, it's not likely to happen."

Sara sniffed. "Ain't *that* the truth."

"In any case, my book illustrations mostly earn only modest amounts. And now, even that outlet is closed to me," explained Eliza. "I cannot ask my publisher to suffer if I am plunged into scandal, so it would be wrong to ask for future work." She cupped her glass, wishing the heat of the wine could seep through her skin. "There must be a way to keep my dream of happiness alive. I just have to be clever enough to find it."

"Let me think on it." Sara raised her glass in salute. "Te happiness. And te the girls who dare to dream that it's within their grasp, if only they are brave enough to reach fer it."

The clink of crystal rose above the crackling of the coals.

"Thank you," said Eliza. She rose and refastened her cloak, suddenly feeling ashamed at the pettiness of her own problems. The other woman probably dealt with far grimmer situations every day. *Life, death.* Real sufferings. And here she was, mooning over a bruised heart.

"Once again you have been kind—more than kind—in seeing me," she added.

"Ye have a place te stay tonight?" asked Sara.

"Yes, a dear friend from childhood has been generous enough to offer me quarters when I come to London. Her husband is away on a diplomatic mission, so she claims my company is most welcome. However, I hate to impose on her generosity more than I have to. I will return to the country tomorrow, and well..." Her sigh blew out the closest candle. "Somehow I shall figure out how to go on from there."

"If ye need a bit of blunt...," Sara offered.

Eliza smiled. "You are truly kind, Miss Hawkins—"

"Oh, please call me Sara. All me friends do."

"Sara, then." The name came very easily to her tongue. "You are very kind, but for the moment I have enough to manage."

"Very well. But if that changes, don't hesitate te come here and ask fer help. Despite its outward appearance, The Wolf's Lair is always a safe haven fer females in trouble."

"Thank you." Eliza moved to the door. "Please don't bother to summon your porter from his duties. I shall see myself out."

Keeping close to the dark wainscoting, Eliza made her way down the corridor, grateful that this part of the Lair was deserted. A curl of gunmetal gray smoke wafted overhead, the only other flutter of movement, save for her own skirling skirts.

"Thank God, I've no witness to my folly," she whispered—and then bit her tongue as the private entrance opened to admit a figure.

Flattening herself against the wall, she turned up her hood and prayed that her presence would go unnoticed.

Bootsteps thudded over the Turkey runner, hurried paces that echoed the pounding of her heart.

Shrouded in shadows, the approaching shape was naught but an indistinct blur of long legs, flapping coat, broad shoulders, tall-crowned hat…*A male.* That much was clear just before Eliza squeezed her eyes shut and offered up a silent prayer.

Keep going, keep going.

The thuds grew louder, louder, and then it seemed that the danger was about to pass. However in the next instant the steps came to an abrupt stop.

She burrowed her head deeper into the folds of the fabric.

"Lady Brentford?"

She didn't reply.

"What in the name of Hades are you doing here?"

There was no use pretending to be a turtle. Squaring her shoulders, Eliza decided to hide her humiliation by brazening it out. "Actually, I was looking for employment, Lord Haddan. Since my art commission has fallen through, I must have some other means of making enough money to survive."

Gryff's mouth thinned to a hard line. "If that is meant as a jest, it's not amusing."

"Basic food and shelter is no laughing matter, sir," she said quietly. "Try going without them."

Limned in the uncertain light, his profile seemed to soften. Shifting his weight from foot to foot, he cleared his throat with a tentative cough. "If you are in need of funds, Lady Brentford—"

"Payment for past services?" Her chin rose, stirring a tiny breath of air. "Thank you, but I'll cling to what little remnant of pride I have left and refuse the offer, generous though it may be."

"I—I did not mean…"

"To insult my integrity? Of course not. According to you, I have none."

She made to pass him, but he moved to block her path.

"Lady Brentford, if I might have a word…"

"Oh, please, sir." Eliza was suddenly finding it hard to breathe. All she wanted to do was escape from the suffocating shadows and all-too-familiar scent of his bay rum cologne. Choking back tears, she angled away from his big, warm body. "I don't see that we have anything to discuss. Indeed, I think we've probably said too much to each other as it is. I have been to see Mr. Watkins and understand that our partnership is at an end. Let us leave it at that."

Gryff hesitated, just enough to let her squeeze by. Quickening her steps to a near run, Eliza fled.

"*Men.*" Sara looked up from her ledger with a scowl as Gryff entered the office. "I swear, women ought to be allowed to run the world fer a change. You all don't deserve te make the rules."

"What new injury or insult has prompted your ire?"

Removing his hat, he ran a hand through his hair and took a seat by the desk.

"Oh, don't ask," muttered Sara, reaching for her sherry.

He watched the candlelight spark through the tawny wine, and waited for her to go on. She was usually garrulous to a fault. But for once, silence seemed to squeeze off further comment. Sara merely sipped, a pensive frown wrinkling her brow.

Gryff crossed and recrossed his legs, then rose again and went to cabinet to pour himself a measure of her special Scottish malt. Its fire hit his belly with a welcome jolt, but the heat quickly dissipated, leaving his insides still caught in a cold clench.

The scuff of his pacing finally roused Sara from her brooding. "Any reason ye are as jumpy as a cat on a hot griddle?" she murmured.

"Don't ask," he muttered.

A brow flicked up, yet to his dismay she respected his request.

Damn, damn, damn. How to broach the subject of Lady Brentford's mysterious visit was proving devilishly difficult. *Women*, he thought, mentally echoing her earlier exasperation. Perhaps he should have sought sanctuary in a monastery rather than a brothel.

"Hmmm." Sara finally made another sound. "I wonder…"

Gryff swung around from his study of the etching.

Her mouth pursed. "Yer rich, right?"

"Yes," he answered.

"How rich?"

"Very."

"Hmmm." The pencilpoint drummed lightly against the open page of the ledger, leaving a trail of tiny smudges.

"Hell and damnation, Sara," he growled. "If you are in need of money, just ask."

"It's *not* fer me," she said somewhat defensively. "The fact is, what with the changes I've made in the taproom, I'm making even more blunt than the Wolfhound. However..." She shook her head. "No, no, never mind. It was just a thought, but I fear it's not a very good one." The last of the sherry disappeared in a quick swallow. "Not that the one I heard earlier was any better."

He carefully set down his glass. "What was Lady Brentford doing here?"

"Oh, ye remember her?"

However fond he was of his old friend, there were times when he wanted to pick her up by her shapely shoulders and shake her until her teeth rattled.

"Yes, I remember her," Gryff replied through gritted teeth. "Now would you kindly answer my question."

"No need to bite my head off." Cocking her head, she fixed him with a look that seemed to strip away his expensive clothing and expose every damnable flaw to the glare of the candle flames.

"Sara," he prodded.

"Oh, very well." A terse laugh trailed off in a sigh. "Lady Brentford came to inquire about how much money a gel could hope to make at a place like The Wolf's Lair."

Gryff suddenly felt a wave of nausea churn in his gut. He had thought her sardonic answer about seeking employment had been merely a cutting quip, a sarcastic retort. Bracing a hip on the sideboard, he drew in a shallow breath. "Good God, what would make her so desperate?"

"Men," answered Sara grimly. "Men who seek to twist her talents to their own terrible advantage, to destroy her dreams for their own bloody selfish gain, to break her spirit for their own evil amusement."

"How so," he asked in a tight whisper.

"Her brother—who, by the by, ought to be boiled in hot oil—has made a deal with the Devil in order to save his own worthless carcass. He owes a fortune in gaming debts to a pair of scoundrels, Brighton and Pearce. And so he is seeking to force her into helping them with some sort of havey-cavey enterprise involving art."

Gryff straightened.

"And apparently marriage to Brighton is part of the bargain, seeing as a wife can't give testimony against her husband."

He sat down again with an audible thud.

"Yer looking a little queasy, milord. Would ye rather pour yerself a tipple of brandy instead of whisky? Spotted Dick just delivered a very fine vintage that he smuggled in from France."

"What I would like," said Gryff slowly, "is to squeeze every last drop of Brighton's lifeblood from his body. Preferably with my bare hands."

"A rather strong reaction." Sara studied him through half-lowered lashes. "Given that the lady is a near-stranger."

"Hold your teasing until later, if you please." Gryff tapped a fist to his palm. "Tell me everything that she said." That he had never asked her about her dreams made his gut twist in a tighter knot. "Everything."

"Ye going te go slay her dragon?"

Gryff winced at the word "dragon." "Let us just say that I intend to fight fire with fire."

The candles seemed to perk up and dance a little brighter.

"Well, she said she intends to return to Leete Abbey on the morrow..."

Chapter Twenty

No." Eliza folded her arms across her chest. "And that is final."

Augustina punched the dough into a ball, then started shaping it into a flattened disc. "I don't see why not. Just because I am older than the hills doesn't mean I can't be moved from one spot to another without withering on the vine."

"It's not a question of your resilience, Gussie. I'll not have you uprooted from friends and familiar surroundings," she answered. "Not when I'm going to be floating like dandelion fluff on the wind, waiting to see where the fickle gusts drop me."

"That's all the more reason for not flying off on your own," countered her friend.

Eliza blew out her cheeks, touched by her friend's stalwart sense of loyalty, but determined to keep her out of harm's way. She had said nothing about Pearce's ugly threat, knowing that it would only spark Augustina's feisty resolve to stand up to the bullies. By heading north, far, far away from her friend's little thatched cottage, she hoped to draw any danger away from her. With luck, she would lose herself in the windswept hills and valleys of Lancaster. Start a new life.

Hell's bells. I've made a muck of the one I have now.

"Please, I—I just want some time on my own," she answered. "Alone, without company, to figure out what I want."

A fine cloud of flour flew up as Augustina dusted her hands and set the shortbread in the oven to bake. A breeze from the open window filled her skirts, and with the delicate powdering of her silvery hair, she looked like a figurine from the last century. Frail, fragile. "If that is what you wish, then of course I shall say no more." The smile belied the hurt in her eyes.

Secrets, misunderstandings, half-truths. No wonder the only friendships that mattered had been twisted into knots.

Eliza looked away, afraid she might break down and admit that the last thing she wanted was to be alone. "Once I'm settled, you can come visit," she said lamely, knowing it would not assuage her friend's bruised feelings.

"Of course." Augustina began a methodical tidying up of the kitchen. Pots banged, crocks thumped, giving voice to the discordant mood that had settled over the room. "Still, I cannot help but ask how you are going to journey north on your own. It is not proper for a lone female of gentle birth to travel by mail coach unaccompanied."

"From now on, I do not plan to stand on ceremony. A governess or housekeeper may make a trip by herself and still be considered respectable. I consider myself to be in the same position—a female who must work for her bread." Eliza picked up the tea tray and carried it to the pantry. "I would much prefer my freedom to living in gilded captivity." Marriage to Brighton would keep her confined to a cage. She had seen the poor lion at the Tower menagerie. Even a lordly beast could have its spirit broken by an interminable existence spent locked behind bars.

Grumbling under her breath, Augustina set down a saucer of cream.

"But in this instance, I did decide to go out in style," she added.

Mouse, the marmalade kitten, scampered out from behind the cupboard. Close on his tail came Elf, his claws scrabbling over the planks as he raced to catch up. Augustina had offered to care for him until she was settled.

"I will be riding in a private carriage, hired to take me as far as Birmingham."

Her friend looked up from the twitching tails. "It is, I know, a large expense, especially when you won't let me add to your purse. But I am relieved to hear it."

Eliza allowed a ghost of a grin. "Don't worry about the money. I decided to give myself a goodbye present, courtesy of Harry. He left that showy chestnut hunter in the stables, the one that Squire Twining has been coveting for last month. So I sold it at a very fair price. Both of us are extremely happy." A pause. "I can't say the same for Harry when he finds out."

A hoot of laughter greeted the news. "What's sauce for the goose is sauce for the gander," said Augustina. "For once, let him stew in his own juices."

Meow. The two cats batted at the empty saucer, sending it skidding across the floor.

"Yes, a celebration is definitely in order!" exclaimed

Augustina. After righting the dish and refilling the cream she took down her flask of medicinal whisky and poured them both a thimbleful.

The clink of glasses dispelled the unsettled air. Like a summer squall, the tension seemed to blow itself out, leaving a clean rain-washing freshness to the kitchen.

"Oh, Gussie." As the spirits hit her belly with a jolt of warmth, Eliza put her arms around her friend and hugged her close. "Nothing would give me greater joy than to have you come live with me in the Lake country. But let us not rush things. We must see what happens with Harry, and then . . . then we can make a better decision."

Augustina sniffed and wiped a tear from her pale cheek. "Even as a child you were always so solidly sensible. I sometimes wondered who was teaching whom."

"Obviously there were some lessons I didn't absorb very well," said Eliza, blinking a pearl of moisture from her lashes. "I would hardly call my dealings with men very sensible."

"Haddan is a fool for not giving you a chance to explain," said Augustina. "A handsome, charming fellow, but a fool nonetheless."

And he likely thinks me a scheming, conniving wagtail, thought Eliza, but saying so aloud would only set off more sparks. Best to let the embers burn down into ashes.

"It was never more than a passing fancy, Gussie. For both of us."

Augustina carefully shifted the jar of cut flowers sitting on the windowsill, her hands lingering on the yellow petals.

Damn, why did daffodils have to mean unrequited love?

"You still don't lie very well," said her friend with a wry smile.

"Don't burn the shortbread," warned Eliza. "*That* would definitely break my heart."

Thank God that laughter was a balm for the spirits. The hot pan was pulled from the oven and they sat at the little table to break off buttery morsels of the still-steaming pastry like naughty children, burning their tongues in the process.

"Mmmm, when do you plan on leaving?" asked Augustina, fanning her lips.

"The day after tomorrow. I have a few things to pack at the Abbey. But now that I have made up my mind, I wish to go quickly, before Harry and Brighton can make any trouble."

"Ha. Just let them try, my dear." A martial tattoo drummed on the scarred oak. "Just let them try."

"I do hope your friends have left one of those sinfully expensive Indian cheroots for me."

Gryff looked around to see Cameron's dark silhouette framed in the doorway of the study. "Help yourself," he replied, setting the carved sandalwood box on the tea table.

"Are we celebrating something?" Shaking the mizzle from his overcoat, Cameron eyed the three hulking figures lounging by the hearth, each of whom was enjoying a large tumbler of expensive brandy to go along with the slim sticks of rare tobacco. Plumes of scented smoke skirled around the carved marble, muffling the rough rasp of laughter.

"The purchase of a painting." Gryff pointed to a large

watercolor propped up against the wall. "In a manner of speaking."

Cameron limped over for a look.

"What happened to your leg?" asked Gryff.

"I fell." His friend plucked at his cuff, revealing a heavily bandaged hand. "Out of a third story window."

The light from the glass-globed sconce showed a shade of bruising running along the left side of his jaw.

"How clumsy of you." Gryff's frown deepened as his gaze moved up to the thin cut on Cameron's brow. "That looks like it was made by a knife. Did a piece of steel do the shoving?"

His friend merely shrugged, and turned to study the painting.

"It appears that I need not have rushed back to Town," he murmured after spending several moments examining Eliza's copy of the Maria Sibylla Merian watercolor. A slanted look cut to the ex-pugilists. "Hell, I do hope you weren't too heavy-handed with The Badger. He and I do a fair amount of business together and he won't thank me if you created any sort of trouble at his establishment."

"There was no trouble at all." Gryff allowed the corners of his mouth to curl up as he raised his voice. "No trouble at all, was there, Georgie?"

"Nay, milord. The Badger was happy te part with the doodle. Ye see, he hadn't yet paid the cove who brought it in, so when he learned that the item was stolen from its rightful owner, he was shocked—shocked!"

His friends guffawed into their drinks.

"And was happy te hear we wuz gonna return it."

"Naturally, I had my friends here give him a token

of my appreciation," added Gryff. "For doing the right thing."

Georgie's slabbed face split into a wide grin.

"Good God, your hidden talents appear to include a knack for vice," said Cameron admiringly. "Perhaps we should go into partnership."

"I'm flattered, but after I finish with this business tonight, I've little interest in any future gropings along the underbelly of London."

Cameron struck a lucifer and lit up a cheroot. "You have another stop to make?"

"Yes. A rendezvous with Brighton and his cousin at The Black Duck, which I'm told is one of their favorite haunts."

The mention of the seedy gaming hell in Seven Dials caused one dark brow to arch up. "It doesn't look as if you need any extra help, but as the encounter promises to be interesting, I might come along to observe."

"We'll be meeting up with an additional party near the gaming hell," said Gryff. "The magistrate."

A lazy exhale blew out a perfect smoke ring. Cameron watched it slowly dissolve before saying, "On second thought, it might not be wise for me to show my face."

"You should be safe enough. The local authority is Mr. Bolt, who handled the investigation into the Wolfhound's recent troubles," replied Gryff. They both had met the man when their friend Connor had been under suspicion of a crime. "And Bolt has decided that his initial impression was wrong and that your features—along with the jewels dripping from your earlobe—are, in fact, *not* familiar."

"How did you manage that?"

"A generous donation to his wife's charity fund for orphans," answered Gryff. "I am always eager to support a worthy cause."

Cameron stifled a smile. "You continue to surprise me."

"I'm planning on giving the baronet and his cursed cousin an even bigger shock to their sensibilities." He signaled to the three men by the hearth. "Ready, lads?"

Glasses clinked down on stone as hobnailed boots shifted over the Aubusson carpet. "Aye, milord," said Georgie, tossing the butt of his tobacco into the fire. "Let's go crack some heads."

"We'll use force only if necessary," Gryff reminded them, though an evil grin shaded his words. "Of course, if they try to slip away from the authorities, it's our duty to see that they don't escape justice."

"Oh, this should be jolly entertaining," said Cameron. "Lead the way."

"Right on time, Lord Haddan." Bolt snapped his pocketwatch shut and surveyed the shadowed silhouettes behind Gryff. "And I see you have brought along your own reinforcements."

"Just in case you could use some extra force. I should like to ensure that these vipers don't slither away."

"Yes, so you said." Bolt lifted a brow. "Any particular reason?"

"My duty as a responsible citizen," replied Gryff without batting an eye. "Once the crime came to my knowledge, honor compelled me to do something about it."

"Very commendable," said the magistrate dryly. His gaze lingered for a moment on Cameron's features before moving on to the trio of ex-pugilists. "And I take it these are other concerned citizens."

"But of course."

A low whistle summoned a quartet of equally beefy men from the shadows behind Bolt. "Follow me, milord."

The magistrate cut between two crumbling brick warehouses and led the way down a narrow alleyway. "Brady and Miller, you two go around and guard the back exits. The rest of you, come along."

A thick cloud of smoke hung heavy beneath the blackened beams of the low-ceilinged room, muffling the sounds of men at play. Dice rattled, losers groaned and sloshed their sorrows with flagons of ale.

Gryff squinted through the haze. "There." He pointed to an alcove, where a half-dozen gamesters were gathered around a table playing *vingt-et-un*.

The room turned unnaturally still, the grunts and groans quieting as Bolt pushed through the tangle of chairs.

Brighton looked up at the group's approach, his red-rimmed eyes dilating in dawning alarm as the *tromp* of boots came closer and closer.

"Sorry, this table is full. Find yourself some other amusement," said Pearce, trying to muster a show of bravado.

Much to Gryff's satisfaction, his bluster rang hollow.

"Sir Brighton. Mr. Pearce." Bolt's voice was a good deal firmer.

The two men scraped back their chairs.

"What do you want?" demanded Brighton.

"You are under arrest."

The other players at the table quickly dropped their cards and slunk away into the shadows.

The baronet paled. "On what charge?"

"Theft, selling forgeries, blackmail, assault." Bolt dropped a sheet of paper on the table. "The rest of the charges are written there. You may read them at your leisure in Newgate Prison."

"Th-that's absurd! The charges are false," exclaimed Brighton. "You cannot prove a thing. Show me one witness who will corroborate such a pack of filthy lies!"

Gryff stepped forward. "Me, for one. And there are others who will back up my testimony." He added his own packet to Bolt's paper. "The proprietor of your flash house has made a full confession, along with a detailed list of all the rigs you are running. They are, I might add, quite numerous." He gave an inward smile as the baronet's face crumpled in fear. The papers were blank, a mere bluff. "In addition, these gentlemen here..." He gestured at Georgie and his two companions. "Will confirm everything."

"How...Who..."

As his cousin stammered, Pearce edged back and then suddenly ducked through a narrow doorway. Gryff signaled to Georgie's two companions. "Go fetch Mr. Pearce and inform him that it would be extremely rude to keep the gaoler waiting."

Brighton was staring at him open-mouthed, gasping for breath like a hooked trout. "H-Haddan, I don't understand. S-surely there must be some mistake."

"The only mistake is yours."

"But what ill have I ever done to you?" The baronet leaned forward, his hot, heavy breath fouled with the reek of brandy. "Come, we are both gentlemen. Name whatever you want, and it's yours. Just make this unwashed scum go away."

Gryff pinched Brighton's lapel between his fingers. It was made of the finest merino wool, soft as a summer solstice cloud. Drawing the baronet closer, he said, "You can take your gentlemanly offer..." He dropped his voice to a rumbling whisper. "And shove it where the sun doesn't shine, you loathsome snake."

It took a heartbeat for the smug smile to vanish from the baronet's face. Twisting free, he drew a knife from his boot and grabbed for a chokehold on Gryff's neck, no doubt intending to trade a hostage for his own freedom.

His strike was quick, as was befitting a poisonous viper. But Gryff's was quicker.

Brighton screamed as his wrist snapped back, the sound punctuated by the crunch of bone and pop of sinew.

The knife clattered to the floor. Bolt kicked it away.

"He broke my arm," moaned Brighton, writhing in pain.

Gryff shoved him toward Bolt's men. "Take him away, before I crack every vertebra in his cowardly spine."

Georgie bent down to retrieve the weapon from under the table. "A fine bit o' workmanship, milord," he said, running the blade lightly across his thumb. "De ye mind if I pocket it?"

"It's yours," said Gryff. He added a few coins to the ex-pugilist's hand. "My thanks to you and your friends for your help."

"Anytime, milord," said Georgie with a tip of his cap.

Turning to Cameron, he said, "Had enough entertainment for the night? Or would you care to make one last stop with me?"

"Oh, please, lead on. I haven't been this amused since the time Connor blackened the eyes of the three brutes who thought it was a great lark to break Sally Fielding's spectacles." His friend cocked his head. "The Wolfhound's temper was no surprise, but I must confess, I've never seen you flex your muscle like that."

"Flex my muscle?" Gryff curled his fingers into a fist. "Trust me, Cam, that was just the first little twitch."

"God save the next miscreant we meet."

"I doubt the Almighty will care to lift a finger to help these miserable slugs," said Gryff. The gamesters in his way quickly cleared a wide path as he stalked by the tables. "I think He'll not object if I continue to play the Avenging Angel."

"My, my, this is yet another face of the devil-may-care Marquess," said Cameron. "Fun-Loving Rogue, Lyrical Writer, and now the White Knight in Shining Armor."

"As you said, we all have hidden facets. It just takes the right situation to bring them out."

"What's next?" As was his wont, Cameron kept up his needling. "The Stalwart Spouse?"

Gryff swung his gaze around. "Are you looking to have your earlobes twisted off?"

Cameron fingered his diamond earring in mock horror. "A fate worse than death!"

"Ass." A smile twitched on his lips. "I don't know why I'm friends with you."

"Who else would have gifted you with a dragon tattoo?"

Gryff kicked open the door and stalked into the night. There was, he realized, something else indelibly imprinted on his skin. *A lady's laugh, an artist's spirit, a woman's passion.*

"Right—I knew there must be some reason. Be assured, you have my undying gratitude."

"I thought so." Cameron grinned, then swore as he tripped over a hunk of rotting cabbage. "Where are we going?"

"To Newgate Prison," replied Gryff. "I've a few things to wring out of Brighton before I'm done with him. If he wishes to save his neck, he'll decide to be agreeable."

"And then?"

"The next task will have to wait until tomorrow," answered Gryff. "However, you ought to stay abed and rest your injuries. I won't need any assistance." His palms slapped together. "I'll handle it quite easily on my own."

Chapter Twenty-One

$\mathcal{T}$he cavernous room of the boxing saloon echoed with the rhythmic slap of leather against leather. Gryff slid his bare feet across the rough canvas, twisting just enough to dodge the padded fist aimed at his jaw.

"Well done, milord. That was one of my better punches."

He acknowledged the compliment by flicking a jab at "Gentleman" Jackson's kidney.

"That's enough for the day," said the famed boxing instructor as the blow grazed his stocky body. "I may have to stop going a few rounds with you, sir, lest my reputation suffer."

Gryff laughed as he caught the towel tossed to him by one of the assistants. "When you go at three-quarter speed, I can land a few blows. But I'm under no illusion that my skills rival yours."

"Seven-eighths," said Jackson with a foxy grin. "You make me work damn hard, milord. I shall have to charge you extra."

"With pleasure," replied Gryff, drying the rivulets of

sweat from his chest. "Thank you for the exercise." His smile hardened as he looked around and spotted Leete and two of his friends in the practice area. The trio was taking turns punching one of the large sawdust-filled leather bags under the watchful eye of a trainer.

Indolent fribbles. Like all the other patrons of Gentleman Jackson's Boxing Saloon the three young men were stripped to the waist—a fact that laid bare their fleshy softness. Their skills were equally unimpressive. But rather than work with any diligence, the trio was teasing and taunting one another, their loud banter drawing glares from the regulars.

However, all that was about to change, thought Gryff with savage satisfaction.

Jackson followed the marquess's gaze to Eliza's brother. "Don't know that I should continue to allow young Leete and his friends in here. They strike me as bad *ton*, if you know what I mean. A lot of prancing and posturing..." The former champion flexed a muscled biceps. "But when push comes to shove, not one of them could break an egg with a punch."

"Very bad *ton*," agreed Gryff after a fraction of a pause. The afternoon sun slanted in through the high-set windows of the saloon, catching Leete's pause to primp at his sidewhiskers with a heavily gloved hand. "But you need not worry. They will not be pestering you for very much longer."

"Then I shall not have to waste my time tossing them out on their fancy arses?"

"No," replied Gryff. "Leave the matter to me."

Draping the towel around his neck, he strolled to the corner of the boxing ring.

Leete looked up and hailed him loudly, as if they were friends. "What-ho, Haddan." Preening for his friends, he gave a cocky salute. "You were in fine form with Jacks, heh?"

Gryff nodded and flashed a quick show of teeth.

Taking it for a smile, Leete puffed out his chest. "Saw you land a few punches on the champion." He gave a jab to the bag. "I'm getting to be quite handy with my fives as well—any gentleman worth his snuff must be able to defend his honor, eh."

"Quite right." Gryff thumped his padded gloves together. "Jackson had to cut my sessions short. I don't suppose you would care to step into the ring and have a friendly little hit."

Leete's face lit up with pride. "By Jove, yes!" he exclaimed, shooting a surreptitious look around the saloon to see who was observing his social triumph. "Vestry," he crowed, waving at one of his cronies. "Be a good fellow and come tighten the lacing of my gloves before I trade a few blows with my friend Haddan."

This time, Gryff's smile was sincere. *You will soon be eating those words—along with several of your teeth.*

They moved to the center of the canvas.

"Ready?" Gryff assumed position while Leete was still making a face at his cronies.

Thump. Eliza's brother staggered back a step.

"Pay attention, Leete," growled Gryff.

Thump. The next blow was just hard enough to bloody the viscount's nose.

"You are going to learn an important lesson this afternoon."

Leete's swagger was swallowed by a look of confusion. He essayed a wobbly smile. "Demme, you've a sharp right cross milord."

"Keep your hands up," warned Gryff. "Remember—a gentleman must always be prepared to defend his honor."

"R-right-ho." Leete threw a weak punch, which Gryff swatted away while driving his other fist into the viscount's belly. The force of it knocked the viscount to the canvas.

"Get up," he said pleasantly.

Grunting in pain, Leete levered to his feet.

"Hands up," warned Gryff again, landing a blow to the chin that snapped Leete's head back. "Show some backbone." With that he began a systematic pummeling of Eliza's brother. Ribs, chest, chin—all were starting to sprout mottled purple bruises.

"A—a break, sir?" gasped Leete through swollen lips.

"No, no, let's keep at it," said Gryff, landing another hard punch to the body.

A look of fear now flooded Leete's blackened eyes. To cry surrender would brand him as a coward, but the unyielding punishment had him close to panic. Crabbing back, he tried to ward off the blows. He was gasping for breath, sweat slicking his carefully curled hair to his skull.

Gryff finally relented, only because he needed the fellow to be conscious. "Come, let's cool off." Taking the viscount's unresisting arm, he marched him into one of the side changing rooms.

Seeing Gryff's expression, the two other occupants hastily gathered their clothing and fled.

"Oh, God," whimpered Leete. "I think you broke my nose."

Grabbing the viscount by the scruff of his neck, Gryff thrust his head into a barrel of water and held it under for several long, long moments before jerking it out.

Leete was sobbing now, the tears streaming down his wet face and mixing with the dark blood from his battered nose. "I don't understand, I don't understand!"

"I am about to explain. So listen carefully, for I don't intend to repeat myself."

Shoulders slumped, Leete sunk down to his knees. At Gryff's command he looked up, one eye completely swollen shut and turning from purple to a ghastly shade of green.

"First of all, repeat after me—a gentleman's responsibility is to look after his family. He protects them."

"A-a gentleman's r-r-responsibility is to take care of his f-f-family. He p-p-protects them."

"Again."

Leete stammered out the two sentences between his low moans.

"Commit that to heart, Leete." Gryff took his coat down from a peg and fished out a handful of paper. "I have purchased your gaming debts, and I have had a little chat with Brighton about a certain unwritten wager. It is now null and void."

The viscount's tears were now ones of relief. "Oh, dear God in Heaven, thank you, sir!"

"Don't thank me," snarled Gryff. "I didn't do it for you. I did it for your sister, who deserves better than to have a miserable little slug like you for a sibling."

"I—I swear," stuttered Leete. "I shall be more careful at The Wolf's Lair from now on."

"In fact, you will not." Gryff separated a sealed packet

from the papers in his hand and tossed it onto the floor. "You will be embarking on a new life shortly—the details are in there, and you will have ample time to read them over during the voyage."

"Voyage?" whimpered Eliza's brother, his unblackened eye widening in alarm.

"Yes. One of the assistants here will be escorting you to your rooms at the Albany, where your servant has already packed your trunk. On tonight's tide, you will be departing for Bombay, where I have arranged a position for you with the East India Company."

"India?" cried Leete. "I—I don't want to go to India."

"No, I imagine you don't. But be assured, you will be on that ship." Gryff shoved the other papers back into his coat pocket, save for one sheet. "And you won't be returning to England until I am satisfied that you've become a man, rather than a sniveling, selfish piece of dung."

Leete started crying, the soft, snuffling sounds gurgling in the back of his throat.

"And know that if you try to bully your sister, or set foot back in England without my permission, I will call you out and put a bullet through your worthless brain," he added. "Do you understand me?"

Cringing, Leete nodded.

"Good. There is one last thing you will do for me. A solicitor is waiting in your rooms. He will officially witness and notarize your signature on this document."

"W-what is it?"

"It gives the legal power of decision-making over all your family property and finances to your sister while you are out of the country. She is a far more worthy steward of the land than you are."

Leete's mouth opened and then closed without making a sound.

"You see, you are already becoming wiser. Now get yourself dressed. I'll send Georgie in to assist you in making it to the docks without delay."

Leete's only response was to fall forward and curl in a fetal position.

Grimacing in disgust, Gryff turned on his heel, anxious to escape the foul stench of sweat and fear that pervaded the air.

Brighton. Pearce. Leete. Three obstacles were now cleared from the path to Lady Brentford's happiness. Whether he could smooth all the bumps and twists remained to be seen.

But at least it was a start.

"What's that noise?" Augustina raised her pruning knife and peeked through the garden bushes. "If that is you, Lord Brighton, come to harass Lady Brentford, be warned that you are *not* welcome here."

Mouse arched against her skirts, adding his own fierce hiss.

"My intentions are entirely honorable, Miss Haverstick." Gryff ducked under the branches of forsythia and brushed the pale petals from his sleeve. "Forgive me for appearing again unannounced. I hope you will hear me out before employing that blade on any portion of my anatomy."

"Hmmph. Certain parts deserve to be snipped." She lowered the tool. "Like your brain and your tongue. You jumped to conclusions, young man, and said some *very* unfair things about Eliza."

He bowed his head in contrition. "Feeble though my mind is, I actually figured that out on my own."

"Well then, perhaps there is hope for you yet."

"I should like to think so." Shifting the large, paper-wrapped package in his arms, he gave a tentative smile. "Might I be permitted to have a word with Lady Brentford?"

Augustina made a face. "I'm afraid you have come a few hours too late, Lord Haddan. She left at dawn this morning."

Gryff felt his heart lurch and kick up against his ribs. "To go where?" he asked softly.

"North," replied Augustina.

"That covers a rather large area. Might you narrow it down just a bit?"

"Might I ask why?" she countered. "She left to escape an unprincipled lout and his unwanted legshackle. As for any other manacles..."

Hoping that his face wasn't as beet red as it felt, Gryff hastily interrupted. "I repeat, Miss Haverstick, my intentions are honorable."

"Hmmph." She eyed him askance.

"Just ask her cat." He spotted Elf flattened beneath the spreading foliage of a rose bush. "He will vouch for my good intentions."

Her mouth quirked upward. "Animals do seem to like you. A definite mark in your favor."

"Ah, good. That's a start. I simply need to progress from felines to females."

The smile was no longer just a tiny twitch. "You're making some headway, sir. And if you turn right at the end of High Street and take the road for Birmingham, you might go even faster."

He reached for her hand and brought it to his lips. "Thank you."

"Don't make me regret it."

"I shall do my best not to." He turned to go.

"By the by, what's that you have under your arm?"

"A message." Gryff gazed at the sun-dappled garden. "In case my own words fail me."

"Ouch." Curtaining the small window, Eliza leaned back against the squabs and massaged at her temples, hoping to dispel the growing ache in her head. Like the carriage wheels, her thoughts had been bouncing in a herky-jerky spin for several hours.

Too much time for introspection was not always a good thing, she mused, trying not to replay her last two encounters with Haddan over and over again in her head. Each time, they seemed to get a little worse.

At this point, she would welcome any distraction...

THUMP.

Something hard and heavy hit the roof, causing the carriage to jolt to a halt.

Tipping her bonnet back from her eyes, Eliza untangled herself from an inelegant sprawl on the floorboards and climbed back onto the seat. "Barker!" she called to the hired coachman. "What is the trouble?"

The reply was too jumbled to make out.

"Drat. It would be just my luck if a falling branch cracked an axle or snapped one of the traces." Her whole life seemed to be breaking apart like a walnut under a bootheel.

Whack, whack, whack. She bit back a snuffle of self-pity.

Whack, whack, whack. The kicks finally popped the doorlatch and a man swung down from the crown of the carriage, his caped coat flapping like great dark wings.

With a small shriek, she slid to the far end of the seat, fumbling in her reticule for her penknife. "If you are looking for money or jewels, sirrah, you have chosen the wrong coach to rob. I haven't anything of value to steal."

"Well then, I'll have to demand some other forfeit," said a low, familiar voice. "How about a helping of walnut shortbread? I know you have a basket tucked away here somewhere, with a batch fresh from the oven."

Her stomach did a slow, spiraling somersault. "Oh, this is *not* funny, Lord Haddan." Pressing up against the paneling, she tucked her skirts tighter to her legs, trying to avoid them touching his thigh.

He inched closer. And closer.

"Th-that's far enough, sir," said Eliza haltingly.

"I've been traveling for hours. I could use a bit of refreshment. How about you?"

Eliza tried to swallow the lump in her throat. Oh, it was like a splash of pure, sparkling champagne to hear his voice, to see his smile. Happiness bubbled through her blood, its giddy effervescence tickling a lick of hope in her chest.

Don't. Don't let fantasy overpower reality, she reminded herself, keeping her face turned to the window to hide her reaction.

"Actually," went on Gryff. "I was hoping for something a little more substantial than just shortbread. Like a picnic, complete with a custard tart."

Talk of tarts reminded her that she hadn't eaten since dawn. Suddenly ravenous, she sighed. A short stop for one last little taste of happiness before heading into a bland future was awfully tempting. But...

"We are in the middle of nowhere, Lord Haddan." Her wave indicated the endless stretch of woodland and fields outside the glass panes. "A picnic is not going to whisk in on a flying carpet at the snap of your fingers."

"No, but it might appear from under the bench of my phaeton."

"It might?"

"Yes, if I rub the magic lamp just so..." He reached up and brushed his fingertips to the brass carriage light. "Yes, I daresay that should do it. But perhaps you should touch it, too, for good luck." In a soft whisper he added, "Please trust me, Eliza. You will not regret the delay."

Her resolve melting, as if a thousand candle flames had leapt to life inside her heart, Eliza lifted her hand. The metal was warm as a sunbeam.

"Shall I tell your driver to turn around?" asked Gryff.

"Yes." She leaned back against the squabs. "B-but only because of the custard tart."

Chapter Twenty-Two

The iron-banded wheels crunching over the stones, the coach swung around. Puffs of dust flew up as the horses broke into a steady trot.

Eliza picked at the threads of her cuff, listening to the jangle of the brass and the clip-clop of the hooves, uncertain of how to go on.

Haddan, on the other hand, appeared completely at ease. Then again, he always did. His devil-may-care charm must be a talisman against inner doubts and fears. *While I spin in circles, awkward and unsure.*

"What are you doing here?" she asked abruptly.

"Enjoying the view." He slanted a sidelong look at her and grinned. "I thought I might write another essay on the beauties of the countryside."

The hedgerows danced by, sun and shadow painting the leaves with myriad shades of green. Wildflowers dotted the verge in front of the weathered stone walls, vibrant splashes of color against the rainwashed grays.

"I'm sure it would be wonderful," she said softly. "Your writing makes me want to take off my shoes and run through dew-dampened meadows."

"I think that's the nicest compliment I've ever received."

She shook her head. "Oh, I'm sure that the London ladies offer far more polished sentiments than that."

"Perhaps I prefer a gem in all its wild, sparkling, natural splendor to a piece of smooth, colorless glass."

Eliza blinked a bead of moisture from her lashes. "Your words are seductive, sir. But I am not sure that I should be doing this. Changing directions, that is. You see, I'm returning to some very difficult conundrums with my brother and his cronies—"

"Actually, you are not," replied Gryff. The boyish grin gave way to a more serious, sober expression. "Brighton and Pearce have been arrested on charges of theft and fraud, among others. They are no longer a threat to you. As for your brother, he is, as we speak, on his way to India. It is my hope that a few years of firm guidance and hard work will turn him into a man."

Shock kept her tongue tied in knots for a moment. "I—I don't understand," she finally stammered. "H-how did all this come about?"

"I took matters into my own hands." Bracing an arm on the back of the seat, he shifted to face her. "Miss Hawkins has informed me that you've been manipulated too much by the men in your life. So I hope that you will forgive me for interfering."

"I..." Her emotions were spinning faster than the wheels. "I don't really know what to say. Except thank you."

His smile slowly reappeared. "I'm relieved to hear that I won't be tied up and tossed onto the first ship bound for Cathay."

"Harry on his way to India," she mused, shaking her head in amazement. "I pray it will do him some good. He wasn't always such a lout, you know. Growing up, he was a sweet, good-natured boy. It was only when he went up to Oxford that he turned ugly."

"So you told me once," replied Gryff. "That's why I arranged this second chance. He'll be working for a former comrade-in-arms, a fine fellow who wields a firm hand in molding the character of men under his charge. Harry has a good chance to shape up into a decent fellow." A pause. "If he sinks into dissipation, that will be his own choice, and it's better that he is far away, where he won't do harm to anyone but himself."

Eliza thought it over. "Being oceans away, he must learn to sink or swim. But Leete Abbey—"

"Leete Abbey is in good hands," said Gryff. "Yours." He went on to explain the legal arrangements. "With a good steward and prudent decisions, there is no reason the estate can't soon be restored to its proper glory."

"I can't begin to...to..."

His finger touched her lips, silencing her stammers. "Let's not talk about such serious things on an empty stomach." The coach drew to a halt. "I can't concentrate on anything when I'm hungry, save for a hamper brimming with rich cheddar, spiced chutney, and creamy custard."

Eliza allowed herself to be helped down to the edge of the road. The scent of sun-warmed grass floated in and out of the sunlight as a gentle breeze ruffled through the foliage.

Gryff waved the coach on its way. "My phaeton is here," he said, leading the way to a small clearing off a narrow side lane. "Whichever way you choose to go when we are done with our meal, I shall be happy to drive you to your destination."

Choices, choices.

He reached up and took down a large hamper, as well as a package wrapped in heavy brown paper.

"What's that?" she asked. "And please don't say it's a box of shortbread. I have already gained several pounds since I met you."

"Are you saying I'm a bad influence?"

His tone was teasing but she gave the question serious thought. "You seem to release a wild woodland spirit in me, Lord Haddan. I'm not sure if it's good or bad. All I know is it's...uncomfortable at times."

"New sensations often are," he replied. "Change can be prickly."

She studied his profile as they climbed a low stile and walked through the high fescue. The crystalline country light accentuated the chiseled angles of his features, showing more clearly the subtle texture and shading. "You speak of change, sir, and yet you appear so comfortable in your own skin."

"Do I?" He deflected her probing with a quick gesture at a spot halfway up the hillside. "That looks to be the perfect place for a picnic."

Quickening her pace to match his stride, Eliza decided not to pursue the matter. "You still haven't told me what's in the package."

"After we dine," he murmured, spreading out a blanket and placing the hamper on a low outcropping of rock.

As if by unspoken agreement, they talked only of trivialities as they ate, the fresh air sharpening the pleasure of the simple tastes, the friendly laughter.

It was only when the last crumbs of the tart had been consumed that Gryff leaned back on his elbows and let out a long, contented sigh. "You asked earlier about change, Lady Brentford."

His gaze drifted over a stand of leafy oak and beech trees to the distant meadow filled with grazing sheep. "Look all around—there is constant change in nature. It is part of the great, glorious cycle of life, and in writing this book of essays about landscape, I have discovered that I greatly miss that elemental connection to the earth. So yes, I am making a change. I plan very soon to return to my family estate and, well, roll up my sleeves and feel the dirt between my fingers."

"You won't miss the glittering ballrooms, the fancy soirees?" Eliza hesitated, then added, "The beautiful ladies, the seductive flirtations?"

"I think I've experienced enough of those things to last a lifetime," he murmured. "One tires of the cloying scent of heavy perfumes, whereas the subtle scent of wildflowers…" He drew in a deep breath and exhaled slowly. "Never ceases to delight."

"Mmmm." Eliza twined her fingers in a twist of clover. Simple pleasures had always resonated with her. "I think I understand what you mean."

"Yes, I know you do," replied Gryff. "You have labored long and hard to preserve the essence of the Abbey—it's your love and your spirit that have kept it alive." His tone turned oddly tentative. "Have you never wanted a place where you could build something for yourself, and watch it grow?"

"I plan to buy a cottage," she answered. "In the Lake District, with views of the rugged hills and the setting sun painting the water with a palette of pinks and mauves."

"I was thinking of something rather larger than a cottage and a backyard garden."

Eliza watched a hawk soaring in slow, silent circles high in the sky, and for an instant the rhythmic motion made her a little dizzy. How effortlessly it floated through life, light as a feather.

"You can see hills from Haddan Hall," went on Gryff softly. "The sun sets over a lovely little lake behind the main manor house, setting it aglow with the fire of twilight. There is a small island in its center, with a Greek folly made of pale marble. The stone gleams as if lit from within. Sometimes I like to sit there and think up stories of ancient heroes and mythical beasts."

"You have a lovely imagination, Lord Haddan."

"So do you." He paused for a moment to pluck a blade of long meadowgrass and hold it between his teeth.

Closing her eyes, Eliza let the sun's bright rays dip and dance over her face. "I shall probably have a hundred new spots tomorrow," she mused aloud, feeling her skin soak in the tantalizing warmth. "I ought to feel horrible about it, but I don't." A hairpin had slipped, and a curl had escaped to tickle her cheek. "In fact, I ought to feel horrible about a lot of things, yet somehow I am content with being who I am."

"Hmmm." He made a funny little humming sound around the grass. "I think you should stay exactly as you are."

Smiling, she laced her hands behind her head, feeling at peace with the world.

"Save for one thing."

"Oh?" One lid slowly lifted.

"I think you should marry me."

The other shot open.

"The cook at Haddan Hall makes a custard tart that can turn cartwheels around the one we just enjoyed."

Eliza sat up and drew her knees to her chest. The breeze played through his hair, setting the long, silky strands to capering across his open collar.

"You think I should marry you because of the *tarts*?"

"Well, no, not just for the tarts. I was also thinking of books as well. Imagine it—with my writing and your drawings, we could create wonderful books for gardeners...for children."

She looked down, trying not to envision little boys and girls with his dark hair and glittering green eyes.

"Sorry—that didn't quite come out as the most romantic of proposals," said Gryff. "So before you say anything, please allow me to add a few more words first." Paper crackled as he lifted the package and placed it on her knees.

"I thought you were going to speak from the heart," quipped Eliza.

"I am." He smiled. "Go ahead, open it."

The ribbon and wrappings fell away. "Oh, Haddan." With an unsteady finger, Eliza traced the outline of the Redouté rose.

"Do you remember what you said when you first saw it?"

"Yes." She did not dare think seriously about the flower's unspoken message. "I suggested selling it."

"No actually, you said that as you couldn't afford to buy it for yourself, you wished that it might find a home where it would be appreciated for its true message. I am hoping that place is Haddan Hall—and that you will be there every day to hear its secret whisper."

She muffled a sniffle in her sleeve.

"Eliza, please look at me." A hint of humor colored his voice. "The flower is paper—it doesn't need to be watered."

"I know, I know." She blotted the tears from her lashes. "It's so beautiful. But…"

"But a lady wants to hear the sentiment said aloud." He cleared his throat with a mock cough. "Forgive me if I stumble a bit. I've never done this before."

Mixed with the sunlight, the delicate shades of the painting seemed to take on an ethereal intensity.

"Not long ago, I knew I was ready to change my life for the better. I am excited about the future, and all the possibilities that it holds. But it would be so much better to share it with a kindred soul. I love you, Eliza. I love your laugh and your intelligence. I love your artistry and your passions. I love your appetite for fun."

Haddan loves me? She didn't dare twitch a muscle or utter a sound for fear that the slightest movement might wake her from this glorious dream.

"Silence? Dear me, that doesn't sound promising." His tone was light, but his eyes were dark, doubt shading their unique sparkle. Shadows flitted beneath the fringe of his lashes, making him look vulnerable.

As if his heart, like hers, had stopped in mid-beat.

"I'm silent because what I feel at this moment is impossible to express in words. So I'll try to answer in a language all my own." Brushing her fingers to his face, Eliza drew slow swirls over the contours of his cheekbones, sketching tiny hearts and roses. The sun had warmed his skin, and as her touch skimmed down the line of his jaw, she could feel his pulse begin to quicken.

Or was it her own? It was hard to tell. The connection between them seemed to resonate as one.

With the crickets chorusing in the background and the breeze whispering through the meadowgrasses, she leaned in and ever so lightly pressed her lips to his, hoping he could hear her heart singing with joy.

"Could you translate that?" he murmured, his mouth tipping up at the corners.

"Was I not eloquent enough?" She kissed him again, tasting the lingering traces of sugar mingled with his own ambrosial spice. "You wish to hear me say it aloud?"

"Please."

"Very well—I shall try, though my phrases aren't nearly as lyrical as yours are."

"I'll be the judge of that," he replied, with a crooked smile that momentarily squeezed the breath from her lungs.

Recovering the power of speech, Eliza said, "Gryffin Owain Dwight." She paused to savor the sound. "I love your name because it captures the very essence of who you are. Unusual and unexpected. Whimsical and strong, imaginative and compassionate. You have poetry and passion in your soul. I think...I think I fell in love with you at the first sight of your glorious, glittering green eyes, so alight with *impish* humor and kindness."

"Thank Heavens you have a fondness for Imps." Gryff tucked a wisp of unruly hair behind her ear. "I think I may have to hand my pen to you, my love. Your words put my own paltry efforts to blush."

"No, let's not change a thing," she whispered, loosening the fastenings of his shirt and slipping her hand beneath the finespun linen. "Things are perfect between us just the way they are."

Gryff lay back in the grass, taking her with him. "Yes, quite perfect." His voice was sleepy, though his long fingers were wide awake. Eliza smiled happily as they inched her skirts up over her knees.

"You paint fanciful pictures on my body and I have my wicked way with you amid the splendor of Nature."

"Haddan!" she squeaked. "Someone might spot us."

"There's not another soul for miles," he murmured, tossing her garters and stockings to the wind. "And my name is Gryff."

"Gryff," she murmured. "Mmmm, perhaps I shall tattoo a gryphon on your flesh. To keep your dragon company."

He laughed. "Oh, my love, I trust that my dragon will not be lonely from now on."

Eliza felt the stirring beneath the flap of his breeches as he rolled atop her.

"There is just one thing missing from our perfection."

"There is?" Eliza arched her hips into his. "I can't think of what." But then, her brain wasn't working all that clearly.

"It's lacking a 'yes' from you."

"Remind me again—what was the question?" Eliza wrapped her arms around his shoulders, reveling in the slabbed strength of his chiseled muscles and the soft caress of his curling hair against her cheek.

"My powers of persuasion must be slipping." Her skirts were now bunched around her waist. Grass tickled her thighs, sending shivers of silky heat coursing through her body. "Here, let me try again," he said just as his mouth possessed hers.

It was some minutes later before she could speak again. Staring up at the sky, Eliza heaved a sated sigh as her body came back down to earth.

"A whoosh of air? I make mad, passionate love to you, and that's all you have to say?" Gryff pulled her close and nibbled at her ear. "I'm prepared to keep you imprisoned here for days—or weeks—until I hear the word I want."

"Hmmm, sounds delicious. But we're all out of tarts."

"Then we'll have to survive on the nectar of love." His lips were now on the hollow of her throat. "Say 'yes,' Eliza."

"Maybe," she murmured, smiling at the huff of surprise that skittered against her skin. "So, the lordly marquess is not used to having anyone fail to bow to his wishes?"

"You know that you'll never need to fear that I will seek to shackle your spirit or your dreams." Gryff lifted his gaze, the gold-green depths turning molten with longing in the slanting sunlight. "I want to watch your marvelous talents blossom, and share a lifetime of growth together."

That look told her all that she wanted to know.

"Yes," she said softly. "Yes."

The glint grew brighter. Lighter. And in it she saw mirrored her own happiness.

"Yes!" This time it was loud enough for the mourning doves nesting in the nearby thicket to hear.

"Yes!" The wind caught the word and swirled it skyward.

"Thank heavens." Gryff grinned. "I was beginning to

worry that I might have to starve you into submission."

"I could stay here forever, just drinking in the sight of you," she said, watching his raven hair dance in wind-ruffled splendor, framed by the cloudless blue sky. "But I suppose we should return to Leete Abbey in time for supper."

"You are hungry already?" Gryff smoothed at the front of his shirt, which was hanging open to expose a deep "V" of bronzed chest. "I can think of a number of ways to take your mind off your stomach during the ride."

"In an open phaeton?"

He flashed a wicked smile. "I'm very creative, remember?"

"Lord Haddan," she said primly. "We must try to rein in our wild impulses. The road is a public venue and we are not married."

"Not yet." He reached for his coat and withdrew a thick sheet of folded paper. "But with this special license, that will soon be remedied."

Eliza peeked at the names written in a flowing copper-plate script. "You were very sure of yourself."

"Not 'sure,' just stubborn. I wasn't going to take 'no' for an answer." His hands stilled and his expression turned more serious. "We shall stay at Leete Abbey for the next few days, so that your friends may attend the wedding ceremony. And then we shall go home."

Home. The word suddenly had new meaning.

"I know that the Abbey shall always hold a special place in your heart," he went on. "But I hope you will now think of Haddan Hall as your real home. A place where you can set down real roots. A place to raise your children. A place to grow old together." His gaze skimmed to the Redouté painting. "I think you will like it very much. The gardens have an exuberant natural beauty. And I can already think of a perfect place for the painting to hang."

"It sounds lovely beyond words," whispered Eliza.

"Then let us gather up our things and set off on the new road." Gryff held out his hand to help her up. "The hardest place of the journey is behind us," he murmured, dropping a kiss on the nape of her neck. "And waiting up ahead lies..." He winked. "I think I shall have a petal-soft bed of roses made up for our first night together at the Hall."

Chapter Twenty-Three

The limestone façade of Leete Abbey glowed in the warmth of the buttery light, and as the phaeton rolled up the long drive, it appeared to Gryff as if the place sensed that a lead weight had been lifted from its bones. The fluted columns stood a little straighter, the classical pediments arched a little higher.

Eliza seemed to feel it, too. Craning her neck to see through the foliage, she exclaimed, "Oh, look how happy the house looks."

"That's because it knows that it is loved," he replied. Eying the graceful lines, he added, "'A thing of beauty is a joy for ever. Its loveliness increases; it will never pass into nothingness.'"

"How beautiful," she murmured. "That is from a poem by Keats, is it not?"

"Yes. 'Endymion.'"

"I admire his work very much."

Gryff smiled, glad that she liked his favorite poet.

Smoothing her skirts—for despite his teasing threat, they were both properly dressed and passed through the roads in perfect propriety—Eliza let out a little sigh. "I must send a note to Gussie. She will be worried."

"Actually, I asked your coach to drive by her cottage and bring her here for a celebration supper." He pursed his lips. "Assuming your brother has left a few decent bottles of champagne in the cellars."

"Trevor and I stashed a number of the fine wines in a place where Harry couldn't find them," she replied. "That was exceedingly thoughtful. Gussie has informed me that if she were forty years younger, I would have a rival for your affections."

"If she were forty years younger, I might whisk you both off to the exotic East and set up a harem."

"Ha! That would be asking for trouble…" Eliza suddenly fell silent, her hands fisting in her lap.

Shifting his gaze, he saw a tall figure stroll out from the shadows of the entrance portico. "Damn," he muttered under his breath, wondering what in the devil Cameron was doing here at Leete Abbey. Whatever the reason, he was not about to let his friend upset Eliza.

"Don't worry, my love." He slanted a reassuring smile, suddenly aware of how protective he felt of his soon-to-be bride. He now understood his friend Connor's fierce reaction when Alexa Bingham had been in danger. "I promise you that I won't let Cam cast a cloud over the day."

Eliza nodded but kept a wary eye on his friend as the phaeton rolled into the courtyard.

"I was beginning to think the housekeeper was mistaken and you had gone elsewhere," said Cameron. Gravel crunched underfoot as the horses came to a halt and he approached.

Gryff shot his friend a warning glance.

Ignoring the look, Cameron held out a hand to help Eliza down from the perch. The other, noted Gryff, was angled behind his friend's back.

"Cam—" he growled, only to be silenced by a flourish of color.

"These are for you, Lady Brentford." Cameron handed her a bouquet of mixed flowers. "I trust that I got the message right. First and foremost, there is purple hyacinth, which says 'Sorry, please forgive me.' I've also taken the liberty of adding lavender heather, which means 'admiration,' and snapdragons, which indicate 'gracious strength.' And lastly, there are sprigs of figwort for future joy, and ivy, which signifies friendship—for I do hope that we will be friends."

Eliza smiled through the pastel petals. "I should like that very much, Mr. Daggett. What a very thoughtful gesture, though in all honesty, no apology is necessary. You can hardly be blamed for thinking what you did."

Cameron gave a cryptic shrug. "I, of all people, should know that things are not always what they seem." Pinching a curling leaf between his thumb and forefinger, he assumed a more playful note. "Perhaps I should have added ox-eye daisies for 'patience,' as you will need it to deal with Haddan. He can be very aggravating, you know." His sardonic grin was directed at Gryff. "But then again, it appears you have no need of advice on how to handle him. From what I can see, another of the Hellhounds has been tamed by love."

Gryff accepted the needling with good grace. "A very impressive recital, Cam. And just how did you come to be so knowledgeable on the subject of flowers?"

"I saw the book by Mary Wortley Montague on your desk and assumed you wouldn't mind if I borrowed it. What a fascinating little compendium."

His amusement faded. "You really have to stop pawing through my private papers," snapped Gryff. "That was meant for Sara."

"I'll pass it on with your compliments." Cameron released the ivy. "And rather than bark at me, you ought to be voicing your gratitude for my less-than-gentlemanly habits. Without them, you might never have rescued Lady Brentford from danger."

"I shall send you a cartload of hydrangea, which, of course, means 'thank you,'" intervened Eliza. "Though flowers seems an awfully paltry way of saying it."

"Your smile, Lady Brentford, is ample enough reward. However, should you be feeling magnanimous, I would dearly love to have one of your paintings."

"It would be my honor," she responded.

Cameron sketched a small bow. "Speaking of art, I left several rare illustrated books with your butler. The markings show that they came from the Abbey library, and after a little chat with Brighton, I learned that he and his cousin had stolen them on one of their visits here."

"Oh, Harry," Eliza sighed softly.

"Your brother did not know of their perfidy. That was how they worked—they befriended impressionable young men and encouraged excessive drinking and gambling in order to fleece them of their money and valuables. The more the authorities dig into their affairs, the more dung is uncovered."

"In the future, we will hope that Leete chooses his friends more wisely," said Gryff.

A low laugh rumbled in Cameron's throat. "I trust that was not meant to voice any personal regrets on your part."

"You can be a thorn in the arse at times..." Gryff eyed his friend for a long moment, thinking of all the scrapes and dangers they had survived together, first in the brutal Peninsular War, then in the skirmishes with Polite Society. "But no, no regrets."

"I'm touched," drawled Cameron, pressing a hand to his heart. But before he could utter any further sarcasm, the clatter of a coach coming up the drive drew his attention. His dark brows rose ever so slightly. "Is that a cat's head I see sticking out of the window?"

"It's Elf," said Eliza. "Gussie was going to care for him until I got myself settled in the Lake District."

"Elf," explained Gryff, "is an Imp of Satan. Though perhaps I should revise my opinion, since without him I might never have *bumped* into my future bride while strolling in the gardens."

A rosy blush spread to her cheeks and he knew that she was thinking of their limbs tangling in a tree. "On second thought," he added, "I'm exceedingly fond of the little devil."

Their gazes met and though she tried to look stern, her mouth quivered at the corners. For an instant, all he could think of was stilling her silent laughter with his lips.

I am besotted, he admitted.

And the feeling was rather wonderful. All around him, the world seemed in perfect harmony with his own mellow mood.

"Welcome, Miss Haverstick!" Shaking off his own sweet musings, Gryff hurried to help Augustina down from the coach.

"Thank you, young man. But first, would you mind taking Mouse?" She handed him a wicker carrying case. "Elf insisted on being set loose as he recognized familiar territory. But Mouse has not enjoyed traveling." She straightened the brim of her bonnet. "I hope you don't mind that I brought the animals. It didn't seem right to let them miss all the fun."

"No, indeed," he agreed.

Seeing Gryff with his hands full, Cameron quickly stepped in to aid the elderly spinster in descending the iron rungs. "Allow me. I am always happy to assist a lovely lady."

"Much obliged." Her gaze narrowed to an owlish squint as he looked up. Tilting her head, she studied his features for a long moment before accepting his aid. "That's a very interesting earring, sir. Why, it reminds me of a bauble owned by the Duchess of Denwick."

"Does it?" After the barest hint of hesitation, he murmured, "You have an extremely discerning eye, Miss Haverstick."

She stared for a moment longer before letting out a little chortle. "I like your friends, Haddan."

"This is Mr. Daggett, Gussie." Eliza hastily made the introductions, then enfolded her old governess in a fierce hug. "Who has helped Haddan save me from certain ruin. Because of them, Brighton—Brighton and his cousin have been arrested, and Harry—Harry is on his way to India. And..." She paused to catch her breath. "And Haddan—Haddan has asked me to be his wife."

"The marquess appears to have been a very busy gentleman over the last few days," quipped Augustina. "By the by, if you didn't say yes, I will think that your wits have sailed to Bombay along with your feckless brother."

"I did," she replied, giving Gryff a look through her lashes that made his insides go soft as custard. "Say yes, that is. But it is a long story."

"Oh, lovely. I adore long stories, especially when they are told over a bottle of bubbly and a festive supper." Augustina pointed to another parcel inside the coach. "I've brought along plenty of walnut shortbread to add to the celebration."

"I'm glad to hear it," said Gryff. "As you know, my wife-to-be has a very healthy appetite."

Her color deepened to the match the fire of the setting sun, but after a moment, she, too, joined in the laughter. "That is because my husband-to-be is a very bad influence on me. I fear I shall soon be as stout as a brandy barrel."

"The key is staying physically active." He grinned. "I shall do my part to ensure that you are kept on your toes."

"And a few other positions, I would guess," murmured Augustina, catching his eye with an earthy wink.

Meow. Peering down from the top of the coach, Elf added his voice to the general merriment.

"Thank you for the vote of confidence," said Gryff. "But if you think I am going to risk ripping my buckskins to climb up there and carry you down, you are sadly mistaken."

A tail twitched and then the cat dropped lightly to the ground and ambled off.

"Smart beast," said Gryff.

"I, too, will take my leave," announced Cameron.

"You won't stay for supper?" asked Eliza.

"Alas, I have a pressing engagement," responded his friend.

"Not out of the country, I trust?" asked Gryff. "I was hoping that you would consent to stand up with me at the ceremony."

Cameron nodded. "It would be my honor. But I hope it will be soon. I do have plans that call for a trip to Scotland."

Eliza was observing their exchange with a pensive look. "Do you not tire of your constant travels, Mr. Daggett? I would think that after a while, one would want to settle down."

A strange flicker lit in his eyes, a fragile flame that in the blink of an eye gave way to a harsher light. "To a life as a county squire, with a pretty wife and a noisy nursery?" He made a self-mocking face. "I cannot think of a life less suited to me. I'm a solitary vagabond by nature."

"People change," said Eliza.

"Yes," Cameron looked at Gryff. "My two comrades have shown that is true. But in this case..." He winked. "Three is *not* a charm."

With that, he crossed the courtyard and headed for the stables, his dark coat and hat blurring into the long shadows of the trees. "Enjoy your evening."

"Oh, I think I've drunk too much champagne." Eliza blew out her breath and took a seat by the fire, savoring the tingle of the effervescence lingering on her tongue.

It had been a festive supper, with good cheer and much laughter as Gryff regaled them with tales of the three Hellhounds and their wild pranks. His self-deprecating humor kept them amused, but it was his quieter kindness and consideration that she loved—Gryff, for all his self-confessed faults, was a man of stalwart character.

A light kiss brushed the top of her head. "Alone at last?"

"Yes, the staff is in the kitchen, enjoying the cask of excellent ale you provided." He had moved to the hearth to stir the coals, but his closeness seemed to warm the very air around her. "As for Gussie, she just retired to her quarters, claiming that all the food and wine had made her sleepy. However, I think she just wanted to let us have a moment to ourselves."

"Tired?"

"Happy," she responded, catching his hand and pressing it to her cheek. "I almost fear going to bed in case I wake up in the morning to discover this was all a lovely dream."

"In that case, might I tempt you to come sit outside for a bit?" asked Gryff. "The stars are lovely, and the back lawns look like liquid silver in the moonlight."

"I can't think of a more perfect ending to the day."

"No?" His whisper tickled her ear as he lifted her up from the soft leather. "Clearly I have a more vivid imagination than you."

The glass doors of the music room opened onto the flagged terrace. The dark stone swirled with shadows cast by the glimmering torchieres set along the railing. A breeze stirred the foliage, the low, leafy rustle a muted counterpoint to the lone hoot of an owl and the cheerful serenade of crickets. A peaceful, pastoral symphony.

"Shall we sit here?" Gryff led her to a bench tucked between a pair of towering classical urns. Jasmine and roses perfumed the air, their scent nearly as intoxicating as the heady wine.

"This has always been one of my favorite spots," she confided, tipping her head up to look at the pinpoints of fire scattered across the black velvet sky. "I would come out here often and sit for hours, just dreaming."

"About what?" he asked, tucking her into the crook of his arm.

"About you."

"You didn't know I existed," he said dryly.

"Oh, yes I did." She waved a hand at the stars. "Amid all those countless winks of light, I knew there was one that shone brightest. I just wasn't sure how I would ever find you."

"Then it's a good thing I dropped into your lap."

Eliza laughed against the soft wool of his coat. "If you recall, it was in fact the other way around."

"Actually, the moment is indelibly imprinted on my mind. And my body." He pulled her into his lap. "Your lush little bum was wiggling against me, setting off all manner of improper urges."

"Oh, I adore your urges." She wagged her bottom back and forth, smiling as she felt him stir beneath her. "Though I'm surprised you didn't toss me over your shoulder. I looked like something that had tumbled straight out of a crow's nest."

He chuckled. "I looked up through the leaves and there you were—the very picture of a wild woodland sprite with your paint-smudged dress, your delightfully bare feet, and your honeyed hair slipping free of restraint." For a moment, the only sound was the steady thud of his heart. "I think I fell in love with you at that very instant."

Eliza snuggled deeper into his hug. "You held me, and silly as it sounds, I knew I would always be safe in your arms."

"I'll never let you go," he whispered.

Looking up she saw moonlight dancing along the curve of his mouth as his lips parted...

"Mmmm, I think I may stay out here all night." She sighed, her body tingling all over from the long, lush kiss. "Simply to smile up at the heavens and count my lucky stars."

"I've a better idea," said Gryff. "I have a present for you to unwrap."

"Another one?" She sat up. "What—"

"Open it and see." From beneath the bench, he pulled out a long, narrow box wrapped in rose red paper. A scarlet ribbon twined around it, ending in a large bow.

"What is it?" she repeated.

"A wedding present."

"We aren't married."

"Not yet. But I'm hoping that this might convince you to hurry along the preparations."

Eliza unknotted the bow and carefully peeled away the wrapping, revealing an ornate rosewood box. She felt her heart begin to quicken. "No. Oh, it isn't..."

The lid opened with a metallic snick.

Nestled on a bed of black velvet was Harry's exotic sex toy, its brass manacles and carved rod winking in the starlight.

"I was thinking that we could rehang it in the guest suite of the Abbey."

"That," she murmured, "would be exceedingly wicked."

"Yes. Exceedingly." His eyes danced with amusement, along with some warmer emotion that made her insides melt into a slow, spinning vortex of heat. "Shall we?"

"The offer is..." Eliza leaned across the box and held out her wrists. "...too tempting to resist."

Can a flame from the past
be rekindled?

Or is it too risky to play with fire?

Please turn this page for
a preview of

Too Dangerous to Desire.

Prologue

The voice stirred a myriad of memories...*None of them good.*

Soft and sensuous as summer sunlight, it tickled around his head, a tantalizing whisper, wrapping his brain in a seductive swirl of honeyed heat and gold-kissed sweetness.

Another word, and the sensation was now like a serpent, trailing its sensuous slither over bare flesh, only to strike with diamond-bright fangs.

Oh yes, he knew that voice—and it was poison to a man's peace of mind.

And yet Cameron Daggett couldn't help edging a little closer to the shadowed door and nudging it open a hairsbreadth wider.

He had just entered the building using the proprietor's private entrance, so no one was aware of his presence. Peering through the sliver of space, he could just make out the two figures standing in the smoky half-light of the corridor walls' sconces. The oil flames were kept deliberately low—the regular patrons of the establishment preferred to come and go discreetly. However, as the whisper had warned, the flickers of gold-lapped light showed the pair who were paused in deep conversation to be females. One of them was the familiar form of Sara Hawkins, the owner of The Wolf's Lair. And the other was...

"This is *highly* irregular, Miss Lawrance," said Sara in a low, taut murmur. "As a rule, I don't allow wives or sisters, or others of our sex to intrude on the gentlemen who patronize this place. It's bad fer business, if ye take my meaning. They expect privacy."

"I understand," replied the Voice from the Past. "Truly I do. And if it were not a matter of the utmost urgency, I would not dream of making such an irregular request. But the truth is...I am rather desperate."

Desperate. Cocking an ear, Cameron held himself very still.

"Yes, I can see that," said Sara, heaving a reluctant sigh. "And so I will make a rare exception. Wait in there." She indicated a small side parlor. "I will fetch the gentleman. But I must ask you to be quick—and fer God's sake, ye must be quiet as well. No tears, no shrieks, no gnashing of teeth, else I will have te ask the porter to remove ye from the premises."

"I will not make a scene," promised Miss Sophie Lawrance, her earnest whisper coiling and clutching at his thumping heart.

"And when you are finished, ye must leave with all possible haste by the same way you came in," added Sara. "Nothing personal, miss, but the sooner ye are gone from here, the better."

Cameron's own inner voice of Self-Preservation

shouted a similar warning. *Turn and run like the Devil. And don't look back.*

After all, he had long ago mastered the art of staying one step ahead of personal demons—not to speak of more mundane threats like bailiffs and Bow Street Runners.

And yet...

And yet, at this moment Cameron found himself incapable of listening to reason. Instead of retreating, he slipped into one of the secret passageways used by the staff and waited for Sara to return with the man Sophie sought.

Low voices. A door opening and closing. The click of Sara's heeled shoes as she returned to her private office.

Moving silently as a stalking panther, Cameron darted out of his hiding place and approached the parlor.

What reason, he wondered, had brought saintly Sophie Lawrance to one of London's most notorious dens of iniquity? Set deep in the dangerous slums of Southwark, The Wolf's Lair was a high-stakes gaming house and brothel that catered to rakehells and rogues who played fast and loose with the rules of Society.

And why, after all these years, should he care?

Because I am a god-benighted fool, thought Cameron with a shiver of self-loathing.

The door was shut tightly with the lock engaged. Drawing a thin shaft of steel from his boot, Cameron expertly eased the latch open. A touch of his gloved fingertips coaxed the paneled wood to shift just a fraction.

Sophie was heavily veiled, the dark mesh muffling her already low whisper. Her companion was speaking in equally low tones, making it impossible to hear their words. However, he saw a small package change hands.

The gentleman let out a low, brandy-fuzzed laugh as he tucked it into his pocket.

Sliding back into hiding, Cameron watched Sophie hurry away down the corridor, her indigo cloak skirling with the shadows until she was swallowed in the darkness. A moment later, the gentleman emerged from the parlor, still chuckling softly. He turned for the gaming rooms, a flicker of lamplight catching the curl of his mouth and the slight swaying of his steps.

Cameron recognized him as Lord Hollis, a dissolute viscount with an appetite for reckless pleasures.

Hollis and Sophie? An odd couple if ever there was one. The Sophie Lawrance he knew was anything but reckless. She was sensible—too damnably sensible to ever throw caution to the wind.

But people change, thought Cameron sardonically. He had only to look at himself—there wasn't the least resemblance between his present persona and the callow youth of...

Shaking off mordant memories, he followed Hollis into the card room. Timing his steps, he brushed by the viscount just as he started to sit down at one of the tables.

"Join us for a hand, Daggett?" called one of the other players.

"Not tonight," answered Cameron. "I've an assignation with an old friend."

The man leered. "A *lady* friend?"

"Pray tell, who?" chorused the man's cronies.

"Gentlemanly honor compels Daggett to remain silent on that question," pointed out the dealer.

Smiling, Cameron inclined a mocking bow and sauntered away, Sophie's package now firmly tucked away in his pocket.

How fortunate that I have no pretensions to acting honorably.

Drawing in a great lungful of the chill night air, Sophie Lawrance forced herself to choke back the urge to retch. *Steady, steady—ignore the sickening smells, the sordid encounter.* And yet, the bitter taste of bile rose again in her throat, and she felt the oozy ground beneath her feet begin to sway. *Breathe, breathe.* She would not—*could not*—give in to fear. Predators pounced on any show of weakness, and this godforsaken slum was perhaps the most savage spot in all of England.

"Allow me to be of assistance." A hand suddenly gripped her arm to keep her upright and a snowy white handkerchief, scented with a pleasant tang of citrus and spice, fluttered in front of her veiled face. "You appear to be in some distress."

"I...I..." Her stomach gave another little lurch. "I thank you, sir." Swallowing her pride, Sophie took the silk square from the shadowy stranger and held it close to her nose. Oddly enough, the fragrance seemed to calm the churning of her insides. She inhaled several slow, deep breaths, savoring the richly nuanced scent.

"Better?"

"Much." Now that her head had cleared, Sophie was eager to escape the dark, filth-strewn alley and the horrid nightmare of the evening. "A momentary indisposition, that is all." She shrugged off his hold and held out the handkerchief. "It has passed."

The stranger made no effort to take it back. "You had

better keep it if you mean to wander around this neighborhood." The alley was dark, with only an intermittent wink of starlight penetrating through the clouds, so for the moment she had only a dim impression of his person. *Tall. Broad-shouldered. Strong hands, surprisingly gentle and warm.*

His voice, however, was coolly cynical. "Though I would recommend a more effective implement of protection if you mean to enter places like The Wolf's Lair. Say, a pistol or a knife. A lady's virtue won't last long without such a weapon." A pause, and then his voice turned even more sardonic. "But perhaps your intentions aren't virtuous."

"I—I assure you, sir," said Sophie tightly. "I am *not* in the habit of coming to...depraved places like this."

"Oh?" Skepticism shaded his voice. "Then what brings you here tonight, if not a craving for danger?"

"That, sir, is none of your business." Lifting her chin, she ventured a look at him, trying to make out some identifying feature.

However, the stranger had his hat pulled low, the wide brim shading his face. In the swirl of murky shadows, Sophie could make out naught but the vague shapes of a straight nose, a sensual mouth. The only clear-cut view was of long, raven-dark hair and the rakish glimmer of a pearl earring.

Danger. His last word seemed a deliberately tickling, taunting challenge. Sophie sucked in her breath, suddenly aware of a strange prickling taking hold of her body, as if daggerpoints were dancing over every inch of her flesh. "In another few minutes I shall be safe from danger. That is, unless I've had the misfortune to cross paths with a pirate," she said, trying to mask her emotions by matching his cynical tone.

A smile curled on the corners of his mouth, half mocking, half...

Sophie couldn't put a name to the flicker of emotion. It was gone in the blink of an eye, so perhaps she had merely imagined it.

"A pirate?" he repeated, making her feel slightly absurd. Like a silly schoolgirl who swooned over novels of swashbuckling heroes rescuing damsels in distress. His voice then took on a sharper edge. "Isn't that just a romantic name for a ruthless cutthroat and a conniving thief?"

Sophie swallowed hard, feeling a shiver skate down her spine. "Who are you, sir?" she demanded.

"Why do you ask?" he countered. "Do you think we might be acquainted? Old friends, perhaps?"

"Impossible," she whispered. "I can't imagine that we move in the same worlds." Her dizziness seemed to have returned, and with a vengeance. Off-kilter, she found herself adding, "And yet you... you remind me of someone I once knew, long, long ago."

"You speak of him as if he were dead." Without waiting for her to answer, he gave a strange laugh. "Perhaps I'm his ghost."

Sophie wondered whether he was drunk. *Or demented.* Inching back a step she looked around for the alleyway leading out to the street where her hackney was waiting.

"You want a name, Madam or Miss Whoever-You-Are?" he continued. "My two friends and I are called the Hellhounds." He let out a low, sarcastic bark. "I'm known as the Sleuth Hound, as I have a nose for sniffing out trouble."

"I am surprised that you admit to such a beastly moniker," she replied slowly.

"I make no bones about what I am," he said softly. "What about you?" His head tilted down and then up, his unseen eyes leaving a trail of heat along her body. "Your manner of dress—sturdy country half boots, modest woolen cloak, prim headcovering—says you are a respectable country lady. But the fact that you are here, visiting a house of ill repute in the stews of Southwark, speaks an entirely different message."

She felt her cheeks grow hot beneath the gauzy veil. That he was right only fanned the flames. "You are impertinent, sir."

"No, I am observant." A pause. "More so than you think. Indeed, from what I've seen, I would say you are playing a very dangerous game. Have a care, for in dealing with those who frequent The Wolf's Lair, you are going up against the most ruthless men in London."

"Including you?" challenged Sophie, though her heart was pounding hard enough to crack a rib.

"Oh, I'm among the very worst of the lot."

"I must be going." Slipping past him, Sophie hurried toward the narrow gap between the ramshackle buildings.

But to her dismay, the Pirate moved along with her. "Allow me to see you to your vehicle. It isn't safe to walk through these alleys alone."

"You needn't bother." She flinched slightly at the sound of scrabbling claws somewhere close by. "I—I will take my chances."

"I think you have gambled enough for one evening," he drawled. "Besides, I'd be willing to wager that you wouldn't care to put your foot where you are about to step."

She stopped short, as a horribly foul odor assaulted her nose.

"Nasty, isn't it?" he murmured.

"I—"

His hands were suddenly around her waist, lifting her into his arms as if she were light as a feather. Beneath the folds of wool she was intimately aware of the lean, lithe flex of muscle.

Oh, what madness has taken hold of me?

Her wits were spinning and skittering topsy-turvy. How else to explain that the moment felt so hauntingly familiar? So achingly comforting.

Madness, she repeated to herself. The meeting with Lord Hollis ought to be reminder enough that youth and innocence were long gone. Only a fool yearned to reach back and recapture the past.

Fisting her fingers, Sophie tried to squirm free. "Please, put me down, sir!"

"As you wish." Her boots hit the ground with a soft squish. "We have passed through the worst. It's just a little farther to where the hired carriages wait. You will soon be back to the respectable part of Town."

Slipping, sliding, Sophie hurried awkwardly toward the weak glimmer of oily light up ahead. The Pirate glided alongside her with a smooth, silent step.

Spotting her hackney parked at the near corner of the rough-cobbled square, she skirted around the snorting horse and quickly unlatched the door.

"Thank you. Though you need not have troubled yourself…" A gust of wind swirled over the stones, catching at her cloak and lifting the thin scrim of her veil just as she turned to take her leave.

"No trouble at all," replied the Pirate. He had moved close to help her climb up the iron rungs, and now their faces were but a hairsbreadth apart. "Indeed, I did warn you that I have a nose for trouble."

And a mouth for sin.

For suddenly his lips possessed hers in a swift, searing kiss.

It was over in an instant. He pulled back, so quickly that she was sure the glimmer of green eyes must have been only a figment of her heated imagination.

"Fie, sir! N-no gentleman—"

Her stammering protest was stilled by a rumbled laugh. *A pirate laugh, redolent with hints of hellfire dangers and storm-tossed seas.*

"Ah, but whoever said I was a gentleman?"

THE DISH

Where authors give you the inside scoop!

♥ ♥ ♥ ♥ ♥ ♥ ♥ ♥ ♥ ♥ ♥ ♥ ♥ ♥ ♥ ♥

From the desk of Roxanne St. Claire

Dear Reader,

BAREFOOT IN THE SAND opens during a powerful hurricane that forces the heroine and her daughter to hole up in a bathtub under a mattress and pray for survival. The scene, I'm sorry to say, took very little imagination for me to write. I've been there. On August 24, 1992, one of the worst hurricanes in the history of this country slammed into Dade County, Florida, and changed hundreds of thousands of lives. Mine was one of them.

Exactly one month pregnant with a baby that had taken four years and a quadrillion deals with God to conceive, I decided to spend the night at my sister's house when Hurricane Andrew approached Miami. Despite the fact that the forecasters predicted the storm would turn north before making landfall, my husband and I had worried that our proximity to the coastline made us vulnerable, and that our east-facing double front doors might buckle with the wind. We braced the doors with the living room sofa and evacuated just eight miles north. My sister's house sustained little damage that night, though freight-train winds ripped her patio screen and took down some beloved trees.

We headed home the next morning, and with each

passing mile, it was clear that the southern section of Miami had taken the brunt of the storm. We sure hoped that sofa had held the doors closed.

We still laugh about that because, well, we never did find that sofa.

When we arrived at what we thought was our street— all the trees were uprooted or stripped bare and not a single street sign survived—all we could do was stare. The sofa was long gone (but our neighbor's love seat was in our driveway!), along with our doors, every window, all the roof tiles, the garage doors, and just about everything we'd ever owned. *Everything*.

Inside, all the ceilings had collapsed, leaving snow-drifts of insulation. My beautiful home was covered in mud, drywall, and broken glass. Every remaining wall was green from the chlorophyll in the leaves that had blown around during what had to have been mini-tornadoes in the house.

I stood in the midst of that chaos and started to cry, of course. Shaking uncontrollably, unable to process what might lie ahead, I could barely suck in shuddering breaths and weep at the sight of my rain-soaked wedding album and shattered bits of my precious Waterford crystal.

Everything we had was gone.

Then my husband gripped my shoulders, giving me a stern shake and silencing me with two words: The baby. *The baby*.

Obviously, not everything was gone. When Mother Nature has a temper tantrum and breaks all your stuff, the only things that really matter are the people who are left.

When I needed the catalyst to set Lacey Armstrong's story in motion and start the Barefoot Bay series, the lessons I learned from surviving and rebuilding after Hurricane Andrew were still fresh in my heart, even almost two decades later. It wasn't hard to imagine riding out that storm in a bathtub; I had many friends and neighbors who had done just that. It wasn't impossible to put myself in Lacey's shoes the next day, digging for optimism in a mountain of rubble.

But I also had twenty years of perspective and knew that no matter what she lost in the storm, Lacey's indomitable spirit wouldn't merely survive, but thrive. She not only found optimism in that rubble, she found love.

P.S. "The baby" turns nineteen this year. And, no, we didn't name him Andrew.

Roxanne St. Claire

♥ ♥ ♥ ♥ ♥ ♥ ♥ ♥ ♥ ♥ ♥ ♥ ♥ ♥

From the desk of Cara Elliott

Dear Reader,

Psst! I've got a secret to share with you about my hero in TOO TEMPTING TO RESIST. Okay, you already know that Gryffin Owain Dwight, the Marquess of Haddan, is rich, handsome, titled, and an incorrigibly charming flirt. But I'll bet you weren't aware of this intimate little detail—he speaks a *very* special language.

No, no, not French or Italian! (Though as a dashingly

romantic rake, he's fluent in those lovely tongues.) It's the secret language of Flowers, a highly seductive skill. For example, he knows that red roses signify "Love," while orange ones mean "Fascination." He can tell you that yellow irises murmur "Passion" and peach blossoms say "I am your captive."

Now, you might ask how he came to know all this. Well, here's an interesting bit of history (as the author of historical romances, I love discovering interesting little facts from the past): Flowers have long been powerful symbols in Eastern cultures, and in the early eighteenth century, Lady Mary Wortley Montague, wife of the British ambassador to Constantinople (and a fascinating woman in her own right), learned of a little Turkish book called *The Secret Language of Flowers*. Intrigued, she had it translated and brought it back to England with her...and from there the romantic idea that lovers could send hidden messages to each other via bouquets was introduced to Europe.

Today, the symbolic use of flowers is still flourishing. Here's another secret! Kate Middleton's bouquet at the Royal Wedding to Prince William was carefully designed using the language of flowers to express special meaning for the bride and groom and their families: *Lily-of-the-valley*, which means "Return of Happiness" (chosen in memory of Diana); *Sweet William*, which means "Gallantry" (isn't that romantic!); *Hyacinth*, which means "Constancy of Love"; *Ivy*, which means "Fidelity, Friendship and Affection"; *Myrtle*, which is the emblem of marriage and love.

Now, getting back to *my* hero, Gryff has a number of other intriguing secrets. He's a man of hidden talents—and hidden passions. It's no wonder that Eliza, Lady Brentford, finds him irresistibly alluring, despite her distrust of rakes and rascals. She too has an interest in flowers, so when she discovers that he speaks their language...

And how does Gryff use this special skill? Well, that's for you to find out for yourself! I hope you'll take a peek at his story and let him whisper his petal-soft seductions in your ear!

Cara Elliott

♥ ♥ ♥ ♥ ♥ ♥ ♥ ♥ ♥ ♥ ♥ ♥ ♥ ♥ ♥ ♥

From the desk of Caridad Piñeiro

Dear Reader,

I've been reading romances for as long as I can remember, going back to when I was twelve and read and re-read *Wuthering Heights* all summer long. At one point the librarian told me I could not take the book out again since other people needed a chance to read it!

Denied my broody Heathcliff and doomed Catherine, I turned my attentions to what some might say were an odd mix: Shakespeare and Ian Fleming.

It's safe to say that those choices as a young reader were later reflected in what I wrote, especially in THE CLAIMED, the second book in the Sin Hunters series.

Action. Adventure. Angst. I've incorporated all those elements that I love into this tale of a determined and broody alpha hero, Christopher Sombrosa, and a woman who is the absolute wrong choice for him, Victoria Johnson.

So why is Victoria *not* the woman for Christopher? Think Romeo and Juliet, Capulet and Montague.

Victoria is destined to be the leader of her Light Hunter clan, while Christopher is not only one of the Dark Ones, he is likewise supposed to assume command of his Shadow Hunter people.

Add to the mix some rather nefarious villains in the form of Christopher's father and ex-fiancée and the betrayal of someone dear to Victoria, and I think you'll find THE CLAIMED will keep you turning pages until the very end.

I am very glad to say, however, that despite the hopeless Catherine, Juliet, and assorted Bond girls who could never win James's heart, there is a path to a new and exciting place for Christopher and Victoria.

I hope you will enjoy their fight for a better tomorrow for not only themselves, but their race of Hunters.

Find out more about Forever Romance!

Visit us at
www.hachettebookgroup.com/publishing_forever.aspx

Find us on Facebook
http://www.facebook.com/ForeverRomance

Follow us on Twitter
http://twitter.com/ForeverRomance

NEW AND UPCOMING TITLES

Each month we feature our new titles
and reader favorites.

CONTESTS AND GIVEAWAYS

We give away galleys, autographed copies,
and all kinds of exclusive items.

AUTHOR INFO

You'll find bios, articles, and links to personal Web sites
for all your favorite authors—and so much more.

GET SOCIAL

Connect with your favorite authors, editors, and
other Forever fans, and share what's important to you.

THE BUZZ

Sign up for our monthly romance newsletter,
and be the first to read all about it.

VISIT US ONLINE AT

WWW.HACHETTEBOOKGROUP.COM

FEATURES:

**OPENBOOK BROWSE AND
SEARCH EXCERPTS**
·
AUDIOBOOK EXCERPTS AND PODCASTS
·
AUTHOR ARTICLES AND INTERVIEWS
·
**BESTSELLER AND PUBLISHING
GROUP NEWS**
·
SIGN UP FOR E-NEWSLETTERS
·
**AUTHOR APPEARANCES AND TOUR
INFORMATION**
·
SOCIAL MEDIA FEEDS AND WIDGETS
·
DOWNLOAD FREE APPS

BOOKMARK HACHETTE BOOK GROUP
@ WWW.HACHETTEBOOKGROUP.COM